He gave her pearls...

a gift of love when she bore his son. But Jonathan Beddoes sold two slaves to pay for Martha Beddoes' necklace. Two human beings were torn from those they loved at Roselawns plantation. Martha Beddoes would not wear her necklace of tears.

But those pearls were passed down to her daughter Prudence, and on to the next generation—a symbol of the love that began the family, the ideals that divided it and the ties that bound them forever.

Passion
and
Proud Hearts

a novel by
Lydia Lancaster

WARNER BOOKS

A Warner Communications Company

WARNER BOOKS EDITION

ISBN 0-446-82548-4

Cover art by Tom Hall

Warner Books, Inc., 75 Rockefeller Plaza, New York, N.Y. 10019

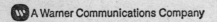 A Warner Communications Company

Printed in the United States of America

Not associated with Warner Press, Inc. of Anderson, Indiana

First Printing: January, 1978

10 9 8 7 6 5 4 3 2 1

BOOK ONE:

Martha

1

In the Lattimer parlor, where the double doors were folded back for the special occasion, Martha Curtis sat on a straight-backed chair with her hands folded primly in her lap and listened attentively to Old Mrs. Lattimer, so called to distinguish her from Young Mrs. Lattimer. Old Mrs. Lattimer was stone deaf and therefore did all the talking, having decided long since that there was no use in pausing for responses that she couldn't hear.

Once every year, in the spring, the Lattimers sent their carriage to convey "Poor Martha" from Martin's Corners to their home in Boston. She would spend a fortnight there amid surroundings to which she was entitled by birth and of which she had been deprived, through no fault of her impeccable bloodline, by her father's heavy and ill-advised investment in the cargo of a ship that had failed to make port. The resultant loss had plunged the Curtis family into bankruptcy, and with a shocking lack of regard for the proprieties, the failure had so undermined Martha's father's health that he had taken pneumonia and died, leaving his wife Nancy penniless.

If it hadn't been for Miss Emily, Benjamin Curtis's sister, who had the stamina that Benjamin had lacked,

7

it's hard to imagine what would have become of Nancy and the infant Martha. Perhaps it was a blessing after all that the two boys had died in infancy, for who would have paid for their education and set them up in business? Even Miss Emily, with all her fortitude, could not have managed that on the stipend she received from the very short end of the elder Mr. Curtis's estate. The estate had consisted of a farm prosperous enough to send Benjamin to Harvard and set him up as an attorney in Boston. The elder Mr. Curtis had as a matter of course presumed that the interest on the small sum he left his daughter would serve her as pin money while she resided, as was proper, with her brother.

But Miss Emily had not elected to live with her brother. She had, instead, bought herself a tiny saltbox house in Martin's Corners, the nearest crossroads town to her former farm home, and set herself up to live in perfect contentment with her garden and her cow and her hens and her tortoiseshell tomcat. As long as she had enough to scrape by without becoming a poor relation in a house where another woman was mistress, even a woman of whom she was as fond as she was of Nancy, nothing would budge her.

For as long as Martha could remember, Aunt Emily, a diminutive spinster with hair drawn severely back from her face in defiance of fashion, had dressed only in dove gray or serviceable brown. Her face did not call for an elaborate setting. It was a no-nonsense face, devoid of beauty, and to squander elaborate hairdressing on it, or fancy apparel on her ninety-five-pound, ramrod-straight body, would have been ludicrous, and Emily knew it. When there was a little extra money left over, Miss Emily bought books, not furbelows, so that her parlor had come to resemble a small public library. The inhabitants of Martin's

Corners considered her a bluestocking but, at the same time, they availed themselves of her generosity in lending her beloved volumes for either reference or pure enjoyment of reading.

When the news of the debâcle her brother had left reached her, Miss Emily had packed a portmanteau with a minimum of personal needs, taken coach for Boston, and arrived in time to supervise as her brother's house went under the auctioneer's hammer. Emily had not been able to reach Boston in time for the funeral because Martin's Corners had been snowbound after a raging blizzard. But Nancy's pathetic letter, when it was finally delivered, had galvanized Emily into action, and she reached Boston in time to battle her way through every inch of the legal procedures preceding the auctioning off of all of Benjamin's worldly possessions to meet the demands of his creditors.

Without Miss Emily's astute mind and her grasp of the value of house and furnishings, Nancy might have been left with a burden of debt still outstanding. As it was, Miss Emily's adversaries were stunned by her competence, and the debts were cleared with even a pittance left over. The pittance helped to pay for moving Nancy and the infant Martha from Boston to Martin's Corners and the shelter of the saltbox house.

There Martha and her mother were accepted not as burdens, but as full-fledged members of a family, in which the three of them made an entity. Each woman had her own tasks, no one more important than another, and Martha, as she grew, assumed her share. There was the cow to be milked, the garden to be tended and the eggs to be gathered, preserves to be put up in season and the cooking and cleaning and washing of clothes. But there was time for reading, as well, and lessons, and long discussion of politics and the classics, of science and invention, of foreign countries and cultures, for Miss Emily's tastes were catholic and her grounding firm. These she passed on, lovingly, to Martha, who absorbed them all like a young plant eager for rain.

There was only one deviation from the routine of the seasons in Nancy's and Martha's lives. Once each year Sarah Lattimer, with whom Nancy had attended a modest Seminary for Young Ladies, invited her girlhood friend and little Martha to her home in Boston. And when Martha became old enough, she was trotted out and put on display to remind reasonably prosperous parents, gently, that she existed, desirable as a daughter-in-law for her pleasing demeanor as well as for the good blood that flowed through her veins. As it was never too early to plant such an idea in the fathers' minds, the visits had begun to take on this extra dimension when Martha had been no more than ten, so that Sarah could evaluate her and scheme where best to peddle her.

So here, eight years later, Martha sat, biting her tongue sharply to remind herself of her manners. There was no use wishing that her own decently full-skirted gown, with its modest neckline, stitched up by herself in Aunt Emily's favorite dove gray, was some sheer, delectable creation smothered with lace and frills. There was very little point in Martha's thinking about clothes at all, because there wasn't the money to follow the fashions, and what she wore, although adequate, had to be practical and serviceable. That was one reason she sat beside Old Mrs. Lattimer and suffered her ramblings. It took her out of close contact with Hester Lattimer, who was only a year older than herself but who was already betrothed to handsome young Joseph Carter, whose family was part owner of a shipyard.

No expense was ever spared on Hester's wardrobe. Tonight the dainty blond beauty sparkled in a pale blue dress, trimmed with yards and yards of real lace, and styled with a low neckline, permissible in the evening, that threatened to expose more than was decent at every movement. And the daintiest of low blue slippers, tied with matching ribbons, enhanced her small feet. Thinking of those dainty slippers, Martha tucked her own feet, shod in decent slippers but not half as dainty, under her sensible gown.

It was all such a waste. No financially solvent father was going to look at her and think, "There's just the girl I want for my second, or my third, son." These visits, although a source of wild excitement when she had been younger, had become, now that she was eighteen, an agony.

Being presented to society, as Young Mrs. Lattimer said, or paraded, as Miss Emily put it tartly, had done no good at all and would do no good in the future. Martha knew by now that she was thought of as "Poor Martha," an object to be dusted off and placed on display in hopes of a customer. In Martin's Corners she was at least thought of as Martha, and accorded the respect due to a niece of Miss Emily. The charming prince does not marry the goose-girl, and if her mother and Sarah Lattimer persisted in dreaming that it could happen, she and her aunt were sensible enough to know better. She would not return next year. No power on earth could make her. Aunt Emily would back her up, and Mama and Young Mrs. Lattimer would just have to make the best of it.

There was a little stir at the door as an elderly man and a younger one, who had arrived together, entered the room. Sarah Lattimer rose from her chair and

11

bustled forward, and Martha saw that her face was flushed with pleasure. That meant that the new arrivals must be of some importance. But the older gentleman was only Mr. Bertram Foster, whom she had met before, and her thoughts returned to her determination never to let herself in for the humiliation of being a rejected piece of merchandise again. She'd marry some farm lad who would appreciate her abilities in the kitchen and garden, or she would be a spinster like Aunt Emily and be just as happy with her books and her tabby, but she would not, she would not. . . .

That was as far as her thoughts went, because the younger of the two new arrivals had come within her range of vision, piloted by the determined Sarah.

"Martha, I want to present Mr. Jonathan Beddoes, a planter from the State of Georgia. Mr. Beddoes, Miss Curtis."

Martha's throat went dry, and the palms of her hands turned clammy. She seemed to be falling into a pair of gray eyes, outlined with thick black lashes, set under dark eyebrows with a disconcerting quirk at the ends. Their owner was doing his best to smile as though he were happy to meet her. His hair, black and worn longer than was usual in conservative Boston, had a tendency to curl, in a Byronic effect, and his features were every bit as perfect as the English poet's. Aunt Emily had copies of almost all of George Gordon Byron's works back home at Martin's Corners. Although Aunt Emily disapproved of Lord Byron's dissolute life, she did not let that prejudice her against his writings. Aunt Emily was not one to cut off her nose to spite her face, or in this case, her intellectual appetite.

On second glance, Jonathan Beddoes was not as prettily effeminate-looking as Lord Byron. Everything about Mr. Beddoes was masculine, from the strong

12

planes of his face to the broad shoulders that strained the broadcloth of his coat, tailored to perfection. He had the narrow hips and long, muscular legs of the horseman, and his skin was darker than that of any of the gentlemen of Martha's acquaintance, except for farmers in the depth of summer.

Even before Martha had come to the end of her quick assessment of him, Mr. Beddoes had turned away to follow his hostess. Sarah's march around the double parlors was a triumphal procession, her manner making it clear that she considered the young man's presence a *coup* of major proportions.

So much for that. The obligatory presentation over, Martha knew that there wasn't the chance of an icicle in hell that he would come near her again. Her frustration and despair churning, she didn't care if she had blasphemed in her thoughts. Drat it, anyway, how much could a girl stand without kicking over the bucket and letting all the milk spill out?

"Harumph!" Old Mrs. Lattimer shouted, fully confident that her voice was pitched at a moderate social level. "He doesn't look like he sprouts horns under all that hair, but you never can tell!"

For a moment Martha was bewildered, and then she understood. Old Mrs. Lattimer had caught the word "Georgia," which was equated with slavery, and therefore in the old lady's mind Mr. Beddoes had to be one of the devil's disciples. The thought sent a shiver through Martha, too. She knew that even in Boston some people owned slaves, as house servants, but she had never, to her best recollection, seen one personally.

Mr. Beddoes was now deep in conversation with Mr. Stacey, who was affiliated with a bank, and there was no use dwelling on him. But it would be something to tell Aunt Emily, she thought. Aunt Emily would be amused by Old Mrs. Lattimer's remark about Mr. Beddoes's hair, and for the first time in her life, Martha wondered how a man's hair would feel under her fingers. Would one of those dark tendrils curl around them, with a life of its own, to make her pulse throb and her heart race? Aunt Emily did not censor Martha's reading, and Martha had had her share of daydreams. Unlike most girls, however, Martha was fully aware that they were fantasy only, and not to be taken seriously.

Enough! she told herself, and she wondered if her face looked as red as it felt at her totally uncalled-for romantic vaporings. But nobody was looking at her. She sat in isolation, protected by the invisible wall that always surrounded Old Mrs. Lattimer.

"Devils, the lot of them!" Old Mrs. Lattimer said, nodding vigorously. And then, to Martha's intense relief, the old lady closed her eyes and went to sleep, leaving her to suffer through the rest of the evening in solitude. As far as Martha was concerned, if she had to suffer, she would much rather do it alone. At least that way, her benefactress and the guests who ignored her forgot to feel sorry for her. As with her Aunt Emily, pity was the one thing in life that was intolerable to the girl from Martin's Corners.

2

"Now for Gawd's sake, remember to be polite!" Jacob Beddoes had instructed Jonathan before the lad had set out on his trip north. Jacob was fuming because he himself could not make the trip. He was, he admitted, jealous of his son, who was going to have all the fun this time around. Even though there was a touch of gray in his thick black hair, it didn't mean that Jacob was ready to give up those special delights that he looked forward to on his twice-yearly trips. Safely away from local gossip, he always managed to indulge himself in a few forbidden pleasures. But this time Jonathan was to be given the pleasant duty. "Don't go getting into any of your damnable pigheaded arguments. We have to depend on those bastards up north, remember!"

"Mr. Beddoes!" Yolande's tone had registered shock. "Such language, and in the house!"

"I wouldn't be in the damned house if it wasn't for this damned leg!" Jacob had shouted, his face an alarming red. "I'd be out in the office where ladies with dainty ears wouldn't hear me cussing! If you don't like it, madam, you can remove yourself! You still have two good legs to walk on!"

Yolande's legs moved, but her face blanched. "Jacob,

in front of our son! *Limbs,* Jacob, limbs!" Having reached the door, she paused to entreat in an agonized whisper, "And don't forget to warn him about. . . ."

"Dammit, I know what to warn him about!" Jacob and Jonathan, so much alike, exploded into laughter as Yolande slammed the door behind her in an almost unheard-of breach of ladylike deportment.

"Well, aren't you going to warn me?"

"Damn right I'm going to warn you! Stay away from cheap places. I don't want you coming back peppered, understand? And confine your tomcatting to New York; don't you as much as intimate that you know the facts of life in Boston! And no fumbling around respectable young ladies even in New York. I've written Lewis Compton there that you're coming. He'll steer you right, even if he is married and never gets the chance any more. But you sprout a halo in Boston, with Foster, or by God I'll lay your back open with my crop when you get back, and don't take a notion that I can't still do it!"

They measured each other, each liking what he saw. Jacob settled in his chair with a grin on his good-natured face. "One more thing. Keep clear of Philadelphia. When I was there years back, those idiots put chains across the streets every Sunday to keep folks from driving, and the dinner party I was roped into was the damnedest thing I ever saw. All the men ate at the table, and the ladies ate standing up, over at the far end of the room. Damned if I didn't get the notion that those folks ain't quite human!"

So Jonathan had avoided Philadelphia and gone directly to Boston, which he'd a sight rather have avoided as well. It seemed a shame to have to waste time in that dull city, when this was the first time he'd ever been farther north than Richmond. Still, New York and Lewis Compton were yet to come, provided he could ever break away from his elderly host, Mr. Bertram Foster, who was determined to educate him for the good of his soul.

In the past week, Jonathan had been subjected to three quiet, "select" gatherings, where the discussions were literary, the refreshments tea and cake, and one or more overaged matron or plain, quivering spinster would honor them with renditions of classical music, trilled in uncertain soprano that would turn shrill on the higher notes. Jonathan was beginning to wonder why he had jumped at the chance to make this journey from Georgia to Boston to consult with Mr. Foster. Bertram Foster was the family's financial adviser in matters pertinent to Northern commerce. Jonathan was to discuss all business and purchases with him, for the young man was here to buy supplies, both basic and luxury, to be transported to Roselawns—all those things that Southern families depended on getting from the North to keep their standard of living at a satisfactory level.

If the genteel evenings were hard to bear, the endless rounds of daytime sightseeing were even worse. Why was it that Bostonians held the belief, deeply rooted, that Boston was the only city of consequence in the Western Hemisphere, and Boston's history of the utmost interest to everyone?

Old South Meeting House, Christ Church, the Old State House, Paul Revere's house, and the Common (forty-eight acres, would Jonathan ever forget?), the wharves, the narrow, twisting streets of the North End. Bunker Hill, King's Chapel, the Boston Latin School, and worst of all, an enforced journey to Harvard. The Harvard tour was accompanied by an endless monologue on what a pity, indeed what a crime against higher education it was, that Jonathan's father had elected to send him to William and Mary in Williamsburg, Virginia, instead of to the very seat of Western culture, Harvard itself.

"William and Mary was built in 1693," Jonathan had got in quickly, when Mr. Foster had been forced to pause for breath. "We're mighty proud of it down where I come from."

"Indeed!" had been the response, which had plummeted Jonathan back into respectful silence lest Mr. Foster decide that the Beddoeses were not, after all, suited to be his clients. His father would skin him alive. Worse, if he failed, Jacob would insist that he become engaged to that goose Miss Amelia Shaw, under the assumption that a married man is a discreet man and marriage itself a maturing factor.

And so here he was in Boston, in this spring season of 1835, after the fields had been well established with this year's crop, carrying out the commissions that Jacob's broken leg had prevented him from undertaking. The most important of them was to purchase a dining table, large enough to accommodate twenty-four chairs, to furnish the new dining room that his mother had browbeaten his father into adding to the house. Originally, the house had been a double log cabin with a breezeway between, but by now it had been expanded into a domicile of respectable proportions, with the original cabins serving as kitchen quarters. The family silver and china had been brought from England by Yolande's grandmother, already heirlooms. But what good were they, Yolande reasoned, without a proper table to display them?

"Hell, get her her damned table and chairs!" Jacob had bellowed, throwing his hands up in defeat. "If this year's crop ain't good, we'll go on short rations, but we'll eat 'em in style. Better to go hungry than to try to buck a woman once she has her mind set!" The likelihood of their going hungry on their enor-

18

mous and prosperous plantation was ridiculous, but Yolande would have subsisted on parched Indian corn and yams with perfect equanimity so long as it was served on her new table in her new dining room.

Since Jonathan had managed to complete his purchases, this was his last night in Boston. Everything must come to an end, even this endurance contest with Bertram Foster. The evening dragged on, without even a recital to break the monotony, and Jonathan's control threatened to snap.

Mr. Stacey's next words did it.

"The railroads are the coming thing. Any man with an eye to the future will do well to look into the possibility of investing in the railroads."

"The steam cars?" Jonathan's quirked brows shot up. "In all deference, sir, I must differ with you. I rode the steam cars for seventy interminable miles on my journey north, just as a matter of curiosity, and I assure you that I wouldn't set foot on one of them again unless my life depended on it! Dirty, uncomfortable, undependable! I was as black as any of our nigras back home by the time I got off, and my clothes were burned full of holes by flying sparks. Believe me, I thanked the Almighty that I was still in one piece! Steam cars are no mode of travel for a gentleman. It would have been better if John Stevens had never invented the contraption. It'll never be more than a toy, and when folks lose interest in the novelty, that'll be the end of the nonsense."

Mr. Stacey looked at Jonathan coldly. "I beg to challenge your opinion, young sir! Why, as recently as '28 the Baltimore and Ohio had only thirteen miles of track, but now in '35, the Mohawk and Hudson have well over a thousand! The facts speak for themselves, Mr. Beddoes."

"That may be, but it just ain't practical. It stands

to reason that nobody's going to ride those contraptions except out of curiosity. And as for hauling freight, why, they ain't in the running." Jonathan failed to notice Mr. Stacey's wince at his grammar, even though that had been one of the things that Jacob had warned him about, Northerners not being natural in such matters. "It's river traffic that keeps this country running. These steam cars are downright outlandish, a few open carriages hooked together, hauled by an engine that can break down any minute, throwing smoke and cinders all over the place. And where's the room for cargo? How many bales of cotton can you stow in a steam car? And what happens when the foolish things go off the tracks, or a storm lays a tree on the rails, or a cow gets in the way? You can keep your steam cars, sir, I'll stick to riverboats by h—" He caught himself just in time, Mr. Stacey's icy stare reminding him that one did not blaspheme in Boston, no matter the provocation.

Jonathan stiffened with incredulous shock as a young female voice broke into the purely masculine conversation.

"Mr. Beddoes, the steam cars spell progress, and no one, not even a Southern planter, can stop progress! This is the age of science, of the machine. Miss Emily is convinced that in a few years, maybe even as little as a decade, the steam cars will interlace all of the unsettled tracts and vast stretches of uninhabited land."

Jonathan turned and looked directly into the face of that colorless young person he had been presented to when he had arrived. A young lady, scarcely more than a child, voicing her opinion on matters she couldn't possibly understand, and to men! If he hadn't been cold sober he'd have wondered if he were hallucinating.

"And who, may I inquire, is Miss Emily, who seems to be such an authority?"

"Miss Emily is my aunt, and she has a mind as astute as any man in this room." Martha's eyes challenged him until she realized, with a jolt, that everyone in the room was looking at her. But drat it, she didn't care! Just because they were men, did they think they had a monopoly on brains? Anyway, the damage was already done, so she might as well be hanged for a sheep as for a lamb.

"And furthermore," she plunged on, her cheeks red with the excitement of battle, "anyone with eyes in his head, who keeps up with the newspapers, must know that progress will not be halted! Do you think that the first boats evolved by mankind were foolproof? If your way of thinking prevailed, Mr. Beddoes, your riverboats would still be propelled by oars! Would you say that it would be better if Mr. Fulton had never perfected the steamboat?"

"Bravo!" Incredibly, Mr. Stacey was applauding this female creature. 'She has you there, Mr. Beddoes. And as for Miss Emily Curtis, I have had the inestimable pleasure of making her acquaintance, and I'd advise you to take her opinions seriously, because she knows whereof she speaks. Remarkable lady, Miss Emily, and by all appearances she has raised another to be as remarkable!"

Great suffering catfish, what kind of a country was this? Back home, among gentlefolk, any young female who voiced her opinions in mixed company would have been reprimanded by her father or her husband, but here was a banking man egging the girl on! Jonathan's eyes took on a glow that would have warned closer acquaintances as he turned them on the young chit who came to stand in front of him with her eyes flashing.

21

Unaccountably, a little shock ran along his veins. Could this be the same girl he'd been introduced to and had dismissed without a second glance? Miss Hester, his hostess's daughter, had caught his attention because she was a delectable piece of young womanhood, but then he'd been informed, in the same breath, that she was already spoken for. But this argumentative young witch hadn't rated a second glance. Until now.

For a moment, he felt uncertain, a state foreign to him. Those green eyes of hers were the exact color of the green glass buttons that ran in two double rows down the bodice of her frumpy gray dress, and as sparkling. His shock deepened as he realized that she was controlling an anger as intense as his own.

Martha stood her ground. She was not going to give way when she was right! It didn't matter anyway. She'd already made up her mind that she'd never come here again. The other young man, a Mr. Flemming, whom Sarah Lattimer had invited for her special benefit, was more horrendous than any of the others to whom she'd been subjected in the past. A veritable ninny-face, well pimpled, and an Adam's apple that jumped up and down like a monkey on a string whenever he spoke. The humiliation of having such a young nincompoop thrust at her with the expectation that she'd be grateful was enough to make her throw all caution to the winds. She had jumped into the conversation on railroads, in part, to escape the unattractive Flemming.

And as for this Southern aristocrat, Jonathan Beddoes, Old Mrs. Lattimer was probably right. There could very well be horns under that unruly black hair, a lock of which, in the heat of the argument, had fallen over his forehead in a most disconcerting manner. Even while she seethed, Martha's hand itched to brush that lock back where it belonged.

Sarah Lattimer, her face red with mortification at this unseemly argument in her own parlor, hurried toward them to intervene. What ailed the girl, she wondered, to make a scene, when she'd always done the best she could for her. It was no fault of hers that Nancy's girl wasn't marriageable. But before Sarah was able to interrupt, the clang of church bells filled the room through the opened windows.

"Fire!" Mr. Stacey exclaimed. As Jonathan watched, open-mouthed, all of the men in the room, including the elderly Mr. Foster, rushed out of doors, sweeping him along with them.

Outside, the street was already filling with people. "Where is it? What's burning?"

No one knew the answer, and so they ran to the end of the street, questioning other men who had come out of their houses. Bertram Foster pounded along with the others, his face alight with excitement. "Where? Where?"

"It's the Brattle Street Meeting House!"

"Nonsense! It's nowhere near there! Listen, it's near Mr. Papanti's dancing school!"

They ran on, rumor and counter-rumor flying as men found breath to question others. Now Jonathan smelled smoke, as more church bells joined in the cacophony.

"There! There it is!"

A fire engine appeared, rounding the corner, pulled by perspiring men. Every place there was room, more hands latched on to help its progress. With most of its buildings made largely of wood, fire was Boston's recurring nightmare. The volunteer firemen fought for the honor of serving and were exempted from militia

23

service as being more important to the city's welfare than soldiers.

The house that was burning was completely enveloped in flames by the time they reached it. The mob was so thick that the men could scarcely locate a well for the suction engine so they could pump water onto the burning structure.

"Too late for this one, get some water on the others!"

Men sweated and grunted, working the brakes to pump the water. As they tired, other men took their places. Another engine arrived; another well was put to use. Dripping with sweat, blackened by smoke, Jonathan manned the brakes in his turn, side by side with Mr. Foster, who now bore no resemblance to the staid, pedantic man Jonathan knew. A woman stood on the outskirts of the crowd, holding her children close, her face stark as she watched all her worldly possessions being consumed in the flames. Jonathan surmised that the man standing near her, his face vacant with shock, was her husband.

The wall of the neighboring house was charred, but the efforts of the firemen and the willing spectators prevented it from catching.

"We did it, boy, we did it!" A grin split Mr. Foster's face, and he pounded Jonathan's shoulders so hard that the younger man flinched. "This calls for a drink!"

Jonathan was in hearty agreement. But, when they finally found a tavern, the drink turned out to be a mild sherry, and only one, drunk as a toast to their success. Philosophically, Jonathan shrugged. One more night in Bertram Foster's house with its heavy furniture placed foursquare against the walls, its marble-topped table in the exact center of the sitting room, was all that was left. One more breakfast when he'd be constrained to choke down the inevitable codfish cakes, codfish being served in some form every day of the year in order to support the fishing economy. Soon he could put Boston behind him. Ahead lay New York, with all its delights.

Once, just before he fell asleep, Jonathan remembered the girl, what was her name, it had eluded him, with whom he had been so angry at the Lattimers'. No matter; he wouldn't be seeing her again and so he had no need to remember her name. He turned over on Mr. Foster's uncomfortably hard mattress and put the girl, and the codfish cakes, out of his mind.

"Leave the girl alone," Miss Emily told Nancy. "That young pipsqueak she ignored would have bored her to death inside a year if he had asked for her hand and she'd been fool enough to accept."

"Aunt Emily, Martha actually entered into an altercation with Mr. Beddoes!" Usually the mildest of women, Nancy was still constrained to protest her daughter's behavior. Sarah would certainly never invite them again!

"He deserved to be argued with, and I have no doubt that Martha came out on top. She'll never see the man again, so where's the harm?"

"We're thoroughly in disgrace with Sarah!" Nancy was close to tears.

"Good. I never could abide the woman. Martha will do well enough where she is. No man Sarah Lattimer might pick out would be half good enough for her."

Martha left them to their argument and went out to milk the cow. It was a comfort to rest her cheek against the warm flank and let her fingers go about their business with no direction from her mind. The milk splatted into the pail, making hissing noises until the bottom was covered.

Young Mr. Flemming with his pimples and his Adam's apple, drat! It wasn't being a spinster she minded, but it would be nice to have children.

"Lucky old bovine, you!" Martha said. "Animals are allowed to have offspring without being married; how is it that women aren't treated as well as animals?" A grin spread over her face. Wouldn't Sarah Lattimer swoon, if she could hear her!

I wonder if there are horns under his hair, Martha thought, and Bossy mooed in protest as she gave a sudden hard jerk.

Drat, drat, drat! She'd never see him again, and she wished she'd never seen him at all. What right did that arrogant creature have to so disturb her peace of mind? She didn't cry, even though she felt like it, because she had been brought up by Aunt Emily not to cry over things that couldn't be helped. Saying drat a few extra times was a sight more satisfying than tears, anyway.

One thing was certain. She wasn't going to let the memory of a man she'd seen only once keep her from marrying some sturdy farmer if and when she felt like it and raising a passel of children, none of whom would have gray eyes under a shock of coal-black hair.

Jonathan swore, long and vehemently, under his breath. He was supposed to be having the time of his life. The dining room furniture was bought, crated, and consigned to Roselawns. The other goods, staples and luxuries, had been contracted for and would likewise arrive at the plantation in good time.

Twenty-four chairs, Jonathan thought! The house, built by his Cavalier grandfather who had come from England, and since enlarged, had been good enough as it was. The three of them would rattle around in

26

that new dining room, because the Beddoes had not run to surviving children. The women had bred well enough. His grandmother had had seven, but most of them had died, carried off by summer fevers or accident, to say nothing of the boy who had been killed by the Creeks during one of the skirmishes that had plagued the country, or the girl who had died of snakebite when she'd wandered off from her mammy. The others, two of them besides Jacob, had been girls, married now, one in New Orleans and the other dead in childbirth.

Jonathan was the firstborn, and Yolande had thereafter given birth, one after another, to five premature, sickly girl-babies all of whom had died. Then her body, directed by a mind that could bear no more heartbreak, had refused to produce any more. That fact had left Jacob with no little bitterness but still with dreams of half a dozen or so strapping grandsons, provided he could browbeat Jon into marrying the giddy Miss Amelia of the ample hips—and whose family ran to boys.

But, please Lord, Jonathan thought, not for a while yet. He had a heap of living to do before he tied himself down to a whey-faced broodmare and a herd of whey-faced young 'uns. He swore again, silently, and turned in bed.

Resolutely, he smiled down into the limpid blue eyes of the rosy Miss Leah. Mr. Compton, true to Jacob's prediction, had set him up well. The sheets on the bed were satin, smooth and sensuous to the touch. His partner's skin was equally smooth and satiny, and smelled of something calculated to make a man's head reel. Leah was young, beautiful, and a mistress of her art. Why, then, did Jonathan keep remembering a pair of eyes as green as glass, a face that held no beauty except for clean, pure lines?

27

Jonathan applied himself. He'd paid for a night's pleasure, and he was going to have it. No little country bluestocking was going to cheat him of it.

Leah writhed, moaned, and gasped with real or feigned ecstasy. Her arms clung to him, and there was real admiration in her eyes. Jonathan wasn't prone to conceit, but neither was he one to ignore facts, and the fact was that he was an extraordinarily good-looking man, one who made female heads turn wherever he went. The very thought of Jonathan Beddoes being intrigued by somebody's country cousin was ludicrous.

Being here was why he'd come north, and this was his first night of freedom. He must be sickening for something, though, for even the wine tasted flat.

He returned to the Compton house before eleven, almost completely sober and as quiet as a lamb, so as not to disturb Mrs. Compton, who was ignorant of his evening's activities.

Damn her. Martha what-was-her-name! What was she but a stiff, priggish little nobody heading for certain spinsterhood, because if a man couldn't even remember what she looked like, what chance did she have to get married? She certainly had nothing material to help her sink her hook into a marriageable male. The way she'd been dressed, she looked like somebody's poor relation. Pounding his pillow, Jonathan gritted his teeth and swore that tomorrow night he'd make up for tonight. There'd been a redhead at Madame Helene's, voluptuous and sultry. Tonight she'd been engaged, but he'd call in early tomorrow to make sure that she'd be available. He'd never have any trouble remembering what she looked like! And she'd remember him, too, if he had anything to say about it.

In the morning, over Lewis Compton's protests and his poorly concealed disappointment at not being re-

28

galed with an account of Jonathan's evening, Jonathan packed a portmanteau and returned to Boston.

Sarah Lattimer's astonishment was profound when her maid announced her visitor and even more profound when she learned that Mr. Beddoes had come to pay his respects, if he had permission, to Miss Martha Curtis. Sarah managed to control her amazement enough to inform the young man that Martha had returned last evening to Martin's Corners.

By midafternoon, Jonathan had rented a livery horse, bought a pair of saddlebags, and was traveling north and west. Sarah rushed off immediately to apprise her bosom friend, Mrs. Greentree, of the earthshaking news that an immensely wealthy and attractive young Southern planter was so enamored of "Poor Martha" that he was on his way to Martin's Corners at that very moment to see her again.

3

The small white house was set well back from the road in a neatly tended yard. A picket fence, with holyhocks growing along it, enclosed the yard and extended around the sides and back to where the outhouses and the vegetable garden were. It was the last house along the road that was the main street of the small settlement. Jonathan had stopped at the general store, which also housed the Post Office, to ask directions.

By now, he felt something of a fool, but having come this far, he determined to carry it through. He'd at least get another look at the girl and set his mind at rest that she was no more worth cultivating than he'd thought she was when he'd dismissed her as entirely without interest to him seconds after he'd met her.

Then, after finding a place to rest for the night, for himself and the horse, he'd return to Boston and from there proceed to New York to collect the rest of his personal belongings and go home to Roselawns. But just for the hell of it, he had to have another look at the girl who had spoiled what was supposed to be a week of riotous revelry in New York, probably the last freedom he'd know before Jacob pushed him into marrying Miss Amelia. If Jacob ever found out about this, Jonathan would never hear the last of it.

But Jacob was a long way away, and there was little chance that he'd find out. Jacob would be satisfied with descriptions of the lovely Leah and of the red-haired beauty that Jonathan had not returned to Madame Helene's to try out.

A rambling rose climbed luxuriously around the small front porch. The black iron knocker, in the shape of a lion's head, was freshly painted. The whole place spoke of an owner with a neat and ordered mind, tempered with a love of beauty that came out in the careful tending of lawn and flowers. There were no weeds in the flower beds, and the window shades were drawn to an exact line, with stiffly starched white curtains showing behind glistening panes.

There was no answer to his knock. He waited, and knocked again, but obviously no one was at home. He heard a cow moo somewhere out back, along with the busy clucking of chickens. To satisfy himself that there was indeed no one about, Jonathan walked around the house and saw a small barn, painted white like the house, its door standing wide to the late afternoon sunshine.

She was there, milking a cow. She had not heard his approach. Her cheek was pressed against the animal's flank, and her hands looked strong and capable as she sent streams of milk hissing into the bucket. A tortoiseshell cat, the biggest Jonathan had ever seen, stood up on its hind legs and pawed at the white stream, and she laughed.

"All right, Jebadiah, you old beggar!" She directed a squirt of milk at the cat, which caught it in his opened mouth, its face and whiskers getting well splattered. The girl laughed again.

"Now, you know that's wasteful! You just be patient

till I get this to the springhouse, and then I'll fetch your saucer. Greedy-puss! No, no more, go on, scat! If you're starving, go find yourself a field mouse!"

Her calico dress, a faded blue, was without adornment, its sleeves rolled to her elbows. It was open at the throat against the warmth of the day, and Jonathan saw a pulse throbbing there and had an insane desire to kiss it. Her hair, as it had been at the Lattimers', was parted severely in the middle and coiled over her ears in shining braids, but a few tendrils had escaped and curled over her smooth forehead. So it was brown, after all. He hadn't been quite sure.

The cat pawed at her again, and she shook her head at it. "Not one more drop! Waste not, want not, you foolish creature. Go lick your chops, there's enough there to hold you till I'm done. Coo, Bossy, you stop that, you pesky imp!"

The cow had flapped its tail in her face, and now it turned its head and butted it against her. "Drat it, you cut that out! I like you, too, but I don't go butting at you!"

Rising from the three-legged milking stool, Martha lifted the bucket without effort, only to find a strong, tanned hand on the pail as she turned. Her mouth opened with amazement, her eyes with shock.

"You! What in tunket are you doing here?"

"Miss Martha, where I come from, that would be called downright inhospitable, to say nothing of impolite. I came here to see you and Miss Emily, of course."

"But why? Why on earth would you have wanted to?" Her face had colored now, as a flush spread down across her opened neckline. With an effort, she collected herself.

"I'm sorry, Mr. Beddoes. You've ridden a long way, you're tired. Miss Emily and my mother have gone to tend a child-birthing. That is, Aunt Emily will officiate; the sight of blood makes my mother sick and she can't bear to hear screaming. Mehitabel Tait does carry on something disgraceful. But Mama makes herself useful keeping the other young 'uns out from underfoot. Goodness knows why Mehitabel carries on so, she drops them as easy as a cow dropping a calf—easier, because the last time Bossy had trouble, and Miss Emily and I had to turn it before it could get out and we were blood up to our elbows." Martha paused for a moment to catch her breath. She realized she was talking too much, but she had never been so surprised and flustered. "I usually go with my aunt to help, but I'm afraid Mehitabel took a dislike to me after the last time because I told her to quit wasting her breath howling and use it to push so's we could get the business over. My goodness, that baby was sweet! It was another girl, of course. All Mehitabel has are girls."

Jonathan was flabbergasted. In his whole twenty-three years, he had never heard mention of child-bearing from any female's lips. It was a subject for women only. Men were supposed to think that their wives retired to their bedchambers with a slight indisposition, and suddenly there was a new baby, out of nowhere—a gift from heaven and a complete surprise, already dressed in frills and laces. But here was this girl, this frustratingly maddening girl, regaling him with details as if it were the most ordinary thing in the world. His mother would go into a decline.

"Come along. There's cold buttermilk in the well. Or you can have coffee. Supper will be a little while yet."

"But I understood you to say that your mother and Miss Emily aren't at home." Jonathan was more perplexed than ever. She couldn't be inviting him into the house, with no elders or even a servant there to chaperone her!

Martha was as perplexed as he was. What ailed the man? Had he come to see them, or hadn't he? "Well, they aren't, but they'll be back as soon as Mehitabel lets them. Come along. Here's the well." Deftly, she pulled up a bucket. "Aunt Emily says the sooner you cool milk, the better it keeps, and she's right."

With an economy of motion, she handed him the smaller bucket, took the larger one with fresh, warm milk from his hand and disappeared into the small springhouse. Returning, she led him through a woodshed and into the kitchen. It was the first time in his life that Jonathan had entered a house other than his own through the back door.

The wide-board wood floor was scrubbed white and brightened with rag rugs. Pots of geraniums sat on the windowsills, and bright copper utensils were interspaced with black cast iron on the walls. A delicious aroma, emanating from the oven set into the wall beside the fieldstone fireplace, filled the room.

"We're old-fashioned here," Martha told him cheerfully. "Every time Aunt Emily gets to the point of buying a proper kitchen range, there's some books she wants more, and so we make do. Use it up, wear it out, make it do, do without. That's an old New England saying. We're experts at making do."

She set the buttermilk on the deal table and went to the oven. Using a thick pair of hot-pads taken from a nail on the wall, she took out a crockery bowl of baked beans and set it on an iron trivet and reached in again to draw out a pan of gingerbread, the source of the mouth-watering smell. "Time these came out, before they burn. Where did you leave your horse, Mr. Beddoes? You can tend it and then wash up, there's a bucket of water and a washbasin and soap

34

and towels just outside the woodshed. I'm sorry we don't have any oats, but there's hay in the barn and plenty of grass in the side yard. Mind you don't let the animal get into Aunt Emily's flowers, or she'll skin you alive, even if you are a guest."

She was still talking too much and she knew it, but she couldn't seem to stop. He couldn't have come all the way from Boston just to see Aunt Emily—it didn't make sense. But as he certainly hadn't made the journey to see her mother, the only other alternative was too overwhelming to contemplate. Drat Mehitabel Tait, anyway! Why'd she have to pick today, of all days? If only Aunt Emily were here!

But she wasn't, and so Martha had to do the best she could. She spread the table with her aunt's best linen cloth and set it with the good china, the service for six that her mother had salvaged from her Spode service for twenty-four. That had been eighteen years ago and not a piece of it broken yet, but if her hands didn't stop their infernal shaking, she would break the first piece and her mother's heart along with it.

When Jonathan returned from hitching the horse in the side yard, he found the table set for four. Martha, her sleeves rolled down now, was placing an iron coffeepot on another trivet.

"I thought we'd go ahead and eat, because there's no telling how long Aunt Emily and Mama will be. You never can tell with Mehitabel. I swear she holds back just to cause as much trouble as she can, because she's sick of having girl babies and her husband'll be mad at her again. I hope you like baked beans. We weren't expecting company."

"I'm mighty fond of baked beans," Jonathan lied. What the hell did he care what he ate? Martha had just smiled, and the plain girl he'd met at the Lattimers' disappeared. The girl who stood in front of him now

35

wasn't pretty, she was a stark, raving beauty. Good Lord, I'm done for! he thought. "We don't get many baked beans down home, it's a treat for me."

He held Martha's chair for her, and when he was seated opposite her, she bowed her head and clasped her hands. "Oh Lord, we thank Thee for Thy bounty, and for all our many blessings. Amen." It was a simple grace, offered as naturally as breathing. Had Jacob or Yolande ever offered grace before a meal? For the life of him, Jonathan couldn't remember. They went to church regularly because it was the thing to do, but Jacob wasn't one to thank God for what he'd carved out for himself with his own two hands.

Evening was coming on by the time they'd finished dinner. In spite of not caring what was set before him, Jonathan had been ravenous after his long ride, and the beans and gingerbread were by far the best he'd ever eaten.

"You go and sit in the parlor while I wash up, Mr. Beddoes. We don't leave dirty dishes to crust over— it makes extra work and that's wasteful. You might find some of Aunt Emily's books to interest you."

Jonathan let his amusement show. "I doubt that a lady's books would be of all that much interest to me. I'm not much on needlework and fashions."

"That's all you know! Why, men come from all over this section to borrow Miss Emily's books, and then more often than not they have to get her to explain them to them!"

There it was again. Her hazel eyes had turned glass green, and the angry set to her mouth made her more beautiful than ever. He wasn't crazy. She was truly a beauty, and as full of pepper as a peppermill. If he hadn't followed his impulse to come and find her, he might as well have thrown away the rest of his life.

"Miss Martha, will you marry me?"

36

She didn't drop the cups she was holding, but it was a near thing. "Oh, Lord, now look what you almost made me do! Mama's Spode, the only thing she had from her old home." Her face was white and her eyes were greener than ever as she looked at him as if she'd just discovered that her tortoiseshell cat was rabid. She put the cups, very carefully, on the stone dry-sink and turned to face him again.

"That wasn't very amusing, Mr. Beddoes." Her mouth was firm, pressed tight at the corners. "I should think you'd have been taught better manners. These dishes are irreplaceable, and I don't care for being made fun of, either. I'm not used to that kind of a joke."

Before Jonathan could open his mouth to protest, Emily, followed by Nancy, entered from the woodshed. Nancy was disheveled. There were stains on her dress, and her hair had come loose from the pins, and there were circles of fatigue under her eyes. But Emily was as neat as a new pin and not at all tired.

"Another girl. This makes five, and Sam's fit to be tied," Emily said cheerfully. "I hope our supper's ready, Martha. All Sam Tait offered us was salt pork and boiled cabbage left over from yesterday. Listening to Mehitabel caterwaul is a day's work, and I'm famished."

The two women, so dissimilar to each other, stopped in the kitchen doorway and looked from Jonathan to Martha and back to Jonathan. Nancy's face flushed, and her hand went to her hair with a fluttering motion.

"Why, it's Mr. Beddoes! How pleasant to see you again." Distressed, she took in Martha's plain cotton housedress and sturdy everyday shoes, and she winced. Why, she looked like somebody's hired girl!

Emily was unperturbed. She held out a small, capable hand to Jonathan. "I'm Emily Curtis. You

37

already know my sister-in-law, Nancy Curtis. Have you had your supper? Good. Martha, just pour me a cup of coffee while I get myself outside of some of those beans. That gingerbread looks delicious; you must have known I'd be starved after tending to Mehitabel. Now, Mr. Beddoes, what brings you to these parts? I shouldn't have thought there would be anything in Martin's Corners to interest you."

"Ma'am, three lovely ladies are of interest to any man!" Jonathan protested.

"Don't listen to him, Aunt Emily. He's insane," Martha said, sounding more than a little desperate.

Jonathan looked at Miss Emily, and there was a twinkle in her eyes, although her mouth told him she wes reserving her opinion of him until she knew him better.

"I asked her to marry me." Jonathan spoke to Miss Emily because it was obvious that she was the head of this family. "That's why she says I'm insane." And maybe she's right, he thought. "I expect I should have asked your permission to address her, so I'll remedy my omission now."

"Not tonight, I hope." Miss Emily's voice was dry. "It's late, and I'm a little tired, and I'm a woman who refuses to be hurried. Besides, if I said yes, on such short notice, it'd be a scandal."

"Aunt Emily!" Martha's voice was anguished. "It isn't funny! What am I, a piece of livestock to be discussed and disposed of without being consulted?"

"You're a girl who's talking when she should be working," Miss Emily told her tartly. "Sit down, Mr. Beddoes. I'm very happy to see you here. I've never had the opportunity to talk in person with a Southern planter, and I fully intend to pick your brains."

Her questions were astute and to the point. Was cotton their only crop? Didn't he realize that planting cotton year after year would ruin the land? Had they thought of trying tobacco, which she understood was a good money crop? She disapproved of tobacco herself, not because smoking was a sin, which it wasn't, but because it seemed an unhealthy habit. What provision was made for the slaves when they grew too old to work, and wasn't slavery a self-defeating proposition in itself? The children had to be nurtured until they were old enough to be of real value, and the old people cared for after they were worn out.

"The South, Mr. Beddoes, is vulnerable. Everything you own is tied up in your land and your slaves. You have virtually no manufactures, you depend on the North for every commodity from table salt to shoes and farming tools. All of your eggs, so to speak, are in one basket. If there is trouble over Free Trade, and I believe that there will be, I rather think that you will find that you have a bear by the tail."

Her grasp of the situation astounded Jonathan, even though he had been warned by both Mr. Stacey and Mr. Foster that Miss Emily was a woman to be reckoned with. He'd like to have his father hear her point of view—Jacob would have apoplexy.

"It ain't going to come to that, ma'am. Not for some time at least. The North needs our cotton. How long would your mills last without it? No, ma'am, your North depends on us as much as we depend on you."

"But we would survive, Mr. Beddoes. I am afraid that the South would not."

Nancy had retired to the room she shared with Martha and made herself more presentable, her mind in a turmoil. To think that just a few days ago, she'd been upset because Martha had wasted her chance to interest that young Mr. Flemming, a third son to be sure, but from a sound merchant family. And now here was Mr. Beddoes, come to see Martha, all this way, and with no warning, and he'd asked her to marry him! Her Martha, the mistress of a vast plantation! What would Sarah think of that? Even Hester's match paled by comparison.

"You sound like one of our neighbors, a Mr. Amhurst," Jonathan told Emily. "He's a Scotch Presbyterian, and always talking along those lines. If it wasn't against the law, he'd even teach his slaves to read and write! As it is he's training his brighter people in carpentry and other mechanics, against the time when they might need to be self-supporting, he says. The rest of the county doesn't hold with his notions. It's causing high feelings among some of the better families."

"Mr. Amhurst sounds like a sensible man. It's too bad that others won't profit by his example. You need industry, Mr. Beddoes, if the South is to know any kind of security."

"We've tried industry, ma'am." Jonathan cautioned himself to patience. "But I'm afraid we aren't worth shucks at running factories, and the Northerners we brought in weren't able to handle the blacks. They can be mighty exasperating, if you'll pardon the expression. No, we'll leave the manufacturing to you Northerners. Cotton is king in the South, and we're content with it."

"A great mistake." Emily helped herself to a second piece of gingerbread. "I'm afraid you'll regret it. But then, I expected your attitude to be exactly what it is. We here in the United States are like two separate countries, more's the pity. The Puritan North, where austerity and hard work is the rule, and your South, peopled with so-called Cavaliers, gentlemen all, used to living off the fruits of other people's labors. Each

40

side, unfortunately, is narrow in its thinking. Sometimes it surprises me that we still speak the same language. The South is evolving into a country apart, and I cannot think where it might end."

"We'll end all right if you Northerners will leave us be! All we want is to be left alone to run our own affairs in our own way, ma'am. We'll make do."

"But we won't leave you alone, Mr. Beddoes. I can assure you that we won't. The North, I'm afraid, looks on the South as a source of wealth, to be milked for all it's worth. It's a matter of business, Mr. Beddoes, and blasphemous as it sounds, most Northerners believe that business, not cleanliness, is next to godliness."

Emily had finished her supper now, and she rose. "There is no inn in Martin's Corners, Mr. Beddoes, and the nearest public accommodation is too far for you to travel tonight." There was a sparkle of deviltry in her eyes. "And as we have but two bedrooms, I am afraid that you will have to sleep in the barn. Martha, fetch Mr. Beddoes a blanket."

Jonathan was speechless. To be invited—no, ordered —to sleep in the barn! He had all he could do not to explode with laughter. Miss Emily knew it, and they grinned at each other, while Nancy's face turned first red and then a sickly white. What would Sarah say!

"One more thing, Mr. Beddoes. A cigar is permissible, but not in my barn. You'll find matches on the shelf, but do your smoking out of doors. Our Northern winters are too inclement for a cow to be without shelter."

Jonathan nodded at her, not at all put out. The matches were where she had indicated. Imported from Germany, these inventions consisted of a cylinder of red paper, four inches high and an inch in diameter.

At the bottom of the cylinder, a little bottle of asbestos was soaked in sulphuric acid; in the top were about one hundred matches made of chlorate of potash. The tip of the match was inserted into the bottle and drawn out aflame, a real improvement over the tinderbox. Well, Germans were Northern people, too, leave it to them to be inventive. Jonathan looked at the flaming match he held in his hand; his eyebrows quirked, and then he tossed it into the fireplace.

"It's a pity I don't smoke. I'd have liked to test that match out," he said. "We'll discuss the other matter in the morning, ma'am. I take it that Martha will be permitted to make up her own mind?"

"Martha has been making up her own mind since she was five. And if your arguments are to be *pro*, Mr. Beddoes, you must grant me the right to argue *con*. She is, after all, my only niece, and there are facets to be explored in depth. As you were introduced to my family under the auspices of Mr. Foster, we need not question your eligibility. The question remains, even if Martha has a fancy for you, could she be happy in an alien environment? If your itinerary does not allow time for me to make sure that she understands exactly what would be involved, perhaps it is for the best. I do not disbelieve in love at first sight. I simply mistrust it."

"I can take all the time that's needed." Jonathan's voice was firm. As Jacob would say, hell's bells, he'd already made up his mind, and he might as well stick with it, crazy or not. There'd been plenty of people who'd thought that the families that had cleared the wilderness were crazy.

"Very well. Good night, Mr. Beddoes."

Looking at Miss Emily's steady eyes, Jonathan was glad that she had promised him that Martha would be allowed to make up her own mind. He didn't relish the idea of fighting that woman, especially as he wasn't at all sure he'd win.

4

The Richmond, Fredericksburg and Potomac Rail Road Company had a train that left New York City at four P.M. and promised, most faithfully, to deliver its passengers, sound of wind and limb, in Baltimore at three P.M. of the following day.

They sat in the first coach and Martha's excitement was at fever pitch. To ride the steam cars was more exciting than the wedding itself, which had taken place at the First Congregational Church in Boston, under the flustered but still capable direction of Sarah Lattimer. Mr. Lattimer, as the closest male friend of the Curtis family, had given the bride away, and Bertram Foster, hastily summoned, had stood as Jonathan's best man. Having Mr. Foster stand for him would go a long way toward cooling Mr. Beddoes's wrath. Jonathan's father, no matter how angry, would realize that Mr. Foster would never have countenanced the marriage if the bride were unacceptable.

Hester, resplendent in the latest Paris fashion, had been Martha's only attendant. Hester's gown of blue shot silk featured the new very sloping shoulders and had a wide lace collar, set off by a cameo brooch. There was lace on the sleeves at the point of the collar and again slightly above the wrist, where they narrowed to a sort of cuff-like effect. The skirt was voluminous, with a wide lace panel running from waist to hem. Hester's bonnet, perched above both real and artificial curls, was festooned with cabbage roses and had a very round brim, which tied under her chin with a wide satin ribbon. Rotundity, Hester had told Martha condescendingly, was the order of the day; the effect must be of roundness. Even the artificial curls had been arranged around Hester's face to enhance its roundness.

There had been no bridal gown for Martha. There was no time to make one, and Jonathan had been thoroughly cowed by Miss Emily's withering glance when he had suggested that he should buy her one ready made. Use it up, wear it out, make it do, do without. In Martha's case, she made do with one of her mother's gowns from her more prosperous days, hastily altered to fit her slighter figure and conform, however slightly, to the mode. And Martha had steadfastly refused to have her hair tortured into curls. She was being enough of a fool, marrying a man she hardly knew and going off to some outlandish plantation, without that.

Now, seated in the train coach, Jonathan teased her. "You only married me because you'd have a chance to ride the steam cars! You'd have married the first peddler who came down the road, if he'd promised you this trip."

"I might have, at that." Martha's eyes were shining. "When is it going to start, Jonathan? What's delaying us?" She bounced up and down in her excitement, forgetful of her new matronly dignity. Married she might be, but riding on the railroad was next to a trip to heaven.

The coach looked for all the world like a boat set on a platform on wheels. It had a roof, but the sides were open. Directly in front of the first coach, an open car that resembled a farm cart acted as a buffer between the coaches and the locomotive that pulled the train. This cart was loaded with bales of cotton, stacked high, to protect the passengers in case the engine exploded. A necessary precaution, considering the fact that on June the seventeenth, 1831, the engine "Best Friend of Charleston" had exploded when its black fireman, annoyed at the shrill sound escaping from the safety valve while the engine had been turned around on a revolving platform, had sat down on the valve lever. The fireman had been killed and two other men severely injured in the resultant blast.

They were going to move! They were moving, with a sudden, violent jerk that sent Martha catapulting forward. Jonathan had to catch her and, pulling her back onto her seat, put his arm around her to brace her. The cars, hooked together with three feet of chain, were far from stable during starts and stops; either they banged together or jerked apart with a snap that never failed to unseat the unwary. The noise was deafening. Billows of black smoke from the smokestack drifted back over the coaches, so that Martha choked and tears flooded her eyes. Jonathan put his handkerchief into her hand and laughed at her.

"This ain't the worst of it. Wait till the sparks start burning holes in your dress. I told you the steam cars are no way for a lady to travel. You'll be glad enough to get shut of them once we reach Baltimore."

"If I were a betting woman, I'd lay you a wager on that!" Martha retorted. She had more to say, but it was broken off when a large spark fell on her sensible brown traveling gown and she had to beat it out, but not before a small hole appeared in the material.

"Told you so." Jonathan was amused. "We should have gone by stage. Not that we won't have plenty of that, and river packets, too. You have quite a journey ahead of you, Mrs. Beddoes."

"And I fully intend to savor every moment of it, Mr. Beddoes."

Her words were spoken with conviction, with all the New England fortitude that had been bred in her, but as the hours passed, she was hard put to keep up her enthusiastic front. She felt, before the first hour had passed, that every bone in her body had been jolted out of place. Her face and hands were grimy; her gown was ruined. Sitting beside her, Jonathan could have passed, except for his impeccably tailored suit, as one of his own fieldhands, and Martha knew that her own hands and face must be as black.

"We've all turned into Negroes! Are you sure some slave-chaser won't pick us up?"

"That's a Northerner for you! There aren't that many escaped slaves, Miss Know-it-all! Mighty few of them even want to escape," he argued. "And you haven't seen anything yet. If that engine breaks down, all of us men will have to get out and push the train to the next station, providing it's close enough. Otherwise, we wait for the crew to haggle horses from some farmer to haul us on in. Outlandish contraptions, steam cars! Only fools would think they'll ever amount to anything."

Martha folded her neatly gloved hands in her lap and reflected on the sermons she had heard that had echoed those very sentiments. Many preachers throughout the country ranted and raved about trains from their pulpits, shouting that the devil was behind the contraption, that they were against both God and nature, and that the people should rise in arms against them before the nation as a whole was damned for condoning them. Such sentiments did not meet with her aunt's approval.

Martha looked at Jonathan out of the corners of her eyes. "Are you implying that Aunt Emily is a fool?"

Jonathan was indulgent. "Miss Emily is a mighty smart woman, but she's wrong about this. It's nothing more than a novelty."

"You are wrong, Mr. Beddoes. Trains are here to stay. When they've made you rich, hauling your cotton more economically and faster than river boats and wagons, I'll remind you of this conversation."

Great jumping hoptoads, Jonathan thought, I hope she doesn't run on like this in front of my father! Jacob might not survive the shock of hearing a woman contradict her husband, much less her father-in-law. It wasn't seemly. It was going to be bad enough, facing Jacob and Yolande with a New England wife they'd never laid eyes on, without her starting right off telling them they were wrong about everything under creation.

There was a sudden, rending shock, women's voices rose in screams of panic, and men cursed, as a length of rail came loose from the roadbed and slammed up through the floor of the car. The train came to a jolting stop that once again sent Martha flying from her seat, this time to land in a heap on the floor. Jonathan, caught unaware, hadn't moved quickly enough to catch her. Her round bonnet, which Jonathan had insisted on buying for her in one of New York's finest shops, jolted askew over one eye.

"What is it? Have we had a wreck? Did we bump into something?" she gasped.

The conductor appeared, apparently unperturbed. "It's nothing to worry about, folks. Just keep your seats. We'll be on our way again in a jiffy." He carried a sledgehammer in his hand—required equipment on the cars—and to Martha's amazement, he calmly and

48

efficiently pounded the end of the rail back down through the floor and the train, with another neck-snapping jerk, backed off it.

"Oh, my!" Martha straightened her bonnet as Jonathan lifted her to her seat and settled her once again. "Does that happen very often?"

"Often enough so they have a name for it. They call it a snake-head." Jonathan's tone was amused. "Are you ready to withdraw your rash statement about the wonders of the railroads?"

"No, I am not! I admit that there may be a few small details that need more study, but the railroads are here to stay!" Martha braced herself just in time as the train started again, the offending rail having been secured where it belonged. "Oh, my!"

Their accommodations for the night were at an inn because the train could not proceed after dark. Attempts had been made in the past to light the tracks by pushing a flatbed in front of the engine, with a bonfire on it to provide illumination, but the smoke and the sparks that came back into the engineer's eyes had proved this method impractical.

Their supper was barely edible, their room poorly furnished, the bed hard and lumpy. Not, Jonathan thought, conducive to a blissful beginning to their marital relations. Because of the lateness of the hour when they had arrived in New York from Boston, and because he had, after all, been raised to regard the fair sex as delicate and in need of consideration, Jonathan had refrained from claiming his marriage rights the night before. Late as it was, Martha had insisted on walking around, as excited as a child, to drink in the sights and sounds of the metropolis. And during their even later supper, served in their hotel room, she had actually fallen asleep over her dessert, worn out by the excitement of the rushed wedding

49

plans and the journey and sightseeing. Jonathan had put her to bed, and she hadn't even wakened when he'd removed her dress and slippers.

Glumly, Jonathan decided that tonight, too, he would have to forgo his marital rights, because today's train ride had been even more rigorous. His bride, after all, was only a fragile female. Being a Southerner and a gentleman entailed disadvantages as well as advantages.

Accordingly, he told Martha that he would join the other male passengers at the bar for a while and let her go up to their room alone. The coarseness of most of his fellow-passengers irritated him, and their nasal Northern twangs grated on his nerves, but he remained there for nearly an hour, so that Martha would be asleep when he joined her.

She had turned the oil lamp on the mantelpiece low, and her eyes were closed and her breathing even when he returned to their room. He undressed, blew out the lamp, and eased himself in beside her as carefully as possible, turning his back on her to try to control his burgeoning desires.

Martha sat up, her hair loosened from its braids and flowing around her shoulders. Her voice was sharp.

"Mr. Beddoes, just what do you think you're doing?"

"I thought you were asleep." To his chagrin, Jonathan's voice sounded sheepish.

"That was last night! Just how long do you expect me to wait to become a real married woman?"

"But I thought . . . the journey was so tiring. . . ."

"Well, you can just think again! I've helped a couple of dozen babies into the world, and it's time I found out what's so all-fired wonderful about conceiving them!"

Jonathan's mouth dropped open, and he looked so

50

ludicrous that Martha laughed. She held out her arms to him, inviting him to come to her.

"You needn't look at me as if I'm some hussy trying to seduce you! We're married, Jon, or have you forgotten? I can be as wanton as I want to be with my own husband; at least, that's what Aunt Emily always told me when I asked her about such things. She was wonderful, Jon! She didn't try to change the subject, or tell me that nice young ladies don't think about such things. She just told me the facts, that as long as a woman has to submit to her husband anyway, and even go to all the work of bearing the babies, then she has a perfect right to enjoy the lovemaking as much as her husband!"

Fire swept through Jonathan's body as Martha's arms went around him, as her parted mouth made contact with his. Even Leah didn't know half, with all of her artifices, of what this bride of his knew by instinct! And Martha was honest, a thing he had never before run into in any decent woman.

He'd kissed girls before, a lot of girls. But none of them had had the power to move him as this slender wisp of a girl whose body flamed against his, pulsing and throbbing.

Even as his senses reeled, the strict instructions he had received since puberty, concerning the correct way for a gentleman to treat his wife, made him cautious. "Martha, do you realize that I'll have to hurt you?"

"Jonathan, do you realize that I love you? I know you have to hurt me. But it's part of being a woman, and there's nothing I'd rather be right now than a woman, *your* woman!"

Impatiently, she struggled out of the hampering folds of her nightgown. Then she was with him again, mouth and legs parted, vibrating with eagerness.

Jonathan had never known that it could be so hard to hold himself back. In spite of her assurances, he didn't want to hurt her. She only knew by hearsay, not by experience, and he knew of too many cases where the bride had been turned against sex on her wedding night and hated that part of marriage all the rest of her life. That mustn't happen to Martha. He had something so infinitely precious here that he'd rather die than inflict the slightest scar on it.

"Jon, Jon!" Martha murmured against his mouth. Her fingers twined themselves in his hair, and her hands ran up and down the length of his back, reveling in his strength, in his male muscularity. A man and a woman, married, free to express their love, free to give and to take to the utmost of their ability! This was what she had been born for.

Her voice, and the feel of her hands, made Jonathan throw all caution to the winds and he entered her. She cried out, her body stiffening, but almost immediately her mouth was soft and warm against his again, her breasts taut with the desire that filled her. Her body began to move in rhythm with his as the warmth spread through every inch of them, enveloping them completely until it built up to the point where the world and their bodies with it disintegrated in an explosion of completion.

It can't be true, Jonathan thought as he lay limp on her, completely spent. No man in the world could be this lucky.

Still lying under him, Martha opened her eyes and looked at him wonderingly. Her voice was awed as she whispered, "Jon, if it's like this the first time, what can it be like with practice? Because if it's much better, then I don't think I could bear it."

He saw that she was crying, but they were tears of joy. He kissed them from her face, and his mouth found hers again, tasting of salt, tender now and sweet and undemanding, filled with love and gratitude.

"You'll be able to bear it," he promised her. "And so will I. Go to sleep now, darling. We have to travel again tomorrow. We're still a long way from Rose-lawns!"

It wasn't until Martha was sleeping the sleep of utter, contented exhaustion in his arms that Jonathan experienced a chill that cut him to the bone. What if he hadn't gone to Mrs. Lattimer's small, select gathering in Boston? He drew Martha closer, terrified by the thought. The one woman in all the world who was his, and he might never have met her!

The frantic grip of his arms roused Martha for a brief moment. "Not now," she murmured drowsily, her mouth curving in a smile. "Later."

Jacob, leaning on the cane that had become the bane of his existence, looked at Yolande, whose face under her wide-brimmed straw hat was pale and whose properly gloved hand was trembling on the handle of her raised parasol. Jacob's face, under his own wide-brimmed planter's hat, was as red as Yolande's was pale, as the packet nosed into its berth.

"Now don't you go swooning. She's Jonathan's wife, no matter how much we hate it, and we've got to face up to it."

"Mr. Beddoes, I've never swooned in my life, and you know it! But the fact remains that I'll never be able to hold my head up in this county again. To think that our son jilted Miss Amelia! The disgrace of it!"

"He didn't exactly jilt her. He'd never asked her."

"But it was understood! That's the same thing!"

"Only to a woman. Miss Amelia'd have bored him into taking to drink within a year. Only I wish to hell . . ." he glanced at Yolande and swallowed, because she might put up with his cussing at home but she didn't hold with it in public . . . "that he hadn't picked a Northern girl!"

Yolande's voice came in a shocked whisper, audible only to him as Jonathan and his wife appeared. The extent of her shock could be measured by the fact that she called him by his first name, right in public. "Jacob, she's dark! She's as dark as a mulatto! She couldn't be, he wouldn't have . . ." Her voice trailed off, smothered by her overwhelming emotions.

Jacob's own keen eyes had now discerned the cause of his wife's distress. Good god, the girl *was* dark! But Jacob's eyes were sharper than Yolande's, and he let out a little grunt of mingled relief and disgust.

"She's tanned, Mrs. Beddoes. You didn't think Jon'd taken leave of his senses up North? She's been out in the sun without a hat or a parasol."

For a moment, Yolande's relief was so great that she thought she actually might swoon. "Why, she must be *ignorant*! How am I ever to whip her into shape so she'll be presentable to our friends?"

"That's your problem. Put a smile on your face— here they are, and folks are watching. We got to hold our heads up, no matter what kind of a wife that idiot son of yours has brought home!"

Walking toward her new in-laws, Martha had a sinking sensation. Jonathan's mother was beautiful, and her clothes! Even at Sarah Lattimer's, she had never seen the like. Mrs. Beddoes's gown had sleeves that were even more voluminous than those on Hester's gowns, and more lace trim. Her bonnet was adorned with a virtual flower garden. She must be wearing at least four petticoats, maybe five or six. Likely she thought that Martha looked like a hired

54

girl in her modest three. Jonathan'd be ashamed of her, and she wouldn't be able to bear it.

Then her inborn sense of her own worth came to her aid. She straightened her back, lifted her chin, and as they came up to the older couple, she held out her hand, first to Yolande and then to Jacob, and her eyes met theirs challengingly.

Generations of breeding camouflaging her dismay at the plainness of the girl confronting her, Yolande held out her arms and gathered Martha into them. She smelled of a fresh, sweet scent that Martha thought might be jasmine, but she didn't have enough experience with perfumes to be sure.

Yolande's complexion, under the sheltering brim of her hat, was as pale as one of Miss Emily's prize white roses. Her eyes were dark, attesting to her aristocratic French Huguenot blood. She doesn't look much older than I am, Martha thought, astonished, and so delicate, like a porcelain figurine. Martha loosened her own embrace so as not to crush the fragile bones. Why, there wasn't a gray hair on her head!

She turned from Yolande to Jacob, who kissed her cheek, and she felt his strength, in spite of the cane that she realized was to ease the leg he had broken. It was a wicked thought, but she was glad that he'd broken it, because if he hadn't, then Jonathan wouldn't have made the trip north, and she'd never have met him.

Taller than his son by at least an inch and a half—and Jonathan stood an even six feet—there wasn't an ounce of excess fat on Jacob's body. He was built as Jonathan was, with the wide shoulders and narrow hips of a man who spends his life out of doors, mostly in the saddle. His hair, when he swept off his wide hat, was as thick and dark and unruly as Jon's, and his eyes were the same startling silvery gray.

"Let's move out of this press," Yolande said, her voice so exquisitely modulated, so soft and sweet, that Martha's ears tingled. Her own harsh New England accent would rasp on these gently bred Southerners. "The barouche is just over there. There's no need to wait for your luggage. It'll come along in the wagon that followed us."

A whole wagon, for their luggage? Martha swallowed a grin. Since most of his purchases had been sent on earlier, Jonathan traveled light, with only two small cases, and all of her own possessions were packed in one small round-topped trunk. Likely her mother-in-law assumed that she'd have brought half a dozen trunks and as many hat boxes and trinket cases.

"Is it far, the plantation?" Her voice did sound harsh, and Martha fancied that she saw Yolande wince.

"It's a good drive. When the men come in on horse-back they cover the distance more rapidly. Are you exhausted, my dear? You must be, after journeying all the way from Boston and New York!"

"I'm not a bit tired. All I had to do on the packet was rest. The steam cars were a little trying, but I was so excited I hardly noticed."

"The steam cars!" Yolande's voice was filled with horror. "My gracious, weren't you terrified? Why, the outlandish things aren't even safe!"

"Even horses and wagons have accidents, and so do riverboats," Martha pointed out. "Didn't Mr. Beddoes break his leg falling off a horse?"

Argumentative, Yolande thought. Whatever was she to do with her?

Joshua, the coachman, was an ebony-black man in his middle years who grinned widely and ducked his head as he evaluated this new bride with shrewd eyes and liked what he saw. "Welcome, Miss Martha, welcome!" he told her, his melodious voice a delight to Martha's ears. He took a good-natured swipe at a stripling, lighter-skinned than himself. "Git on there, you Tod! Young mistress want to be gittin' on home, move them splay feet, you hear?"

Martha was appalled. "Doesn't the boy resent being pushed around?"

Yolande looked at her without comprehension. "Resent it? Why should he?"

Worlds apart, Aunt Emily had said, and how right she was!

It was nearly sundown when they arrived at Roselawns, and the glow from the setting sun turned the white clapboard house a rosy tint in the darkening air and set the windows to blazing.

Martha's breath caught in her throat. A long verandah, or gallery, ran the length of the house, while a sheltering roof, supported by tall white columns, shaded the ground floor and the first story. The house itself was not as large as she had expected; indeed, none of the plantation houses they had passed on their journey had been as magnificent as Northerners believed they were. Where, she wondered, were those castles built by the sweat and toil of an enslaved people, whip-driven to keep their masters in sinful luxury? Martha had seen larger houses in Boston. Nevertheless, Roselawns had a grace and charm that could not be denied. The evening air was filled with the scent of honeysuckle and roses, from vines planted close around the house, lending a fairy-tale enchantment.

"Like it?" That was Jacob, beaming at his new daughter-in-law, ready to bask in her approval. Jacob was proud of his house, with a good deal of justification. "It's some different from the way the family started, back when my papa had to chase the Creeks off the land and build himself a cabin and tame his acres. We've come a good way since then." His voice held a world of self-satisfaction.

"I'm speechless!" Martha paused, searching for words. "Jonathan told me about it, but I had no idea how lovely it would really be. Oh, look! Look at all the people!"

"They're our people, come to bid you welcome." Jonathan's voice was as filled with pride as Jacob's. "Stand up, Martha, so they can get a good look at you."

The field people stood well apart at the edge of the yard, a respectable distance from the house people who had lined up in front of the gallery. There were so many! Martha stood up, her eyes wide with wonder. "I feel like royalty, like Marie Antoinette when she entered Paris."

She ain't so uneducated after all, Jacob thought, surprised. "Eighty-odd field hands and artisans of one sort or another, and half a dozen house servants. Roselawns isn't the biggest plantation hereabouts, but it isn't one of the smallest, either. We make out."

Martha turned back toward the slaves, and the field workers broke out in song. They seemed to be making up the words as they went along, one voice picking up the refrain and carrying it forward from another, while the rest joined in to repeat them in swelling cadence. So many workers meant a lot of land, and all of it belonged to Jacob, and after Jacob, to Jonathan. All this would one day belong to their children.

Impulsively, Martha's hands went to her bonnet, and she removed it so that the slaves would see her better. Her face lighted up in a smile that set Jacob back on his heels. By God, I see it now, he thought.

Jonathan's got himself a real woman there. She ain't pretty, she's better than that, she makes Miss Amelia look like a bowl of curds.

There was a clapping of hands and a rhythmic stamping of feet as the slaves showed their appreciation of Martha's gesture. "Welcome, welcome, new bride's come! Happy day!"

5

Dressed in one of her three daytime dresses, a plain brown muslin with braiding on the bodice, the sleeves nowhere near full enough to be in fashion and the shoulders with a regrettable lack of slope, Martha made her way downstairs on her first morning at Roselawns to find Yolande already in the sitting room.

Even at this early hour, Yolande's morning dress, of sheer sprigged muslin, made her look as though she were about to set off for a tea party. By comparison, Martha was downright dowdy. Where she came from, folks didn't dress up in the morning, with a full day's work ahead of them.

"Did you sleep well? I told Rebecca not to wake you because I knew you'd be tired. Come and have breakfast, dear, and then we'll see about choosing a maid for you."

Martha hoped that the breakfast wouldn't be as heavy and greasy as last night's meal had been. Fried ham, fried chicken, grits, gravy, not a salad or a feather-light biscuit in sight. Even the layer cake had been heavy. And the coffee had been thick and black, making her yearn for a cup of Miss Emily's delicately brewed tea.

"A maid? I don't need a maid. I wouldn't know what to do with one!" she protested.

Yolande looked at her patiently, and Martha could read her thoughts almost word for word. What else could one expect from a girl from that heathenish North!

She noticed Yolande's hands, as soft and white as flower petals, and felt a compulsion to hide her own, brown and calloused from working in the garden, from churning, from scrubbing. But she was young and strong, and it would have been a disgrace for her to leave the heavy work to Aunt Emily and her mother, although they had both done their share.

Her chin went up. In Massachusetts, where house-keeping was an art and every house was supposed to be in "dying" condition at any hour of the day or night, work was no disgrace, and she'd be dratted if she was going to apologize for it.

A young woman entered the sitting room in re-sponse to Yolande's tinkling silver bell. Tall and slender, her body a study in grace, she stood straight and proud, with no hint of deference. Her soft brown hair was pulled back from a serene forehead and caught in a neat coil at the back of her neck. Her eyes were hazel, much like Martha's own, her brows swept in a graceful arch, her mouth was sensitive and delicately molded.

Martha, who had sat down gingerly on a brocade-covered chair, rose again to her feet. Another relative, and young, not much older than Martha herself, how wonderful! She must have arrived very early, because Martha hadn't seen her last night. I hope we'll be friends, Martha thought. She wouldn't feel half as out of place if she had a friend of her own age.

"Yes, Miss Yolande?"

"Miss Martha is ready for her breakfast."

"I'll bring it right away."

Thoroughly confused, Martha sat down again, rather too fast, so that her posterior thumped against the chair seat. "I'm sorry. I was surprised, that's all. I hadn't realized that you had a white maid. I'm afraid I took her for a relative."

Miss Yolande had just picked up her delicate Limoges cup and was in the process of taking a sip of coffee. She choked, and her face turned as red as a raspberry in midsummer. Alarmed, Martha leaped to pound her on the back, her alarm making her forget Yolande's delicacy so that she hit too hard and nearly knocked her out of her chair. At least the blow had the desired effect. Miss Yolande stopped choking, although her face was even redder than before.

"Rebecca is my personal maid. She is a slave."

"But I don't understand." Martha was in a sea of bewilderment. "How can a white girl be a slave?"

"Rebecca is not white. She is what is called an octaroon. Mr. Beddoes obtained her for me at Savannah five years ago, when my Ernestine unfortunately succumbed to an inflammation of the abdomen. I'm afraid we won't be able to do as well for you, my dear. Highly trained girls like Rebecca, and of such a light color, are not easily come by, and I'm afraid the expense—"

Yolande broke off, annoyed with herself. Money was never discussed, except among the menfolk when they estimated their profits at the end of the season. "But we will find you somebody suitable. We have two housegirls who might do, with a bit of training."

While Martha was trying to digest all this, her mind still refusing to believe that Rebecca was a black person, Rebecca returned with her breakfast on a tray. One look at breakfast made Martha's stomach roil. A plate of grits, swimming in drippings, a slice of fried ham, burned, and more of that thick black coffee. Oh, Aunt Emily, I want a boiled egg!

"Will there be anything more?" Rebecca directed her question to Yolande.

"Not at the moment. But see that Pansy and Marguerite are available when Miss Martha has finished, so that she can choose between them."

"Doesn't she ever smile?" Martha asked, as she ordered her jaws not to lock in protest against the food in front of her.

"Smile? Certainly she smiles. Why should she not? She has a very easy life. She was fortunate to be bought as my personal servant." There was no hint of why Rebecca had been so fortunate in her voice. Ladies were not supposed to be aware that a girl as lovely as Rebecca might well have been bought for a different purpose. "I hope you haven't those strange notions prevalent in the North that we here in the South mistreat our people."

"Of course I haven't. It wouldn't be practical to mistreat them." Martha swallowed a mouthful of grits, held back a grimace, and decided that the burned ham would have to be better because there was no way it could be worse.

"Exactly. A sullen slave is not a good worker. I'm glad that you understand, my dear. Of course you must be firm with them. They're like children, they need guidance and discipline in order to be happy."

"Yes, ma'am." Martha struggled with the ham. It wasn't as bad as it looked, but there was so much of it! Defeated, she pushed her plate away. "I'm afraid I can't eat another bite."

For the first time, Yolande's face showed real approval. Martha's waistline was miniscule, and as long as she kept it that way, she could be dressed to advantage. "Then we'll send for the two girls for you to choose your maid."

"I'd like to see the kitchen first, if you don't mind. I'm interested in how the house is laid out." How was she to choose between two girls? The longer she could put it off, the better. If she could put it off long enough, maybe she could persuade Jon to convince his mother that she didn't need a maid.

"If you wish." Again, Yolande's face showed approval. A lady must be thoroughly acquainted with her household in order to keep it running smoothly.

The kitchen was reached by way of a covered passage, open at the sides. Seeing Martha's surprise, Yolande explained. "It helps to keep the house cool in the summer, of course, but even more it's because of the danger of fire. If a fire started in the kitchen we could hope to contain it there without damage to the main structure."

"That makes sense. We're mightily afraid of fire ourselves, back in Massachusetts. But our winters are too cold for kitchens to be separated like this. We just have to be careful."

The room they entered was large, with an enormous fireplace hung with cranes and kettles, and a monstrous black iron range. At a large deal table standing in the center, a young black girl was plucking a brace of chickens all the while tears streamed down her singularly homely face. She couldn't have been more than fourteen and was painfully thin, and her shoulders were hunched as though she were used to cringing from sudden blows. That couldn't be true, of course. The Beddoeses did not mistreat their people.

Over this girl hovered another black woman, hands on enormous hips. Middle-aged, shapeless, her hair completely hidden under a scarf, the woman found fault with the younger girl's efforts in a steady, shrill voice.

"Mind you do a clean job this time, you Cleo! Git all them pinfeathers out or you'll be sorry!"

The knife the girl was holding to help get out the pinfeathers slipped, and blood gushed from the thumb of her hand. She thrust the thumb into her mouth, her terrified eyes widening at her tormenter.

The cook threw her hands up in the air in despair. "I done told you, Miss Yolande, this girl's witless! I cain't put up with her no more. We give her her chance, but I got to have me somebody that don't fall over her own feet in this here kitchen, and that's the truth! This one, she ain't fitten for nothin' but field work!"

The despised feet, innocent of shoes, wriggled their toes, and then one foot began to rub up and down the other skinny leg. Clearly, their owner wished that she could hide her feet, but her dress was too short.

"All right, Juliette, we'll see to it. I'm afraid you're right about Cleo." She turned to Martha, realizing that this Northern girl would need instruction in the simplest matters. "We like to give all our people the opportunity to be trained for something other than field work, but in this case I guess Cleo will have to be furnished with a hoe instead of with kitchen implements. I was afraid of that when she was sent to the kitchen. Some of them, unfortunately, are not trainable."

Martha's mouth tightened. Yolande spoke as though the object of her conversation were not in the room, or as though she were an animal, a horse that had proved unsound or a cow that did not produce enough milk.

"Don't you think we'd better see to her thumb?"

Yolande looked at her, puzzled again. "Her thumb?

Certainly it will be looked after, but a clean cut like that shouldn't give any trouble."

"I'd like to look at it, if you don't mind."

Yolande swallowed her annoyance. Her son's bride at least showed suitable concern for keeping the people in good physical condition, and it was never too soon to start training a future mistress to care for the slaves' sicknesses and hurts.

Cleo looked at Martha with dumb misery as Martha pulled her thumb out of her mouth.

"Ain't nothin', mistis," Cleo mumbled, struck almost speechless by this white lady's concern.

"It looks quite deep, but it bled enough to lessen any danger of infection. Could I have a clean cloth for a bandage, please? We want to make sure that it stays clean. And Cleo, when I've bandaged it, you must remember to keep the bandage dry."

"Yes'um."

Juliette, who had watched the doctoring procedure with contempt, took a swipe at the girl. "Go on, git along now! Tell that Mose to put you to work where you belongs!"

Cleo's shoulders drooped. Her eyes looked like those of an animal that doesn't know why it is being kicked. She hung her head and started to walk toward the open kitchen door.

"Wait!"

Cleo looked over her shoulder, her face now swept with terror. Lawdy, what had she done now? She stood still, head hanging, drawn in on herself, to see what further punishment would be meted out to her for her clumsiness. She didn't mean to be clumsy— all she wanted was to please—but her hands and feet wouldn't mind.

"Mother Yolande, I've changed my mind about having a maid. I've decided that I'd like Cleo."

For a few seconds, the shock of her words kept even Juliette from voicing a protest. Yolande looked at Martha as if she were suddenly speaking Greek or some equally incomprehensible language.

"Cleo? That's out of the question! You can see for yourself that she's quite unsuitable. If she cannot even learn simple kitchen duties, how could she ever learn to care for your wardrobe or dress your hair?"

"My hair doesn't need dressing. I always wear it in these plaits, and I'm capable of doing it myself. Please, Mother Yolande, I've taken a fancy to Cleo, and I'd like to try her."

"Well, I never! I don't know what Jonathan will say, I'm sure. He'll think you've lost your wits and I've lost mine in the bargain, to allow it!"

Cleo looked at Martha with blind adoration, as if Martha were a saint descended from heaven to take her up to paradise. The pure devotion in her eyes hardened Martha's resolve.

"May she start now? She can help me lay my things away, and we'll see if any of them need mending, or a button, or to be pressed."

"Trust that Cleo with a smoothin' iron?" Juliette's voice rose, scandalized. "Lawdy, Miss Martha, you must have lots of clothes if you're ready to let her go burnin' holes in 'em before you sends her out to the field where she belongs!"

An amazing transformation came over the cringing girl by the door. She turned on Juliette in fury. "I won't burn 'em! I won't! I'll be keerful!"

Like a worshipful shadow, Cleo followed her new mistress back through the passageway and up the stairs, her eyes shining with mingled terror and ecstasy at this first time she had ever set foot in the big house. Her fingers caressed the polished balustrade reverently, and her toes curled around the carpeted risers, fearful of sullying them. Cleo had added another deity to those she already worshipped. Jesus, and Mary, and Saint Paul; her lips moved soundlessly as she added Martha to the list.

"She has two left hands, and two left feet. I despair of ever being able to teach her to fold undergarments neatly or to sew on a button without making a complete botch of it."

Martha paused, nibbling at the tip of the quill pen. She was writing to her mother and aunt, as the late afternoon sun slanted into the bedroom. "Yesterday, I caught her eating a cake of soap, and I declare that when I saw the froth on her mouth, I thought she had been taken with a fit. Still I cannot find it in my heart to have her sent to the fields."

Martha's writing was tiny, the words spaced as closely together as she could manage and still have them legible. Postage rates were outrageously high, and a one-sheet letter, folded over and sealed, would cost an entire shilling to send as far as Boston. The shilling had to be paid by her mother as the recipient. Thirty miles cost six cents, thirty to eighty miles ten cents, eighty to one hundred and fifty miles, twelve and a half cents, one hundred and fifty miles to four hundred miles, eighteen and three-quarter cents. A shilling was roughly twenty-five cents, and her mother did not have too many shillings to spare. Two sheets, of course, cost double, and three sheets, triple, and no packet of more than three pounds could be posted at all.

Martha smiled, remembering that Jonathan had told her how he had been loaded down with letters, entrusted to him by friends and acquaintances, when he had set out on his fateful trip north. With postage rates so high, anyone traveling any distance was importuned to carry letters to be dropped in the post at the nearest point of delivery. Indeed, mailcoach drivers often carried more letters in their personal pouches, as a favor, than were in the Post Office bags.

Still smiling, Martha resumed writing. "Cleo aside, I find the life here pleasant and rewarding, although I must confess that I have had more than one run-in with my father-in-law. How I wished that you were here, Aunt Emily, to back me up! But I would not back down. You did not raise me to be a coward, and just because a man is a man does not mean that he must always be right! Yours with all my love, Martha."

Holding a stick of sealing-wax over a candle flame until it bubbled, she let a round glob drip onto the folded sheet and pressed it with Jonathan's seal, embossed with a full-blown rose, a pretty conceit based on the name of the plantation.

Her face itched. Impatiently, she left the little escritoire and went to the washstand. The mirror that hung above it, framed in gilt, showed a face that might have been in the last stages of some dreadful disease. A concoction of honey and lemon was spread over it from hairline to chin and down over her throat.

Pouring water into the basin, she took up a cake of soap, perfumed and imported from France, an extravagance that made her New England soul cringe. It was sinful to use such a luxury to wash with, let alone see it being consumed, like candy, by a slave girl. Cleo was sitting in the corner by the window, waiting for another duty to be assigned.

"Cleo, go fetch the buttermilk and several slices of fresh cucumber."

The child jumped to her feet so precipitously that she tripped over her skirt and fell again.

"Yes'um! Right away, I'll run fast!"

"You don't need to run, Cleo. I'm not in that much of a hurry."

"I'll run anyway. Don't you fret, Miss Martha, I'll have that old buttermilk and cucumber up here 'fore you kin say scat!"

Martha sighed and began to scrub the revolting mess off her face. She must bleach out her tan, Yolande had told her. Thus the honey and lemon, buttermilk and cucumber. Well, it was working, after a fashion. But why shouldn't it? She had not set foot out of doors without a wide-brimmed hat and a parasol since she had arrived at Roselawns. Martha still bubbled with laughter at the memory of the gardener's face the afternoon she had stripped off her gloves and knelt to get her fingers into the soft earth of a flower bed. She wished there had been room in her letter to tell Aunt Emily about that.

A terrified expression on his face, afraid to reprimand her himself, the gardener had called to a naked child and sent him to the kitchen to tell Juliette to tell Rebecca to inform Miss Yolande that she'd best come out *right now*! And Miss Yolande's face, when she'd discovered her daughter-in-law grubbing in the dirt with ungloved hands! Lordy, if she'd kicked over the last bucket of milk Bossy was going to give before she freshened, Aunt Emily wouldn't have laced into her like that! The price of becoming a Southern gentlewoman, Martha was discovering, was somewhat excessive.

Cleo, having slopped more than a quarter of the buttermilk in the process of transporting it from kitchen to bedroom, watched with round eyes as Martha rinsed with it and rubbed the cucumber slices over her face.

"You sure is gittin' pretty!" Cleo said admiringly. "You think that old buttermilk'd work on me? I'se so black!"

70

"I think no such thing. All the cows in the world could not produce enough buttermilk to whiten your face, Cleo." Martha's lips twitched, but she spoke kindly. "God gave you the color of your skin, and you must be content with it."

"Yes'um." Cleo sat down on the floor again, her face doleful. It would be nice to be lighter—being light was a matter of prestige.

Then she brightened. Even if she was black, she was in the house, not breaking her back in the fields. Miss Martha had saved her from that, and no matter how clumsy she was or how many mistakes she made, Miss Martha always told Mrs. Beddoes that she was learning and that she was satisfied with her.

"Jesus bless Miss Martha," Cleo whispered, a ritual she went through at least a hundred times a day. "And keep that Rebecca away from Massa Jonathan, 'cause he belongs to Miss Martha, and Miss Martha wouldn't like it!"

She thought a little more, and added, "And bless Sam, 'cause he keeps watch that that Rebecca don't git close to Massa Jonathan." Satisfied at last that her prayer was complete, and seeing that Martha had no immediate use for her, she went back to her corner to rest.

6

The footsteps taking the stairs two at a time could belong to no one but Jonathan, and Martha's face brightened as he came into the room. He crossed over to her with his long, free stride, and put his forefinger under her chin, tilted it, and bent and kissed her. "So here's where you're hiding! You'd better get ready for supper. It's early tonight—I have patrol duty."

He felt her stiffen, and he chided her gently, laughing. "Now, honey, you know I have to do it! We all have to take our turn."

Martha did know it, or at least she had been made to understand that it was necessary. Ever since the Nat Turner insurrection in Southampton County, Virginia, in August of 1831, the Southern planters had kept up these nightly patrols. They rode the roads to make sure any black they came across had a pass from his master. They also checked slave quarters in search of weapons or implements that could be used as weapons. All white men over sixteen had to take their turns. The Nat Turner insurrection had brought home to them how vulnerable they were, so vastly outnumbered by their slaves. Sixty whites had been slain in that insurrection, and it must never happen again.

"I know that you're in no danger, Jon." There she went again. Yolande would have a conniption if she heard her call Jonathan by his given name. No matter how upset or angry she was, Yolande rarely failed to call her own husband Mr. Beddoes. "It's just that it seems so outlandish to have to live like this, always uneasy about the slaves. Back home, we didn't have to be afraid of our servants."

"Afraid of them!" Jonathan's face tightened, and he paled a little under his tan. Two red spots appeared on his cheekbones. "Now, that's about as ridiculous a statement as I ever heard in my life. We aren't afraid of them, Martha. We have them well in hand, and besides, they're contented, they have no idea of rebelling, everybody knows that. It's just a precaution. Being afraid of them doesn't enter into it."

"You said yourself that it's a *necessary* precaution!"

"Northerners! You'll never understand. You don't even want to understand! This is our way of life, and you might as well get used to it." Jonathan struggled to control himself. "What have you been doing all day, while I toiled for you?"

"Anything your mother would let me." Martha's voice was tart. "I went for a stroll around the lawn, but she came out after fifteen minutes and told me I mustn't overdo. Good heavens, any sensible person knows that a body must have exercise! Jonathan, mayn't I have a horse? I'd so dearly love to learn to ride. I feel like a prisoner, I swear I do!"

"Ride! Are you bereft of your senses? You stay away from horses, you hear?" Jonathan glared at her, tapping his riding crop against his boot with a furious tattoo. "Damn it, I see I'll have to give orders that any slave that saddles a horse for you will have the skin taken off his back!"

Martha stood up and faced him, and now her

dimples came through, playing around the corners of her mouth, sending her face into that sudden, startling beauty that never failed to take Jonathan's breath away. "I thought you never whipped a slave, or even threatened one!" she mocked.

"Well, we don't! You go threatening them, they'll run. But this ain't a threat, it's a promise, so you might as well get that sneaky look out of your eyes and forget about learning to ride until after it's happened."

"Until it's happened!" Martha mocked. "Why can't you say till after the baby's born? A baby, Jonathan! I'm going to have a baby!"

Jonathan clapped his hand over her mouth, looking green. "Stop that! You want Jacob to hear?"

Martha bit his hand, and when he snatched it away, with a curse, she doubled over with laughter. "What's the matter, doesn't Jacob know where babies come from? Didn't his mother ever tell him? How does he think you got here?"

"Someday I'm going to lick the tar out of you!"

"Not unless you can catch me!" Tauntingly, Martha ducked under his arm and raced for the door and through it. Her feet flew down the stairs at a run, while Jon plunged after her, his face white.

At the foot of the stairs, Yolande's face was also white. "Martha! Have you gone mad? Stop that this instant, what will the servants think?"

"I'm sorry, Mother Yolande. It's just that I feel so good, it seems I can't keep my feet from running. I'd like to run for a mile, just to take off the razor edge, as Aunt Emily used to say when I was young and full of beans."

"You are not a child now. You are a respectable young matron." Yolande's mouth tightened at the corners. How the girl tried her! How was she ever to

74

introduce her into society, when one never knew what she might do or say from one moment to the next? What if she were to start arguing about how to run a plantation properly, when gentlemen were present? Worse, she might even point out that the slaves didn't seem to breed well in captivity, so that the cost of buying new hands ate into their profits. *Full of beans*! Lord preserve us, what a vulgar expression!

Neither Martha nor Jonathan realized that Yolande kept her mouth compressed to quell the smile that struggled to get out. Once, she too, had been young and "full of beans," and she knew how Martha felt.

7

Martha paced up and down the winter-blasted garden. Six paces to the rear, Cleo walked, ever watchful. Ten paces behind Cleo, Sam kept faithful vigil. As if having Cleo spy on her wasn't enough, Jonathan had exasperatingly set his own body-servant, Sam, to dog her footsteps. Cleo, Jon had argued, couldn't be trusted, but he'd trust Sam with his own life.

Drat, drat, drat! Did they all think that she was made of glass? If they didn't quit smothering her, she'd scream. A body had to have breathing space.

The first pain took her so much by surprise that she stiffened, a look of astonishment on her face, but it was Cleo who screamed. Sam was at her side immediately.

"I'll send someone to fetch Mister Jonathan. Cleo, help your mistress into the house!"

Martha slapped Cleo's hand away and glared at Sam. "Don't be an idiot! I'm perfectly capable of walking by myself. Cleo, you run ahead and see my bed's made up with that fresh-ironed linen like I showed you and that the other linen's ready. Mind you scrub your hands well! And take that terrified expression off your face, I'm only having a baby, I'm not going to die."

When they reached the gallery, Sam looked at her beseechingly. "Hadn't I better send for Mister Jonathan?"

"He'll only be in the way." Martha's expression softened as she saw Sam's concern. "Go on, then, send for him. You're a mighty good friend. See that Jonathan doesn't go to pieces, will you? He'll be needing you."

"I'll do that." The slave's eyes met Martha's, and there was perfect respect and trust in both pairs.

The heavy draperies had been drawn across the bedroom windows. The fire had been built up in the fireplace until Martha felt she was being cooked alive. What was that fool doctor about? Hemming and hawing, looking grave, patting her on the shoulder and telling her to be brave.

"A little more laudanum, I think," Doctor John said. "It's a difficult birth.'

Martha already knew that. She'd attended enough birthings with Aunt Emily to know that this one wasn't normal. The baby wasn't coming straight, it needed to be turned, and this bumbling old fool was obviously afraid to try. They'd only sent for him when Yolande had become worried, and they'd have been better off not having him around at all.

It had been ten hours, now. Martha could hear Jonathan pacing up and down outside her room instead of remaining properly downstairs as he should, pretending ignorance of what was going on over his head.

Yolande, her face white and strained, looked at the doctor pleadingly, and he shook his head, his lips forming words that Martha couldn't hear but that she understood. She gripped Cleo's hands again, and the black girl did not flinch, as Martha fought against the pain, against bearing down because it would only batter the baby that couldn't find the passage out. She screamed, again and again, and when the pain subsided she spoke to the doctor, her voice filled with venom.

"Get out of here, you imbecile! You hear me, get out!"

"There, there. Take this, child. . . ."

Martha slapped the laudanum out of his hand, and it flew across the room. Her words were evenly spaced. "Cleo, put him out."

"Martha, you must not—" Yolande looked ready to break.

"You shut up. Cleo, did you hear me? Put him out and lock the door!"

Cleo's face went gray. Lay her hands on a white man? A slave could be put to death for that, if the master so chose. To lay a hand on a white man meant, at the least, a whipping that would make you wish they'd hung you instead.

Martha's body arched again and another scream tore the air of the room. Cleo put her hands on the doctor's shoulders and pushed. Her love for her mistress gave her a strength that was supernatural. She catapulted him out into the hallway and slammed the door behind him, in Jonathan's startled face, before either he or Sam could move to stop her. Shaking, Cleo leaned against the door while Jonathan pounded on it, shouting for her to open it.

"Come here." Martha's lips were drawn back from her teeth, her body was soaked with sweat. "Cleo, open that dratted window! Mother Yolande, listen to me, and listen good, because I'm too used up to tell you more than once. Thank you, Cleo, that's

78

better. Now, both of you, scrub your hands. No, no, use fresh water! And lots of soap. Mother Yolande, here is what you must do, and you'd better have the guts because if you can't do it, then Cleo will have to, and her hands are bigger than yours."

Yolande's lips formed a prayer, but she moved to obey.

Outside, Sam looked at Jonathan. "Shall we break down the door?"

Jonathan shook his head. "Leave her be. You heard what she called the doctor? Well, she was right."

The doctor was downstairs drinking peach brandy and telling Jacob that his insane daughter-in-law was going to die. Sam grinned. "Yes, sir. I believe that Miss Martha was right. It's the best chance she's got."

Downstairs, Jonathan heard Jacob bellow, "Jon, I'm fetching some of our strongest hands. We'll have that door down in a minute!"

"Damn you, don't you dare!" Jonathan bellowed back. He turned again to Sam. "Oh, God, Sam! God, God! Is she going to die? Am I going to lose her?"

"I think that it would take more than a baby reluctant to be born to kill Miss Martha," Sam said, with such conviction that Jonathan's shoulders slumped with relief. "I think we should wait. After all, Miss Yolande is in there, and she'll unlock the door if it's necessary."

They waited, and they heard Martha scream again, the sounds torn from her suffering body. When the silence fell, it was even more shattering. Jonathan, his face pale, raised numbed eyes to Sam. "She's gone," he said. "Oh, God, Sam, God!"

And then, incredibly, they heard Martha laugh, a triumphant laugh in spite of the exhaustion behind it, and the tiny, mewling wail of a newborn infant.

They waited again, for what seemed an eternity, before Cleo opened the door.

"Miss Martha says, massa, that iffen you fainted, she ain't never going to speak to you again. Miss Martha says to tell you you got you a son."

The doctor was gone, well fortified with peach brandy, so highblown that Jacob had sent young Tod, on a mule, to see that he got home without falling off his horse into a ditch. A double fee for his services, and the doctor's own conviction that he'd be a laughingstock in the whole county if it ever got around that he'd allowed a fifteen-year-old slave girl to put him forcibly out of a room, was reasonable assurance that he'd make no trouble about having had black hands laid on him.

Jacob poured himself another tot of brandy as Yolande entered the sitting room. Yolande looked as if it had been she, rather than Martha, who had gone through the brutal hours of labor.

"That crazy-woman!" Jacob ranted. "What kind of insanity has Jon introduced into our bloodline, anyway? She's stark, raving mad. I should never have let Jon go on that trip—see what's come of it! For all we know, the child'll be insane, too!"

For the first time in her married life, Yolande raised her hand to her husband. The slap she administered across his purpled face could be heard across the room. "Jacob, you shut up!"

The sound of singing roused Martha from her exhausted sleep the next morning. Cleo was sitting beside her in a straight-backed chair, her eyes wide open and watchful in spite of having only dozed fitfully, in the chair, ever since the baby had been born.

"It's over," Martha said. "Lordy, it's over, and we

pulled it off, didn't we? In spite of that doddering incompetent, we pulled it off." She began to laugh. "Cleo, you were wonderful! I swear that that doctor's feet lifted right off the floor when you pushed him out!"

Cleo's face was gray with dread as much as with fatigue, but she gave no indication to Martha of the terrors that crawled in her mind. The whipping post, her back laid bare, cut to the bone. As long as Miss Martha and the baby were all right, it didn't matter. She'd do it again, if need be.

"Where's my baby? Was I dreaming, Cleo, or do I have a son?"

Cleo's face split in a grin. "He's fine, Miss Martha. Miss Yolande, she said he's the finest baby she ever done see! Ain't nothin' wrong with that baby!"

"But where is he? I want him!"

"He's nursin'. Miss Yolande had Petulia in to feed him. She's got aplenty milk, her gal-baby was borned 'bout a month ago." Cleo broke off, her grin fading into alarm. "Now you stop that, Miss Martha! You lay back on them pillows again. You cain't set up yet, what's gotten into you?"

Martha leaned back, but her fury didn't abate. "Cleo, you are to fetch me my baby this instant. A wet-nurse indeed! My baby isn't going to have any wet-nurse when he has a perfectly good mother to feed him! Look, my milk's already coming in, I'm all wet in front. Run now, you hear me? But don't you dast run on the way back with my baby!"

Cleo's face crumpled. "Miss Martha, I ain't goin' drop our baby. Only what iffen they won't let me take him?"

"Then tell them that I'll come and get him myself!"

Within minutes, both Yolande and Jonathan were in the room expostulating with Martha. "You can't

81

feed the baby yourself, it's unheard-of! Only white trash feed their own babies. Petulia is a strong, healthy girl. Be reasonable, Martha. You're overwrought because of your ordeal."

"Poppycock! Bring me my son! Do you think I went through all that to hand him over to somebody else? Bring him!"

Jonathan and Yolande looked at each other, defeated. There was no telling what this girl was capable of if she were crossed.

A celebration went on all that day and into the early hours of the night. Jacob had declared a holiday for all his people. Flames from huge bonfires leaped into the air as the slaves danced and sang and feasted on a pig butchered for the purpose, with generous portions of rum for all those who wanted it. Holding her infant Rory against her breast, Martha listened to the singing. She could make out some of the words, even from this distance, because the window was open a few inches to cater to her fetish about fresh air. Neither Yolande's warnings nor Jonathan's threats had been able to convince her that her baby's death would be on her head if he took a chill from the air. It was more likely, she had said tartly, that Rory would choke and die from the overheated, smoketinged atmosphere that they thought essential to an infant's well-being.

"New young massa's borned! New young massa's here! Glory day, glory!"

Jacob Rory Beddoes belched and let Martha's nipple slip from his overflowing mouth. Martha looked at Jonathan. "We'll call him Rory, of course. Otherwise it would be confusing. Jon, isn't he beautiful? He's going to be your image."

"He'd better be." Jonathan was complacent. Who

the hell cared what people thought of Martha feeding her own baby? Rory was the finest young 'un ever born in the State of Georgia and had the finest mother. What other namby-pamby county girl could have thrown the doctor out and directed her own difficult delivery? God bless Miss Emily, Jonathan thought.

"Does the singing bother you? Shall I tell them to tone it down?"

"Don't be foolish. They're singing to our son. Jon, I'm the happiest woman in the world."

Two weeks later, on the occasion of Martha's first appearance at the supper table after Rory's birth, Jonathan laid a long velvet case in front of her. Jacob was busy filling slender-stemmed wineglasses with imported wine, not the usual local peach brandy.

"Open it, darling." Jonathan's eyes were shining. "It's our gift to you, in partial payment for your gift to us."

Martha's fingers trembled as she opened the case, and her gasp, when she saw the contents, was one of pure awe. The pearl necklace seemed to glow with inner life against the blue velvet lining, each pearl perfect.

"You're out of your minds!" Martha said. "I know what a strand like this costs! We can't afford it! The price of cotton is going down all the time!"

"Miss Martha, for once in your life, I'll thank you to be quiet," Jacob told her. "If your husband and I chose to make you a gift, it was our right. As for the price of cotton, it's none of your business. Jon, put those pearls around her neck. I want to see how they look. Blamed if they don't become her!"

Martha reached up to touch the pearls, already warm from contact with her skin. "For once in my life, I'm going to obey you, Father Jacob. They're beautiful, and I love them. They're almost as beautiful as Jacob Rory." Her heart was so full that she was afraid that she was going to cry.

The house was strangely subdued the next day as Martha made her way around the downstairs rooms. Something was wrong, she could feel it. Pansy, dusting the sitting room, had no smile for her. Come to think of it, the whole house had been abnormally quiet these last few days, and she hadn't heard the usual laughter and bantering from outside workers as they neared the house. After the wild joy that had prevailed following Rory's birth, it was too strange to be normal.

"Pansy, is something wrong?"

Pansy ducked her head, her plump face carefully impassive. "No, ma'am."

It was no use questioning her. The slaves did not talk when they chose not to talk. But Martha was not so easily defeated. She returned upstairs to where Cleo was straightening their bedroom.

"Cleo, something's wrong, and I want to know what it is."

Cleo's face took on that look that meant she'd rather be whipped than have to tell her mistress something that she wouldn't want to hear.

"Cleo, I'm waiting."

"Master Jacob and Master Jonathan . . ." Martha had been working hard to improve Cleo's grammar . . . "sold Clem and Brutus."

Martha sat down in the nearest chair and stared at Cleo with disbelief. "You must be mistaken. We don't sell our people, we simply don't."

"Did, all the same."

"But why? Were they unsatisfactory? Were they hard to handle?"

84

"No, Miss Martha. They was fine, good men. They done sold them to buy your beads."

Martha found Jonathan and Jacob in Jacob's office. The small, one-room cabin stood at a distance from the house, well out of earshot of the womenfolk in case talk out there got rough or gentlemen chose to indulge in an extra tot of rum.

"Why did you do it? How could you have done it? Two human lives, for a bauble!"

"We didn't sell them into misery, Martha, for God's sake!" Jonathan defended himself. "We haven't enough work to keep the hands we have busy, and you know yourself"—his voice took on a tinge of sarcasm—"that the price of cotton isn't what it should be. John Renault's been after those two boys for years. Brutus is a fine hand with animals, and Clem can turn his hand to carpentry. They'll have a better home at Swanmere than they had here. Neither of them was married, so we broke up no families to sell them. They'll be well treated."

"All the same, you didn't consider selling them until you wanted to buy the pearls. And they didn't want to go. Pansy, and the others, wouldn't be so upset if they had."

"Damnation, woman, be silent!" Jacob barked. "I'll sell my slaves if and when and where I choose, do you understand? Do me the kindness to return to the house where you belong."

"I will not return to the house where I belong! I want you to return the pearls and buy Clem and Brutus back."

"And I will not be ordered around by my daughter-in-law!"

Jonathan put his hand on Martha's arm. "Honey, John Renault wouldn't sell them back even if we

85

offered. As I told you, he's wanted them for a long time, and a bargain's a bargain. There's our honor involved."

"Honor! Your blasted Southern honor! Well, I don't think much of your Southern honor, hear?" Gathering her skirts in her hand, Martha swept out of the office, leaving the door reverberating behind her.

In her room, she put the velvet case with the pearls in the bottom drawer of her chiffonier, under a stack of undergarments. It would be a long time before she'd want to look at them again. She wasn't even sure that she wanted to look at Jonathan again.

8

Martha drew rein at the edge of the field the slaves were planting to cotton, and her mare cavorted a little, tossing its head, impatient at the delay. Beside her, Rory sat his pony with the ease of an accomplished horseman. Martha breathed deeply, drinking in the April air, sweet with the fragrance of spring.

It didn't seem possible that this was her eighth April at Roselawns. Rory was seven and, back at the house, four-year-old Prudence played with her doll-babies under the supervision of Dulcy. Prudence adored Dulcy, who was sweet-tempered and utterly reliable.

A little smile twitched at the corners of Martha's mouth. Prudence wasn't the only one who adored Dulcy. Martha was convinced that, at any time now, Sam would ask permission to marry the pretty, shy girl who had been bought to act as nursemaid when Prudence was born. No one but Cleo was allowed to care for the new babies—a right she was ready to defend to the death—but since little Crissy's birth, Cleo had had enough to do.

Rory, as impatient as Martha's mare, made his pony prance. A little behind them, as was proper, Sam raised his voice in reproof.

"That's enough of that, Master Rory. You're hurting his mouth. Your father'll skin you if he catches you treating a horse like that."

"Dancer ain't a horse, he's only a pony." Rory's dark brows, so like his father's, drew together. "I'm sick and tired of having to ride a pony! When am I going to get a real horse, like my papa's?"

"When you've learned enough self-control to handle one properly," Sam told him. "And when your legs are long enough. You have all you can manage under you, right now."

"I can handle a horse! I could ride yours, right now, or Mama's, if Mama didn't ride that silly side-saddle! Come on, get off, Sam, and I'll show you! I'll show you I can handle a full-sized horse!"

The approach of another figure on horseback proved a distraction. It was Victor Slade, the new overseer Jacob had hired when the former one had decided to pull up stakes and move on west to get a little piece of land for himself.

Sam didn't like Slade, even though he was well out from under Slade's jurisdiction. As for the hands, they hated Slade worse than poison. Slade wasn't quality folk, he was an upstart redneck who dared to ape his betters by getting an education of sorts and hiring himself out as an overseer. He was white trash, no matter how he dressed up and put on airs, and no matter how efficient he was at his work.

Martha had only glimpsed Victor Slade once or twice after he'd come to Roselawns and moved into the overseer's cottage. He was a tall man, only two or three years older than Jonathan, with sandy hair and very pale blue eyes. His efficiency had impressed Martha favorably, the little she knew of him. He understood cotton, and Martha was intensely interested in the cultivation of cotton.

In April, or as soon as the land dried out and was arable, holes were drilled three feet apart and cotton was planted. If the land were not worn out, ten acres of cotton could be produced by one top field hand. Under ideal conditions, two thousand pounds per field hand could be hoped for, but the figure seldom ran as high as that. Martha estimated that here at Roselawns, a more accurate estimate would be twelve hundred pounds.

At Liverpool, in England, the price of cotton fluctuated between eleven and nineteen cents a pound. Cotton, Martha had long since decided, in agreement with Aunt Emily, was a highly speculative business and extremely risky. Any natural disaster, such as drought or storm, or such as the panic of '37, could ruin a planter, or force him to borrow so heavily against future crops that there remained little hope of his ever getting out of debt.

In return for their labor, the slaves were housed in rough shacks, clothed in coarse materials, the younger children running stark naked in the summer-time. On the better plantations, such as Roselawns and Swanmere, which belonged to the Renaults, and the Amhurst place, they were supplied with one pound of meat, usually salt pork, one peck of corn, and some salt, each week per person, as well as receiving medical care of some sort.

The hands were better off, the planters maintained, than the poor whites, who grubbed a meager living from a few acres and suffered from acute malnutrition and hookworm. Their miserable holdings brought in five to six bales, each year, which were brought to the larger plantations to be ginned, at a toll of one in eleven pounds.

Victor Slade had sprung from just such a small holding, one of eleven children, and the only one who had had the gumption to better himself. He had, by means of offering himself for odd jobs to the local schoolmaster and parson, managed to come by a little schooling, and he had worked himself up from there. Here at Roselawns, he was as high as he could ever hope to get, and he was doing a good job even though there was some muttering among the slaves.

Trotting toward them, Slade sat his saddle as straight as Jonathan himself, and when he swept off his broad hat and bowed to Martha, the sun glinted on his hair and along the hard, lean lines of his face. When he spoke, his accent was more cultivated than either Jacob's or Jonathan's.

"Good morning, ma'am. I trust you're enjoying this warm sunshine."

"I am indeed. How is the planting going, Mr. Slade?"

"We'll get the job done. If we have the proper amount of rain we can look forward to a bumper crop."

Martha had been watching the workers, admiring their rhythmic motions as they moved along the rows. "Isn't that man a little slow? See, the one just there. Isn't he limping, Mr. Slade?"

"It's only a cut foot. We'll see it's doctored, come sundown."

"I think he should be sent in now. We don't want him getting hookworm, or having the cut fester."

"As you please." Slade bowed again and raised his voice. "You, Gabe, get back to the quarters and have that cut attended to."

"Thank you, Mr. Slade. I'll be getting back myself, and see to it." Until Martha had come to Roselawns, Yolande had done most of the doctoring. But she was only too glad to delegate the responsibility to Martha, once she had seen how efficient her daughter-in-law was in such matters. Miss Emily had acted as unofficial doctor for all but the most serious hurts and ailments, back in Martin's Corners, and Martha had followed in her footsteps as naturally as breathing.

Sam was displeased. It wasn't proper for Miss Martha to be so friendly with Victor Slade. A simple nod of her head in return for his greeting would have been sufficient. He was glad when Martha touched her mare with her heel and wheeled to return to the house. Rory pouted, scowling again, because he resented having his ride cut short.

"Mama, why do we have to go back now? It's only a nigger, you don't have to fix him right this minute!"

"All cuts must be tended promptly, Rory. Infection is a nasty thing." Martha's mouth compressed at the corners. "And Gabe is a Negro, a person, not a 'nigger'! He is one of our people and entitled to care and respect." Raising her son on a plantation, and trying to instill some sort of responsible humanity in him was a task that seemed to grow harder every day. It wasn't that Rory was naturally callous, because he wasn't. He fretted over a sick puppy or a bird with a broken wing. But he'd accepted the idea that slaves were property, rather than human beings, from the time he'd learned to walk and talk.

At seven, Rory was already a small autocrat, and there were times when Martha wished, fervently, that her aunt were handy to use a switch on him where it would do the most good. She did it herself, occasionally, but it never failed to cause a raging flare-up with Jacob.

Riding easily, Martha felt the inequity of the fact that she, who was perfectly able-bodied, should ride in ease, while Gabe, with his badly cut foot, had to hobble along the best he could in her wake.

Sam still kept his respectful distance behind her as they entered the hospital shed, where the sick or injured slaves were treated. There was only one other occupant at the moment, an oldster who was suffering from a grippe of the bowels. Even so, Martha could not be allowed to tend either him or Gabe without an attendant, and Sam had long since taken over this duty when he was not needed by Jonathan. The fact that he, a black man, was allowed this privilege was a measure of the Beddoes's family trust in him.

Martha marveled at Gabe's impassive face as she cleansed the cut, using strong lye soap. Turpentine was next, and Martha knew that it stung, but Gabe only grinned when she asked him if it hurt.

"Jesus bless, mistiss. Jesus bless," Gabe said. "It'll do me fine, now. I'll be back to work in no time!"

"Not for at least a week!" Martha's voice was sharp. "Tell Mr. Slade that those are my orders, Gabe."

"Yes, mistiss." Gabe's eyes shone with appreciation. "I'll tell he that." Under his breath he muttered, "He won't like it none, but I'll tell him and he cain't do nuttin', 'cause Miss Martha done said!" Why, Miss Martha had even ordered, and made it stick, that a woman who gave birth was to have two weeks off to get strong again and have a little time with her child. 'Most blew the plantation apart, that had, but what Miss Martha said mostly stuck, no matter how much Massa Jacob and Massa Jonathan bellowed.

In her bedroom Martha poured fresh water into the washbowl and scrubbed her hands thoroughly. The washbowl, with its delicate tracery of vines and roses had, like nearly everything on the plantation, come from the North. Drat that Jacob! He ranted and raved, like all the other plantation owners, about the inequitable tariff, but like all the others, he refused to try to depend less on such imports in order to encourage home manufactury. Their arguments on that and other issues were hot and heavy, invariably ending with Jacob red-faced and shouting because a chit of a girl, and a girl from the North at that, dared to try to instruct him in matters that were entirely the prerogative of the male.

The acrid odor of the hospital shed still clung to her riding habit, and Martha wrinkled her nose as she stepped out of it. "Take this to the drying-yard, Cleo, and air it. And don't forget to bring it in again— it might rain and I can't afford to have it ruined, that velvet cost a fortune!"

"Yes, ma'am." After nearly eight years of Martha's training, Cleo was no longer the clumsy girl she had been when Martha had chosen her as her personal maid. Martha's patience and kindness had released the hidden vein of intelligence in the girl. Her loyalty to Martha was absolute, and not even Rebecca ventured to intrude on her domain. Indeed, there was a tacit enmity between the two that puzzled Martha, because she could not find any reason for it.

After she had washed, Martha sat down in her wrapper to reread the latest letter from home, warm with the feeling of closeness the written words brought her.

Mehitabel Tait had given birth to yet another daughter—this made seven so far—and Sam was fit to be tied. On her last excursion to Boston, Aunt Emily had ridden a railroad car and noted that they had been vastly improved.

Nancy, Martha's mother, still visited her friend Sarah Lattimer, and Sarah, that inveterate matchmaker, was now trying to find a husband for her. "But Nancy, I fear, has little interest in the proposition, still being loyal to your father's memory," her aunt wrote.

"How I wish I could see your newest baby, your sweet Crissy, and Rory and Prue as well. As a spinster lady I take a lively interest in the rearing of other people's children, a common failing, I hear."

By the same post, Miss Emily had sent a poster that she thought would amuse Martha.

MOTHERS LOOK OUT FOR YOUR CHILDREN! ARTISANS, MECHANICS, CITIZENS!

When you leave your family in health, must you hurry home to mourn a
DREADFUL CASUALTY!

Philadelphians, your RIGHTS are being invaded! Regardless of your interests, or THE LIVES OF YOUR LITTLE ONES, THE CAMDON AND AMBOY, with the assistance of another Company without a Charter, and in VIOLATION OF LAW, are laying a

LOCOMOTIVE RAIL ROAD!

Through your most Beautiful Streets, to the Ruin of your Trade, annihilation of your RIGHTS, and regardless of your PROSPERITY and COMFORT!

Rails are now being laid on BROAD STREET to connect the TRENTON RAIL ROAD with the WILMINGTON AND BALTIMORE ROAD, under the pretense of constructing a City Passenger Road from the Navy Yard to Freemount! This is done under the auspices of the CAMDEN AND AMBOY MONOPOLY!

RALLY PEOPLE IN THE MAJESTY OF YOUR STRENGTH AND FORBID THIS OUTRAGE!

Martha had laughed when she first read the diatribe, but Jacob and Jonathan, still as opposed to railroads as ever, had digested every word of it, adding their own scathing remarks. Although their comments had been no more than Martha had expected, they had set off another heated argument, and the air at Rose-lawns had been thick for days.

Now she put the poster aside and returned to musing over Aunt Emily's letter. How she, too, wished that Aunt Emily and her mother could see her hand-some Rory, and sweet little Prudence, who already gave promise of being an exact replica of Martha herself. As for the baby, Crissy, she was a paragon among babies, her coloring a throwback to Nancy's, her hair spun gold, her eyes as blue as an October sky in Massachusetts, altogether the most beautiful infant that Martha had ever seen, and Martha was given neither to conceit nor bragging. Even Jacob, whose heart had been set on another boy to make up for his disappointment at Prudence's sex, was enthralled with her.

Martha looked up as Jonathan entered the room, his scowl so exactly the counterpart of Rory's earlier one that it made her heart turn over with love for him. What was it now, she wondered? Hadn't the rum punch that Sam always had ready for him when he returned to the house been exactly to his taste? Had that new stallion of his been overly fractious, the beast that Martha had pointed out had cost far more than they could afford, at least until this year's crop was in?

"Rory tells me you went to the field this afternoon. He says you talked to Slade."

"We did happen to see Mr. Slade. Naturally, he

95

was there supervising the work. I asked him how it was going."

"Don't you know any better than to talk to a man like Vic Slade? Not only do you hang around the fields, you have to compound the felony by treating that peckerwood like an equal! If Jacob gets wind of it, there'll be the devil to pay. Ain't you ever going to learn?"

Martha stood up. "Mr. Slade seems a perfect gentleman to me, certainly more of a gentleman than you're acting right now. Besides, I wasn't alone. Both Rory and Sam were with me."

"I should hope Sam was with you! I'd take the skin off his back, if he wasn't! Even you know better than to ride out alone! Don't go changing the subject. You ain't to talk to Slade, Marty. Not in the fields, not if you meet him near the house, not at any time or for any reason. You hear me?"

"I could scarcely help but hear you. They must hear you clear to the quarters." Martha's voice was cold. It was the old clash of wills, the constant friction caused by her independence and the South's artificial protection of its womenfolk. "I must say that Mr. Slade looked more the part of a gentleman than you do right now, Jon. Your boots could use a cleaning, and you smell of horse."

"Damn it, Marty, cut that out! You know what I mean. I don't have to draw a picture for you. I will not be shamed and humiliated by having it get around that my wife talks to my overseer, especially one like Vic Slade! I knew it was a mistake to put him on. I told Jacob so, at the time. It's a disgrace. You behave yourself, damn it!"

"And you keep a civil tongue in your head!"

Jonathan's face paled. His eyes were like molten steel. "Damn Miss Emily!" he gritted through clenched

96

teeth. "Damn her free-thinkin' hide! Sometimes I think she ruined you past all redemption." He slammed the door as he went out, shouting for Sam.

Cleo crept in, uncertain of Martha's temper. When her mistress and Mister Jon had a set-to, it was wise to move softly.

"Cleo, fetch the pen and paper." Martha's chin was set, and Cleo sighed inwardly. There she went again. Every time she and Jonathan had a difference, Miss Martha got back at him by giving Cleo lessons in reading and writing. If they ever got caught at it, the sky would fall. It was against the law and Miss Martha knew it, she did it for pure orneriness.

The quarrels between Martha and Jonathan were so frequent that, by now, Cleo knew her letters, both to read and to write them. Small letters and capitals, she knew them all, and she could read words, too, if they weren't too very long or complicated. She could even put sentences together on paper. Rebecca could both read and write—she was an educated woman—but she had been that before she had come to Rose-lawns. Her white father had seen to it before he had died, leaving his quadroon mistress and his octaroon daughter without his protection.

"Miss Martha, one of these days Mister Jonathan is going to catch us at this, and then we'll be in a peck of trouble."

"If he catches us, and tries to interfere, the trouble will be on his side. Are you ready, Cleo? The word is tyrant. T Y R A N T."

Cleo wrote the letters, carefully. Her writing was clear and legible.

"What does it mean, Miss Martha?"

"It means a Southern planter. Next word, Cleo. Bigot. B I G O T."

9

Dulcy looked so beautiful that tears filmed Martha's eyes. She had taken infinite pains with Dulcy's wedding dress. Rebecca had stitched it up and done all the tedious work, but Martha herself had spent hours on the embroidery and braidwork.

The plantation carpenter had built a bower on the front lawn, an arched trellis that Pansy and Marguerite had interlaced with roses and greenery. Long trestle tables had been made by laying planks over sawhorses. A huge pit had been dug, and a freshly butchered pig, even now, was filling the air with its aroma as it was barbecued for the coming feast. Not only that, but there was a wedding cake, with real sugar icing, and platters of long-shortening cookies, and a keg of rum which Joshua, the coachman, was to guard, making sure that no slave had enough to make him drunk, but enough to make him happy. Benjamin, Jacob's majordomo, was acting as best man, and to Cleo's rapture, she also had been stitched up a new dress, so she could serve as Dulcy's bridesmaid.

Martha was ready to wager that in all the South, no slave had ever been given a finer wedding, or one that could anywhere near touch it. In fact, Jonathan had told her that some of the other planters were objecting, claiming that they were setting a precedent for spoiling the slaves.

Vic Slade was thinking along those same lines, his pale eyes narrowed, his handsome face brooding. It was crazy to throw a shindig like this for a nigger. Jacob must have taken leave of his senses. Slade resented any special consideration that was shown to the blacks. As did nearly all of his class, he believed that they should be kept in their place and treated harshly, because after all, they weren't quite human. Not one of his own sisters had had a wedding like this, or could ever hope to. It wasn't only ridiculous, it was downright wicked, and a slap in the face to every decent white man.

Work had been called to a halt an hour early that afternoon so that the slaves could get ready for the celebration. Now, just before twilight, they had all gathered on the lawn, dressed in whatever bits of finery they could come by, their faces alight with anticipation.

Sam took his place under the arbor, and Dulcy came from the big house where Martha herself had supervised her dressing. Dulcy's blood was no more than a quarter white, and her features were delicate, her bone structure beautiful. In her wedding dress, with the lace and the camellias crowning her hair, she was so lovely that people caught their breath as she walked, with graceful dignity, to stand beside Sam.

They made a beautiful couple, Dulcy small and dainty, Sam tall and slender, his face classical in its features, attesting to some Arab blood in his ancestry. Sam's eyes glowed with love and pride as they rested on his bride, and the look she returned was one of breathless rapture.

Slade took another swallow of rum. It went down the wrong way, too fast, and he choked before he felt the smoldering anger in him intensify. He'd been after that piece himself, but she'd always managed to elude him. She'd known what he was after, and she'd never left or returned to the cabin she shared with Pansy and Marguerite and an old granny without someone with her. And Slade hadn't dared to order or force her into the overseer's cottage because Jonathan would have raised hell if Dulcy had complained. Dulcy was Miss Martha's pet, the same as that Cleo—she spoiled them rotten, treated them as if they were white, for God's sake.

There she was herself, Miss Martha, up there on the gallery, looking like she belonged in a painting. Just to look at her made Slade's blood rise. Until he'd come to Roselawns, he'd never seen a woman like Martha or even imagined that there was one.

And he, Slade, wasn't as much as allowed to pass the time of day with her. That damned Jonathan had made that plain to him. He could work like a sonofabitch, maybe even build up to a plantation and slaves of his own, but he'd always be trash to the Beddoeses and the Amhursts and the Renaults, not good enough to speak to their wives and daughters. The men might nod to him, in passing, but their womenfolk would look right through him and never see him.

The smoldering hatred inside him was a raging fire, fed by the rum he had consumed. His eyes left Martha and passed on to Rebecca. Now there was a delectable piece of poontang, but he had about as much chance to get next to her as he did to Miss Martha. Rebecca even slept in the big house. She wasn't sent to the quarters at night like the other slaves, but had a small cubbyhole of her own next to the sewing room. And she thought she was quality! She, too, looked at Slade, if they happened to meet, without even seeing him.

100

The ceremony was over. The slaves had exploded into jubilation, their hands clapping, their feet stamping. They formed a circle around Sam and Dulcy, and Dulcy was so radiant that Slade felt his rage turn murderous.

It wasn't right. It wasn't right that a nigger, even if he was Jonathan's personal boy, should have a piece like Dulcy. As overseer, Vic should have his pick of the wenches. But did he? "Keep your hands off the wenches," Jacob had told him the day he'd been hired. "I don't allow any messin' with them, you understand? You need a woman, you go find yourself a white gal down in shantytown. There's plenty of them there'll be glad to take up with an overseer."

A soft voice spoke from behind him. Susie, that was her name. Fourteen, fifteen, at a guess. But ripening. "You want some pork, Mister Vic? I'll load up a plate for you."

She spoke diffidently, aware that Slade was in a bad mood, hopeful that if he had enough to eat and drink he wouldn't be so hard to please when they returned to work tomorrow. He'd laid her pappy out this morning for tripping, and threatened to whip him, and Susie loved her pappy.

Vic looked around the milling celebrants, his eyes narrowed. Nobody was looking their way. "I need you for something. Come along," he ordered.

Susie's nostrils flared, the fear emanating from her causing a noticeable odor that served to excite him further.

"You come!" he said, his voice filled with menace. "Or do you want me to take special notice of your pappy tomorrow? Your mam, too. She's got a big belly again, ain't she? Most ready to drop her foal. Well, are you comin' or ain't you?"

Susie's heart beat sickeningly against her immature

breasts. She could run, or yell, but she'd never, in her fourteen years, attracted the attention of the white folk. To Susie, the embodiment of all white authority lay in Vic Slade. Shaking, nausea rising in her throat, she followed him.

The overseer's cottage was pitch-dark as Slade pushed Susie through the door and pulled her dress, the only garment she wore, up above her hips. He shoved her down onto his bed, the cornhusk mattress rustling as he bore her down under him. His hands found the warm soft area between her thighs, pushed them apart, then his knee took the place of one of his hands to keep her legs spraddled while the hand found her breasts, tender and nubile. He squeezed, and Susie whimpered with terror when pain shot through her as he twisted her nipple.

"Gawd, Massa Vic, don't hurt me!" she begged. "Please don' you hurt me like that!"

Vic's voice was gloating, thick with lust, as he twisted harder. "What you fixin' to do about it? You goin' tell your mammy, tell your pappy?"

"No, massa, I ain't tell! Jes' lemme go!" Susie was crying in agony, her tears scalding against Vic's hand as they fell.

"Like hell I'll let you go! I got my rights . . ." His voice broke off as he pressed his face into Susie's breast, his teeth finding the nipple, clamping down. Her voice rose in a shriek, only to fall muffled as his hand clamped over her mouth. His male member was throbbing, probing at her, seeking entry, hugely swollen, and he cursed as Susie's tight virginity prevented the entry. He got his other hand down there to use his fingers to spread her wider, and Susie's body arched with unbearable pain.

"You bastard!"

Strong, ruthless hands grasped Vic's shoulders and

hauled him off his intended victim. "Rebecca was right, you did bring this child to your house! It's a damned good thing she saw you, Slade, or you'd be off this place tomorrow with no letter to help you find another place even on some small peckerwood's holding! You can consider yourself damned lucky that I don't want to raise a stink that'd get Miss Martha all upset and spoil Sam's wedding! Susie, you get home to your ma! Have her take a good look at you, see if you're hurt. If you are, you come tell me tomorrow."

Susie scrabbled off the bed and through the open door, running like a terrified fawn even though she was still doubled over with pain, her hands clutching at her vagina. Vic's body thumped against the opposite wall as Jonathan hurled him from him, his voice filled with barely controlled fury.

"Sober up, you bastard! And if you had time to hurt that little wench, you'd better be off this place before I find out about it!"

On Monday morning, the field hands rolled their eyes at each other nervously. Slade had gone on drinking all through Sunday, and he was in an ugly mood. That wedding had been somethin', all right, but now the celebration was over, and Slade was just looking for somebody to cross him. They'd better toe the mark today, and that was no lie.

Their very nervousness made them clumsy. Keeping one eye on Slade, Luther, who was ordinarily one of the best hands on the plantation, missed his stroke with the hoe and chopped down a tender cotton plant instead. A moment later, even as he stood open-mouthed with fright, Slade's whip came down on his shoulders.

All work stopped as the whip rose and fell and

rose again. Lord have mercy, he was killing Luther! He was killing him as sure as Judgment Day! Luther's screams split the air, as the others cowered, their limbs shaking, their faces strangely gray under their dark pigmentation.

Luther was down, now, flat on his face in the dirt, his shirt ripped clean off him, his back running blood. He wasn't screaming any more. Maybe he was dead. And still the whip rose and fell.

One of the others, a boy no more than a stripling, broke and ran. Slade, seeing him go through a red haze, took after him, but he'd dismounted to whip Luther, and his horse, frightened by Luther's screams, had sidled off. The young black's feet seemed to have sprouted wings. Behind him, Slade stumbled and fell to his knees, his curses turning the air blue. The young black ran faster, terror lending him speed of which he would otherwise have been incapable.

Now that Luther's screaming had stopped, the horse had come to a standstill. Slade got up and ran to it and swung into the saddle. Glancing back over his shoulder, the boy ran faster, his ribs working in and out like an accordian.

The horse, its eyes rolling and showing red, foam flecking its mouth, bore down on him. The boy screamed as the horse reared, yanked up by the bit so hard that the foam on its mouth showed blood. The hooves descended, and the boy wrapped his arms around his head and rolled.

"He ain't dead. The hoof didn't any more than graze him. I had no intention of hurting him, the horse reared, that's all." Slade was defiant, his face sullen and belligerent. "He had no business running. What was I supposed to do, let him get away with it? The next thing you know, we'd have an insurrection on our hands."

"Pack your gear and get out." Jacob's face was stern under its flush of intense anger. "You'd been warned, Slade. Now git!"

"But he ain't dead! Luther ain't dead, either. Maybe I laid it on a little harder than I should have, but he was damned careless. You want me to let him go on choppin' down cotton plants instead of weeds?"

"Two prime hands disabled, the others in a panic. I'm not telling you again, you bastard. Get off my property." Jacob turned his back and moved toward his desk in a gesture of dismissal.

His face murderous with rage, Slade left the office.

10

Jonathan had the pony on a leading-rein, but Prue's chubby little hands grasped the reins with determination. Her face was flushed with excitement. "Let him go, Papa! I can do it alone, let him go!"

"Not just yet, young lady. You got to get the feel of it first."

Prudence gave her father a pained look. "You don't lead Rory."

"Rory's a big boy. And he rides astride, and that's safer than sidesaddle. He can hang on with his knees and you can't."

Prudence was a little mollified, but not much. "I can keep my balance. Dammit, Papa, let go!"

Martha gasped. "Prue! Such language! I shall have to wash your mouth out with soap!"

"Papa says it! He says it all the time."

"Your papa has no business saying it. Cursing is an indication of an inadequate vocabulary, as well as a sin."

"Then wash his mouth out with soap, too," Prudence said reasonably, and jerking the leading-rein from Jonathan's hand, she gave the pony a hard kick with her stirruped foot so that it began to canter. She sat ramrod-straight, her long dark hair streaming out behind her, her cheeks flaming with triumph. "See, I told you I could do it!"

"You do that again and you'll get a whaling!"

Prudence laughed up into Jonathan's face. She wouldn't get a spanking, at least not from her papa. But her mother was another matter entirely. Martha didn't spank, she used a switch cut from a tree, and it stung like the . . . it stung like anything. Looking at her mother's face, Prudence decided that it would be wiser, at the moment, not even to think a bad word.

Jonathan was standing there, still holding Prudence with one arm and the pony with his free hand, when Sam approached them.

"Miss Martha, Mister Jon, have you seen Dulcy this morning?"

Martha sobered when she looked at Sam. He was obviously worried, and that wasn't like him. "Why, no, I haven't. Have you asked Miss Yolande? Surely Dulcy must be around somewhere."

"No, Miss Martha, she isn't. We've looked everywhere."

"Sam, that's downright impossible! She has to be here," Jonathan said, frowning. "When did you see her last?"

"She had a little time off, she got through with the dusting early, and Miss Yolande told her she could go to our cabin to work on the curtains she got new material for. Only she never came back, and when I went to fetch her, she wasn't there. Just the curtains she'd been working on, in a heap on the floor, and she wouldn't have left them like that, she was too proud of them."

Martha began to be worried, too. "Are you sure you haven't had some misunderstanding? She might be keeping out of sight because you've had words."

107

"No, Miss Martha, Dulcy and I haven't had words." Perspiration beaded Sam's forehead.

"We'll find her, Sam. We'll get every person we can spare to hunting her right now." Jonathan set Prudence on her feet. "You run to Grandma. Your mama and I are going to be busy for a while."

An hour later, they were sure that Dulcy had been taken from Roselawns by force, and they were sure who had taken her. Young Tod, the stableboy, who was Joshua's right hand, was the first to spot the hoofmarks where they left the outer limits of the Beddoeses' holdings going east.

Jacob, who had had considerable experience in tracking, back in the days when the Creeks had been on the rampage, confirmed that the marks had been made by Vic Slade's horse. But it was Tod's keen eyes that spotted one of Dulcy's shoes, half a mile beyond, where Slade had taken to an area of scrub away from the roads. Fuming because one of them had to stay on the plantation, it being unthinkable for all white men to be away at the same time, Jacob returned to the house and reluctantly let Jonathan lead the search party to recover Dulcy.

"He got a mighty long start on us." Jonathan slackened the pace a little and frowned. It was no use wearing out the horses. Beside him, Sam also drew up and nodded. Sam was mounted on a horse, one of Roselawns's best, although the other blacks rode mules. In the South, blacks were not allowed the use of their masters' horseflesh; if necessity compelled them to be mounted, mules had to do.

"Too long, I'm thinking, Mister Jonathan. The mood Slade was in, anything might happen. Mister Renault's Caesar had a pass into town yesterday afternoon, and he stopped by here on his way back, and he told us that Slade was there, drinking heavy. Drinking and mean, poison-snake mean."

"That figures. The bastard!" The muscles along Jonathan's jawline knotted. "Well, we'll get him, Sam. And Dulcy's a healthy girl. Likely she'll be all right, only mauled a little."

He shouldn't have said that. It was bad enough they were all thinking it without putting it into words.

Young Tod, who, as a yard pickaninny, had listened while Jacob told his hair-raising tales of the Indian troubles, and who had emulated his master by patient development of his own skill at tracking, pointed off to the south and east. "He went thataway, Massa Jon. See there? Look like he headin' for the swampland."

Jonathan studied the faint tracks. "You're right, boy. He's making for Okefenokee; likely he's bent on getting down into Florida. But his horse is carrying double, remember, and it'll be getting mighty tired by now. Let's get on!"

Grimly, the little party that was comprised of Jonathan, Sam, Tod, and two strapping field hands kicked their mounts into action.

Jonathan didn't like it. If Slade made it to the Okefenokee, they'd have the devil's own time laying him by the heels. Not one of the blacks with him knew the first thing about the swamp, and Jonathan didn't, either. And it was doubtful if they'd be able to persuade any local poor white to act as a guide. Even hard money would not tempt them into entering a planter's business. They hated the aristocracy's guts, and they hated blacks even worse. Likely they wouldn't turn a hand to help Slade, either, but that wasn't much comfort. Slade knew the swamps; he'd been raised on their outskirts, and he wouldn't need any help.

The hell of it was, it was coming on night, and

they'd have to lay over. You couldn't track at night. If he'd had a grain of sense, he'd have stopped by the Renaults' and got John's hounds, Jonathan realized. But he'd had this notion in his head that the less folks knew about this business, the better Sam would feel when they got Dulcy back. Slade could be charged with trying to kill Luther and Caesar, and Sam wouldn't have to bear the humiliation of having everybody know that Slade had manhandled his wife. Once caught, Slade would keep his mouth shut. Stealing a slave was far more serious than beating one.

Just before dark they came on a cracker's cabin, two log rooms connected by a covered passage. The lantern-jawed owner didn't go all out to make them welcome, but the sight of hard cash persuaded him to show the blacks to a shed and to show Jonathan where he could roll up in a blanket in the cabin. Cornmeal mush and fatback were doled out, with a bitter concoction, boiled up out of herbs by the owner's wife, to pass for coffee. The young 'uns, half a dozen of them like stairsteps, alternately hid behind their mother's skirts or scattered whenever Jonathan looked at them.

The woman couldn't have been more than in her thirties, but already her teeth were rotting out from chewing snuff, and her hair, unbound, fell lank and straw-like around a face darkened by years of bending over open fires. Jonathan felt a sadness in him looking at her, looking at the young 'uns, as wild as wood animals. Uneducated, fiercely independent, they'd choose to stay here, eking out a bare existence, even if a better offer came along. Vic Slade had come from just such a family, but he was an exception. Jonathan wondered what had given him that touch of ambition.

Dulcy's back was raw from being ground into the

rough ground beneath her, her throat was swollen from the screams that the gag stuffed into her mouth prevented from reaching the air. On top of her, Slade grunted and thrust like a boar in rut, each thrust bringing new moans of agony into Dulcy's throat. Blood from the bites on her breasts trickled down toward her waist, where her bunched-up skirt absorbed it.

She couldn't stand much more. She'd die under Slade's vicious attack, the third that night since he had made camp. She'd been gently raised, the daughter of her former master's cook, and her master and mistress had been pleased when Jonathan Beddoes had asked for her to be nursemaid for his children. The Johnsons had been middle-aged and childless; although they had hated to sell one of their house people, they'd had no need for Dulcy and they'd been satisfied that her new owners would be as kind to her as they themselves had been.

Moaning against the filthy gag, Dulcy screamed silently for Sam. Slade was hurting her, he was killing her. Dulcy had had no experience with men who acted worse than beasts. Her body was delicately made, unsuited for such treatment.

With several last, vicious thrusts, Slade's body collapsed on Dulcy's, his breathing heavy, gasping his exhaustion in the thick, hot night air. He was drunk. He'd started drinking from a bottle of rum the moment they'd stopped, and he'd continued drinking between his assaults. Numb with pain, numb of mind after what had been done to her, Dulcy realized that he had fallen asleep on top of her.

Slade was a big man, and heavy, and Dulcy's hands were bound behind her back, the wrists chafed raw and bleeding. It took her a long time to work her way out from under him, terrified that he'd wake up

111

and beat her again, as he'd beaten her, without mercy, when she had resisted him the first time.

She rolled free of his body at last and struggled to her knees. It took her even longer to gain her feet. Each step she took, hot blood seeped from her vagina, torn and mutilated by Slade's inhuman handling. Her mind, filled with the cruelties that had been inflicted on her, knew only one thing. Sam was out there somewhere, and she had to get to him, so he could hold her violated body in his arms and protect her from further horror.

The men were up before first light, gulped down leftover mush, stone cold and held in their hands, and were on their way. Looking over his shoulder, Jonathan saw the cabin's owner spit after them as they rode out of his clearing. Jonathan cursed as he scratched at the flea bites he'd accumulated during the night, cursed because the man had refused to rent his four scrawny hounds. The mush sat like lead in his stomach.

Sam was silent, his cheekbones showing prominently under taut-stretched skin. His eyes were somber, unreadable. Jonathan was wrenched with pity. That was Dulcy that Slade had, and knowing Slade, Dulcy'd be in bad shape by now. Damn it to hell, why'd this had to go and happen? If it wasn't that the country was beginning to pride itself on being law-abiding, he'd strangle that bastard Slade when they came up with him.

Tod's mule shied and reared, sending him cata-pulting over its head. Another second, and the two horses were going crazy, snorting and plunging and trying to back up or turn around and bolt for home.

112

By the time they had the animals under control, they could smell it, the rotten, fetid odor of death.

"Stay back, Sam!" Jonathan's voice was like a whip. Sickened himself, he walked, stiff-legged, toward the clump of brush where a scrap of blue calico showed, barely visible. When he parted the bushes and looked down at Dulcy, his stomach roiled, and he turned away and retched, until it felt as though his insides were torn loose.

She'd been bitten by a snake, and her body was swollen grotesquely. Cottonmouth, Jonathan thought. Her feet, both of them bare now, and her legs were cut and torn and scratched, as were her arms and face. Her hands were still bound behind her back, the swollen flesh almost enveloping the cord.

The story was plain enough. She'd got away from Slade, somehow, and hit out for home. But a cottonmouth had got her—likely she'd never seen it. It would have had to be during the night, while Slade was asleep, drunk, most likely.

Jonathan heard a moan and straightened up just in time to see Sam go to his knees. "Dulcy, oh, my God, Dulcy!" The cry was torn from Sam's soul.

Jonathan took his arm and tried to bring him to his feet. "Don't, Sam. Don't! We can't help her now. Remember, there's still Slade. We'll get him, Sam! I promise we'll get him, if it takes from now to kingdom come!"

"We ain't goin' to leave her here! We ain't goin' to just dig a hole and roll her into it!"

"No, no, of course we aren't." Jonathan tasted bile in his throat again. "You can take her home, Sam. Tell Jacob to arrange for the funeral."

"I'm going with you. She was my wife. I've got to see Slade brought in. I couldn't live if I didn't see him caught."

113

Jonathan understood. Catching Slade, seeing him brought to justice, was the only thing Sam could do for the woman he'd loved so deeply. Was it possible that just three evenings ago they'd celebrated the wedding that had made John Renault and a lot of others say that the Beddoeses spoiled their people and it'd end up causing trouble?

He shook his head to clear it. Noah, the elder of the two field hands, could be trusted. He wouldn't try to run away. Jonathan had no means with him to write out a pass, but any chance patrol would have to believe his story if they came across him carrying Dulcy home.

"Get her back to that cabin, Noah. Buy a blanket off those folks to wrap her in, and then take her on home." He reached into his pocket for a gold piece and placed it in Noah's hand. "You'll have to pay him. He wouldn't part with a blanket, else."

It took some time to balance Dulcy's body over the back of the nervous mule, and Noah didn't relish his task, but Jonathan knew that he'd carry it out. "Set Jack to making her a coffin as soon as you get there. Tell him to make it a good one. Miss Martha'll give him something to line it with." Anything, to take some of that grayness out of Sam's face, that death out of his eyes.

If Sam heard, he gave no indication. They watched Noah set off with his pitiful burden, and then they pressed on, sick at heart, but with steel-hard determination prodding them on.

It was sundown when they found him. He'd been back-tracking looking for Dulcy, and his horse had gone lame. The tracks, one of them shoeless, led to another shanty.

The horse was tied under a chinaberry tree, its head

114

drooping to its front feet, standing hip-slung to ease its lame hind foot. Only trash would treat a horse like that. The bastard hadn't even watered it, or rubbed it down.

Slade came out of the shack as they approached and yelled something to the owner who loomed up behind him. "Shoot, damn it!"

The other man had a rifle in his hands, but he didn't raise it. This was none of his affair. A man showed up sick, his horse lame, and he'd taken him in, but the man's quarrels were none of his.

Slade had a gun, a handgun, and he fired, but the bullet went wild. Jonathan began riding him down as he headed for the scrub. The horse's shoulder caught the former overseer just as Slade threw the empty gun into Jonathan's face. It struck Jonathan squarely between the eyes and jolted him out of the saddle, and he landed heavily, all the wind knocked out of him.

His head ringing, Jonathan rolled to his knees so he could shake the confusion out of his brain. Tod and the other black, Big Arnie, were shouting, and as his eyes cleared, Jonathan swore and catapulted himself up to drag Sam off Slade.

A knife, still dripping blood, was clenched in Sam's hand. Damn, where'd he got it? Jonathan had never thought to search Sam before they'd set out. It was his fault, he should have allowed for this. If Sam had killed the bastard—

Slade wasn't dead, but Sam had done a good job on him. The wound in his shoulder was gushing. Still cursing, Jonathan shouted orders. "Arnie, hold Sam! Damn you, hold him, I said! Tod, get that shirt off your back and hand it here."

Sam fought like a catamount, but Big Arnie stood six three and had muscles to match. In spite of Sam's frantic struggles, the larger black wrestled him to the ground and sat on him, twisting his arms behind his back.

Jonathan ripped Tod's shirt in two and made a wadded patch of half of it and pressed it against Slade's wound to staunch the bleeding. Slade's eyes were open, baleful. Two days' stubble of beard did nothing to hide his increasing pallor as he lost blood.

"You bastard," Slade said. "You mother-fucking bastard! You always win, don't you? You and your kind, you always win! But I'll get you, Jonathan, I swear to God I'll get you one of these days!"

"You bastids git offen my propity!" the man at the cabin snarled at them. "I don't want no trash dyin' on my propity, you hear? You're tresspassin'! Load that bleedin' bastid on his horse and git out of here before I open up on you!"

"Keep a civil tongue in your head. This man is a fugitive and we have every right to apprehend him wherever he may have been hiding." Jonathan's face was as white as Slade's. Jesus God, Sam! He was almost of a mind to tell Sam to get going, to run. Then he shook his head. He couldn't do that, not in front of Arnie and Tod. Besides, Sam wouldn't go. He still had Dulcy to bury. Oh, Jesus, Sam!

"All right, Arnie. Help me get Slade across my saddle. Tod, you lead Slade's horse. We'll be heading on back."

116

11

"You can't do that!" Martha's face, as she faced Jonathan, was as white as Massachusetts snow, and her eyes were dark with disbelief. "Jonathan, you can't have him whipped! He had a right, he had every right! Dulcy was his wife, he loved her, and that beast killed her!"

"He attacked a white man." Jonathan sat slumped in a chair in their bedroom, his hair disheveled, his chin unshaven since he'd started out on the manhunt. "He has to be punished, Martha."

"A white man!" Contempt made Martha's voice take fire. "You call Slade a man, after what he did? If Sam were white, if Dulcy had been white, and Slade had taken her, and she'd been snakebitten and died while she was escaping from him, would Sam be punished for trying to kill him?"

"That has nothing to do with it. Sam isn't white. He's black, and he's a slave. He has to be whipped."

"He's your friend! He's as close as a brother! I've seen you with your arm around his shoulder, Jon! I've heard you laughing together, joking together! You told me you loved him, that your earliest memories are all wrapped up with Sam! You said he'd lay down his life for you. Is the friendship, the loyalty, all on his side? What kind of a monster are you?"

Jonathan rose, his fingers tugging at his hair. "Shut up. Just shut up, Martha." He strode from the room, but Martha wasn't finished. She ran after him and grasped his arm.

"I won't let you do it! Do you hear me, I won't let you do it!"

"Get back to your room!"

"They're going to do it now, aren't they? That's why you've been drinking this past hour, because you haven't the moral courage to watch it unless you're numbed with drink! Has anybody given Sam rum or brandy, so the pain won't be so unendurable?"

"Get back in there, I told you!" Roughly, furiously, Jonathan caught her arm and half dragged, half pushed her back into their bedroom. "Stay there, you hear me? This is no concern of womenfolk! For once in your life, be quiet and let us run our own affairs the way they have to be run!"

Before Martha realized what he was doing, Jonathan took the key from the lock and shut her in, locking the door behind him. He had actually locked her in! She paced the floor, so furious she could hardly see straight. She knew that Yolande was in her own room, probably crying, but completely helpless in the face of the written and unwritten laws of this horrible land.

She threw herself on the bed and pounded the pillow in a frenzy of anger. Where was their civilization, their highly touted chivalry? All gone, a thin veneer that could not withstand their constant, underlying fear of the people they owned and ruled. Sam had attacked a white man, and so Sam must be punished, in front of all the slaves, punished brutally, as an example.

118

Aunt Emily had been right, Southerners were an alien race.

Sam's eyes met Jonathan's, and Jonathan's were the first to drop. Bound to the whipping-post that had not been used in Jonathan's memory, Sam stood, his shirt ripped to his waist. Big Arnie, who had been chosen to wield the whip, looked at Jonathan beseechingly.

For a moment, Jonathan almost tried to stop it. But Jacob was there, implacable, as sorry about it as Jonathan but convinced that he must uphold the laws of the land. This was better than turning Sam over to the civil authorities, who might go harder on him, even in the face of the evidence. If a planter punished his own slaves, the authorities were apt to look the other way. No gentleman cared to cause embarrassment to another gentleman.

"Go ahead, Arnie. Let's get it over with." Jacob's voice was heavy.

Jonathan winced as the blacksnake whip rose and fell. Sam's face was stolid, expressionless, after that first blow. Arnie's face ran with sweat and it was obvious that he'd rather have been taking the whipping himself as his arm rose again.

The whip fell, rose, and fell again. After a first, wailing moan, the other slaves stood silent, expressionless, only their eyes showing the extent of their emotions.

At the fourth blow, Sam moaned. His eyes looked directly into Jonathan's as he turned his head, painfully, to look at his master. Jonathan felt nausea rise in his stomach.

The whip fell again, and this time Sam's moan was louder. Red weals were rising on Sam's back. Again, and again, and again. Jonathan had lost count, although he had determined to keep track and stop it as soon as the twenty lashes had been administered.

The sound of the blows went on, the whistle as the whip lashed through the air, the sickening plop as it landed on Sam's back, bleeding now, the blood running in rivulets down into his trousers. At the next blow Sam screamed, the scream breaking off in a gurgle as his head flopped limply onto his shoulder.

"Jacob, for the love of God!" Jonathan cried hoarsely. "It's enough! Have him cut down!"

Jacob's face looked green. "Three more," he said.

All the hands were looking at him. He had to stand there, he had to be the Almighty Planter, upholding the law, while the last three lashes fell. He wished that he were dead.

Martha was too angry to cry. She didn't cry until an hour later, when Cleo came to let her out of her room with the key Yolande had given her.

She raised her head from the bed, her hair in wild disorder. "Is it over?"

"Yes, Miss Martha."

"Did you see?"

"Yes, ma'am. We all had to see."

"Was it bad?"

Cleo's mouth shook, and she put her hand over it and dashed for the slop basin.

Martha waited until her retching had passed. "Where is he? Where is my husband?"

"He lit out on his horse, like the devil was after him."

"And Sam?"

"In the hospital shed. But don't you go, Miss Martha. Rebecca's taking care of him. There's no need for you to see it."

120

Without answering, Martha brushed past her and hurried down the stairs.

She'd known it would be bad, and Cleo had confirmed it, but even that hadn't given her sufficient warning. Sam's back was laid open to the bone.

Rebecca disapproved of her presence here. "He's still unconscious, Miss Martha. He'll stay that way for hours, God willing. It's better so. There's no need for you to stay."

She stayed anyway, and helped Rebecca replace the wet packs on Sam's back.

"What did the doctor say?" She knew that one had been summoned beforehand to attend Sam when it was over.

Rebecca's face was noncommital. "He didn't know."

"Did you see it?"

Rebecca's face did not change. "No. My presence was not required." Martha was sorry that she had asked. Rebecca's status was ambiguous. She had never given any indication that she considered herself a slave, and Yolande treated her as she would have a white employee. Rebecca had no dealings with the other slaves except to help direct them in their work when occasion required. Martha did not know whom she pitied more, Rebecca or the people who accepted the fact that they were black and held in bondage.

Toward evening Jacob came in. Sam had begun to toss and turn, and Rebecca had gone to fetch laudanum.

"Damnation!" Jacob looked from Sam to Martha and apologized. "It's a blasted shame that this thing had to happen. I should have listened to Jon in the first place and never put Slade on. But you oughtn't be out here, girl. What's Jon thinking of?"

"Jon hasn't come back, as far as I know. He went galloping off hours ago, or so Cleo told me."

"So he did. Well, he was mighty cut up about this affair."

There was no humor in Martha's reply. "Not as cut up as Sam."

Around ten o'clock that evening, she allowed Rebecca to persuade her to return to the house. Jon still hadn't come back, and she was glad about that. She was tired, more tired than she had ever been, but the anger was still raging in her.

"Cleo, help me gather up Jonathan's things."

Cleo's face showed her consternation. "Miss Martha, you aren't fixing to shut him out of your room? Ain't no Southern lady locks her husband out of her bedroom."

"I'm not a Southern lady, and I'm proud of it!" Martha told her. "Hurry up, I'm tired, and I want to get this over with so I can get to bed."

In the light of a single candle, Rebecca looked at Sam. She hadn't given him more laudanum yet, because he hadn't seemed to wake from his semiconscious state enough to swallow it. She was mildly sorry for Sam, but she thought, half in anger, that he'd brought it on himself. He'd known what would happen if he attacked a white man, even trash like Vic Slade.

Rebecca sat very still, her hands folded in her lap, her eyes withdrawn as she drew deeper into her thoughts. Martha was almighty angry with Jonathan, and it might be turned to her advantage. Rebecca knew that Martha had removed Jon's belongings from their bedroom and locked the door against him. The black grapevine did its work well. On her way to the quarters for the night, Cleo had told no one, but still they knew, and Rebecca had heard it discussed, in low, frightened voices, by Joshua and Tod when they'd

122

paused outside the hospital shed to ask one last time after Sam before they sought their own beds.

Jonathan's going to be furious, Rebecca thought. And if she keeps him locked out, he's going to need comforting. The thought made her blood run fast, and her face took on a radiance that would have startled anyone who might see her. But there was no one to see.

Rebecca had loved Jonathan ever since she had come to Roselawns. She had been well aware of her good fortune. Jacob had paid twenty-five hundred dollars for her when her mother's master had died, leaving them unprotected. If Jacob had not bought her for Yolande, she would have ended up like her mother, the plaything of some other white man, or worse, sold to a house in New Orleans where she would have been handled and used by any man with the price.

Rebecca hated the black blood in her veins. She was white! Her father had been just as much of an aristocrat as Jacob himself. She had a right to love and marriage, to a fine house of her own, to the respect of the community. She had been grateful when Jacob had bought her, but her resentment at her status in life had not been tempered.

When Jacob had brought her into the house to present her to Yolande, Jonathan had been with his mother, and the moment she saw him, Rebecca was lost. If Jon had favored her, taken her as his mistress, she would have been content with her lot. But in all this time, even before he had gone north and returned with Martha, he had never asked her to share his bed, even though she had given him every opportunity. She had finally given up hope.

But tonight, Martha had locked Jon out of their bedroom. Jonathan would be exhausted when he returned from wherever his mad gallop had taken him, he'd need his wife, the warmth of her body, her arms, her lips, to blot out his grief.

Sam was still quiet, apparently sleeping naturally. Just as quietly, Rebecca rose from the chair beside him and glided from the hospital shack. She entered the house as silently as a shadow, and there was no one to see her passing. All of the white folk were in bed and the slaves had long since retired to the quarters.

She made her way, without the light of lamp or candle, to the cubbyhole next to the sewing room, the place Yolande had given her because she'd felt that Rebecca should not be housed with the other slaves. There she had, beside her narrow bed, a chest that held her few belongings, and it was to this chest that she went, and raised the lid.

She found the potion that old Hannah had made for her. Even Jacob knew that Hannah had set herself up as a sort of witch-woman, dispensing simple medicines and complicated charms for everything from childbirth to spider-bite to revenge on an unfaithful sweetheart or a potion guaranteed to so inflame the blood of your beloved that he would be powerless to resist.

Rebecca knew some of the ingredients of the potion that she had obtained from Hannah some time before, when she'd hoped that Jon's enforced absence from Martha's bed because of her pregnancy with Christine might make him vulnerable. Three drops of blood from a live snake, mixed with a pinch of ground spider-dust, stirred into half a cup of green corn squeezings. It never failed, Hannah had told her, gloating over the thick slice of ham and the length of calico that Rebecca had brought in payment.

Rebecca did not actually believe in the potion.

She was too well educated for that. But she had seen it work, and she suspected that Hannah had put in still another ingredient of which she knew nothing.

Carrying the jar with her, Rebecca returned to the ground floor. When Jonathan came home, he would find his bedroom door locked against him and he'd come back downstairs in search of brandy. And she'd be there, and this time Sam would not be there to stand as a buffer between them, his watchful eyes filled with suspicion.

Her breathing became softer in the darkness, and her heart beat fast.

Riding home through the night, Jonathan was exhausted both physically and mentally. Damn it, Sam, why'd you go and do it, he kept thinking over and over. I'd rather have taken the whipping myself, don't you know that, you black fool? But I'll make it up to you! I can't set you free, there's a law against that, but I'll find a way! I'll take you north myself and turn you loose with your papers; just don't let those cuts fester and go dying on me!

He was still drunk in spite of the miles he had ridden. He'd headed, first, into town, to a tavern, after his first wild gallop had threatened to kill both himself and his horse. It had been the horse, not his own neck, that had stopped him. He couldn't ride a good animal to death just because he felt like Judas.

He could have gone to friends, but he had had no desire for the company of anyone he knew. The story of Slade's abduction of Dulcy and Sam's subsequent whipping for trying to exact his own revenge had spread like wildfire. Even to the tavern. The sight of Jonathan's white face and steely eyes, however, had kept any of the patrons from speaking to him or even mentioning the subject among themselves in whispers for as long as he stayed. He'd sat by himself, bolting down fiery rum as though it were water, until the other men had looked at each other uneasily and wondered how he could remain upright.

The rum seemed to have almost no effect. After an hour, Jonathan left the tavern, to remount his rested horse and set off again to ride through the night with thoughts even darker than the night itself.

Much later, the rum found its way to him, and he felt its full effects. He'd ridden on until he had sobered up a little, but then he stopped at another tavern on his way back, because he didn't like the encroaching sobriety. He didn't have as much, the second time—just enough to see him home. He'd need those extra drinks to give him the courage to face Martha. Now, turning into the stableyard, he wished he'd had a little more.

His step was unsteady as he dismounted and shouted for Tod to come and take his horse. When Tod, rubbing sleep from his eyes, responded, Jonathan turned toward the hospital shed, where the light of a single candle showed through the curtainless window.

Sam lay where he had been placed, on a cornhusk mattress on a rough wooden cot. Except for Sam, the shack was empty. Luther and Caesar had both recovered enough to return to the care of their own families in the quarters yesterday.

Jonathan entered and, crossing to the cot, he stood looking down at his servant. Sam's eyes were open a slit, and Jonathan thought there was recognition in them but he couldn't be sure.

"You hurry and get well, you hear? I can't get along without you, you know that."

There was no response. Jonathan began to sweat a little, lightly, in spite of the coolness of the hour. "Now you see here, you know we had to do it! I

126

didn't want it done, and you know that, too! You get well, and I'll take you north and set you free where there ain't any laws against it, but what the hell I'll do without you, don't ask me! You're like my right arm, damn your hide!"

Sam lay without stirring. Defeated, Jonathan's shoulders slumped, and he left the shack. Sam was drugged, that was it. He'd come back later, after he'd made his peace with Martha.

God, he was tired! Tired to the bone. And lonesome. He wanted Martha; he needed her more than he'd ever needed her in his life. He hurried to their room. His hand reached for the doorknob, trembling.

At first he couldn't believe that the door was locked. Then he thought, groggily, that Martha had been so upset when she'd gone to bed that she hadn't noticed what she was doing.

He rapped softly and waited, listening. He heard Martha move in the bed, but no footsteps came toward the door; there was no soft voice telling him to wait.

She'd locked him out. For a few seconds, his impulse was to break down the door. But that would rouse the whole house and the story would be all over the plantation by morning. Damn her, Jonathan thought. When's she going to get it through her head that she doesn't know everything there is to know about running a plantation, about keeping the people in check?

He turned back toward the stairs. He needed something to drink. How could she have done this to him—tonight of all nights? If she was any kind of a wife, instead of a hot-headed, stubborn wildcat from Massachusetts, she would have known how he'd be feeling.

A soft touch on his arm startled him, and for an instant his heart leaped, for he thought that Martha had relented and followed him. Then Rebecca's soft voice, hardly more than a whisper, told him who it was.

"Your things are in the yellow bedroom, Mister Jon. You'll be wanting a drink. I have some brandy here."

Her hand still on his arm, she guided him to the bedroom.

"Just lie back. Here, drink this, and then I'll help you off with your boots."

Good girl, Becky. She had the habit of being around when she was needed, Jon thought fuzzily. And she could be counted on not to spread the story of his being locked out of his room. Cleo wouldn't talk, either. Jon swallowed the brandy and lay back, his head throbbing.

He felt Rebecca remove his boots, one at a time. She leaned over him, her hands at the buttons on his shirt. They were soft and caressing. She put one arm around him, helping to lift him a little so that she could get his shirt off. Her breasts brushed against his bare skin.

"Sam . . ."

"Hush." Her mouth was against his, silencing him. "Don't think about it. I'm here, I'll help you."

Her arms were soft; her mouth was like fire.

"Don't think," she whispered again. "Just let me help you."

There was a fragrance about her, sweet and heady. She lay down beside him, pressing the length of her body against his. She guided his hands to the soft fullness of her breasts and moved a little until she could cradle his head against them. Her hands were busy again, touching, caressing. Jonathan felt his manhood stir and then burgeon, wanting her, needing her, needing the oblivion from pain that she was offering him. Martha had locked him out, but Becky was here,

128

doing the things that a man needed when he was filled with guilt and grief.

His arms went around her, drawing her close, and his hands explored the warmth of her supple body. Her breasts were taut, the nipples standing out. Her waist was small, curving deliciously into her hips and thighs. He drank in the smell and the feel of her.

Her body melted into his as he rolled over on top of her. A muffled cry of pure delight escaped from her lips as the union was made. She curled her legs around him, and rose to meet each thrust, moaning, her arms straining him against her as if she meant to consume him. She was consuming him, enveloping him within the fire and passion that spread and grew until it blotted everything else out, until the images that had tormented him were swept into oblivion. There was nothing but Becky's body under him, eager, giving, demanding, molded to his as if they had been made for each other.

Jonathan's senses reeled as their rhythm quickened, became wild. Each thrust now sent pulsating waves of sensation through him, drowning out past, present, and future. There was nothing but this moment, this delight.

He thrust again, and Becky bit into his chest to muffle her moans as her fingernails raked the length of his back. She began to shudder under him, and the shuddering went on until it reached a volcanic crescendo, carrying him with it. He was floating down, down into the soft warmth of her, into forgetfulness as his body took fire from hers. He scarcely knew that it wasn't Martha under him, giving him the surcease he needed, the comfort he had to have.

Somebody was trying to kill him with blows from a sledgehammer, on his head. He opened his eyes, and the morning light, just seeping into the room, made him flinch. What the devil was going on? This wasn't his bed; Martha wasn't beside him.

He groaned, remembering. The locked door, Rebecca, the brandy. He sat up, and the pain in his head exploded. God! If Marty ever found out she'd never forgive him. And there'd be Jacob to contend with. Jacob hadn't ever permitted him to amuse himself with the slave girls, and he'd make no exception in this case. Jacob's conviction that white blood shouldn't be tainted with black was absolute. Jonathan was in one hell of a mess.

He'd dreamed that he'd heard screaming, and the echos of the dream still reverberated in his skull. It went on and on, high and earsplitting.

It wasn't part of his dream, or part of his hangover; it was real. And now Jacob's voice was added to the din, shouting "Shut that noise, damn you! You hear me, stop it!"

The screaming stopped. There were heavy footsteps on the stairs and then a loud knock on a door at the front part of the house, his own bedroom. "Jon? Jon, wake up! There's something you have to know."

He got out of bed, found the robe that Rebecca had draped over the bedside chair before she had crept away sometime in the night, and managed to thrust his arms through the sleeves. When he rounded the turn in the corridor he could see his room, the door already open and Martha standing there, still in her nightgown, her hair in thick braids over her shoulders.

"No!" The words were torn from her. "Oh, no!"

"What is it?"

Jacob turned, his face, under its years' accumulation of sun and wind, white. "Jon . . ."

"What is it?" Jonathan's voice was harsh, sharp, filled with a premonition that clawed at his vitals.

"It's Sam. Jon, I'm sorry, boy."

"Dead? He died?" Jonathan's voice was loud, denying. Sam couldn't have died! He'd taken a bad whipping, but he was young and strong.

"He hung himself." Jacob's feet were planted wide apart, as if to steady himself, and his words came reluctantly.

"Sometime during the night. Tod found him just now. Sam was hanging from the rafter, with a piece of harness he must have got from the stable." He paused and put his hand on Jonathan's shoulder. "I'm sorry, boy. I know you thought a heap of Sam. Come on downstairs, you need a drink."

Jon looked at him but didn't see him. He saw Sam, swinging, twisting, turning, his head at an impossible angle, his eyes bulging. Slowly, like a sleepwalker, he turned and went back to the room where he had spent the night, and Sam walked with him, two steps behind as was proper.

12

Martha sat on the gallery with Coralie Amhurst and they watched their children, Rory and Prudence and young Burke Amhurst, who was a year younger than Rory, race around the broad expanse of lawn. "That ain't fair, Rory! Prue can't run as fast as we can, we have to give her a head start! You know, a handicap."

"She don't have to play with us. She's only a girl." Rory's voice was impatient.

"She can't help it if she's a girl. Come on, we'll start over. Prue, you stand there by that bush, and the goal's that magnolia tree. Rory and I'll stand back here and when I say go, run like anything!"

"I wish Rory were more like Burke," Martha said to her friend. "Burke seems to have human kindness built right into him."

"He's a good boy." Coralie spoke without pride. Burke could hardly take credit for being a good boy, or she take credit for training him, when he was so much his father's son.

Martha had been visiting the Amhursts for three weeks, come tomorrow. Yolande had suggested this alternative to packing up and going back to Martin's Corners.

"You're so upset over Sam that you can't think

straight, Martha. Not that I blame you. There's no accounting for men, if I do say so myself. I'm not very happy with Jacob at the moment, either." She'd said Jacob, not Mr. Beddoes, so Martha knew how upset she was.

"Go to Coralie Amhurst, dear. Stay there for as long as you like. Evan and Coralie Amhurst can help you sort things out if anyone can. And remember, Jon's going through his own hell, too. Don't do anything irreversible, in the heat of your anger. Leave the door open at least a crack."

And so she had come to the Amhursts and been welcomed without question. The Amhursts had known when to speak and when to remain silent. The fact that they had never had a slave whipped made it easier for Martha to stay with them while she tried to sort out her life.

"I'm going to call the children in." Coralie rose from her wicker chair. "It's getting too hot for them to run like that. We'll have lemonade out here, instead of coffee. Have you come any closer to making up your mind, Martha?"

Martha shook her head. "I love Jon, but I can't live like this, Coralie. If Jacob and Jon were like your Evan, I'd be able to bear it, but they aren't. They just close their eyes to facts and insist that there's no reason to change their way of life. Worse, they insist that their way is the only right way."

"So it is with most planters, unfortunately. Things being as they are, I'm afraid it will be a good many years before they change, and so we must just do the best we can. We—at least, you and I and others like us—can make sure that our own people are not mistreated, and we can make our convictions known to others. We need you, Martha, and that's one reason I hope you will stay in the South, as well as the fact that we love both you and Jon and wish for your happiness."

How good Coralie was! Her face, long and without any hint of beauty, was nevertheless so sweet that the lack of beauty didn't matter. Coralie's convictions shone through her plain features and gave them a beauty of their own.

"It's all so stupid, the whole system!" Martha burst out. "If men could see beyond their own noses they'd realize that in the long run slavery can never be profitable! Jacob's up to his ears in debt right now, and when I point it out to him he just gets angry and tells me it's men's business."

"Jacob isn't the only one. With the exception of my own Evan, all of the planters I know are in debt. It's fortunate that Evan cares so little for luxuries, so that he doesn't overspend. And of course, he's looking toward the future. He's in complete agreement with you, that the slave system must eventually topple."

Martha's face was set. "Coralie, I'm mortally convinced that sooner or later there's going to be a war. But can I convince Jacob or Jonathan? I might as well talk to a stone wall!"

Coralie's face was as grave. "Evan, too, is sure that there will be trouble, but he thinks not yet."

"Jacob is certain that the North will never fight. He says that if the South decides to secede, it will be carried off peacefully, and that then it will be like the millennium, with cotton forever king and the South rolling in riches that the North can no longer bleed from us. I cannot get it into their heads that it will not be that easy. You don't know how I wish that Aunt Emily could talk to them! Some of the most astute men in Boston respect her opinions."

Coralie sighed. "You love Jon. Bad times occur

134

in all marriages, but as long as the love endures, the rifts can be healed. We must endure, and try to understand and forgive, if there is to be any happiness at all."

Coralie stood up, remembering the children, who were still playing their game. Prudence's excited shrieks attested that Burke's insistence that she be given a handicap had paid off. "I won, I won!" Prudence shrilled.

Her screaming broke off as Burke shaded his eyes with his hand. "There's someone coming. See, down the road. I think it's your father."

"It is my father!" In his eagerness to see Jonathan again, Rory pushed Prudence out of his way so roughly that she went sprawling. Prue's voice rose again, in an outraged wail.

That was how Jon found them, when he reined in his horse. Rory, clamoring for his attention, Burke lifting Prue to her feet and dusting off her pinafore, and Martha, her face pale, looking at him with a question in her eyes.

He swung from the saddle and handed the reins to a stableboy who had come at a run to take his horse. "Well, Marty, are you ready to come home?" When she hesitated, he lost his control. "Damn it, I want you home! I need you! I can't go on without you, and that's the whole of it!"

He swept her into his arms, fiercely, and kissed her just as fiercely, oblivious to the interested audience. Martha felt her bones melt in her body, and she strained against him and kissed him back just as fiercely. One word, one touch, and all her resolve was as nothing. Jonathan was her man, and she had to have him.

"Children, come inside." Coralie shooed the children ahead of her into the house in order to afford

135

Martha and Jon privacy for their reunion. She needn't have bothered. Her two friends were oblivious to every presence in the world except each other's.

Martha had thought that Savannah was the most beautiful city in the world, but that was before she saw New Orleans.

She had been surprised when Jon had informed her, peremptorily, that they were going on a second honeymoon. "New Orleans? Jon, you're daft, you're stark out of your mind! We can't afford it. Jacob's already borrowed against this season's crop—you men don't have a lick of sense between you!"

"Hush up. We're going. It's time your narrow New England views were broadened a little, and I'm the man to teach you. There are more things in the world than cotton crops and melting candle stubs to save money, you little New England Puritan!"

How many more things, she could not have dreamed. New Orleans was unbelievable. Jonathan never returned to their hotel room without an armload of flowers purchased from the vending carts. They haunted the French Quarter and spent hours sitting in delicate chairs at sidewalk cafés. They ate fresh hot shrimp; they stuffed themselves with gumbo. They attended an opera, a real opera, something that Martha had always hoped to do. They went to the theater. Aunt Emily did not consider the theater wicked, but Martha wasn't sure about some of the other forms of entertainment that Jonathan insisted she sample.

And they shopped.

"Jonathan, you're mad! What in the world will I do with another gown? You've already bought me three!"

"You must have this one the color of your eyes, and think how your pearls will look with it! You're going to model it for me the minute we get back to our room."

The modeling session proved to be short-lived. The new silk gown lay like a pool of seawater on the floor as Jon introduced her to the delights of making love in the middle of the afternoon, while the cries of the street vendors came through their jalousied windows and the heady scent of massed flowers made her senses reel.

The sunlight filtering through the slats of the jalousies made patterns on their naked bodies as they lay on the huge bed, arms and legs entwined. Where the sunlight fell, their skin took on glowing warmth, adding to the sensual excitement that was already gathering strength as Jon's mouth found hers and forced her lips apart to drink in the sweetness of her kisses.

There was a magic about those afternoon love-makings, a quality that in spite of all the delight that Martha had always taken in Jon's body had eluded her up until now. The sight of his muscular body, as well as the way it felt under her exploring hands, added to her excitement, made her feel limp and helpless with wanting him, with pride that out of all the women in the world, she had been chosen to belong to him and he to her. The exotic setting, the sounds, and the heady aroma of the flowers all added to her pleasure until she felt that she must burst with the joy of it.

"Tell me you love me!" Jon demanded, his mouth against hers.

She told him. She could have sung it, like singing a hymn in church. The notes of the music were in her mind, glorifying their love, sanctifying it. She wished that this moment might never end, that she could be here forever, until the end of time, in Jon's arms, with nothing but their love to fill the universe. How could she have lived for so many years without experiencing this ultimate delight? Or had it been saved for her, like something infinitely precious, the ultimate gift after a lifetime of gifts?

Their lovemaking had always been so good that she'd have sworn that there was no way it could be improved, but those hot, sultry afternoons in New Orleans taught her that up until now they had only skimmed the surface. There was a wildness in their passion, an all-consuming fire that burned her and yet somehow left her whole and restored.

The children were jumping up and down with excitement as their parents arrived with a baggage cart trailing them. All except Crissy, of course. Crissy wasn't even crawling yet, and she slept through the arrival.

After she kissed Prue and Rory, Martha threw off her hat and hurried upstairs. Where in tunket was Cleo? A slight frown marred her smooth forehead. It wasn't like Cleo not to be on hand to greet her. Could she possibly be ill? Mother Yolande would have told her, surely!

Cleo was not in the nursery, nor was she in Martha's room. Martha gathered up her skirts and ran back down the stairs to burst in on Yolande, who was calming herself, after all the excitement, with a cup of tea in the sitting room.

"Mother Yolande, where is Cleo?"

Yolande put down her cup, carefully, and Martha knew by her expression that something was wrong, something she wasn't going to like.

"Cleo isn't here, dear. The Renaults needed a girl to help with their children—they've got way beyond their Beulah, Gaylord especially. And as surprising

138

as it is, one of their men has had his eye on Cleo for some time, and he asked John Renault to buy her. I know you'll miss her, dear, but it was such a wonderful opportunity for her! No one ever dreamed that anyone would want to marry her. We felt we had to let her go. She's a good girl, and she deserves a husband and children of her own."

"I don't believe it!" Martha ran her hand through her hair, disheveled from all the hugging and kissing of the arrival. "I don't mean I don't believe you, Mother Yolande. I mean it's so hard to believe that Cleo would leave me and the children!" A quick suspicion crossed her face, and her voice turned hard. "You didn't go selling her to finance our trip, did you?"

Yolande looked hurt. "My dear! Of course we did not! Cleo wanted to go. She'll miss you dreadfully, of course, but it isn't as if you'll never see her again. We visit the Renaults occasionally, and she'll be right there."

Martha returned to her bedroom much more slowly than she had come down. Cleo, to be married? She felt bereft, betrayed, and she chided herself for it. She loved Cleo and she wanted her happiness above all things. But for her to leave while Martha was away . . . !

Now don't be selfish, Martha told herself. Cleo knew we'd still be seeing each other. Likely she thought she'd better go right away before that man that wanted her changed his mind. She wouldn't be likely to get another opportunity.

Who was taking care of Rory and Prudence and Crissy now, she wondered? But she could trust Yolande to have chosen someone reliable, someone they would like. It had been hard enough to replace Dulcy, whom they had adored as much as they'd adored Sam, and Martha was uneasy about letting anyone but Cleo look after the baby.

And what about herself? She'd have to choose another maid. The thought made her smile. What a Southern lady she was turning into, after all! But with all those new clothes, she'd need a maid to look after them. All the same, she wanted Cleo. Another girl would never be quite the same.

Jonathan was out in the office with Jacob, giving him an accounting of their trip, and likely they'd be at it for an hour or more. Martha washed herself thoroughly, sponge-bath style, because she felt so grubby from the trip and didn't want to wait for any of the house servants to carry up buckets of hot water for a proper bath.

Standing on a towel, she dried herself, and then moved to the bureau to find clean underthings. She put them on and reached for a petticoat, and then another, but hesitated before donning a third, propriety or not. It was so hot! It had been hotter in New Orleans, and she wanted to feel cool for a change. She'd wear the pink dimity; it was light and cool even if it was more than three years old and Jonathan might frown on it.

Cleo would be all right. Miss Bella would treat her well. She'd even move up in the slave hierarchy, because the Renaults were a great deal wealthier than the Beddoes family, their house much larger and more impressive. She shook out the third petticoat, feeling virtuous.

Something fell out of the petticoat's folds, and she stopped humming as she bent to retrieve it. It was a piece of paper, folded into a very small square. Frowning, she unfolded it and spread it out.

It was a note, in Cleo's handwriting.

"Dear Miss Martha:"

Martha smiled. How well Cleo could write now. And she hadn't left without a word, after all. Wouldn't the Renaults have a conniption fit if they knew that their new nursemaid could read and write?

"*Dear Miss Martha:*" she read again. "*They're selling me away. Rebecca is with Master Jonathan's baby.*"

The words blurred in front of her, and the room seemed to turn a bright red.

13

"All right! It's true, I've admitted it!" Jonathan's face was as white as Martha's. They'd been quarreling for nearly an hour, behind the locked door of their bedroom. "I've admitted I took Rebecca to bed, I've admitted that Cleo was sold to keep you from finding out about the baby! What more do you want?"

"It happened more than once. You took her to bed more than once!"

"Yes, I took her to bed more than once! Good Lord, you wouldn't let me near you for weeks after Sam hung himself! And then you went off to the Amhursts, and we had one hell of a time persuading you to only go there instead of back to Massachusetts! I was suffering, too, remember? *Sam was my friend*! I had to have somebody, something, or I'd have gone crazy."

"How could you! If you couldn't think of me, you might at least have thought of your children!"

"It was more your fault than mine." Jonathan's face was set as he hurled the accusation at her. "Yes, your fault that Sam died, too! If you hadn't locked your door against me, I'd have come to you that night. I needed you, Marty, God knows how I needed you! I was torn apart and you knew it, and yet you locked me out! And when Rebecca brought me brandy, I drank it. And when she came into the bed you'd banished me to, I let her! If I'd been with you, I wouldn't have drunk any more, I'd have got up and gone back out to see Sam again, and maybe he wouldn't have killed himself!"

"So now you blame me for that, too! In your mind, it's all my fault! A Southern gentleman is never wrong! The system that lets such things happen can never be wrong! But I can't live like this, Jon, and I won't! I'm going home, back to Mother and Aunt Emily. I'm going home where I belong!"

"Like hell you are! You think I'm the only man who ever fathered a child on a good-looking slave wench? Do you think the other men's wives don't put up with it, accept it, and pretend they know nothing about it? They do, because that's the way it is. It ain't as if it's a habit of mine. It never happened before, and it would never happen again. I'm sorry it happened this time, but that doesn't give you any license to leave me."

Martha was quiet now, and that frightened Jonathan. He'd rather she'd go on ranting and raving than have that set, rockbound New England expression on her face.

"It isn't because of Rebecca I'm leaving you. At least, not entirely. It's because I cannot and I will not go on living in a society where things like this can happen, where a fine man feels he has to end his life because the friend he trusted betrayed him, where men can thwart all the rules of decency in the name of The System! I will not have my children raised by such false standards. Sam, and Dulcy, and Cleo, and now Rebecca. I want my children to have a moral upbringing, to have real values, and I'm going to see

143

that they get it! I can't breathe here, Jon. I can't breathe any more where there's such moral decay!"

"I'll send Rebecca away. You'll never have to see her, or the baby. The children will never know."

"Another wrong, to make a right by your twisted Southern standards! Certainly, sell her off, sell your own unborn child! We'll never think alike, Jon. We could live together and love each other for a lifetime and never think alike. That's why I have to go."

"You love me! You just said it!"

"I love you, and it doesn't change a thing. I have to live with myself, too. And our children will have to live with themselves. And we can't do it here, nobody can do it here unless they grow as twisted as you Southerners. Yes, I love you. I'll go on loving you because I can't help it. But we're an alien people to each other, Jon."

"We're all Americans! You're talking crazy!"

"Alien races," Martha repeated. "Aunt Emily tried to warn me, and I wouldn't listen, but she was right."

"Well, you ain't going! If you think you're leaving me and taking the children with you, you're almighty mistaken!"

"What do you intend to do, lock me in my room again? But you can't keep me locked up forever. It'd be a scandal, and you don't like scandal, do you? Oh, yes, I'm going! And if you try to stop me I'll divorce you, I'll stand up in court and tell the world why, and you'll find out what scandal means."

"What I've done isn't cause for divorce, not even up north! A man's allowed to have affairs as long as he supports his wife and children."

"So he is. But I can file for divorce and spread your infamy from one end of the county to the other. I can claim that our children's souls are in mortal danger because of your immorality. There'll be sermons preached on it! Oh, not in your fine churches that cater to aristocrats only, but there are other churches, and preachers who'll jump at the chance to tell their congregations how a fine man died because of your inhumanity to him while you were wallowing in bed with a slave girl!"

She'd do it, too. Jonathan knew she would. But still he would not back down. "If you leave me, I'll bring you back."

"And beat me, in the bargain. That's your right! I'm fully cognizant of the law."

"Damn it, who said anything about beating you?"

"As your wife, I am your property. Sam was your property, and you had him beaten."

Jon raised his hand and Martha thought that he was going to strike her, but she neither flinched or tried to avoid the blow. "Go ahead. You might as well get in some practice, because if you force me to stay, you're going to have to do a lot of beating, I promise you! I won't stay quietly, Jon. I'll raise all the hell it's possible for one woman to raise."

Cursing, Jon dropped his hand and slammed out of the room, his boots beating a furious tattoo on the stairs as he descended them.

14

"Is that the *house*?" Rory's voice was incredulous. Why, it was little, it was hardly bigger than a peckerwood's cabin, even if it was white clapboard, instead of logs. "I thought Miss Emily was a lady, Mama!"

"Miss Emily is a very great lady." Martha's voice was sharp. "And this is the kind of house that ladies and gentlemen live in, in Massachusetts, unless they're rich and live in a big city like Boston. Money has nothing to do with being a lady or a gentleman, or the size of the houses they live in."

The front door had opened, and the slight, straight figure of Emily Curtis hurried down the path, hands outstretched. Her hair had a few more streaks of gray in it, but other than that, she hadn't changed a mite. And right behind her, crying with joy, was Nancy, lifting her skirts to run, calling out Martha's name.

Aunt Emily offered her cheek to be kissed, as calmly as though she had seen Martha only yesterday, but the shining of her eyes betrayed her feelings. "So these are the children."

She smiled as she looked at Prudence, but the smile faded a little as she studied Rory with a longer look. Rory was studying her just as carefully, and he didn't

146

smile at all. *"That one,"* Emily said to herself, *"will bear watching. It sticks out all over him."*

Martha, seeing her aunt's look, put her hand on Rory's shoulder and smiled. "This is Rory. Sometimes he's a bit of a handful, Aunt Emily, but he's bound to learn."

"And this is the baby." Emily's eyes crinkled. "She inherited Nancy's coloring, I see; she's as pretty as a picture!"

Prue, who had been standing quietly, now slipped her hand into Aunt Emily's. "I'm not as pretty as Crissy, but I'm good."

Miss Emily's mouth quirked at the corners. "Pretty is as pretty does. Being good is of more value and apt to last longer." She turned to Jacob, who was standing beside the hired carriage with Cleo, who held Crissy in her arms. Jacob was distinctly uncomfortable at dumping this passel of children, as well as his daughter-in-law, on the frail-looking woman who stood before him.

Emily held out her hand. "How do you do? Supper is almost ready. We were expecting you, of course, Mr. Beddoes. This is Mrs. Curtis, Martha's mother."

The older children were already being smothered in Nancy's arms, as she covered them with kisses and tears. "Oh, Prue is a love, she's simply a love! And Rory's so handsome, my, he's the handsomest boy I ever saw in my life! Martha, you look radiant. I can hardly wait for Sarah and Hester to see all of you! We've been invited to visit them, of course."

"But not tonight, thank the Lord!" Miss Emily laughed. "Come in. Nancy, unhand that boy and look at the beans—we don't want them burned. I have biscuits all ready to go in the oven. Mr. Beddoes, I am very sorry that our house is not large enough to offer you accommodation. There are only two bedrooms, and

I don't believe I'd care to suggest that you sleep in the barn, as I did Jonathan. I took the liberty of engaging a room for you at the inn. There was no inn when Jonathan was here, but Martin's Corners has progressed, and we have quite an acceptable one now. You'll take supper here, of course."

"If there wasn't an inn, I'd be perfectly happy in the barn." In spite of himself, Jacob was taken with the woman. He knew good stock when he saw it. "I'll just go along and have the horse and rig taken care of and come back as soon as I've made myself presentable."

Cleo had held back, filled with confusion at meeting Northerners, but now Emily walked toward her and took her hand. "You're Cleo. I'm happy to welcome you. Martha wrote of you often."

In all her life, Cleo had never had a white person hold out a hand to her in greeting, but something stirred in her and she returned the pressure of Emily's hand. All Cleo's terrors at making this move into a strange country were laid at rest. She was happier even than she had been when Master Jacob had brought her back from the Renaults' and told her she was to go north with Miss Martha.

The moment was disrupted by Rory's voice, filled with outrage. "Cleo's a slave, Aunt Emily! You don't shake hands with slaves! You just tell them what to do, and they do it."

Emily looked at him, her eyes steel-gray. "Cleo will be a guest in my home, albeit a working guest. We all work here. Come along, Cleo. I've fixed up a comfortable enough room for you in the summer kitchen. Martha will share Nancy's room with the baby, and Prudence will share mine. We've had a cot put in the box room, in the attic, for Rory, and a chest of drawers and a chair, and made it into a respectable bedroom. It's small, but there's a window."

"Who's going to be my boy?" Rory demanded. "They wouldn't let me bring Jimmy with me."

"You'll be your own boy. Boys don't have boys, here in Massachusetts. You'll soon get used to it. As I remember, young men of your age do not like being different."

Prudence had transferred her hand to Nancy's. "May I help you in the kitchen? I never got to help in a kitchen before. Juliette would never let me."

Nancy's face crumpled. "Oh, my darling! Of course you may. You shall help me to set the table, and to pour out the milk, and to put the napkins around."

Her face shining, Prudence skipped along beside her "new" grandmother. Something told her that she was going to be very happy here. If she could help in the kitchen, she wouldn't even miss the dollhouse that her papa had brought her from New Orleans. She wished that Papa had come with them, but if he couldn't be here, then working in the kitchen would make the time go faster until they would all be together again.

It took Jacob only a short time to have the horse and rig taken care of and wash the dust of the journey from his face and hands. When he returned, Miss Emily took him into her sitting room while Martha and the others were busy settling their belongings in their new quarters.

Seated on Emily's stiff, unyielding horsehair sofa, Jacob took measure of this woman who had played such an important part in the lives of his family even though he had never met her until today. At first impression, the diminutive woman seemed as unyielding as the horsehair surface on which he sat, but a closer scrutiny convinced him that, while she was

149

surely strong and dependable and enduring, she knew the meaning of give and take.

Now that he had finally met her, Jacob felt a sense of personal loss to think that he had resisted making her acquaintance before. Every year, on his trips to Boston, he had pleaded pressure of business to excuse him from making the short side trip to Martin's Corners. For no other reason, he admitted to himself now, than that he had had no wish to meet a woman as strong-minded as Emily Curtis, the woman who had instilled all those nonsensical ideas into Marty's head. Without ever having seen her, he had put her down as his enemy. Bertram Foster had urged the meeting; he had told Jacob that it would be well worth his while. But Jacob had been determined not to waste any of his all too precious freedom on a woman who could do nothing but make him angry—and who, because she was a woman, his Southern chivalry would have prohibited his shouting down!

Just as he had surmised, Emily Curtis, now that they were face to face, was direct and to the point.

"How bad is it between Martha and Jonathan?"

Jacob met her honesty with his own. "It's bad. I'm not sure it can be patched up, although Yolande thinks that a separation might do the trick."

"Absence makes the heart grow fonder? Well, maybe, although I've never subscribed to such story-book beliefs. I'm glad to have my niece and the children here for a visit, and they'll be welcome for however long they wish to stay. But I am convinced that Martha loves Jonathan, in spite of their differences, and that she will never be happy apart from him. The Curtises have always been one-man women, Mr. Beddoes. In any case, you can be sure of one thing. I will not say, or indicate, anything that would keep this breach between our young people alive. I'll listen,

150

but Martha must make up her own mind. For both their sakes, and for the sake of the children, I hope that they will be reconciled."

Jacob's smile was spontaneous. There was one thing that he and this woman agreed on, at any rate! He already felt better about leaving Martha and the children here. Miss Emily Curtis was not a meddler in other people's affairs. She might not approve of the South or of any of its customs, but as long as Martha was married to Jon, she wouldn't say one word against him.

For the next hour, Jacob found himself both amazed and flabbergasted as Emily questioned him about affairs in the South. No wonder Martha had had such a grasp of the situation, a grasp that had outraged him when she had presumed to argue with him! Emily Curtis was a woman to be reckoned with. All the same, though he was forced to respect her for her thorough grounding in matters that rightly belonged to men, he was glad that he wasn't married to her. And glad that there was no woman in the South, at least none that he had ever met, who knew so much and who would dare to hold her own with the menfolk!

As the supper hour approached, Emily rose and held out her hand, and Jacob found her clasp firm and steady.

"We will hope for the best," she told him. "Under the circumstances, it is all we can do." Her voice was dry as she added, "Although a little prayer might not hurt, both for Martha and Jonathan and for the North and the South."

Jacob left for Boston, and then home, the next morning, stopping in only long enough to say a brief goodbye. Prudence was in the kitchen with Nancy; Emily was playing a game of checkers with Rory and to Rory's intense annoyance beating him without effort.

"Didn't I hear a carriage just now?" Rory asked.

"Yes, your grandfather is leaving."

The checkerboard was swept to the floor as Rory jumped to his feet and checkers flew in every direction.

"He's gone! And you didn't even tell me! You had no right! I didn't want him to go, I wanted to go back with him!"

Which was exactly, Martha thought, why Aunt Emily had kept him busy. They'd both known that Rory would make a scene about wanting to return home.

Nancy came hurrying in, her face filled with consternation. "Rory, darling, don't you like it here?"

"No, I don't! I think it's horrid. My room is ugly and little, and I don't even have a horse to ride, and I want Jimmy!"

"Well, never mind, darling. You'll have a good time in Boston. We'll be going there soon, to visit friends, and you'll like it there. They're quite wealthy, and they live in a fine house." Nancy's face lighted up. "I can hardly wait for Sarah and Hester to see Martha in her beautiful gowns, and wearing her pearl necklace!"

"She can't wear her pearl necklace. She didn't bring it with her." Rory's face was still sulky. "She and Papa had an awful fight about it. Mama said she hated it, that every pearl was bought with the tears of a human being held in bondage. That's silly. What does a nigger have to complain about, anyway? They're taken care of and they never have anything to worry about. Mama's crazy, that's what she is. She has to be crazy, or she wouldn't have brought us here!"

"Rory, the woodbox is almost empty. Go and fetch in an armload." Miss Emily had had quite enough of

Rory's temper, and she knew, from experience, that the best way to keep a boy happy was to keep him busy.

"That's nigger's work! Send Cleo!"

"Rory, I do not make it a habit to speak twice. And one more thing. You are never again to refer to a person of color, even a slave, as a nigger. Now march!"

For a brief moment, Rory stood up to Miss Emily and returned stare for stare, while Nancy fluttered her hands helplessly. Then, his head high, his face flaming with fury, Rory marched out. Watching him, Miss Emily shook her head. She knew that the clash of wills was by no means over. Rory was going to be a handful.

15

David Lawrence read the handwritten article brought him by Miss Emily Curtis, standing up, his composing stick in one hand. The editor of the Martin's Corners *Clarion* was a tall man in his late thirties, with brown hair that was usually rumpled and a trifle inky because of his habit of running his hands through it. His intense blue eyes needed glasses if he was to see across the room, but he seldom remembered to wear them.

The editor's expression changed from mild interest to intense surprise. When he came to the end of the article, he started again at the top and read it through a second time.

"If this doesn't knock them right off their horse-hair sofas, nothing will! Miss Emily, you're a genius. I'm going to run it in this week's edition."

"Not I, David. My niece Martha Curtis Beddoes wrote it, at my urging. I thought the people of Martin's Corners, at least, should become acquainted with the real facts of plantation life and the institution of slavery."

"Then your niece is a genius! You know what this piece makes me feel like doing? It makes me feel like going south myself and bringing the slaves out! This story about the slave Sam, and his Dulcy . . . Miss Emily, I just don't know what to say!"

"What you can say is that you will give Martha employment in your newspaper office. We could not only use the extra money, although her father-in-law sends enough to cover her expenses and those of her children while they visit me, but Martha finds time heavy on her hands and needs to be kept occupied. She has a talent to offer; you have the means of using that talent."

David Lawrence's face filled with consternation. "A newspaper woman, in Martin's Corners?"

"And why not? She writes as well as or better than any man, and your mother is always here, handling the social news and such trivia, so the proprieties will be observed. Well, David?"

David was reading the article for the third time. "Miss Emily, if this article brings in the response that I think it will, your niece has a job."

The printing office was a revelation to Martha. Her interest in every phase of the work was avid. She spent time examining the Washington hand press on which the *Clarion* was printed, marveling at the ingeniousness of bringing the square metal platen, by means of a lever, down on the type-bed to make the printed impression. Her fingers itched to get into the typecases, with the brevier-size type, and learn to set it herself in the stick, letter by letter to make words, word by word to bring information to people who would actually read it.

The newsprint itself caught her interest. The paper had to be cut to the correct size, twenty by twenty-four inches, and two weeks before it was used it had to be dampened so that it would handle more easily and take a better impression. This was accomplished by wetting sheets of burlap a little larger than the sheets of paper, inserting a piece of burlap about every twenty-five sheets of paper, and weighting the whole stack down with boards so that the moisture would penetrate evenly.

To David's consternation and his mother's cry of anguish, Martha insisted on trying her hand at cutting the paper with a plow, an ingenious contrivance that consisted of a knife-like blade hung between rollers, which looked something like a fat rolling pin with its handles in the middle. The plow was rolled back and forth over the stack of paper, in a trough, to cut it, and it required considerably more skill than was apparent to the uninitiated.

Martha also tried her hand at preparing the ink to be applied to the type, her dress covered by a long, black apron as she wielded the inkballs. The ink was very thick, and placed in small balls covered with leather and mounted on the ends of sticks. When the balls were well covered with ink, they were then used to pound the type, already locked up in the chase, until the letters were neatly coated.

"Miss Martha, you'll go home looking like one of your own black slaves!" David's mother protested. Short and plump, with a kindly face and spectacles perched on her short nose, Mrs. Lawrence was habitually as fluttery as a mother hen. "Whatever will Miss Emily think if I let you do such dirty work?"

"Miss Emily wouldn't care, as long as I'm doing useful work, and learning."

"I didn't employ you to work in the pressroom." David smiled, in spite of his stern tone. "I employed you to wield a pen! It's too late for this week, but in between copying out any items our townfolk bring in, I would like you to write another article about life in the South."

The first article had been printed a week ago, and by closing time of press day Martha had been a celebrity. Mrs. Blaisdel, whose husband owned the mercantile store, had come in to congratulate her and had become so emotional that she had had to be assisted home by her husband.

Mr. Hamilton, a beefy man with a florid face, who owned the feed and grain store, had pumped Martha's hand until she'd been afraid it would fall off. And on Monday morning, the first person to enter the outer office had been the Reverend Smith, of the Congregational Church, to inform her that the ladies of his congregation had requested that she speak at a specially called meeting at the Church Hall.

"I've never spoken in public in my life!" Martha had protested.

"But the ladies would be most gratified. Miss Emily is, of course, invited, as is your dear mother."

When he had left, closing the door softly behind him, Martha had burst into laughter. "They must really want me, to invite Aunt Emily! She was all but drummed out of the church by these same women, years ago, for what they termed her revolutionary and unladylike ideas!" Martha controlled her laughter to take a sheet of paper that Mrs. Lawrence handed her, an article on the birth, to the Tait family, of seven female kittens. "Miss Hattie, I really don't believe we should print this item at all. It might cause some people to tease poor Sam about the preponderance of females in his family."

Even though she was about to become a public speaker, Martha could not neglect her duties, and David had already taught her that the foremost rule in printing local items, other than spelling the names right, was never to cause anyone embarrassment.

Jacob studied the newssheet that John Renault had brought back with him from his recent trip north. Disquieting rumors of the antislavery pieces in the Northern papers, in the vicinity of Boston, had already reached him, but this was absolute proof. Not only was the scurrilous article right here in black and white, it even bore Martha's name.

"The South has two classes of slaves, the black workers, and the womenfolk of the aristocratic planters. Although the second class is technically free, they are no less slaves than the toilers in the fields. Every moment of their lives is restricted. They have no freedom of movement, of speech, even of opinion. They must never venture beyond the immediate environs of their homes without being accompanied by an adult male of their family, or by a trusted guard. Indeed, the white, adult male is almost as restricted, as they live in constant fear of uprisings.

"The so-called cherishing of the Southern Lady as a creature of delicacy, who has to be protected from all danger and unpleasantness, is no more than a myth. These delicate creatures are up at sunrise every morning, to supervise their household slaves. Every item used for housekeeping has to be kept under lock and key, and doled out as it is needed. Even the best trained of the slaves come to their mistresses to be directed as to their every duty. The mistress rarely can go to her rest until ten or eleven at night, only to have to rise the next morning at sunrise and begin her tedious routine over.

"This delicate creature, the Plantation Mistress, is expected to nurse the sick slaves, no matter the nastiness of their wounds or the virulence of their maladies. While their stronger menfolk, who so protect them, give wide berth to the hospital sheds, their delicate

wives are exposed to whatever illness lies within, to
whatever vile retchings and fetid odors prevail. . . ."

With an exclamation of rage, his face choleric, Jacob threw down the newssheet and rose to his feet, his forefinger outstretched toward Jonathan.

"Your wife!" Jacob bellowed. "Martha Curtis Beddoes! We're disgraced, boy! How're we ever going to be able to hold up our heads again, in front of our friends and neighbors? The whole county's buzzing with it by now, you can depend on that! She's made us a laughingstock, and worse. She's made us relatives of a criminal, because that's what she is, a criminal, spreading lies, rabble-rousing, working against her own kith and kin! Any white man here in the South talked like that, he'd find a rope around his neck, and no questions asked. Well, what are you going to do about it? She's your wife, dammit, it's up to you to put a stop to it!"

"If you'll recall, it was as much your idea as mine to let her go." Jonathan sounded bitter. "Let her go, you said, give her time to simmer down, she'll come back, wagging her tail behind her and ready to behave herself."

"How was I to know she was crazy? Who would have thought she'd write pieces like this and get them published? Good Lord, Jon, I wouldn't be surprised if a delegation of planters called on us and demanded an explanation."

"They know us better than that. They know that this is no doing of ours. The worst they'll say is that I was a fool to bring home a Northern wife."

"And they'll be right, won't they? Not only a Northern girl, but a damned bluestocking, at that! You're likely to have to call somebody out over this, Jon. To say nothing of some hothead burning our

159

barns to teach us a lesson. Go get her, damn it! Pack your saddlebags and get moving!"

It had been midsummer when Martha arrived in Martin's Corners, just going on to fall. Now summer was approaching again. The maple trees were in full bud, and the grass in the meadows was showing green patches as the last snow of the winter melted off, leaving everything soggy underfoot. It didn't seem possible to Jonathan that Martha had been gone for that long, but, certainly, she had been north long enough to cause all sorts of mischief.

Not only was Martha's work published in the Martin's Corners *Clarion*, but other newspapers had picked it up, even a large one in Boston. She was rapidly becoming notorious as her scathing denunciations of the slavery system issued forth in printer's ink.

Jonathan was grim as he alighted from the stage in the courtyard of the inn, the only passenger to disembark on that blustery March day. Carrying his own carpetbag, he set off on foot for Miss Emily's house. He had not let Martha know that he was coming. He hadn't wanted to give her time to marshal her defenses against him.

A boy rounded the corner of the house from the direction of the barn. His face and hands were weathered and chapped, and there was a wisp of straw in his hair. Jonathan stopped, uncertain, and swallowed against the sudden lump in his throat. It was Rory, although at first glance he hadn't been sure.

Rory also stopped, frozen in his tracks, his face a mask of astonishment. Then he hurtled forward and nearly knocked Jonathan off his feet as he threw himself at his father.

"Easy, Rory! Hold up! You want us both wallowing in the mud?"

"Papa! I don't believe it! Have you come to take us home? I hate it here, you don't know how awful it is! When can we go, can we start tonight?"

He broke from his father and raced toward the house, shouting at the top of his lungs. "Prue, Grandma! We're going home! Papa's here and we're going home!"

Miss Emily appeared in the doorway, calm, as always. "Well, Jonathan? I've been expecting you. Martha is still at the newspaper office, but she'll be home directly. Rory, stop that shouting. I'm well aware that your father is here. You go and clean up, you're a sight."

"No wonder I'm a sight! You make me work like a nigger!" Rory's outrage blazed in his eyes as he recounted his grievances to his father. "I have to milk the cow, Papa, and chop kindling and bring in wood and clean out the barn, and now she's got me cleaning out the root cellar!"

"Root cellars have to be cleaned out to make ready for the new crop. Cleaning out the old straw is honest work; I've done it all my life, and so has your mother."

"It ain't for a gentleman!"

"Rory, that's enough whining. Jonathan, here comes Prue."

Once again Jonathan felt the hard lump in his throat. Prudence, too, had grown, and she looked more like Martha than ever. Pretty, why, she'd be the prettiest little girl in Georgia, once he got her back where she belonged. But unlike Rory, Prudence's face was grave and unsmiling, and her greeting to her father was restrained.

"How do you do, Papa? I'm glad to see you." There was a wariness in her eyes, a reluctance to

161

accept him. Damn them, they'd turned her against him!

Crissy, too. There she was, tagging after her older sister, but she stopped short of Jonathan and hid behind Miss Emily's skirt, looking at him with wondering eyes. She didn't even know him! Martha had a lot to answer for, and by God, she was going to!

"Aunt Emily, is Uncle David coming to supper? I need to know how many places to lay." Prue's voice was soft and pleasant to the ear.

"Uncle David?" Jonathan's heavy brows shot up in a question.

"Oh, yes. Mr. Lawrence, you know. He comes quite often. He isn't really our uncle, but Crissy and I call him that." Her omission of Rory's name was obvious.

"Lawrence. He's that editor who's egging Martha on, isn't he?"

"Hardly egging her on. They're doing valuable work." Miss Emily's voice was steady.

"And what does Mrs. Lawrence think of their association?" Jonathan spoke evenly, holding back his sudden suspicion.

"Oh, David's mother approves of everything David does!" Nancy, who had come in just in time to hear Jonathan's question, answered him as she went over to give him a welcoming kiss.

"I hate him!" Rory, who had disregarded Miss Emily's orders to go and clean up, took Jonathan's hand. "He's always hanging around here, making eyes at Mama. If it wasn't for him I'll bet we'd have gone home a long time ago!"

"Jonathan, where are you going?" Miss Emily asked sharply.

"Where do you think? I'm going to have a look at David Lawrence!" Jonathan tossed his carpetbag to Rory. His face set in angry lines, he strode off

162

through the puddles in the road toward the *Clarion* office.

In all these months, Martha hadn't written to him, not even once. Miss Emily had written, to report on the health of the children and to say that Martha was also well. But there had been no mention of David Lawrence. As he walked, Jonathan's rage grew and expanded until he felt that he would burst with it.

At the *Clarion*, David called from the pressroom, "Martha, will you come here for a moment?"

Martha laid down her pen and went into the pressroom where David, composing stick in hand, stood in front of the typecases. At the hand press, Jeb Addison was making some minor adjustment, muttering to himself. Two months ago, the sixty-year-old journeyman printer had arrived in Martin's Corners, suffering from a bad case of the shakes brought on by over-indulgence in his favorite beverage.

When he had sobered up, Jeb had applied to David for a job. And David, well aware that dozens of such journeyman printers suffered from the same malady, had followed the general rule among printers that such men were to be given at least a day's work.

To his surprise and Martha's astonishment, Jeb had proved to be a capable man. As long as he was sober, there was nothing he could not do around the shop. And David had kept him on, with the provision that he report to work reasonably sober.

"What is it, David?" Martha stopped beside him.

"Look here." David nodded at the sheet of copy he was working from.

"*Last Wednesday, Martin Smith celebrated the birth of his third son, and received the congratulations of all the patrons at the local inn, with the exception of Sam Tait. Mr. Tait became abusive and threw his ale in Mr. Smith's face and had to be subdued by the land-*

163

lord and some of the patrons, and he was locked up overnight until he became sufficiently sober to be allowed to return home."

"Oh, my lands!" Martha said.

"My mother has been at it again. Only, how did it get by you, Martha? I had it half set up before I realized what I was setting!" David began to laugh. "And how in the world did Mother come by the information?"

Jeb grunted, and Martha and David looked at each other. The only gentleman who could have been at the inn that night and seen the ruckus and related it to David's mother was Jeb.

They were laughing, looking into each other's faces, Martha's hand on David's arm, when Jonathan appeared in the pressroom doorway. What he saw made his rage explode into a red haze.

"Lawrence!" Jonathan shouted.

They both turned, startled. Martha opened her mouth to speak Jonathan's name, and David groped in his pocket for his glasses.

Martha screamed as she saw the gun appear in Jonathan's hand. "Oh, Jon, no! Oh, my God—"

The shot caught David in the shoulder, and he staggered from the force of it, a look of utter amazement on his face. When he fell, the glasses he had extracted from his pocket shattered on the floor.

Jonathan stood there, bewildered. "I thought he was reaching for a gun! I thought he was going to shoot me! What else was I to think, when his hand went to his pocket like that?"

Martha's face, when she raised it from where she knelt beside David, his blood seeping into her skirts, was as white as David's own.

"Get help! Go next door to the feed store, and have Mr. Hamilton send for the doctor!" Her voice

shook, but her hands were steady as she tried to un-
button David's shirt and ended by ripping off the
buttons so that she could lay the wound bare. Martha
folded a clean towel and pressed it against the oozing
hole.

"Harder!" Jeb grunted. "Here, let me do it. No,
my hands are dirty. Lay down harder, girl, you want
him to bleed to death? That man'll hang for this!
We're witnesses, and he'll hang!"

16

Jonathan and Martha faced each other, and Jon knew, even before she spoke, that she had made her decision.

Even if David Lawrence had decided to press charges, which, because of Martha he had not, Jonathan could not have been plunged further into the depth of despair. Right at the moment, he was unable even to recognize how lucky he was that his aim had been bad and that Lawrence hadn't died. He felt that he had made a reasonable mistake. After all, he had suspected that Lawrence, who was taking his wife away from him, had had a gun. Under the circumstances, any man might have done as he had done, believing that he was defending himself.

He knew that by due legal process and with the help of a good lawyer he could eventually force Martha to return home. But if he took such measures, he would have no wife at all. The Martha he had married and this solemn woman in front of him were two different people. If they had grown to hate each other, it would have been easier. The fact that they still loved each other made it a tragedy.

"I realize that your shooting David was a mistake, Jon. But that is just the point. I will not return, nor allow my children to be returned, to a place where every gentleman believes he has the right to shoot another man, where every gentleman goes armed as a matter of course, whether to defend his so-called honor or to defend his own life because of the customs of that area."

"Marty, you're talking as if Georgia is on another continent!" Jonathan exploded.

"It might as well be. Who but a Southern gentleman would have armed himself to talk to the editor of a country newspaper?"

"I'd been traveling! Any man would be a damned fool not to carry a weapon when he's traveling!"

"That may be true, but you were not traveling when you went to see David. And you were not back in Georgia, where you go armed whenever you supervise the fields or go on patrol, as a matter of habit."

Martha's face crumpled, her first show of emotion. "Jon, I'd made up my mind to go back to you before you ever came to get me! I was going to leave everything I know is right and just and try to be a good wife to you. Living without you all these months showed me that I'm only half alive without you. Why did you have to do it, Jon? Why have you smashed our last hope of happiness?"

Her voice rose, and she clasped her hands together and fought to control herself. "I love you. I'm afraid I'll always love you. But I cannot, and I will not, go back to you."

"I take it you want a divorce? No doubt you're ready to accept David Lawrence as your comforter, to help you forget your undying love for me!"

Martha's head came up. "No. Not now. Not ever! Yes, David loves me, if that's what you want to know. And I love him, in a way completely different from the way I love you. We could have a happy and peaceful life together, except for one thing. I'd be cheating him, and he'd know it. No, Jon, no divorce, unless you yourself institute it and divorce me."

"You're talking crazy. You love me, but you won't live with me! You were going to come back to me, but now you won't, because of something that was a pure accident!"

There was complete honesty in Martha's face as she answered him. "I admit that one of the reasons I was going to go back to you was because of David, because I was afraid of hurting him if I stayed on. And I admit that I took a great deal of pleasure in writing those articles. I caused you and others like you a good deal of embarrassment, and that is exactly what I set out to do. If having the truth published is embarrassing, then you deserve it, and more besides! But I thought that I had done all I could to broadcast that truth and that I could return to Georgia with a clear conscience. But now it is too late. I will not sacrifice my children on your altar or permit them to grow up worshipping your false idols, not even for my love for you!"

Jonathan left the house, carrying his carpetbag. He would rent a horse at the inn, as the stage was not due for another two days. It had been made clear to him, by the town marshal and Mr. Blaisdel and Mr. Hamilton and the doctor, that his presence was far from welcome and that he would be wise to put as much distance as possible between himself and Martin's Corners as soon as possible. If one accident could happen, so could another. David Lawrence was well liked in Martin's Corners, and the town did not appreciate a stranger—and a Southerner at that— shooting him.

Jonathan felt as though he were walking into a void,

that there was nothing ahead for him but emptiness.

"Papa! Papa, wait for me!"

He stopped, looked back, and saw Rory struggling with Martha. Rory was fighting like a wildcat. "Let me go, Mama! I'm going with Papa and you aren't going to stop me! If you stop me now, I'll run away the first chance I get! I'll get home somehow, even if I have to walk all the way!"

"Rory . . ." Jonathan's voice was ragged.

Miss Emily appeared behind Martha in the doorway, and Nancy behind Emily, wringing her hands, her face streaked with tears. Emily put her hand on Martha's arm.

"Let him go, Martha. You'd already lost him, before you came back. He'd never be happy here, and there's no way you can keep him. You still have your girls."

Rory didn't even look back at his mother as she released him. He raced after Jonathan, his face alight. "I'm coming with you!" he cried.

Jonathan looked at Martha. Her shoulders were straight, but her face was torn with grief. He tightened his hand around Rory's. Martha stood watching them for a long moment, and then she closed the door. This must be killing her, Jonathan thought. But Rory was his, his son! If Martha kept his daughters, he had a right to his son.

Half an hour later, the young lad from the feed and grain store delivered a small valise, packed with Rory's clothes, to the inn. Jonathan and Rory rode out together, with Rory up behind his father on the only horse the innkeeper had to rent. Rory's face, already turned southward, glowed with happiness.

If it had not been for the necessity of keeping the *Clarion* running, Martha might have broken down

169

during the next few weeks after Jonathan left with Rory. Rory was her flesh and blood, her firstborn, conceived from the passion between her and Jonathan, and delivered in agony, while Martha had fought for his life and her own against the ignorance of old Doctor John. Losing him as well as Jonathan was like having a part of her own body torn away.

"You're biting off a mighty big piece to chew," Doctor Bryant told her. "Nobody, at least around here, ever heard of a woman running a newspaper."

"Then they'll hear of it now." Martha replied. She was frightened at the job ahead, but she refused to let anyone see it. Only Aunt Emily realized how the prospect appalled her, and she kept her own council.

"Jeb Addison's an able enough man, but if David couldn't keep him sober and working steady, how do you propose to do it?"

"I'll pray a lot. And maybe even cuss a little. But I'll do it." And in spite of the opposition of a few of the townswomen who disapproved, and the doubts of nearly all the men, Martha and Jeb managed to keep the paper going during the two months that David was laid up. Martha was aware that David's friends did a great deal to smooth her path. For one thing, Jeb found it impossible to buy a drink, and nobody would give him one. Mr. Hamilton, from the feed and grain store, sent over his son Jody to act as a general printer's devil. And more small ads came in than ever before.

David returned to work much thinner, his face pale from his weeks of confinement. But his newspaper was still running, and solvent.

When he walked into the office his first day back, Martha stood up from the desk where she was going over copy, a glad cry on her lips. "David! Are you sure you're strong enough to be here?"

"Not only strong enough, but ready to take the paper back away from you." Martha found it difficult to read the expression on his face and decided that it would be better not to try. "I did a lot of thinking about Jonathan while I was laid up, Martha, and most of it wouldn't bear repeating. But now I'm only sorry for him. I don't believe that he knows what he lost when he lost you."

Jeb came bristling out of the pressroom. "It's hard enough to get the ink workable, without you letting in all outdoors! Mebby it's May but that's a durned chill breeze." He slammed the door shut and then held out an ink-stained hand to David. "Glory be, man, you're back! And about time, too. One more day without a drink and I'd be the next one to be laid up for a couple of months. It ain't natural, stayin' sober for so long! My system can't stand it."

He took off his leather apron, tossed it into the pressroom, and set out across the street, heading for the inn. Halfway there, he turned around and came back, looking sheepish. "On the other hand, I ain't finished my day's work. Guess I can wait till tonight, after all."

17

In the early eighteen fifties, emotions between North and South ran high. A surprising number of wealthy Northern businessmen were pro-slavery, although an understanding of their motives made it less surprising. Slavery meant profits, as the Southerners borrowed more money to buy more land, and more slaves to plant their crops. And the crops were distributed by Northerners, while the South used any profits, and borrowed against future profits, to buy luxuries and necessities from the North.

Demonstrations were common in the larger cities. Sometimes the demonstrations grew violent and resulted in damaged property and broken heads. It was not unusual now, when Martha traveled to Boston or other communities to speak, for her to suffer through heckling and catcalls, and she was no longer surprised when fistfights broke out in the audience.

But Martha's fighting spirit was only fanned by the opposition. Her husband was lost to her, Miss Emily and Nancy and Cleo took care of Prue and Crissy, and the only thing she had left to give meaning to her life was her campaign to help rid the country of slavery.

"I have too much respect for my beliefs to let them scare me out," she said, when David tried to persuade her that it was becoming too dangerous. It was just as dangerous to spend too much time with David. She knew that his love for her was outgrowing its bounds, and she was fond enough of him to feel a growing tug of passion when she was too near him. He needed her desperately, and she needed . . . someone. She was in the full bloom of womanhood, and her body cried out for the physical relief that only a man she loved could give her, whether it was the burning, destroying love she had for Jonathan or the calmer, softer love she felt for David.

"No one has hurt me yet," she pointed out. "The worst I've experienced is a few rotten eggs and tomatoes dirtying my clothes."

"There's always the first time. You can do as much good staying at home and writing your articles. They're being picked up by more newspapers all the time. You're becoming famous, do you realize that?"

"I don't feel famous. I only feel tired." Martha tucked a stray wisp of hair back into one of her coiled braids. David saw how her hand trembled, and no power on earth could have stopped him from catching it and raising it to his lips.

"Marty, you can't go on like this, half killing yourself trying to forget your husband! Either go back to him or divorce him and marry me! God knows I'd try to make you happy. I love you . . ."

Martha's tired body rested against his, and then it took fire. In all this time, David had never taken her in his arms or begged her to return his love. As their lips met she began to tremble, and her hands were frantic as she held his head, stroking his hair, forcing the kiss to go on.

Jeb poked his head out of the composing room,

and they broke apart. David's face was racked with agony, and a cry of pure shame escaped from Martha's throbbing mouth. While Jeb pulled his head back and pretended that he hadn't seen a thing, Martha escaped from the building and walked for more than an hour, beating down the fire within her. Then she went home and wrote an antislavery article that took its fire from her own veins, almost scorching the paper.

The *Clarion* with the article came out on Thursday afternoon, press day. On Friday night, while the town slept, the newspaper plant was vandalized. The type was dumped from the typecases and strewn around the floor, ink was smeared over work surfaces and walls, and water was poured over the stock of newsprint, reducing it to useless pulp. The composing stick was stolen, David's desk was rifled, and everything that had been written in advance was destroyed.

"Someone took exception to your article," David told Martha, as she looked at the destruction with white-faced shock. "I've been expecting something like this. The *Clarion* is becoming well known as a leader in the fight against slavery. It's a wonder men from Boston and other communities haven't been sent in before, to teach us a lesson."

"I'm going to get me a gun!" Jeb stopped cursing long enough to put together a few coherent sentences. "I'm gettin' me a gun and I'm going to sleep right in the pressroom, and if any . . ." Martha, her hands over her ears, marveled that one small, elderly man could give voice to such a variety of words . . . "dare come in here there's going to be somebody shot!"

"Right now you're going to help clean up this mess. It'll take two days just to un-pi that type. And there'll be no gun. Martha, do you think you and Jeb can get started here? I'll have to hire a horse and wagon

174

and get to Boston to bring back another stock of paper."

"It's getting to be a war, isn't it?" In spite of her effort at self-control, Martha was shaking.

"It's been a war for some time now. Disturbances, riots, vandalism. Only last month a New York paper had its press dragged out and dumped in the river." His face was very serious. "Martha, I'm firing you. I want you to go home and keep yourself out of the limelight before you find yourself hurt."

"No, David! As long as you and others like you go on fighting, I'm going to fight. You can discharge me, but that won't stop me. Darn it, David, I'm angry! It's my battle, too, and I am going to stay in it!"

No one but Cleo knew of Martha's sleepless nights. From her room off the kitchen, Cleo often heard Martha as she rose in the dark hours when everyone else lay asleep and came down to light a lamp and find a book to try to keep her thoughts at bay.

At first, Cleo would get up, too, and offer to stir up the fire and make Martha warm milk or a cup of tea or coffee, but Martha always told her to go back to bed, apologizing for having disturbed her. Cleo's heart ached for Martha, but she knew that there was nothing that she or anyone else could do to ease Martha's sorrow.

During those dark hours, Martha sometimes feared that she was on the verge of losing her sanity. Where was Jonathan now? Was he, too, wakeful in the night? Did he get out of his bed and go downstairs to find solace in brandy? Or worse, solace of another kind, one that drove Martha nearly mad as she struggled for sleep that would not come. Was he even now in Rebecca's bed, forgetting her as he reveled in Rebecca's soft arms, her warm, yielding body?

Martha knew that Rebecca's child was a girl, that she had been named Naomi, and that Naomi lived in the big house, neither slave nor free, a shadowy figure with no place of her own in the world. She knew that the child was lovely. Coralie Amhurst wrote to Martha regularly and had told her these things, even though Martha was too proud to ask. Through Coralie, Martha knew that Jonathan had made no move to secure a divorce.

But that, Martha thought, did not signify. There would be little advantage in a divorce, as far as Jonathan was concerned. No family of any standing would allow their daughter to marry a divorced man. Did Jonathan chafe against this restriction, did he curse her for condemning him to a life alone? Jonathan, with his hot, red blood, had never been cut out to lead the life of a celibate. Did he find release with the girls from the "houses" in Savannah, or did he turn, again and again, to Rebecca?

On top of that torment, Martha was worried about her mother. As the summer wore on, Nancy's vitality seemed to weaken. She insisted that she wasn't ill, but she tired much more quickly than she had used to. When they had first arrived at Martin's Corners, Nancy had been happy to stay up late at night, first playing with Prudence, helping her to cut out paper dolls or to sew doll clothes, or to play endless games of checkers or backgammon with Rory. Rory always preferred his grandmother for a partner, because Aunt Emily invariably won. She refused to give him any edge, or cheat a little so that he could win, and Rory was not a good loser.

But now, Nancy would go to bed soon after the supper dishes were washed up. "No, I'm fine, I'm only a little tired," she would apologize. "It's just a headache, it'll be gone in the morning."

It took both Martha and Aunt Emily to persuade her to see Doctor Bryant, but outside of prescribing a tonic the doctor could find no reason for what had become plain to all of them as failing health. "She's going through a difficult time of life," the doctor told Martha. "The tonic will probably help her, but make sure that she gets plenty of rest, and don't let the children wear her out."

Not letting the children wear her out was easier said than done. Nancy doted on them and encouraged them to demand things of her. She would also insist on doing her share of the work until either Martha or Aunt Emily ordered her to rest.

Martha and Aunt Emily tried to hide their growing concern about Nancy from each other, but each knew how worried the other was. Sometimes, during those black hours, Martha's whole being yearned to turn to David, to accept the love and comfort he had to offer. She, as well as Jonathan, had never been meant to live alone.

But there was no way. In a town as small as Martin's Corners, it was impossible for them to meet alone. It was equally impossible for David to absent himself from town at the same time that Martha was away. Even if she had been willing to subject her family to the scandal of an affair, such an affair would have put an end to her usefulness in the fight against slavery. Any woman known or suspected of having such an affair would be barred from public speaking, and her articles would be turned down by the newspapers.

When the sharp days of fall drew in, Nancy contracted a severe cold that she couldn't seem to shake off. Aunt Emily dosed her, but after she had had it for several days she called in Doctor Bryant, who gave her additional medicines and strict orders to rest and keep warm.

The orders were carried out. Nancy was kept in bed, and Prudence or Cleo carried her her meals. Cleo bathed her and changed her bed linens daily and nursed her with a devotion that brought tears to Martha's eyes. Still, in spite of all their care and nursing, the cold developed into pneumonia.

The efforts of everyone in the household doubled and redoubled. Aunt Emily and Cleo watched by the suffering woman's bedside in shifts through the nights. Doctor Bryant called in twice every day. Prudence tiptoed around the house, her face drawn, her eyes pools of anxiety. Crissy kept to her room and stared with frightened eyes at the ceiling, her hands clenched into fists by her sides. Martha kept on with her work at the *Clarion* only because Aunt Emily demanded it.

"There's nothing you can do here but worry yourself to a shadow. Cleo's the best natural nurse I ever saw. It would fret your mother if you stayed home because of her. But *pray*, Martha!"

Nancy was laid to rest in the family plot on a fall morning when scudding clouds presaged snow. Crissy, who had adored the grandmother who had petted and indulged her, wept with bitter grief. But Martha, Miss Emily, and Prudence stood beside the open grave, their skirts whipped around their ankles by the wind, dry-eyed, their faces calm to hide grief so deep that it could not be relieved by tears.

Where had the years gone? Prue was fourteen, and at Roselawns, Rory would already be a young man. There might be a touch of gray in Jonathan's dark hair. Martha herself was approaching what was considered middle age, although her face remained unlined and she still had the figure of a girl. Was this all there was to life, a succession of meaningless days and nights, with only a yawning grave at the end?

Martha's body cried out, "Traitor! Cheat!" even as she fought to control her mind.

Cleo, too, struggled with her own grief as much for Martha and Miss Emily and Prue as for the woman whose wasted beauty was now being consigned to cold earth. Cleo wasted little sympathy on Crissy. She had her own opinion of Crissy, never hinted by word or expression, but nonetheless there. Crissy, Cleo thought, should have returned to Roselawns with her father and Rory. That girl was born to bring trouble to those who cared for her.

18

"I don't give a hang what you say!" Jonathan faced Jacob, in Jacob's office, a newspaper held in his hand, brought from the north by packet. He had just finished reading an account of the brutal burning of the *Clarion* plant in Martin's Corners and of how the woman abolitionist, Mrs. Martha Beddoes, whose pen had stirred people's hearts and urged them to action, had entered the burning building to salvage type and been burned.

"A heroine," the Boston newspaper said. "A true heroine, of whom we can all be proud, and this newspaper wishes to express its most hearty wishes for her rapid recovery and her renewed fight against the evils of slavery."

"Damn fool woman! Female suffragist!" Jacob's voice was strangled. "She brought it on herself, Jon, with that poison pen of hers and those scurrilous speeches she gave. It says here that that's why the newspaper building was burned. High time somebody burned that one and a lot more!"

"She's going to end up getting herself killed if I don't stop her!" Jonathan's face was white, his eyes dark and burning. "I'm going to fetch her home, and this time she's coming even if every man in Martin's Corners meets me with a gun!"

"You bring her back here, she'll likely be lynched!" Jacob said, pounding on his desk with his fist, so that the decanter and the glass rattled together.

"Not while I'm alive, she won't. She's my wife. She's Mrs. Jonathan Beddoes, and nobody's going to look crossways at her, much less lynch her! Since when ain't the Beddoes family capable of protecting their own?"

"Think what it'll do to your mother! A female rabble-rouser, a notorious woman, under our roof!"

"Mother understands. I've already told her, and she's packing my saddlebags for me right now. She has more guts than you do, Jacob. She said that if anybody as much as raises their eyebrows at Martha, she'll spit in their eye!"

"Yolande never said that!"

In spite of the seriousness of the situation, Jonathan could not suppress a grin. "She said a heap more than that. She said that every word Martha's written or said in her speeches is true. She said that the women of the South know it, even if the men don't! She said she wished she had Martha's nerve." Without waiting to see how Jacob survived the shock, Jonathan walked out of the office.

An hour later Jonathan left the plantation, cantering down the curved driveway on the first leg of his journey.

"The damned fool!" Jacob spluttered. "He didn't even take his gun!"

"Shut up, Jacob," Yolande said. "I don't want to hear any of your asinine ravings."

Jacob's face turned purple. What if any of the house people had heard her use his first name, heard

181

her speak to him in that tone of voice? God almighty, what had got into womenfolk these days?

A howl of rage intermingled with utter astonishment issued from the room that Yolande had just entered. It came from Rory, who had also made the mistake of opening his mouth to say something to his grandmother and had received the back of her hand.

Jonathan was exhausted when he arrived in Boston. He'd traveled fast and pushed himself hard. When he was ushered into Bertram Foster's inner office, his father's old friend hardly recognized him.

Later, after Jonathan had downed two brandies and consumed the meal that Mr. Foster had sent out for, Mr. Foster leaned back in his chair and studied Jonathan.

"We can force Mrs. Beddoes to return south with you, certainly. She's still your wife, and the law is the law. I foresee no legal trouble on that score. But did you know that Mrs. Beddoes is in Boston at this moment, Jonathan?"

Jonathan's mouth dropped open, and he started. "No! Why didn't you tell me that, instead of letting me rant on?"

"I wanted to get things clear in my mind. And there is not that much hurry. Legal proceedings take time. Mrs. Beddoes is to speak tonight, at seven o'clock, in the assembly room of a fraternal organization." Mr. Foster drew a large pocket watch from his pocket and opened the case. "As it is now after six, you have just time enough to get cleaned up and attend the meeting."

"The meeting be damned! That's why I'm here, to keep her from doing any more public speaking!"

"I'm afraid you'll have to attend the meeting, if you want to make contact with your wife," Mr. Foster explained patiently. "I do not know where she is staying, you see. It will be with a private family. As she cannot travel alone, being a lady, some family man and his wife or sister or daughter, always escorts her from Martin's Corners and gives her accommodation, so that the proprieties will be observed. So you see, the earliest contact you can make with her will be at the meeting. And you should hear her speak, Mr. Beddoes. I myself have done so, and although I disagree with almost everything she has to say, I have to admit that I have the utmost admiration for the way she says it. To hear her is an experience."

"I'll be damned if I'll sit there and let her make a fool of herself in public, with me listening!"

"Mr. Beddoes, I have to contact a lawyer and have legal papers drawn up. I have to have them signed by a judge, and I have to arrange for an officer of the law to properly serve them on her. Until these things are done, you can hardly carry your wife off bodily, without causing a riot."

Cursing under his breath, Jonathan capitulated. It was maddening to think that Martha was here in the city and that he had no way of finding her until she stood in front of an audience making another of those speeches that were setting the country on its ear. Blast Marty, anyway! Why couldn't she have been in Martin's Corners, where he'd expected to go once he was armed with the authority to make her behave herself?

What would she do when she saw him? How would she look, after all these years? What business did she have, after having been burned like that, to be gallivanting around the country still stirring people up, still causing trouble? What if she said she hated him, what if her hate showed in her face, her voice?

No matter. If she did, she would still have to go

with him. This time she would have no choice. He should have taken this step years ago. Only his own pride, and the fear that she'd hate him worse than ever, had kept him from it.

Damn it, Marty, why'd you have to go and have those ridiculous principles, why couldn't you have settled for being happy?

Arriving at the assembly room just as the meeting got underway, Jonathan was totally unprepared for the crowd that packed the place. They swarmed around him, hundreds of them, so that he was forced to stand in the back, no more seats being available and men elbowing others for room. Was everybody in Boston crazy? Who would have imagined that so many supposedly sane people would turn out to hear a woman talk?

The platform on which Martha was to speak was well lighted. The crowd stirred, and a murmur of excitement swept through the hall. Somewhere a lady exclaimed as she was jostled; a man cursed. The hum of hundreds of voices trailed off to silence as Martha stepped up on the platform, escorted by two dignified-looking men in black suits.

Jonathan's heart seemed to stop. Martha was the same and yet not the same. She was older, but if anything, more beautiful than she had been the last time Jonathan had seen her.

She was dressed in dark gray, the modest neckline relieved only by a small white collar with a cameo brooch set directly between the rounded points of the collar. Jealousy surged in Jonathan's body. Had Lawrence given her that brooch? Martha, in an inexpensive dress, a plain bonnet, when she should have been gowned by Worth, wearing her pearls!

There was a storm of applause, as well as a few catcalls. Martha stood quietly, her hands clasped in

184

front of her, until the noise subsided. She had no notes, Jonathan saw, and he could not help marveling at her self-possession. How in the world had he ever come to marry a woman like that! Only, she hadn't been a woman then, he remembered, his throat dry. She'd been a girl, hardly more than a child, showing only a hint of the beauty and self-possession she would attain with the passage of years.

"I wish to thank you for coming to hear me," Martha said. Her voice was softly modulated, but it carried well. It was obvious that she had had considerable experience at speaking. "And to thank those who invited me to speak to you. It is heartwarming to realize that our cause has so many friends, and that your numbers increase with every passing day."

"Get on with it! Tell us about the slaves!" a voice called.

"That is why I am here, to tell you what I know, what I have seen with my own eyes, having lived, for several years, on a plantation in Georgia." Martha was not ruffled. Her smile was friendly, as if she realized that their impatience to get to the heart of the matter was because of their belief in the cause.

Martha talked on, her voice taking fire as she spoke, stirring her audience. She described the cotton fields with their long lines of black workers, bent double as they dragged their heavy sacks behind them, or chopping weeds, their feet bare, such clothing as they wore saturated with their perspiration as they toiled under a relentless Southern sun.

She told of whippings for minor infractions, on plantations that prided themselves on their humanity toward their people. She told of the inadequate diet, of their sicknesses and heartbreak and pain. Many of the women sobbed as she described children torn from their mothers' arms, brothers and sisters separated when they were sold off. She did not exaggerate. She made it clear that many plantations had a policy of never selling individual members of a family except in case of dire necessity.

"But in other cases, a slave might be sold in order that some luxury, something that could easily have been done without, could be bought, merely because the slave-owner thought the occasion merited something special."

Jonathan winced. God, how he wished that he and Jacob had never decided to sell Clem and Brutus to buy those pearls! That was what had started this whole thing, turned Martha against the South even before the tragedy of Sam's death.

There was a growl of anger from her audience as she went on to speak of light-skinned Negroes, the sons and daughters of their masters or their masters' friends, but still slaves to be bought and sold, to be used for profit or pleasure as their masters saw fit. She told them how some planters encouraged the practice of siring light-skinned Negroes because of their high monetary value as house slaves. "Not all masters encouraged this practice, but . . ."

A loud voice interrupted her speech. "I know about you! Who are you to stand up in public and talk about morals, about decency? A married woman who won't stay with her lawful husband where she belongs! There's names for women like you, who leave their husbands and try to do a man's work, consorting with other men . . ."

Fury almost strangling him, Jonathan looked around to try to locate the man who had just insulted Martha, but now another voice rose.

"Go back south where you belong! We don't need you up here, stirring up trouble! You talk about morals, about decency, but it's right in the Good Book about how slavery was commanded for the blacks by the Almighty Himself!"

The two men who shared the platform with Martha rose to their feet, held up their hands, and begged for order. "Gentlemen, gentlemen! You shame our fair city! Let the lady continue! There are those here who wish to hear her!"

"Well, we don't want to hear her, and she's no lady!"

"Shut up, you!"

"Be quiet there! Be quiet!"

"Let her talk!"

"Send her packing, send her back where she belongs!"

The entire audience was on its feet. Insults and recriminations were hurled back and forth, but Jonathan wasn't alarmed. He had heard how hired rascals were sent to such meetings to disrupt them. The more fool Marty, to try to hold her own against such rabble!

"Where are the police! Clear these rascals out and let this meeting continue!"

A bench was overturned, and fists began to fly. Still Jonathan was only disgusted. Why didn't Martha have sense enough to know when she was licked? She was still standing there, waiting, when the first tomato was thrown. It splattered against her dress and left an ugly smear. She looked down at it, but she didn't move. Another tomato, and then rotten eggs began to fly, and the crowd was getting completely out of hand. Fist fights started up. The officers who had been posted to keep the peace were completely overwhelmed by the numbers, unable to perform their duty.

"Harlot!" someone shouted, and the cry was taken up by other voices, while still others called, "Shame! Shame to treat her so! Have done with it!"

187

Men who had escorted ladies were now trying to elbow and shove their way from the hall, to get their womenfolk out of the melee. Canes were brought into play as weapons, and out of the corner of his eye Jonathan saw one valiant old lady laying around her with her parasol. He tried to reach the woman's side to protect her, his Southern chivalry aghast that any man would lay a hand on an elderly female, as a red-faced ruffian wrested the parasol from her.

Before Jonathan could fight his way to the woman's side, the first casualty howled with pain as a cane landed against an unprotected head. This wasn't a demonstration any more, it was a full-fledged riot. Jonathan plunged through the crowd, maddened by his need to reach the platform, to get Martha off it and to safety.

The dignitaries with Martha had already seen the danger, and they acted, urging her off the stage, keeping her in front of them as they headed for a side exit. But others, with the same idea, spilled out after them as the hall emptied, and the fighting went on.

Jonathan also gained the side door but his frantic eyes caught no sight of Martha, so he let himself be swept along with the crowd to the front of the hall. Martha was there, speaking to one of her escorts, who was apparently urging her to come away. Jonathan called her name, and miraculously, she heard him, even through the tumult, because she looked his way, her face startled, her lips parted.

"Jon!" He could see her lips form the word, even though her voice did not carry to him. Her face lighted up, and for a moment it was as though the years had rolled back as her radiant smile transformed her into a glowing beauty. She threw off the hand of the man who tried to hold her back, her

188

own hands outstretched. "Jon!" she cried again, and this time he heard her.

To Martha, Jonathan's appearance was a miracle. Even now, with him directly in front of her, separated only by the milling crowd, she could hardly convince herself that she was not experiencing an hallucination brought on by the nightmare around her.

But he was there, she must reach him, she must tell him that she was sorry she had ruined his life, ruined their life together. She must tell him that she loved him, that she was tired of fighting against him, that she couldn't live without him.

She had almost reached him now, as they both struggled against the mob that separated them. Another moment and she would be in his arms, and all the empty years between them would be as nothing.

Jonathan stood frozen to the spot, disbelieving, when she went down. Then he was fighting his way forward again, a man gone mad, until he reached where she lay, her face ashen, blood streaming from her forehead. Her eyes were open and glazed.

"Marty, Marty!" Jonathan knelt beside her, fighting off the hands that were trying to lift her. "Don't move her, damn it! Get a doctor, somebody get a doctor, she's hurt bad!"

The stone, thrown by some furious hand, was there beside her, spattered with her blood.

Jonathan was only dimly aware that the rioting had stopped, that people were standing quietly, their stunned faces turned toward the tableau in front of them. A gray-haired man, his hat missing, his hair disheveled, made his way forward. He knelt in the grass beside Martha and placed his fingers on her pulse, turned back one of her eyelids, and shook his head.

"You're a doctor? How badly is she hurt? Do something!" Jonathan's voice was strangled.

"Her skull is fractured. There is nothing I can do, nothing anyone can do."

He didn't believe it. It wasn't true. Not Marty. Oh, God, not Marty!

For just a moment, her eyes seemed to clear, and she looked him full in the face. A little smile struggled to appear at the corner of her mouth. "Jon?" she whispered. Then her head fell to the side.

Jonathan still knelt there, holding her. "Marty, Marty!" he said, his voice choked with unbearable grief. "Not like this, it can't end for us like this! Marty, why'd you have to do it?"

BOOK TWO:

Prudence

Part One

19

"There it is," Jonathan said. "That's Roselawns."

Prudence tried to look at the house that loomed before her, at the slaves who had lined up to welcome her and her sister home, but their images wavered through the mist of tears that filled her eyes.

"It hasn't changed," she said, because she felt a need to be polite. She knew that her father was suffering just as she was suffering. "It's just as I remember it."

"Oh, it's beautiful! It's a mansion! I didn't know we were so rich!" Crissy cried. In her excitement, she stood up in the barouche, and Rory put his arm around her to balance her. How tall he was, Prudence thought. And how handsome! He was going to be every bit as handsome as Jonathan. He'd probably break the hearts of half the belles in Georgia before he went north this fall, to Harvard College. But there was still the summer for her to get to know him again. She hoped he would be nicer now than he had been when he had lived in Massachusetts with them.

"I love it!" Crissy cried. "Are all those slaves ours? Papa, will I have one of my very own, a lady's maid? Will we have parties, and great balls?"

"Christine, sit down." Prudence's voice was sharp

in spite of her effort to control it. "We can't have parties or balls for at least a year. We're in mourning for Mama."

Crissy's face fell. For a moment, in the excitement of this homecoming, she had almost forgotten. But that didn't give Prue any call to look so sour. How could she help but be excited? She'd been too young when they'd left Roselawns to remember it at all. Why, it made Aunt Emily's house in Martin's Corners look like a hovel! And they were rich, they must be rich, to have a house like this, and so many slaves, and it didn't really matter about the parties because she was only eleven. Well, almost eleven. And she was prettier than Prue. She didn't need the admiration she saw in every pair of male eyes to know that she was beautiful. She knew what she saw in the mirror, and she was glad.

Prudence sat quietly, her hands folded in her lap to control their trembling. Grandmother Yolande was very pretty and very kind, but she wasn't Mama and she wasn't Aunt Emily. For just a few moments, when her father had asked Aunt Emily, very sincerely, to come with them to Georgia and make her home with them, Prudence had hoped that Aunt Emily would accept. That had been foolish of her. Aunt Emily was part and parcel of New England. And Mama, and Grandmother Nancy, and all the others, were still there, buried in Massachusetts soil, just as Aunt Emily herself would be some day. She could never leave there.

"Thank you for asking, Jonathan, but I'll stay where I am. I'm too old to transplant," Emily had said.

Cleo had been there. They had just returned from the churchyard, and Cleo had just stood and looked at Papa.

"Mr. Jonathan, I'd like to stay with Miss Emily.

She needs me, and you don't." Cleo's reluctance to be taken from Martha's grave had been apparent, as was her reluctance to leave Miss Emily, who was second only to Martha in her esteem.

Jonathan had inclined his head in silent agreement. Miss Emily said, "Thank you, Cleo. I confess I'd be mighty lonesome without you."

"I'll give you your freedom. You've earned it, many times over," Jonathan had said, but the black woman had shaken her head.

"I'm as free now as I ever want to be. No paper could make me want to go anywhere or do anything I'm not doing right now. Thank you kindly, Mr. Jonathan, but freedom would make no difference."

Remembering, Prudence turned her face away quickly and looked toward the fields as the barouche started forward again, so that the others wouldn't see her tears.

"They're beautiful, Jon," Yolande said, laying her small hand on his. "We'll do our best for them. As soon as it's decent, we'll have those parties that Crissy wants." Her eyes were shining, filled with plans. "The Beddoes family will boast the loveliest belles in the South! As soon as I can get them out of those somber clothes and properly dressed they'll be the talk of the county!"

Parties, balls, gowns. Jonathan turned his face away. Martha hadn't needed frilly dresses to make her beautiful. She'd been as beautiful as a goddess, standing there on that platform, dressed in sober gray. And they'd killed her, those bastards had killed her.

He swallowed. He had to begin facing the truth sometime. If he'd gone to her before, if he hadn't waited so long to make up his mind that keeping her was worth giving up Roselawns, worth giving up his Southern ideals, she'd be alive today. Too late, he realized that if God gave people second chances, he'd have done just that.

Intuitively, Yolande knew what he was thinking.

"Life isn't easy, Jon. It never has been, and it never will be. But you have your children to think of now, especially your daughters. Rory will be all right, he's you and Jacob all over again. But your girls need you. For their sakes, you must put the past behind you."

As the family came up the steps, Naomi stood apart from the other house slaves, at the farthest end of the gallery, half in the shadow of the honeysuckle vine. Her mother, Rebecca, had not come out with the others to welcome the young daughters home, but Naomi's curiosity had drawn her. The younger of the two girls must be only a little older than she was, and Naomi thought that she had never seen such a beautiful creature in her life.

Christine, her name was, and she was prettier even than Miss Yolande, prettier than Rebecca. The other girl was older, and not nearly as pretty. So Naomi's eyes went back to the younger, with her golden hair showing underneath her bonnet, her skin as white and creamy as a gardenia, her eyes as blue as Naomi's dress had been before it had faded.

She's my sister, Naomi thought, that beautiful girl is my sister. Naomi was well aware of her status in the Beddoes household. The old master, Jacob, often looked at her as if he didn't really see her, but Miss Yolande was unfailingly kind. Jonathan's attitude toward her was harder to understand. He tried to be nice, but at times, when he looked at her, his eyes held an expression of unutterable grief and shame. It made Naomi sad when Mister Jonathan looked at her like that.

Miss Yolande, leading the two sisters past the line

196

of house folk, introduced everyone. "Prudence, you remember Benjamin, of course. And Juliette, our cook, you must remember her. Pansy, and this is Rose, she's new, and Jimmy, Benjamin's son, Rory's boy."

They came to the end of the line, and Naomi shrank farther back into the shadows, but it was not necessary. Miss Yolande and the girls entered the house, and Naomi had not been introduced. A little chill made her skin feel cold in spite of the warmth of the summer day, and she blinked back sudden, shameful tears. What a ninny she was! Of course she hadn't been introduced! What was Miss Yolande supposed to do, say, "And this is your half-sister, your father's bastard"?

Upstairs, Crissy bounced up and down on the huge fourposter bed with its tester. The mosquito bar was drawn back, its novelty already examined and passed over. Now Crissy jumped down, ignoring the footstool that was beside it because it was higher than any bed that Crissy had ever imagined She landed lightly, as graceful as a spring breeze, and danced and twirled around the room.

"Look at it, Prue! Just look at it! And it's all ours! Did you ever see such curtains? They're made of *velvet*! And did you ever see such a rug, all those bright, pretty flowers in it? The fireplace is made of real marble! To think we could have lived here all along! We didn't know what we were missing! I feel positively cheated."

Prudence tried to turn off her sister's lilting voice. The room was beautiful, far more beautiful than she had remembered. Of course, Miss Yolande had had it redecorated especially for them.

But in spite of its luxury, her heart ached for the bare, wide-planked floor of their tiny bedroom in Aunt

Emily's house and for the rag rug that Grandma Nancy had made to keep the chill of the winter boards from their toes when they got out of bed. She would rather have her old patchwork quilt than the expensive bedspread on this big bed. Their room in Aunt Emily's house had been plain, almost austere, but safe, secure, filled with Aunt Emily's own serenity.

"Prue, there was one servant we weren't introduced to. Or maybe she isn't a servant, maybe she's a friend or a relative. I wonder who she was? Her family can't be rich, because she only wore a plain old dress. Maybe she's some kind of a poor relation."

Prudence's breath caught. She, too, had noticed the girl, only a little younger than Crissy, who had stood apart from the others. But unlike Crissy, she had a very good idea who the girl was. Crissy had been only a baby when Mama had taken them away from Roselawns, but Prue remembered. There had been the devil to pay when Mama and Papa had come back from Savannah. Prudence hadn't been sure why, but it had all started when Sam died. She remembered crying for days about Sam and Dulcy, and even now thinking about them made her feel sad.

Looking at the girl in the shadow of the honeysuckle vine had given her a shock. She'd known who she was at once. She'd heard Grandma Nancy and Aunt Emily discuss her several times. Furthermore, Naomi had a remarkable family resemblance to Jonathan, and some resemblance to Prue herself, although it wasn't as marked. Naomi's eyes were blue rather than Prue's greenish hazel, and her hair was darker, not as dark as Jonathan's, but a deeper brown than Prue's. Anyone would have known that Naomi was the result of Jonathan's affair with Rebecca.

Prue's face was pale, her eyes dark with the knowledge of a duty that must be done. It would never

198

do for Crissy to prattle to the others about the girl she had seen on the gallery. She must be told, and it was up to Prue to tell her, right now, before she upset the whole family.

"Honey, you're too young to remember when we left here. But the reason we left was because Rebecca was going to have a baby." How could she put it, not to shock Crissy too much? "I think that that girl is her baby. And Papa is her father."

"But that can't be!" Crissy frowned with incomprehension. "Mama was Papa's wife, and we're his children, you and Rory and me!"

"It can happen." Prue found the conversation more and more painful. "People can have children even if they aren't married to each other. It's a sin, but it can happen."

Crissy began to understand, and now her own face was pale. "Like Mama said in the pieces she wrote for the *Clarion*. I wasn't supposed to read them, but the other girls told me what Mama wrote because they heard their parents talking about it, so I read a couple, only I thought they were boring."

"Yes." Prudence nodded. "So you mustn't ask about her, Crissy. We must pretend that we simply don't notice her, until we see what's expected of us. Do you understand?"

"No."

"Then just do as I say. When I find out how we're supposed to act toward her, I'll tell you." Prue's eyes turned a shade darker, with pain. "Of course, I don't mean you should be impolite to her, or hurt her feelings. It must be terribly hard for her, knowing that her mother wasn't married to Papa."

"All right." Crissy's voice was doubtful, but then, Crissy-like, her eyes fell on a pair of figurines on the mantel and she darted across the carpet to look at them. "Look, Prue! Oh, they're just too beautiful, Aunt Emily never had anything like this in her house! I'm so glad we've come home!"

I can't cry, Prue thought. There's no place I can go to cry, without everyone knowing. It was all for nothing, Mama. You gave up your life, and you died, and everything is just the same here in the South.

If it were in any way possible, she, like her mother, would return to Massachusetts, to Martin's Corners and Aunt Emily. But it wasn't possible. She had no choice but to stay here, no matter how she was crying inside.

Rebecca had known, from her first glimpse of the returned girls, that her life at Roselawns was going to be untenable. Especially when she'd seen Prudence's green eyes appraising her, cataloguing her, seen the pain in those eyes. Jonathan obviously worshipped the ground Prudence walked on, because she was the image of her mother.

Not that things had been as Rebecca had wanted them, during the years since Martha had left. Jonathan had been wild with grief and anger, and the first night that Rebecca had gone to him, to offer him comfort, he had actually struck her and shouted at her and told her to get out of his sight.

He'd apologized, later, but Rebecca knew that he still blamed her, even though he had no way of knowing how deliberately she had planned her seduction of him. Once or twice, Jonathan had come to her, when the blackness was on him and he couldn't bear it, but he'd hated himself afterwards, and hated her, too.

But Rebecca had gone on hoping. He couldn't remarry, even if, as she hoped, he divorced Martha for desertion. No nice girl would have a divorced man. But if he'd reconcile himself to Martha's loss, and put all thoughts of her behind him, then Rebecca would do her best to take her place.

It hadn't happened, and when Naomi was born, Jonathan had looked at her with pain, and with pity, and with something a little like love, but then he had turned away. Rebecca's heart had roiled with bitterness.

As the months had passed after Naomi's birth, Rebecca had prayed that Jonathan would come to her again. She'd prayed for another child by him, anything that would bind him more closely to her. But it had never happened. She could see in his eyes that the thought of doubling his guilt with another child filled him with revulsion.

The time when Jonathan had gone north to bring Martha home, and returned without her because he'd made that crazy mistake and shot a man who wasn't armed, he'd walked around like a zombie, like he wasn't there at all. And then he'd gone wild, and gone out carousing, gambling too much, drinking too much. He'd nearly beaten a man to death for making a slurring remark about Martha and her abolitionist writings, not calling him out, as a gentleman should have, but using his hands on him. The disgrace had nearly killed Jacob. He hadn't spoken to Jonathan for weeks.

Jonathan had grown quiet again after that. He'd tended to his work, except for the times when he'd disappear for two or three days. For Rebecca, those were the worst times of all, because she knew that he'd gone searching for a woman, any woman, rather than turn to her.

But she could still see him, be near him, and stubbornly, her hope had refused to die. Except for the accident of birth, she would have been as acceptable

201

to him and his family as any other county girl. Her father and her grandfather had been aristocrats, their blood as good as the Beddoes blood. She could pass anywhere in the country as white. She was sure that someday he'd look at her again and realize what he was throwing away.

Now that was all over, of course. Prudence and Christine made all the difference. Now that they were home, Jonathan would never come to her.

Rebecca's bitterness was deepened a hundredfold when Naomi, of her own desire, became Crissy's personal maid. While Crissy accepted Naomi with careless unconcern, Prudence was invariably kind to her half-sister and treated her with gentle and affectionate consideration.

Her very kindness toward Naomi made Rebecca realize that Jonathan was lost to her irretrievably. It was a daily reminder to Jonathan of exactly what he had done, and of its consequences. Rebecca knew this, and it ate at her like a cancer, until she could no longer bear it.

Jonathan's face displayed only his usual courtesy when Rebecca waylaid him as he was returning from inspecting the fields, early the following autumn after Prudence and Crissy had returned.

"Yes, Rebecca? Was there something you wanted?"

"I want to leave Roselawns, Mister Jon."

For a moment his face was blank. "You aren't serious. Do you mean you want to be sold?"

"No." Rebecca stood proudly, meeting his eyes without flinching. "I just want to leave."

Jonathan's voice was gentle now. "You know I'd be glad to give you your freedom, but my father would never hear of it. You know how he feels about freeing slaves. But we'll do everything we can to place you in a fine home, with a mistress who will be as gentle as my mother, if you really have your heart set on leaving."

"I want to go to New Orleans, and not as a slave. I can make my own way, Mister Jon." How it galled her to have to call him mister, when she wanted to call him by his name, to have the right to use it. "You needn't give me my freedom. All I need is a little money, enough to get me there and keep me until I can find work."

"It's unthinkable! Anything might happen to you in New Orleans! It's a wicked city, filled with wicked men. The only way you'd be safe there would be for you to take menial work in some private family's house, and you'd be worse off than you are here because there would be no one with an interest in protecting you."

"I still want to go."

"And what about Naomi?" His daughter's name on his lips cut Rebecca to the quick. "Are you willing to leave her behind, never see her again?" His voice was incredulous.

"Of course I'm not. I'm asking you to let her come to me as soon as I'm able to provide for her. Even your father won't cavil about letting her go. He'll be glad to see her leave; she'll no longer be an embarrassment to him."

Jonathan realized that Rebecca intended to pass as white, to work her way up in the world by any means at her disposal. It was impossible. Jacob would blow the roof right off the house.

"I'm going to go, Mister Jon. Whether you give me permission and money to help me or not, I'm going."

She meant it. She'd run away empty-handed. Without money, the chances were greater that she'd be caught and either returned to Roselawns or sold elsewhere, be manhandled and abused. He spread out his hands. He had never felt so utterly defeated since Marty had looked at him with those clear hazel eyes of hers after he'd shot Lawrence and he'd known that she was lost to him forever.

Jacob looked up from the column of figures he was toting up at his desk when Jonathan entered his office. He knew his son well, and he knew that something was wrong by Jonathan's whole demeanor.

"Let her go? Give her money, a good sum of money, and let her go, just like that? You're out of your mind, boy! You must have been out in the sun too long!"

"If we don't let her go, she'll run away."

"She wouldn't get far. She's too well known, she couldn't go a mile without being recognized and brought back."

"And that's why we have to give her our permission. And money. How much can we spare?"

Jacob looked at Jonathan as if he had never seen him before. "You're dead serious!"

"Yes, I am. If she wants to go, it's her right. God knows she's had nothing but grief from the Beddoes family."

The battle raged. For an hour, two hours, Jonathan fought his father until he brought him to a standstill.

"Five hundred dollars," Jacob said at last.

"A thousand."

Jacob almost strangled. "You think we're made of money? The crop ain't even sold yet! I couldn't lay my hands on a thousand dollars in cash if our lives depended on it."

"Then I'll sell Martha's pearls. She hated them anyway, she said they were bought with human bondage. She'd like it, to have them pay for Rebecca's freedom; she'd consider it a victory."

For a moment, he thought that Jacob was going to have a stroke. Jacob's hand shook as he reached for the decanter and slopped brandy into his glass.

"Those pearls are to go down in the family, they're for Rory's wife, just as this plantation is to go to Rory and his son after him." Jacob lifted his glass and drained it. "All right. A thousand. I'll scrape it up somehow." He filled his glass again. "I curse the day I bought Rebecca as a present for your mother so she could have the finest lady's maid in the county!"

20

"Are you going to accept him, if he asks you?" Crissy twirled around in front of the pier glass, making her crinolines sway. Crinolines were absolutely the most beautiful creations in the world.

"If who asks me what?"

"Oh, Prue, don't act so obtuse! You know perfectly well who I mean. If Gaylord Renault asks you, and I heard Grandmother telling Grandfather that it's almost a sure thing, will you accept him?" Crissy twirled around again, frowning at her inadequate bustline. If only Grandmother would let her pad it! Here she was, the prettiest girl in the whole of Georgia, with the tiniest waist, but her barely budding breasts spoiled it all.

No matter. If she stuffed something down there skillfully enough, Grandmother Yolande wouldn't suspect. "Isn't it wonderful that somebody invented crinolines? We never had anything like this up north!"

"They didn't have anything like it here in the South, either, when we lived in Martin's Corners. They haven't been patented that long." Prudence smiled at her younger sister and surveyed her own reflection in the mirror. She, too, was pleased with what she saw.

Against Yolande's wishes, Prue's dress was less elaborate than her sister's, whose skirt had row after row of flounces, each flounce trimmed with lace and scattered with embroidered rosebuds that were echoed around the decolletage that was much too low for a girl of Christine's age. Aunt Emily would not have approved, Prudence thought. But then Aunt Emily wasn't here and Jacob was, and Jacob let Crissy have anything she wanted, even over Grandmother Yolande's protests.

Both ballgowns were white, but Prudence's gown was not cut as low as Crissy's, even though she was well developed. Both girls wore their hair in long curls over their shoulders and swept up in back. Crissy was going to wear a wreath of camellias around hers, but Prudence had shaken her head at the suggestion of such adornment for herself.

"Flowers in my hair would not suit me, Grandmother. I'd feel like a fool."

"I believe you are right, my dear, although what Bella Renault will say, I don't care to think. She'll be sure to believe that I neglect your appearance."

"She'll think no such thing. You can't make a silk purse out of a sow's ear, now, can you?"

"Really, Prue! What an inelegant expression! And it isn't true, not at all. You have your own beauty, and although Crissy does rather outshine you, right now, I have an idea that your looks will last long after hers have faded. You have superior bone structure."

The occasion was Gaylord Renault's twenty-first birthday. The young man had already graduated from Harvard College and had taken the Grand Tour, his reward for graduating without the stain of failing grades or any undue campus scandals. Ever since he had returned from Europe, every girl of marriageable age in the county had been swooning with love for him.

And not without reason, Prudence admitted. Gaylord was beyond doubt one of the handsomest young men to walk the face of the earth. He was as fair as Jonathan and Rory were dark, with hair—the color of cornsilk before it has ripened—that tended to curl where it met his collar. His eyes were the deepest blue that Prudence had ever seen in a human being and fringed by lashes that would be the envy of any girl.

If those attributes were not enough, Gay was blessed with a tall figure, broad of shoulder, narrow of hip, and the lithe muscularity of the natural athlete. The product of generations of French Huguenots, aristocrats all, Gaylord had brought the bloodline to its culmination of physical perfection. And to top it all, his family was the wealthiest in the district, maybe in the entire State of Georgia.

"I hope he doesn't ask you!" Crissy preened herself, tilting her head first one way and then the other, experimenting with the exact angle that would show off to the best advantage her delicate curve of cheek and throat. "I can't help it, Prue, I just hope he doesn't! In another year or two, I'll be old enough, and I'm so much prettier than you are that he'd be bound to want me!"

Realizing what she'd said, her hand flew to her mouth, and she looked at her sister warily to see whether her tactless remark had made her angry.

Prudence laughed. "I agree with you perfectly. You're much, much prettier than I am. And if Mr. Renault asks me, I promise I won't accept him."

"Prue! You're making fun of me!"

As a matter of fact, Prue was not. It was not the

desirable Gaylord Renault she hoped would ask her, but someone far less handsome.

Naomi came into the room carrying a delicate ivory fan carved in a lacy pattern. It was one of the trifles Martha had brought back from New Orleans years before, and Prudence thought it much more beautiful than the popular fans made of chicken skin and painted with flowers or peacocks.

"You look beautiful, Miss Prudence," Naomi said. The two girls' eyes met, and there was quick pain in Prue's. Except for their dresses and the way their hair was done, there was not much difference between them. If Naomi were white and . . .

White! Prudence was beginning to hate the word. Naomi was whiter than Rebecca, only one-sixteenth Negro, and yet she could never hope to marry well, and therefore she could never hope to marry at all, to have her own home, her own children.

Years ago, Aunt Emily had told Prue that in southern Europe, nearly every white person had some colored blood because of the nearness of Africa and the intermingling, throughout the centuries, of the races. But no one thought of them as tainted. It was only here in the South that people were so prejudiced.

Where was Rebecca now, Prudence wondered. Naomi's mother had not been heard from since Jonathan had escorted her to Savannah where he put Rebecca on a packet for New Orleans, with a paper that had given her her freedom. For the first few months Naomi had asked, her eyes filled with longing, where her mother was. She had not asked for a long time now. She had substituted her devotion to her half-sisters for her devotion to her mother and done her best to make the best of her tragic situation.

Prudence never had to wonder why her mother, Martha, had chosen to become an abolitionist. She knew. And only a small part of the reason had to do with Jonathan's infidelity. Multiply Rebecca and Naomi's fate by thousands . . .

Swanmere Hall was far larger than Roselawns, and this evening flowers and candlelight made it shimmer like a palace out of a fairytale.

Gaylord Renault was standing out on the wide gallery to greet his guests, his fair hair shining in the late afternoon sun. His mother, Bella, greeted the ladies and turned them over to a maid to be escorted upstairs to the various bedrooms assigned to them, while John Renault saw that the gentlemen were fortified immediately with the finest imported brandy after their long rides to attend this celebration.

Gaylord! Crissy's heart turned over just to see him. She imagined herself standing beside him, her hands extended graciously to her guests. Gaylord's wife, the fabulous Christine Beddoes Renault, the target of every gentleman's eye and the envy of every lady.

To Crissy's chagrin, Gaylord only smiled at her and turned immediately to Prue, his smile widening into one of delight. "I'm mighty glad you could come, Miss Prudence. Remember, I'll expect the first dance, and every alternate dance after that, and the supper-dance, so mind you keep your card free until I've filled it in!"

"Must I commit myself so early?" Prue's smile was serene, her eyes clear and serious, enough to drive a man crazy.

"But I want you to commit yourself! It's my birthday, Miss Prue, and I'm entitled to have what I want, don't you agree?"

"I'm not sure that I do. I'm not at all sure that

210

anyone on earth is entitled to what they want just because they want it."

Beside her, Yolande refrained, with an effort, from gritting her teeth. It wasn't that Prudence was stupid, or lacking in social graces. She'd absorbed Yolande's instructions in etiquette effortlessly, she simply didn't bother to put them into practice. She should be smiling, coy, she should appear flustered and flattered, and here she was arguing as if this were a serious event, instead of a gala!

"Come, Prudence, we must freshen ourselves." Yolande put her hand on Prue's arm and drew her away, and Prudence said "Ouch!" when her fingers bit in. It was embarrassing in the extreme, but the pinch had been so unexpected that the exclamation had been involuntary. Crissy tittered, and then there was a deeper laugh, filled with genuine amusement, and Prudence's heart leaped.

He was here, after all, even though Coralie hadn't been sure, last week, that he would attend. Rory had had an errand to Amhurst Hall, and Prudence and Crissy had cajoled him into taking them along. For Prue, any occasion on which she might see Burke Amhurst, if only for a moment, was something to be treasured for weeks.

How well she had remembered Burke through all the years she had lived in Martin's Corners! He had been a serious boy, much more serious than Rory, and more gentle by nature. Prudence had worshipped him even then, when she had been only a child. And each time she had seen him since her return, Prue's liking for him had increased, until now he was the single most important person in her existence.

Burke was there, holding out his hand, and Prue felt warmth spread through her as she placed her own in his far larger one. He'll never change, she

211

thought, not if he lives to be a hundred. She knew he was nowhere near as handsome as Gaylord, but the gentleness was still in his hazel eyes, which were lighter than her own.

Adam was tall as Gaylord but not as broad of shoulder and his brown hair was usually rumpled from running his long, sensitive fingers through it. Even now, dressed up for this occasion, his cravat was a little askew, and Prudence reached to straighten it. His eyes, nearly always filled with gentle humor, laughed at her concern for his appearance.

"Don't let Gay take up all of your dances! I'm a fish out of water at doings like this, and I won't have any notion of what to say to all those other fluttering young females. I'd appreciate a few moments, now and then, of intelligent conversation, when I won't have to watch my tongue every minute for fear of saying the wrong thing."

"Cutting up cadavers and studying the effects of different physics isn't exactly a course in how to please young ladies." Prue's smile was almost a grin. In an abrupt deviation from custom, Burke had decided against a conventional education, which would have prepared him for nothing except to be charming and witty, and had enrolled in the College of Medicine at Baltimore. Simply attaching himself to an established physician, as many young men did, to learn by observation was not enough for Burke. The county had been flabbergasted at his decision. As Evan Amhurst's only son, his duty was clear. For a second or third son, a career in medicine or the law would have been acceptable, but for Burke to turn his back on the plantation in favor of tending ills and broken bones was more than anyone could fathom. It almost made him a traitor to his class.

But Prue was glad that Burke was looked on

askance. It had kept other girls from cornering him and extracting a proposal from him. From the first moment she had seen him, after her return to Rose-lawns, Prudence had known that Burke was hers. Her memory had not played her false. Burke was just as she had remembered him. He had to be hers, he could never belong to anyone else.

Because of Burke's studies in Baltimore, Prudence saw little of him, not nearly enough to satisfy her, but when he was at home they managed to spend every possible moment together. Not that Burke showed any inclination toward romance. Rather, he had pounced on Prudence as being the only sensible person, outside of his parents, with whom he could hold a serious conversation. And for now, that was enough for Prudence.

Often, they would relax under a tree after a hard gallop on their horses. Burke would chew on a blade of grass, a smile on his lean face. Prue would encourage him to talk.

"Glory, Prue, if I mentioned the way Doctor John bungled Dorothy Meyer's confinement to any other young lady, she'd slap my face first and then swoon! It was all I could do not to lay hands on the man. He was as good as could be had in his day, but he never had any formal training and he's too old to go on practicing. He's doddering, and still everyone in the county swears by him."

Prudence had thrown back her head and laughed. "As I understand it, my mother swore at him, not by him, when Rory was born! And she made her Cleo lock him out of the room. She told Grandmother Yolande and Cleo what to do, and Rory was born perfectly all right, but they'd both have died if Doctor John had had his way! I remember Aunt Emily saying that she was glad she'd raised Mother to cope with

213

things that had to be coped with. I guess Mama gave Grandfather and Grandmother fits, all the while she lived here."

Burke's laughter had matched her own. "So my mother tells me. You're like Miss Martha, Prudence, and I'm glad. I don't think I could stand it if you were like the other girls around here." He tossed away the blade of grass and picked a fresh one.

Prudence and Burke's conversations took many forms. They discussed the deeper implications of slavery, the opening up of the country as it pushed westward, year by year, as the railroads opened the way to vast uninhabited tracts. They spoke of commerce, of the importance of foreign trade and the inequities of the tariff, which resulted in the South being paid less for their raw cotton and having to pay more for everything they had to import in order to exist.

They discussed philosophy, religion, the classics, and mundane things such as the preservation of the soil by the careful rotation of crops, by letting fields lie fallow for a year, by spreading manure.

"Manure!" Rory had exclaimed, when he'd come upon them discussing the subject. "Whoever heard of a young lady speaking of the spreading of manure? It's that Aunt Emily, she's the one to blame! You'll just have to excuse my sister, Burke, she doesn't know any better."

"I think I'd give a year of my life to know Miss Emily," Burke had replied. "If Prue is an example of her as her pupil, it would be a privilege to meet the teacher!"

Rory's face had turned dark. "I hope I never have to see her again, as long as I live. I had all I wanted of Aunt Emily when I was a boy."

"You were a spoiled brat," Prudence had informed

214

him. "Sulky, sullen, and always thinking you were better than other people. She only tried to instill some common sense and decency in you."

Now, as she stood facing Burke in the Renault home, Prudence's heart felt as though it were beating audibly in her breast. She hadn't allowed herself to hope too hard, but he was here, and she felt alive, vibrant, her very blood singing in her veins.

"I've promised Gay the first dance. I could hardly refuse, as it's his birthday. But after that, you may have as many as you want. I'm just so glad you've come, Burke! I've missed you."

"We must go in and freshen up." Yolande was still at Prudence's side, impatient to get her away from Burke, who was acceptable but not nearly as desirable a young man as Gaylord Amhurst.

Burke released Prue's hand, which he had taken as soon as she had finished straightening his cravat. "Hurry back, Prue!"

"Prue indeed!" Yolande was visibly displeased. "You're a young lady now, and you'd think that with Burke's upbringing he'd at least know enough to call you Miss Prudence!"

"That," Prudence said, with that simple calmness that Yolande often found maddening, "would be silly."

21

Over and above the fact that he had a tremendous admiration for Gaylord Renault, Rory liked attending any affair at Swanmere because Swanmere boasted a bachelor cottage. Rory had tried, these last several months, to persuade Jacob to build one for himself and his friends, but Jacob had turned a deaf ear.

It was downright unfair, Rory thought with resentment. He was a grown man, and a bachelor cottage was the epitome of worldliness. He needed a place where he and his friends could entertain without supervision, as befitted the scion of a wealthy planter. But Jacob showed no sign of relenting. There were, Jacob said, quite enough light-colored slaves in the community without Rory and his profligate friends siring more.

The ball had gone on until four in the morning, although some of the guests who lived near enough to return home that night had left earlier. Now, a little after four-thirty, Gay and Rory and half a dozen other young men had repaired to the bachelor cottage, which was situated far enough from the main house so that they could go on carousing for as long as they wanted to without danger of disturbing the family or the other guests who wanted to sleep.

Gay was drunk, but not as drunk as Rory. It made Rory angry that he felt so giddy. He had few opportunities to spend the night with Gay, and he wanted to make the most of it, but his eyes wouldn't cooperate. They showed a remarkable tendency to go out of focus, and once in a while they closed altogether, in spite of his efforts to keep them open.

Absalom, Gay's valet, moved about quietly, replenishing glasses, holding matches to cheroots, offering sandwiches and fruit to anyone still hungry after the collation of baked ham, roast pork, fried chicken, salads, breads, cakes, cheeses, and ices that should have sated the most rapacious appetites. Damn if this wasn't the way to live, Rory thought, blinking and swaying a little on his feet. He wanted to sit down, because the walls kept moving closer and then receding, the floor undulating under his feet, but he was afraid that if he sat down he'd fall asleep and miss the rest of the fun, the best part of this whole damned wonderful evening.

Gay was in a bad mood. He'd been in a bad mood for hours, because as impossible as it seemed, Prudence had spent the entire evening avoiding him. Stuck-up little chit, with those eyes that looked right into your brain and found it wanting. Who did she think she was to treat Gaylord Renault, the most eligible bachelor in the county, as if he were nothing? She was nothing herself but a cold little Massachusetts bluestocking, that's what she was! It wasn't even as if she were all that pretty.

What the devil did Prue see in Burke Amhurst, anyway? Why, his folks weren't even rich, not in the accepted terms of the South, because Evan Amhurst pampered his people disgustingly. The Amhurst slave families had much larger parcels of ground to raise vegetables for themselves than other planters allowed.

Amhurst gave them young livestock to raise for meat and provided them with luxuries like sugar and flour, even spent a ridiculous amount on their clothing to make sure that they were warm in the winter. Evan Amhurst was crazy, the way he pampered his people, and he'd raised Burke to be just as bad.

A bone-setter, a dispenser of physics! And there was Prudence, hanging on his every word, egging him on, her eyes shining, her mouth smiling, as if Burke were next to God instead of the crazy son of a crazy planter. Burke wasn't even good-looking, much less as affluent or as charming as Gay.

If Crissy were a year or two older, Gaylord thought, he'd show Prue! That Crissy was going to be the beauty to end all beauties, when she developed a little more. It was too bad, but she was too young, even by Southern standards, where a single girl of sixteen was on her way to being an old maid.

The room was filled with smoke from the cheroots his friends were smoking, the best Havana tobacco, supplied for the occasion by his father. The discussion of wenches was in full spate, and Absalom paid strict attention, because he'd be the one sent to fetch them. Absalom's face was impassive, betraying no emotion, even though he felt, privately, that when they'd been drinking, the young masters behaved no better than pigs. Rutting pigs, mindless of anything except satiating their lust.

Not that the wenches would mind, most of them. Chloe, for one, sassy as a jaybird, always rolling her eyes and her hips at the gentlemen, and Pearl, as plump as a partridge and big in front, who giggled. Petulia, who was pretty near half white, held herself above the others. Raylene would enjoy their attentions, and Jeannette, who had French blood and who wasn't exactly pretty, knew tricks to set a man's blood

218

on fire. She should be in one of those fancy houses, Jeannette should. Absalom ticked them off in his mind. Like as not they'd be waiting, ready and eager.

"I'll take Raylene, if nobody else wants her," a stock, sandy-lashed youth said. "How about you, Rory?"

"Don't know. Haven't decided yet." Rory's voice was thick.

"Pearl's sassy and plump, and always willin'."

"That one? Oh, that one! No, I don't guess so."

"Give him Jeannette. He's the youngest, he ain't hardly broke in yet, Jeannette'll give him a workout that'll educate him! I'd take her myself, only Rory needs her more, he's still ignorant."

"Ignorant be damned! I'll show you who's ignorant! Bring her in, I'm ready for her, we'll see who teaches who a thing or two!"

"Whom." Gaylord's voice was languid, a sure sign that he was out of sorts. "I see Harvard hasn't done you a mite of good, Rory. You still can't speak correct English."

"*Who, whom*, bring 'em both!" Rory muttered. There was still a little brandy in his glass and he finished it, shuddering a bit. That one's going to be sick before this night's over, Absalom thought, and I'll have to clean up after him. He hasn't got the head for it—Mister Jacob and Mister Jonathan keep him on a pretty tight rein, and it's too bad Mister John doesn't do the same with Mister Gay.

Now they'd all chosen except Gay himself, and Absalom looked at his master questioningly. "Ruby for me, then, if Rory has to have Jeannette."

"Ruby's young." Absalom spoke softly. He might get a fist in his face for his pains, but Ruby was too young. Mister John wouldn't like it if Gay hurt her and Miss Bella found out about it.

"I said Ruby." Gay's face was suddenly ugly. "Get a move on, you lazy black bastard, or do I have to help you on your way with a foot in the seat of your pants?"

Absalom left, silently, shaking his head when he was outside and out of Gaylord's eyesight. But he didn't like it. Ruby wasn't old enough or big enough; there'd be trouble. He considered going to Mister John, and decided against it. Mister John and Miss Bella would be asleep, and it wasn't Absalom's place to go carrying tales to their bedroom in the middle of the night. White folks' business was none of his business; he was there to do what he was told.

Ruby's ma woke up when Absalom went to their cabin to fetch her, and she made a fuss, while Ruby's eyes grew big with terror. Ruby's father, Pete, clenched his hands into fists and shook his head numbly, filled with misery. "Ain't he drunk enough he wouldn't know the difference if you took somebody else?"

Absalom wanted to hit out at something. "No, he ain't. I'm sorry, Pete, but you know Mister Gay."

Absalom herded the girls in front of him through the quiet quarters. He wished that Burke Amhurst had stayed. Mister Burke would have put a stop to Mister Gay's taking Ruby, but he had ridden off two hours ago, hell-bent to get back to town and check up on some cracker he'd patched up. And Miss Prudence, she'd said she was tired, and gone on up to bed, although Miss Yolande had given her a look fit to kill. That's what made Mister Gay really hot under the collar, and he still was.

"Cut out that snivelin'!" Petulia told Ruby. "You'll like it, after the first time or two. It ain't so bad. And maybe you'll get a present. The rest of us will. We most always gits presents, money, and we gits to keep it to buy ourselves somethin' pretty. Ain't nothin' to

220

bawl about, it's bound to happen sooner er later, anyways."

Ruby hung back, her face puckered up. "I don't want to!" Absalom had to grasp her arm and pull her along.

Jeannette was pleased when she found that she'd drawn Rory Beddoes. Next to Mister Gay, Rory was the best looking, and Jeannette liked them young. If she were in one of those fancy houses, she'd try to pick them young every time. Being in a fancy house, getting paid for what she liked to do better than anything else, having beautiful clothes, being able to lord it over common plantation slaves, was Jeannette's favorite dream.

Filled with liquor, their minds dulled by the alcohol and the cigar fumes, the young men were ready to start on this last phase of the evening's entertainment. Rory, a foolish grin on his face, led Jeannette to the bedroom that had been assigned to him. He located the bed on its third trip around the room and plunged for it and fell across it, half on top of and half off Jeannette.

Jeannette wriggled out from under him, got out of her clothes, and lying down beside him again, took his hand and laid it on her breasts. A stentorian snore was the only response she awakened. Furious, she leaned up on one elbow and looked at him. She patted at his face, nibbled at his shoulder, undulated against him, but he slept on. It wasn't any use. He wasn't any good to himself and a lot less use to her.

Shrugging, Jeannette put her head on the pillow and closed her eyes. She'd have liked having him, but likely he wouldn't remember, come morning, that he hadn't taken her, and he'd reward her anyway. In the meantime, she'd enjoy sleeping in this good bed, instead of on her cornhusk mattress.

In his own room in the bachelor cottage, Gaylord looked at Ruby with disgust. He should have paid heed to Absalom. The girl just huddled there on the bed, clutching the dress he'd ripped off her to her underdeveloped breasts, shaking and bawling. Now that she was naked, he could see that there wasn't anything there to interest him. The sight and sound of her sniveling enraged him, and he cursed her. But she had to learn that she had to do as her master wished, and he had nothing better to do than to teach her.

He fell on top of her, forcing her legs apart with his knees. He thrust against her, but she was too small and tight, he couldn't get it in. Ruby screamed, clawing at him, her eyes rolling wild as a terrified animal's. Gaylord tried again, and as the pain of his attempted entry tore at her, Ruby's entire body began to shudder and she looked as if she were going into a convulsion.

"Damn it, get the hell out of here, you worthless slut!" Gaylord grabbed her shoulder and pushed her off the bed. She landed on her face, and her nose spouted blood. Wailing, she scrambled to her hands and knees and scuttled around the room, still wailing.

Absalom, in the sitting room, risked a look through the bedroom door. "Get her out of here!" Gaylord shouted. Absalom retrieved the torn dress and pulled it over her head. "Scoot!" he told her, patting her skinny bottom as he pushed her through the outer door.

Gay lay on the bed, his hands behind his head, scowling. Ruby! Who wanted Ruby? It wasn't Ruby he wanted, it was a slim girl with white skin, with satin-smooth brown hair and eyes that burned from hazel to green when she laughed, a face that lighted up into incandescent beauty when she smiled, even though it seemed plain when it was in repose.

He pulled the pillow out from under his head and thumped it. No use thinking about Prue. Even if he asked Jonathan tomorrow for permission to address her, it would be at least six months before he had her in his bed, where he could teach her what it meant to be loved by Gaylord Renault.

In spite of all the alcohol he had consumed, the fiasco with Ruby had left him unsatisfied, inflamed. Damn it, he needed a woman! And there wasn't a wench on the place he'd be satisfied with.

Absalom was nodding in a straight-backed chair when Gaylord shook him awake. "Get up off of there, you lazy black bastard! You know where that wench of the Beddoes' is beddin' down?"

Coldness spread through Absalom's body. "You mean that little girl of Miss Prue's? You mean Naomi?"

"Yes, I mean that one! Who the hell did you think I meant? Go fetch her!"

Dread turned Absalom's bones to water. "I can't do that. Mister Gay, you're drunk! You don't know what you're saying. She ain't ours, she belongs to Mister Jacob! We can't fetch her here!"

"I didn't ask your opinion, I gave you an order! Who gave you leave to think?"

"But Mister Gay, she's only a child! She ain't but fourteen! And she's most white, she's Mister Jonathan's own—"

Gaylord struck him, hard, across the face. His drink-fogged mind was no longer capable of reason. "Get her."

"There'll be trouble. . . ."

"Get her."

There wasn't any way he could get past Mister Gay

to get to Mister Rory. Moaning a little, Absalom went to do his master's bidding. Lord, Lord, he wished he were Evan Amhurst's slave. Things like this didn't go on at Amhurst Hall. He'd rather work in the fields, every day of his life, than belong to Gaylord Renault.

He had to stop for a moment, to be sick. He almost wished he were dead. But he'd be better off dead if he didn't do what Mister Gay had told him.

Yolande and Prudence hadn't wanted Naomi to accompany the girls to the Renaults', but Crissy had raised a fuss and Jacob had taken her part, as he always did. Even so, Yolande would have forbidden it if Naomi herself hadn't been so eager to go.

Naomi worshipped Prudence because her older half-sister was so unfailingly kind and gentle with her, but Crissy held a special place in Naomi's life simply because she was so beautiful. No one could do Crissy's hair to suit her except Naomi, who had a natural talent for coaxing the long, flaxen curls into picture-perfect order.

Just to see Swanmere, to get a glimpse of all the quality in their lovely party clothes, to be given a share of the delectable food—and Prudence would see that she received some of the choicest—had set Naomi's blood racing with excitement. She had spent days helping Crissy get ready for this event, and to have to stay at home and not get to see any of it with her own eyes was more than she could bear. In all her life, she had never been away from Roselawns, and she wanted to go so badly that it was a physical ache.

Naomi's pleading eyes, with their heartrending appeal, had made Yolande capitulate. As desirable as it was not to flaunt Jonathan's slave child in public, Yolande hadn't been able to resist that mute appeal. Bella Renault was a sensible and discreet woman. She would understand the situation at a glance and arrange for Naomi to be bedded somewhere in the house, away from the other servants and away from the knowing glances of her guests. So, Yolande gave her permission.

It had been every bit as wonderful as Naomi had known it would be. Under her ministrations, Crissy had looked like an angel when she descended the grand staircase. From a vantage point behind the balustrades of the shining mahogany stairway, Naomi had watched Crissy's grand entrance to the ball with shining eyes. The other guests looked like people who had stepped out of a fairytale, but Crissy outshone them all.

Miss Bella herself had sent a plate heaped with delicacies to the sewing room, where a pallet had been improvised for Naomi's sleeping accommodations. Naomi had feasted and crept out to watch again, her eyes ever seeking her own two young ladies, happy because Prudence was so happy dancing with Burke Amhurst. Tonight, at least, Naomi thought, Prudence was fully as beautiful as her sister.

Naomi was sleeping dreamlessly when Absalom entered the sewing room. He touched her shoulder softly, afraid of startling her into crying out.

"Don't make a fuss, Naomi. Mister Rory wants you. He says come now, it's important." The lie had come into Absalom's head at the last moment, as a way to persuade the girl to come with him without question.

Sleep left Naomi slowly, so that she fumbled in pulling her dress over her head. "Oh, dear, he must be sick! Miss Prue said he'd been drinking too much! But shouldn't you fetch Mister Jonathan instead of me?"

"He said to fetch you. Come along, and be quiet. We don't want to go rousing the house."

Still groggy with sleep, Naomi followed him, wondering why it was she that Mister Rory wanted.

The sleep dissolved into a nightmare as she stepped through the door of the bachelor cottage and a hand clapped across her mouth.

"Come into my parlor, said the spider to the fly! And here you are, sleek and plump for the eating!" Gaylord's voice was thick, thicker than it had been only a few moments ago when he had ordered Absalom to fetch her. The quantity of spirits he had drunk during the night had caught up with him. It was a shame that they hadn't put him out like Mister Rory, Absalom thought, as Gay jerked his head toward the door.

"Get out, but stay close. I'll need you to take her back when I'm done with her."

Absalom closed the door behind him, his face gray in the pre-dawn blackness.

The pain was like nothing Naomi had ever known before. She couldn't scream, because Gaylord had stuffed a handkerchief into her mouth. As he pawed at her body, mouthing her breasts, his fingers wrenching and twisting at her flesh, she prayed that she would die before such shame and pain could go on.

But it went on, for an eternity. Her body went rigid with shock as Gay pushed into her. She felt as if her insides were being torn to pieces. She felt blood spurt between her thighs. She beat her hands against the bed, against Gaylord's back, but he was oblivious to her frantic writhings and poundings. He thrust and thrust again, savoring her smallness, savoring the fact that she was Prudence's half-sister, that he was taking his revenge on Prudence by violating this child who was almost white, who was lovely to look at, who was innocence personified.

Only half-conscious, driven, at last, into darkness by the pain, Naomi barely heard Gay's vicious voice as he shook her. He was still on top of her, still inside her, but he had gone limp, now, he no longer thrust into her, making her pray for death.

"You know what'll happen if you tell? You'll be sold away, that's what'll happen! I'm going to marry Miss Prudence, and the Beddoes family aren't going to let any scandal spoil things for her, do you understand that? They'll sell you and you'll end up in the fields more likely in a place where this will happen to you every night, only worse. You don't know how much worse, because it won't be just one man, it'll be half a dozen, taking their turns. . . ."

Naomi's throat was so swollen from the screams that she hadn't been able to answer him. Gaylord shook her again, more viciously than before. "You understand?"

Naomi nodded, her face soaked with tears.

"They'll give you to a nigger, a big buck nigger, and what he'll do to you will make this seem like heaven. Miss Prue will hate you. Miss Crissy will hate you. . . ."

Absalom had to support her more than halfway to the house. When they entered, he had to carry her up the stairs. His own face was wet with tears.

"Poor little child," he murmured. "Poor little nobody's child!"

He hoped to live to see the day when Mister Gaylord would get what was coming to him, but he had no real belief that it would happen. White folks didn't get punished for their sins. It was the way it always had been, and the way it would be until the end of time.

22

Joshua cracked his whip, and the perfectly matched team of bays moved out, their necks arched, their sleek hides glistening in the morning sun. Jacob moved to stretch out his game leg to ease it, and Jonathan passed them on his horse, making the hunter curvet, waving his crop in salute.

Prudence was worrying about Naomi. Her half-sister had left an hour earlier, in the baggage cart, and Prudence was certain that the younger girl was not feeling well. As soon as she got home, she'd check up on her and see if she were really ill, or just over-tired from all the excitement. There had certainly been dark circles under her eyes this morning, and Crissy, in a mean mood because she'd sneaked a great many too many sips of wine last night and was suffering from what Prudence suspected was a hangover, had slapped her for being clumsy with her hair.

Sometimes Prue thought that her mother and Aunt Emily had not had any influence on Crissy at all. It was certain that Crissy had not inherited any of their Curtis traits.

"Well, Prue?" It was Jacob speaking, his voice jerking Prudence back from her thoughts.

"Yes, Grandfather?"

"It looks like we've made a match. Gaylord spoke to your father this morning, and he'll come callin' on you any evening now. How does it feel to be a young lady on the threshold of marriage?"

"But I'm not on the threshold of marriage. I have no intention of marrying anybody for a good many years." Prue spoke pleasantly, as if they were discussing the weather, and Crissy marveled at her older sister. Why, she was as crazy as Mama had been! Not grab at the chance to marry Gaylord Renault? She had to be crazy! Crissy gritted her teeth against the nausea that the motion of the carriage aggravated, cursing the fate that had made her the younger.

"You aren't serious, girl. You're of marriageable age, of course you'll marry, and right soon." Jacob was not pleased. "Gaylord's a good match, we couldn't have done better if we'd looked all over the South. You ought to be dancin' with joy."

"I am serious. I have no desire to marry at present, and I have no intention of marrying Gaylord at any time in the future. He will just have to look elsewhere for a bride."

"It's that Burke Amhurst!" Yolande said, her exasperation sounding in her voice. "I couldn't believe that you'd be so rude last night, to leave the dancing as soon as Burke left! I was so humiliated I nearly cried. I declare, Prudence, I don't see what you see in that young man! What has he to offer you, in comparison with Gaylord?"

"A very great deal, only he hasn't asked me." Prue laughed, she actually laughed! "He can't yet, with all that schooling still ahead of him, and then a practice to establish. It won't be easy for him to wean the people around here away from old Doctor John. But it's of no matter. Folks will soon see that Burke's a much better doctor, and I can wait."

229

"You just see here, young lady!" Jacob exploded, his face a dangerous red. "You can't high-handedly turn down Gaylord Renault! You want the whole county to think something ails you?"

"I'll be sorry if they think that, but it won't greatly affect my life. Besides, all the mamas will give sighs of relief because it'll mean that their daughters are still in the running, so I don't really anticipate any trouble over it, Grandfather."

"You got to be sensible!" Jacob spluttered. "You can't just throw away a chance like this! We'll see what your father has to say about it, once we get home!"

"Yes, we will, won't we?" Prudence was not at all perturbed. She knew that Jonathan would never urge her to marry against her will. She leaned out of the barouche and pointed to the fields. "Look there! See how that yearling prances in the grass! Isn't he altogether beautiful?"

"Don't change the subject. You're a willful girl, Prudence."

Prudence turned her head to look at him, her glance level and unafraid. "Like my mother?"

"We'll just stop this discussion here and now!" Yolande said firmly. "I will not have a quarrel in this carriage!"

"I'm not quarreling, Grandmother. Your husband is." Prudence folded her gloved hands in her lap. Once she was married to Burke, she wouldn't wear gloves every time she stepped out of the house. She'd get her hands in the dirt again, because Burke wouldn't care how brown or calloused they got. Her fingers ached to feel good soil crumbling between them as she tended flowers and vegetables. Life on a plantation was much like being a wax doll. She remembered how Bossie's flank had felt against her cheek when she

230

milked her, and she could almost hear the tinkle of the milk as it swished into the bucket. She missed Miss Emily and Cleo so much it hurt.

"Watch your hat!" Yolande told her. "It's about to blow off. Tie the ribbon more securely, Prudence. Don't you ever give a thought to your complexion?"

Prue's face took on a look of pain. "All right, but only because it might frighten the horses if it blew in front of them." Crissy smothered a gasp. The implication was clear that complexions were not important and that Prudence found her grandmother frivolous.

Yolande didn't answer. Prudence was too old to take a switch to, even if she was her granddaughter. And besides, she had an uncomfortable feeling that most of the time the girl was right.

Jacob was not as forbearing. "Prudence, I will not tolerate such sassiness toward your grandmother!"

Yolande's voice was calm, almost sweet. "Mr. Beddoes, please be quiet."

Women! Unpredictable, the whole lot of them! Jacob wished to hell he was home; he could use a drink. At least they had Crissy. A proper young miss, Christine. He'd never have any trouble with her. When her turn came, she'd know enough to be grateful for a good match. All the same, coping with females was a thirsty business, and it hadn't changed over the years and probably it never would.

Several times Gaylord Renault happened to call at Roselawns at the same time as Burke, but Burke didn't even seem to be aware that Gay was there as a rival suitor. Even Gaylord's annoyance at finding him there escaped Burke's notice. It wasn't that he was obtuse, he simply had other things on his mind.

Roselawns was something like an armed camp during that period. Jonathan, just as Prudence had thought, refused to push her into a marriage she didn't want. Jacob, on the other hand, lost no opportunity to make caustic remarks about girls who didn't know what was good for them and were too Northern-uppity to listen to their elders.

Yolande, surprisingly, remained neutral. It would be a wonderful match, the prestige of the Beddoes family would soar if Prudence finally tired of waiting for Burke and accepted Gaylord, but Yolande had seen too many marriages of convenience. The unhappiness of the women who were tied to men they didn't love was sad indeed. Her own marriage to Jacob had been a love match, and Jonathan and Martha had had several years of almost unbelievable happiness, even though it turned out tragically in the end. If Jonathan had married Amelia, Yolande's grandchildren would have been placid and exasperatingly dull, rather than the beautiful, lively young people of whom she was so proud.

"Miss Prue, I don't understand you! It just isn't natural for a girl to say she isn't interested in marriage! My sister's your age, and she was married over a year ago!"

"I could hardly forget it, Gay. I was one of her bridesmaids."

The casual use of his first name was another annoyance to Gay, but one that intrigued him. Prudence had none of the artifice of current manners, and he found her directness refreshing after the cloying sweetness of other eligible girls.

"You're enough to drive a man mad!" he accused her. "Don't tease me, Miss Prue. If you're waiting around for Burke to ask you, you're wasting your time. He's a born bachelor, and that's a mercy because any girl who married him would lead a miserable life. He wouldn't have any time for her, he'd always

232

be too busy taking care of crackers and peckerwoods who couldn't even pay him!"

"Don't you think that that depends on the girl?" Prue looked at him so levelly that he flushed.

Yolande, who had been sitting in the rose arbor, close enough to keep a proper eye on the young people but far away enough not to eavesdrop, came into the house. A moment later, Naomi appeared carrying a silver tray with cool drinks and a plate of cakes. From her vantage point, Yolande had seen that Gaylord's session with Prudence was not going well, and she deemed an interruption advisable. She had no wish to make an enemy of Bella Renault because her granddaughter refused Bella's son.

"Come along, you two, sit here in the shade," Yolande invited, as she followed Naomi. She herself sat down and moved over on the bench so that her crinolines would make room for Prudence. "Mr. Renault, is your mother quite recovered from the ball?"

"She's fine, Miss Yolande, never better." Still flushed, Gaylord accepted a cake and looked a little balefully at the glass pitcher, which contained nothing stronger than lemonade.

Naomi's hand shook as she poured, and as she handed Gaylord his glass, his hand brushed hers accidentally and she started, the glass dropping from her fingers.

"What on earth ails you, child?" Yolande got to her feet and wiped at Gaylord's riding coat with her napkin. "I do declare you aren't well! Now just look, there's broken glass all over. Do pick up the pieces, and fetch another glass, there's a good girl."

Her face pale, Naomi knelt, but her hands were still shaking so badly that she cut herself. With an exclamation, Prue took her own napkin and wrapped it around the spurting gash.

233

"I'll send Benjamin with another glass, grandmother. I want to get this washed and bandaged." She put her arm around Naomi and led her into the house. Under Naomi's thin dress she felt the younger girl's heart beating like a wild bird against the bars of a cage. "Naomi, you are ill! You should have told us, and stayed in bed!"

"I'm not, Miss Prudence. I . . . just happened to drop the glass, that's all. I'm sorry."

"Well, I'm sorry you cut yourself! I wish Burke were here, it's bleeding hard, but I think I can stop it. Naomi, you're shaking like a leaf! Has Crissy been sharp with you again? I'll speak to her."

"Please, Miss Prue, it isn't Miss Crissy. It isn't anything." Naomi shook her head and her eyes clouded over. "I was just dizzy for a moment. It must be the heat."

Prue looked at Naomi, puzzled. It wasn't that hot, and the heat, even in midsummer, had never seemed to bother Naomi before. Then her face relaxed. Naomi was just at the age when her recently started monthly periods must be painful. Goodness knows Crissy made fuss enough, staying in bed all day, complaining that she was going to die, while Yolande spooned ginger tea into her and babied her. Prudence had never paid much attention to her own periods except to consider them a dratted annoyance, but that didn't mean that Crissy and Naomi might not really suffer. She'd ask Burke about it, the next time she saw him. Or would she? Even Burke might be a little taken back by such a question from a young unmarried girl. The idea made her smile. Men! Sometimes she wondered if even doctors knew all the facts of life.

"Go and lie down for a while," she told Naomi, after she had stanched the bleeding on her hand and

234

applied a bandage. "Would you like me to make you some ginger tea?"

Naomi shook her head, and Prudence saw fine beads of perspiration on the younger girl's upper lip. She firmed her chin and made up her mind that she would ask Burke about it, anyway. With all these new things he was learning, he might know something that would make it easier for Naomi, and Crissy, too.

But she had no opportunity to ask Burke. Rory came home later that afternoon with news that hurt.

"That Burke does beat all! He went rushing back to Baltimore just because he got a letter from one of his instructors that some European doctor is there, some bigwig from Germany. Went galloping off like the world'd come to an end if he didn't get to talk to him."

Prue waited to see if Burke had sent her any message through Rory, but Rory said nothing more. Instead, he went stamping out to find Jonathan and Jacob in the office, in search of a before-supper drink. Prudence pushed down her disappointment. Of course Burke had been excited, and gone rushing off! He'd write to her and tell her all about it.

All the same, the disappointment was there. She'd been sure, a couple of times last week, that Burke was going to declare himself and ask her to wait for him.

And that was nonsense, too, she told herself impatiently. He doesn't have to ask me to wait, he knows I will. There was that between them that made putting perfectly obvious things into words unnecessary.

She picked up a piece of needlework, not the company kind, embroidery or needlepoint, but a prosaic petticoat with the hem coming out. How she wished that she could study nursing, so that she could work beside Burke and be a help to him when the time came!

But that was idle dreaming. Jacob, and even Jonathan, thought that while what Miss Nightingale had accomplished was remarkable, for a woman, no gently bred female should soil her hands doing professional nursing. Here in the United States, only the coarsest women, the dregs of society, lent themselves to such things. That stupid male thinking again! It was all right for a lady to nurse sick or injured slaves, but to actually study the subject, to enter into it as a career, would be unthinkable.

I'll make Burke teach me everything he can, anyway, Prue thought, jabbing at the petticoat viciously. I can help him with the women patients, at least. He'll be glad of my help, and nobody will be able to stop me.

Her short-lived bad temper gone, she settled to making tiny stitches. If a thing was worth doing at all, it was worth doing right, and this was one hem that wouldn't come out again. She smiled, thinking of Aunt Emily and the patient hours she had spent teaching her to do things right. Aunt Emily, at least, would be proud of her when she took her place beside Burke.

23

Naomi's usually quick, deft movements as she helped Crissy with her morning toilette were unaccountably slow on the first morning of October. Prudence, who merely plaited her own hair and wound it around her head, never needed Naomi's help, but Crissy wouldn't dream of appearing at breakfast without every curl arranged to shining perfection. It pleased Jacob to see her looking always at her best, and pleasing Jacob was very much to Crissy's advantage.

"What ails you, Naomi?" Crissy spoke impatiently. Prudence had already gone down, so Crissy could be a little sharp if she felt like it. "You're slower than molasses in January!"

"I'm sorry, Miss Crissy." Naomi tried to work a little faster, but her hands were shaking. Suddenly, her face turned green and the brush dropped from her fingers. Clasping her hand over her mouth, Naomi hurried to the slop bucket, and was thoroughly and revoltingly sick.

"Oh, my land! You've come down with something, and now I'll get it!" Crissy wailed. "Stay away from me! Who knows what you've got?" Forgetting about her unfinished hair, Crissy rushed from the bedroom

237

and downstairs, to burst in on the rest of the family already seated around the table.

"Naomi's sick, she looks fit to die! And if I get it, I won't be able to go to Ruth Ann's party, and I just won't be able to bear it!"

Yolande started to rise, but Prudence was already on her feet. "It's all right, Grandmother. I'll go up and see to her. You finish your breakfast."

"I hope she hasn't fever!" Yolande looked worried. "We've been so fortunate this summer, hardly a case among our people. Now, now, Crissy, don't take on so! Likely it's only something she ate."

"If she's really ill, we'll send for Doctor John," Jonathan assured his pouting daughter. His face was expressionless, but his anxiety was real, for all that. Legitimate or not, Naomi was his daughter, as much as Crissy or Prue, and he was concerned about her. In fact, the conventions that made him feign indifference galled him. "He'll fix her up, so you can set your mind at rest."

"Well, he'd better!" Crissy sat down and began to eat with a hearty appetite. She liked grits and gravy, ham and eggs, and it was hard for her to eat lightly so that she wouldn't spoil her figure, which was beginning to blossom out at last. She'd almost given up in despair, before her breasts and hips began to change. If Prue was imbecile enough to turn Gaylord Renault down, in no time at all now Crissy would be very much in the running.

Prudence found Naomi in her little room off the sewing room, curled up on her narrow bed with her face pressed into the pillow. When Prue spoke to her, Naomi lifted her head, and she saw that a thin line of perspiration glistened on the girl's forehead. Naomi's face was pale, and there were shadows under her eyes.

"I'm sorry you don't feel well." Prue put her hand

on Naomi's forehead and frowned, puzzled. There didn't seem to be any fever. "Do you hurt anywhere, or are you just sick to your stomach?"

"I'm just sick to my stomach." Naomi's voice was low, hardly more than a whisper, but Prue's eyes, trained to observe symptoms among the blacks, saw an unmistakable flicker of fear on her face.

"Naomi, tell me what it is. You haven't been yourself for the past few weeks. You haven't been taking some concoction that Old Hannah brewed up, have you?" Old Hannah's remedies were the bane of Prue's and Yolande's existence, because while most of them were harmless and some even did some good, others did more harm than good. "Honey, she's so old she probably doesn't even know what she puts into her potions any more; it'd be downright dangerous to take anything she mixed up!"

"I haven't taken anything. I wouldn't be that foolish!" Naomi denied. "I haven't even seen Hannah."

Prue's fingers sought Naomi's pulse, a skill she had learned from Miss Emily. The pulse was racing, and Prue frowned again. She'd swear that it was fear that made it race, and not illness, because outside of the nausea there were no other symptoms.

Prue studied the girl on the bed and noted how she had filled out this last summer, so that her young breasts strained at her bodice. Naomi needed some new dresses; she'd outgrown the ones she had; Prue would speak to Miss Yolande about it.

A cold little suspicion nibbled at the edges of Prue's mind, and she tried to thrust it aside. It was ridiculous, impossible. Naomi wouldn't, and even if she would, who? There was no young man at Roselawns who could possibly have caught her fancy. Besides, Naomi wasn't a slave wench; none of the young bucks would have dared.

But this wasn't the first time that Prue had noticed that Naomi hadn't been well in the mornings, and there was her recent habit of dropping small articles, and her absentmindnesses, her withdrawal. Naomi had been keeping out of sight whenever it was possible.

Prue spoke almost doubtfully. "Naomi, have you been seeing some young man?" Oh, God, don't let it be that! It would kill Jonathan, if Naomi were pregnant, and Yolande would never be able to bear it. As for Jacob, she didn't dare even contemplate his reaction. There were few light-colored Negroes at Roselawns because Jacob wouldn't stand for that sort of thing.

Naomi's face grew a shade whiter, and now the fear in her eyes couldn't be denied. "No, Miss Prue! You know I haven't!"

"But this sickness every morning . . ."

Naomi pressed her face back into the pillow and her shoulders shook as sobs racked her. Oh, God, Prudence thought, as she went back downstairs. God have mercy on all of us! Who? Who?

Yolande looked up as Prudence appeared in the doorway of the dining room, beckoning to her. "Yes, Prue? Is it anything serious, do you think?"

"I'm not sure. I'd like you to come and see her for yourself after all, Grandmother."

"Bother!" Crissy threw her napkin down, her face petulant. "I wanted to take her with me to Ruth Ann's, to help me dress and do my hair! Why'd she have to go and get sick now, of all times!"

"Christine, stop that this minute!" Jonathan's eyes rested on her with cold disapproval. "If Naomi is ill, you should feel sorry for her and not go on wailing because of your hair!" Crissy stared at him with open-mouthed amazement. All this fuss just because Naomi was sick to her stomach! Then understanding filtered

240

across her face, and she bit her lip. Of course, Naomi was really Papa's daughter. Sometimes Crissy forgot, but it explained why Papa was so concerned.

"Let me know how she is," Jonathan said. "I'll be in Jacob's office." He left the table without finishing his breakfast, a grim look on his face.

When her father's back was turned, Crissy scowled. All the same, even if Naomi was sort of special, it wasn't fair! She needed her. Naomi could have picked some other time to get sick!

Rory's face was white and defiant as he faced his family. Crissy had been packed off to Ruth Ann's a day ahead of time with a note from Yolande asking Ruth Ann's parents to keep her indefinitely, as there was illness at Roselawns and they wanted her away from possible infection.

"Gaylord Renault," Jonathan said, his voice curiously flat. "It happened the night of his birthday ball. Naomi was brought to the bachelor cottage, and you didn't lift a hand to stop it."

"I tell you I don't remember! Can't you understand that? I was drunk. I just plain don't remember!"

Prudence's face seemed to burn with an inner fire that would sear him if he touched it. "Rory, she's your sister! Your own sister, and you let it happen!"

"Damn it, what do I have to do to make you realize I didn't know a blamed thing about it? I remember Gay sending for some wenches, but then I passed out."

"Prudence, leave the room!" Jacob seemed to realize, for the first time, that his eldest granddaughter was present at this conference.

"I will not. What would be the point? I know about it, and I'm directly concerned. She's only fourteen,

Grandfather! Only fourteen, and now what's going to happen to her?"

Jonathan stormed at Rory, "I ought to take a whip to you! I ought to take every inch of skin off your back!"

"That would be a great help, wouldn't it?" Prue's tone was scathing. "Just to lash out and hurt somebody, because you've been hurt!"

"It's Gay Renault I'm going after!" Jacob raged. "The arrogant, filthy young puppy, doing a thing like that and then daring to present himself here, in this house, as Prudence's suitor! John Renault's going to hear a thing or two about that son of his, and if he doesn't punish him within an inch of his life, I will!"

Of them all, Prudence, who was shaken to the core, kept her wits about her. "Yes, that would be the thing to do. Call him out, kill him, cause the worst scandal in Georgia's history! Why aren't you thinking about Naomi, about what's best for her?"

She spoke to Jacob's back, because her grandfather was already leaving the room. Prudence turned her clear eyes on Jonathan and Yolande.

"Papa, go after him! If you don't stop him, there's no telling what he might do!"

Jonathan looked at her peculiarly. It could have been Martha standing there, looking at him as though she wasn't sure he was quite human.

"You're right. I'll go along, or there'll likely be a shooting."

In spite of his age and his game leg, Jacob must have ridden like a demon, because though he had only a few minutes' head start, he had arrived at Swanmere a full five minutes before Jonathan. As the Renault majordomo, his eyes filled with the fear that quarrels among the white folks always generated,

242

ushered Jon into the library, Jacob's voice could be heard all over the house, roaring out his accusations.

Jonathan crossed the room with long strides and grasped his father's arm. "Jacob, tone it down!" he demanded. "You want the whole county to hear you? By this time, every black at Swanmere knows what's going on, and it'll be a miracle if it doesn't come to the ears of our friends."

"And how do you expect to keep it a secret?" Jacob shouted. "Things like this can't be kept under cover! You can't hide a baby, not a white baby!"

Gaylord stood beside the mantel, a hastily poured drink in his hand. His face was pasty, while his father looked both furious and stunned.

John Renault turned to Jacob. "Jacob, I don't know what to say. I guess it goes without saying that I'm damnably sorry."

Like Rory, Gaylord tried to defend himself, and his excuse was the same. "I swear I don't remember! I remember the others wanting some wenches, and I sent Ab to fetch them, but I just plain don't remember anything after that." His words carried little conviction, and his expression showed that there was a more than flicker of memory brought to the surface by having his act pushed in his face.

Gay sensed their hesitancy and leaped to attack as the best line of defense.

"The girl's probably lyin'! She's been with some buck on your place, and she's tryin' to crawl out of it now she's been caught."

Jacob sprang at the young man, and Jonathan barely caught him in time. For all that Gay was so much younger, Jacob's rage-inflamed strength might have done irreparable damage if he'd got his hands on him.

John Renault spoke deliberately. "All I can think of is for us to take the girl. I'll fix her up in a cabin of her own, make it comfortable, see that she has the best of everything. You know we'll take good care of her, and the child, as well. They'll never want for anything. If the child is a boy, we'll see that he gets some education so he can fill a responsible position when he's grown. If it's a girl, we'll be able to place her to advantage. You have Miss Yolande and the two girls to think of, and Roselawns is no place for her."

Jonathan was white with rage. Get rid of her, hide her, remove the embarrassment. That was his daughter John Renault was talking about, not some high-yellow field wench! He seemed to see the room through a haze, and for a moment he felt dizzy, he who had scarcely suffered a sick day in his life.

Send Naomi here, where that young puppy standing there guzzling his drink could get at her again? According to Gaylord's way of thinking, there'd be no reason to leave her alone, now that she was already ruined. Jonathan waved away the glass that John Renault offered him.

John Renault's mouth was a grim line. "I hold Absalom directly responsible. He wasn't drunk, and he knew that he had no business fetching your girl for such a purpose."

He stepped to the door and called for his major-domo. The man appeared so quickly that Jonathan knew he had been standing within earshot. "LeRoy, bring Absalom here."

Absalom tapped gently at the door a moment or two later, his face taut with apprehension. He already knew what this ruckus was about. The voices could be heard clear upstairs where he'd been straightening up Mister Gay's possessions, so he hadn't needed LeRoy's warning to know that he was in for it.

"Ab, on the night of Mister Gay's ball, you brought

244

Naomi, the Beddoes girl, to the bachelor cottage. Will you tell me why in the world you did such a thing?"

"I was ordered, Mister John."

"You were ordered!" The words were an explosion. "You knew that your master was the worse for drink. You knew he didn't know what he was doing. And yet you obeyed him, instead of reporting the matter to me! Damn it, Ab, you have to be punished, you know that, don't you?"

Absalom began to shake. "Yes, sir."

Jonathan's gorge rose. "I don't see any point in whipping Ab. He only did as he was told."

"It'll teach him better the next time! He knows he's held directly responsible for my son when Gay's in that condition! I will not tolerate any insubordination among my people, Jonathan, any more than you do among yours."

Absalom stood with his eyes downcast, not even daring to look at his masters.

"And Jacob, you needn't worry about Gaylord bothering your girl once she's at Swanmere. Gay is to remain in his room until I decide that I want to see him again. In the meantime, I'll arrange for him to visit cousins of ours in Louisiana for an indefinite period. Ab, go with your master and stay there until I send for you."

"Yes, sir." There was no hope in Absalom's voice, no hope in his heart. He was going to be whipped, and it wouldn't be light. He was going to be whipped within an inch of his life. If there were any place to run, any way to run, he'd do it, even if he knew the patrol would catch him. He'd take his chances. Only there wasn't any way to run or any place to run to. He wouldn't get as far as the road before he was caught, and that would only make it worse.

One thing was sure in his mind. He wasn't going

245

to hang himself, the way that Sam had hung himself. Absalom knew all about that; it was still talked about in the quarters. He'd live, and if he ever had a chance to get even, he'd do it. As Absalom followed his young master from the room, hatred was born in his heart, a hatred deeper than his fear.

Prudence was waiting for them when they returned home. Jonathan found it difficult to speak to her, to answer her unspoken questions. "They're going to take her," he said. And at the look on her face he burst out, "What else could we do?"

"If she were a stray dog or cat, you could drown her."

"Damn it, Prue, don't look at me like that!"

"She's my sister. Am I supposed not to care? And do you think that sending her to Swanmere is any answer? Well, I don't!"

"She won't have to go right away. She won't begin to show for a while yet."

Prudence spoke calmly. "Papa, promise me you won't send her until I've had an answer from Aunt Emily."

"What do you mean, until you've had an answer from Miss Emily?"

"I've written to her. I did it as soon as you and Grandfather left. I sent Tod to town to post the letter on the first fast packet."

"And what is Miss Emily supposed to do about all this? She isn't possessed of magical powers."

Jonathan's obvious wretchedness softened Prue's answer in spite of his sarcasm.

"I asked her if we could come to her. I asked her if I could come home and bring Naomi with me."

For a moment, Jonathan couldn't speak. He wouldn't let her go! He'd lost Martha, did he have to lose

Prue, too? But when he spoke, his words formed themselves with no will of his own.

"Prue, will you ever come back?"

Prudence put her fingers on his face and traced the planes of his cheek, her touch gentle.

"I will if I can, Papa. But not as long as Naomi needs me."

24

Michael Donovan straightened his back to ease his aching muscles and wiped a soot-grimed hand across his forehead. The riverboat had nosed in to the bank several minutes ago, and all hands had been set to loading wood. It was customary for farmers, at that time, to earn extra money as well as rid their acres of unwanted trees by supplying the needs of the riverboats. A sign tacked to a post beside the huge stack of wood read:

NOTIC

To all persons takin wood from this landin, pleast to leve a ticket payable to the subscriber, at $1. 75 a cord as per usual.

Andy Skykes

When he had wiped the sweat out of his eyes, Michael saw the girl again. She, along with other passengers, had got off the boat to breathe in the fresh, crisp air and look around, glad to have a view unimpaired by bales of cotton for a few moments, at least. The shipping season was in full swing, and the riverboat's decks were piled high all the way around, so that the passengers had to move about under lamplight even in the middle of the day.

There were three in the girl's party, the girl herself, an older girl, and a gentleman planter. Michael had ascertained through discreet questioning that the man was the older girl's father, but he hadn't been able to decide whether the younger girl was also his daughter or some more distant relative. Her relationship to the man and the older girl was not important. What had struck Michael was the hopeless look in her eyes. What could have caused such sorrow in a girl so young?

Michael hadn't been able to get the girl out of his mind ever since he had seen her when her party had boarded the riverboat. His glance then had been brief, because his duties were in the engine room.

None of the black slaves who worked as roustabouts or servants on the boat were allowed near the engine room. In case of an accident, an explosion, the blacks were valuable property, and their maiming or death would constitute a serious loss to their owners. As an immigrant, Michael and the other Irish had no value. They were, to put it bluntly, fully expendable.

The work was hard, and the pay was insultingly low, but Michael, a fugitive from the Irish landlords and the repossessing of farms that had followed the potato famine in the forties, took what work was offered without complaining. If he had complained, there would have been twenty other immigrants eager to step into his shoes.

The Irish were not kindly looked upon in this land of opportunity. But no matter how little they were paid, the small sums they could send to their relatives starving in Ireland were still essential. Jobs were scarce, and the competition for them was fierce.

This girl now, the one who had been so constantly on his mind since he had first seen her, reminded Michael a little of his sister, Meg, except that Meg was scrawny from hunger, her pretty face marred by ill-tempered resentment of the landlords. Likely by now Meg was married. Shawn O'Leary had had his eye on her these three years past. Letters were a long time in coming, but Michael wouldn't be surprised to get word, any day now, that Shawn and Meg were on their way to America, too. Shawn wasn't one to listen to the voice of experience; he still thought that the streets of New York were paved with gold.

Well, Meg, at least, would be able to find employment. The ladies of Boston hired Irish girls in droves, to wash their clothes and scrub their floors. They, too, received almost no pay but a roof over their heads and enough food to keep their souls in their bodies.

"Donovan!" The engineer's voice snapped Michael out of his daydreams. "Get a move on, you lazy Irish bastard! Heave that wood—you think we got all day? We got a schedule to meet, damn your hide!"

Michael looked once more at the girl, who was re-embarking now with the others. He'd never seen her smile, but she was so lovely, in her sadness, that he felt an urge to take her hand and reassure her.

His muscles rippled as he bent to his work again. Lazy Irish bastard! If he ever saved enough to buy a piece of land, no matter how poor or how small, no man would ever call him that again.

In the dining-salon that evening, Jonathan kept a determinedly cheerful smile on his face and urged Naomi to take a little more fried chicken. "At least try the rice, honey. We can't deliver you to Miss Emily looking like we never fed you. She'd skin us alive."

His feeble attempt at humor brought a smile to Naomi's face, more to please him than because she felt like smiling. In spite of Jonathan's and Prudence's kindness, she was frightened. Miss Emily sounded formidable, and everything in Massachusetts would be strange to her. Miss Emily might think she was bad, even if Miss Prue had told her that she wasn't.

She'd have to remember to stop calling Prudence Miss Prue. Prudence had told her to start practicing, but she kept forgetting. She was supposed to be Miss Prue's cousin, a young widow whose husband had been killed in a hunting accident. A young white widow! She'd never be able to do it; she'd make some slip and Miss Prue and Mister Jonathan would be disgraced.

"Papa, look out. That servant carrying that lamp looks a little tipsy to me. Don't let him drip oil on you—" Prudence's warning broke off with shattering abruptness as the boat lurched and ground to a stop.

"Sandbar!" They heard someone shout. "We've run aground!"

The next instant, the man carrying the lamp had fallen, jolted off his feet by the sudden stop. The lamp fell from his hand and landed on their table, and its flaming oil spread. Prudence had seen the man fall and thrown her chair aside as she got out of the way, but Naomi was saturated with the oil in a split second, and it burst into flames even as it spread across her dress.

"Papa, help her!" Prudence screamed, as she struggled against the milling people all around her. "Help me get to Naomi!" Cries of fire, panic-stricken voices screaming and cursing, added to the bedlam.

251

Jonathan, too, had been jolted from his chair, and now he had trouble rising because of the press of hysterical passengers. He shook his head, half dazed, and fought his way to his feet, an animal-like cry of horror escaping from him as he saw Naomi's dress aflame.

He plunged toward her, knocking other men out of his way, but someone else reached her before he could. Men went flying as Michael tore through the dining salon to reach the girl, who was standing, her eyes wide with shock, futilely beating at the flames that were enveloping her skirts.

Michael reached her and bore her to the carpet under their feet with his own weight, spreading himself over her, muffling the flames with his own body and hands. The room was filled with acrid smoke, but now the crew were at hand to stamp out the fire that had spread to the carpet.

"It's all right, folks. No cause for alarm. We're in no danger of burning or sinking. Just keep calm, we'll be backed off the sandbar in no time. You, there, Donovan, get back where you belong!"

Michael stood up and helped the girl to her feet. As far as he could see, she was unharmed. Those wide crinolines were good for something, if only to keep fire away from a woman's body. But his own hands were severely burned.

The older girl was beside them now, making sure that the other girl wasn't hurt, then examining his hands. She glared at the captain with her eyes flashing.

"Can't you see he's burned? He needs a doctor. Is there a doctor on board?"

There was not.

"Don't fret yourself about the Irishman, ma'am. We'll daub a little grease on him and he'll do all right."

"But he can't work with his hands burned like this!"

"He won't have to. He's fired. We can't carry him along for charity, ma'am. We'll put him off at the first stop."

"You bastard!" Goaded beyond endurance, half crazed from the pain of his hands, Michael lunged at the captain. Jonathan threw himself between them, using both of his arms to hold the furious Irishman back. It took all Jonathan's strength, as well as that of two other gentlemen who stepped in to help him.

"Take it easy, lad. Knocking down the captain will only get you in trouble. You don't want to spend the next six months in jail. Easy, boy!"

"So he wants to fight!" The captain looked at Michael with contempt. "Troublemakers, the lot of them! I'll just have him tied up till we can put him ashore, to make sure he doesn't go berserk."

"Papa!"

Jonathan didn't need Prudence's cry to stir his own anger. Irishman or not, this young man had saved Naomi from being severely burned, maybe from death.

"You'll do no such thing. I'll pay his fare, and he'll remain on board as a passenger until we reach the next port of call, where he can receive the medical attention he needs."

The captain was disposed to dispute this, but other voices, notably those of ladies, were added to Jonathan's. The brawny young man had been brave, he had saved the young lady, and he should not be treated so badly.

"Prue, can you do something about those hands? Naomi, one of these ladies will be kind enough to accompany you to your stateroom. I think you had better go right to bed."

"Indeed she must!" a motherly woman declared.

"Come along, child, and let me tuck you in. What a fright you must have had! My own heart is still pounding, I declare!"

Naomi allowed herself to be led from the salon, but she paused at the doorway and turned to look Michael directly in the eyes. "Thank you. Thank you very much."

For a minute, Michael's hands didn't even hurt.

Michael spent the rest of the journey in a daze. It still didn't seem possible to him that he was to accompany Jonathan and Prudence and Naomi all the way to some place called Martin's Corners, just because his hands were more badly burned than had at first seemed apparent. The older girl, Prudence, insisted on it, saying that they owed it to him for having saved her cousin's life, and her father had not been hard to persuade. A debt was a debt, Jonathan said, and he made it a habit to pay his debts.

"It's as bad as that, is it?" Jonathan asked, when Michael, his hands swathed in bandages, told him something of his life and of the difficulties of finding employment in America. "And from the looks of it, you won't be able to work for some time."

"I'll get along." Jonathan approved of the pride in Michael's eyes, but he strongly suspected that the young man would not be able to get along. Michael had only a few dollars saved, and when that was gone, what would he do? Charity was even harder to come by than employment, and it would gall the lad to accept it, in any case.

"I think you had better come with us. Prudence would raise the roof if I took those hands of yours out from under her supervision before they're completely healed. And I know that Miss Emily is quite a doctor in her own right. After that, we'll see." The

254

more Jonathan saw of this young man, the better he liked him. "I could use you on my father's plantation. Do you think you could handle slaves? There's always room for a good overseer."

Michael's blue eyes clouded. "I'd like working in the open, on the land, but I'll tell you frankly that I hold no brief for slavery. In Ireland, on the land, we were near enough to being slaves ourselves to know what it's like."

When Prudence dressed Michael's hands again that afternoon, bathing them in very strong cold tea the way Miss Emily had taught her, Naomi stood beside her, holding the basin. By Saint Patrick and all the other saints, Michael thought, but she was a beauty! When Naomi looked at him like that, those huge eyes of hers all melty with gratitude, it did something to his heart.

"Does it hurt terribly?" Naomi asked him, biting her lips to still their trembling.

"Hardly at all. 'Tis nothing, colleen, believe me," Michael lied.

"I wish Burke were here!" Prudence fretted. "These burns are deep, and Miss Emily said there was danger of infection with burns. We'll have to keep your hands well covered, and for goodness' sake, don't get the bandages dirty!" She dipped clean bandages into the solution of cold tea and began to wrap them, deftly covering the wet cloths with dry ones to hold the moisture in as long as possible.

Naomi saw Michael wince, in spite of his determination not to worry Naomi.

"It does hurt! M . . ." She caught herself before she made the mistake of saying "Miss Prudence." "Prudence says that I'd have been dreadfully burned if it hadn't been for you. She says that you saved my life."

"I just happened to be passing the door and saw you were in trouble, is all." He'd have to see a priest pretty soon, he was doing so much lying. How long had it been since he'd been to confession? These riverboat captains didn't give time off to attend church. Heathens, they were, and no wonder, Protestants all, and knowing no better. Michael had made an excuse, a deliberate lie, to get out of the boiler room and pass the salon door, just in the hope of glimpsing her. He'd said he was sick and going to heave. If any of the officers had caught him, where he had no business being, he'd have been fired right there, instead of after he'd burned his hands.

The trouble was, he was in love, and being in love made a man lie a lot. And she so young, he should be ashamed of himself. The next priest he confessed to would have a penance or two to lay on him, for certain.

All the same, he was going on to Massachusetts with them. After this journey was done, he'd never set eyes on Naomi again, and that would be penance enough.

25

There it was, small and sparkling white, its windows flaming with the sunset, the garden still as neat as a pin, no weed daring to encroach along the picket fence where a riot of blue morning glories rivaled the blue of the sky. Prudence's breath caught in her throat so painfully that tears misted her eyes, and for a moment all the outlines dissolved into a haze of blue and white and green and the red of the sunset. And then her eyes cleared, and she saw the front door open and the two women step out onto the porch, one small and straight, the other, standing slightly behind her, tall and rawboned.

"Aunt Emily, we're here! I can hardly believe it, it's so beautiful, everything is just the same, nothing has changed at all!"

There was the clean, fresh smell of Aunt Emily's starched apron, the faint scent of the rose and geranium potpourri that her great-aunt laid in sachets among her clothing, the familiar odor of soap as Prudence pressed her cheek against Emily's.

And then Prudence's breath caught again, painfully, because Aunt Emily had changed. She was older, incredibly older, her face a network of lines, her eyes deep-sunk in her face. Aunt Emily was old! A sudden sense of outraged loss was almost more than Prudence could bear.

"So you're here at last. We've been ready for you for days, but you made good time, for all that." One thing hadn't changed. Aunt Emily's voice was exactly the same—crisp, authoritative, with a warmth that made things all right with the world.

How tiny she was! She was nothing but skin and bones. Her collarbone stood out sharply under her skin where it showed beneath the prim neckline of her dress. Prudence could have lifted her in her arms, for she weighed no more than a child. She was even afraid to hug her too tightly for fear that the delicate, brittle bones might snap under her grasp.

But Cleo hadn't changed. It might have been only yesterday that Prudence had left her. She remembered looking backwards until the coach had rounded the bend in the road, to keep these two in sight until the last possible second, her chin set with resolution against the tears that had threatened to engulf her. She hadn't cried, but only she knew the effort it had taken.

Prudence let go of Emily at last, remembering her manners, and turned to draw Naomi forward. The younger girl hung back, her face pale, her eyes enormous, filled with the shame and dread of meeting this woman of whom she had heard so much.

"Aunt Emily, this is Naomi."

Emily took both of Naomi's hands in her own, kissed the pale cheek, and then held her off to appraise her.

"You're beautiful, but we must put some weight on your bones. Child, you're trembling! Cleo, take her inside, show her up to their room, and help her into bed; she's exhausted. There, child, it's all right. You're home now."

Cleo's face had crumpled. "Land, you're the image of Mister Jon, and you have a look of Miss Yolande about you, too. And Prue, she's a young lady, as pretty as a picture, just like her mama."

Cleo gathered Naomi into her arms and held her until the girl's trembling eased. "Don't you go fretting, child, Miss Emily and Cleo's going to take care of you now. Nothing bad can happen to you now, only good. Which is your valise?"

Michael touched his forelock as Jonathan motioned him forward.

"Miss Emily, this young man is Michael Donovan, who rendered us all a great service by saving Naomi from being burned by oil from an overturned lamp after our boat ran up on a sandbar. Since he suffered severe burns himself, and the captain discharged him, we managed to persuade him to come along with us."

Emily held out her hands, but instead of taking Michael's to shake, she turned them over, a frown between her eyes, as she traced the forming scar tissue with skillful fingers.

"They're a mite stiff, aren't they? Yes, I can see that they are. We'll start rubbing them with cocoa butter, several times a day, and exercising them. After what you did, we can't have you going through life not able to make a living because of your hands."

Michael's face lighted up, and eager relief showed in his eyes. Although he had never mentioned it, he had been worried that his hands would not heal properly, and an Irishman without the use of his hands was as worthless as a piece of offal, to be cast as thoughtlessly aside.

"Do you think it will help, ma'am?"

"Of course it will help. There's nothing better. All it takes is time and perseverance, and we have plenty of both. You'll have to bed in the barn, Michael, but outside of that, you're a member of the family until you are fit to leave and find new employment."

I might be back in Ireland, Michael thought. Never, since he had boarded the stinking immigrant ship, had he encountered such warmth and human kindness. Jonathan's attitude had been kind enough in its way, but Michael knew that that was the result of a debt that had to be paid. Prudence's concern had been warm and sincere, but this little lady, a very great lady, had a quality that struck Michael to the heart.

"I've slept in worse places, and will again. And hands or no hands, I can pull my weight and be everlastingly grateful."

"I am sure you can." There was a twinkle in Emily's eyes. "And you may be sure I'll hold you to it. We all work here. If I thought he knew how, I'd set Jonathan to milking the cow."

A cow, was it? Holy Mother Mary, fresh milk to drink! Michael's face looked like an Irish sunrise. His father's cow had died many years ago, before the old man himself, and there had never been the money to buy another.

Miss Emily turned to Jonathan. "Well, Jonathan?"

Jonathan winced. It seemed that every time he had occasion to meet Miss Emily face to face, she greeted him this same way.

Emily smiled, her eyes softening. "Come inside, there's coffee on the stove, and gingerbread still warm in the oven, to stay you until supper. I want to hear all about everything, especially the railroads."

They sat in the kitchen around the table with its immaculate linen cloth. Prudence was almost ashamed of her appetite as she wolfed down the gingerbread, made as Emily had taught Cleo to make it, rich, spicy, as light as a feather. The old familiar fireplace was still there, but its hearth was swept clean of ashes and a black iron range stood directly to one side of it, a stovepipe let into its chimney. The autumn afternoon, close to dusk, was growing chill, but the fire in the firebox of the range made the kitchen snug. The inviting aromas of coffee and gingerbread and ham baking in the oven filled the room.

Prudence was still excited about the river trip. "I knew cotton was king, but even living on a plantation, I had no idea of the immensity of the trade! Imagine the boats so loaded that we had to have lamplight in the middle of the day!"

"It's an experience I would love to have shared," Emily said. "Still, I am afraid that there is trouble ahead. And if the trouble explodes, as a good many knowledgeable men think it will, what then, Jonathan? If your markets should be cut off, even your market in England, what will you do?"

"England will always buy all we can produce!" Jonathan's tone held a touch of belligerence. "We don't need the North, as long as we have England!"

"There may be an embargo."

"Nonsense. That isn't going to happen. Why, if the worst came to the worst, England would come in on our side, everybody knows that."

"That is wishful thinking. England is far too practical to become embroiled in a conflict between our States. Granted that her industry would suffer and that there would be widespread unemployment, but England would still keep her skirts clear."

"Begging your pardon, ma'am, but you're wrong."

Emily's hand trembled a little as she placed her cup back in its saucer. "I can only hope that it is never put to the test."

Prudence's eyes were fastened, with shock, on her aunt's hands. Then Emily folded them in her lap, out of sight under the table, but Prudence had seen their tremor, the sign of weakness that had never been there before. Was her aunt not well? That couldn't be; Aunt Emily was never ill, she was as sturdy as a New England rock.

Jonathan stood up. "I think I'll take a walk down to the *Clarion*." There was an embarrassed look on his face, but determination as well. "I'd like to see David Lawrence, see what he's up to these days. Don't worry, Miss Emily. I'm not armed." Only a little bitterness crept into his voice. "I think it's time I told him I never held him responsible for Martha's death. Nothing would have stopped her, and if it hadn't been Lawrence's paper, she'd have found some other way to stir up trouble."

"He's still fighting slavery for all he's worth." There was a little smile at the corners of Emily's mouth. "I trust you won't start an argument, Jonathan, else you'll be there for hours and miss supper. Tell David that I'll expect him and his mother for supper tomorrow night. You gentlemen can have your discussion then, where the presence of ladies will keep your tempers within bounds."

Michael entered the kitchen, his smile stretching from ear to ear. He had milked the cow, ignoring the condition of his hands, and he was near to heaven. "I put it in the springhouse, Miss Emily. What rich milk! What a fine animal she is, the darlin'!"

"Coffee, Michael? Or milk?"

"Milk, if it's all right." Michael had not touched a drop, although refraining had taken a great deal of effort.

"Prudence, fetch him a glass of milk. Sit here, Michael, and have some gingerbread."

It didn't seem right; it was beyond anything Michael had ever experienced, to have a young lady of quality wait on him. He looked at Prue half fearfully, and

262

then at Jonathan, expecting a protest. To his amazement, neither of them turned a hair. It gave him the courage to ask the question that had nagged at him even during the almost unbearable pleasure of milking the cow.

"Is Miss Naomi all right?"

Emily gave him a brief, searching look, and she understood. "Naomi will be fine, Michael. Cleo took her up a light supper, and she's already asleep. You'll see her in the morning."

Michael's face turned bright red, and he applied himself to the gingerbread.

By noon of the next day, Emily had been forced to include Doctor Bryant, and Mr. Hamilton, and Mr. Blaisdel, along with their wives, as well as the new Reverend Parker from the First Congregational Church, in her invitation to dinner. All of the men were anxious to talk to Jonathan and to get firsthand his views on the Southern situation.

"If Lincoln wins the Presidency, we may yet come through these troubled waters without foundering," Reverend Parker said ponderously. "It is my belief that he is the only man strong enough to be trusted with the helm of our ship of state in these perilous times."

"I expect that Mr. Beddoes favors Douglas," Doctor Bryant said, looking at Jonathan from underneath beetling brows. "Most Southerners do."

Jonathan twirled the stem of his wineglass in his strong, slender fingers, a thoughtful frown on his face. "I'm not altogether sure of that, sir. Where I come from, men are talking of nominating the Vice President, John Breckenridge, if Lincoln manages to snare the Republican nomination. Not that that's likely to

263

happen. Even up North here, intelligent men will have better sense than to vote for a backwoods oaf."

"Jonathan, your Southern arrogance is showing," Emily said. She looked tired, but her eyes were alert. "Just because a man happens to have been born in a log cabin doesn't necessarily detract from his intelligence. As I understand it, a good many of your most aristocratic planters made their start in log cabins, before they began to realize enormous profits on their crops."

Jonathan had the grace to look slightly ashamed. "Granted, Miss Emily. My own family, for one. But you must realize that they were people of culture in the first place, not like this Lincoln. As for our enormous profits, where are they now? You Northerners have seen to it that we get d— blamed little."

"I should think that the entire South would stand behind Douglas, because of the Kansas-Nebraska Bill of '54," Doctor Bryant mused. "His popular sovereignty proposal, that territorial slavery should be left up to the individual States, should swing the votes for him."

Jonathan's smile was wry. "There's that, but we all know that Douglas backed the Nebraska territory business to clear the way for a transcontinental railroad to make Northern speculators rich. And his stand on the Dred Scott case caused a considerable rift between Northern and Southern Democrats. We have too much at stake to pin our hopes on somebody like Douglas, for all he was a good man, in his time."

The argument waxed and waned. If Jacob had been there, it would have turned into a free-for-all, Jonathan thought, as the men finally shook his hand and collected their womenfolk and left. Cleo came downstairs and shooed Prudence and Emily out of the kitchen.

"I'll clear up here. You go to bed, Miss Emily, you hear?"

"Thank you, Cleo. Jonathan, how long can you stay? There will be others who will want to talk to you."

"Not long, I'm afraid. Jacob will need me, and it still takes an almighty long time to travel from Massachusetts to Georgia, in spite of those railroads you're so enthralled with. And I must make a few purchases in Boston. A day or two more and I'll have to be on my way."

Prudence waited with Jonathan for the stage to be readied for departure. Michael had insisted on helping him take his luggage to the inn, and he would escort Prudence back to Miss Emily's, but now he stood a little apart so as not to intrude on the leavetaking between father and daughter. Michael was happy, because he was not only to stay in Martin's Corners, where he would see Naomi every day, but Mr. Hamilton had told him to come around to the feed and grain store as soon as his hands were in better shape, and he would give him some employment. "I can always use a husky young fellow like you. I'm not as young as I was, and hefting those sacks is getting to be harder every day. If you aren't afraid of work, I can use you."

Prudence's head was primly bonneted, her hands properly gloved for this last goodbye. She owed that much to her father, but she vowed that from now on, for as long as she remained in Massachusetts, she would wear gloves only to protect her hands from the cold.

"I have something for you." Jonathan drew a slim velvet case from his pocket and handed it to Prue.

Surprised, she opened it, and saw a magnificent string of pearls.

"Papa, what is this? Isn't it Mama's necklace? But you mustn't give it to me! Things like this go to the oldest son, and that's Rory, to be given to his wife." Prudence's throat hurt, and she hoped that the tears she felt like shedding didn't show.

"It was your mother's, and now it's yours, Rory be damned," Jonathan said. "I want you to have it, baby. I want you to wear it, and remember your mother, whenever things are hard for you. Rory doesn't deserve it, and you do. Your mother would want you to have it."

He lifted the necklace from its case, and his fingers trembled as he clasped it around Prudence's throat. For a moment, it was as if something crazy had happened to time, as if it were Martha there before him. How Marty's eyes had sparkled when she'd first seen it! And what hell she'd raised when she'd found out they'd financed it by selling two slaves.

"Wear it for Martha, and for me," Jonathan said, his voice strained.

Prue's laugh broke the spell. "In Martin's Corners? Papa, even you couldn't expect that! Except at Thanksgiving, maybe, and Christmas. It would hardly be appropriate for digging potatoes or churning butter."

"Wear it anyway. Pearls are meant to be worn, or they lose their luster. That's why they look dull now, but they'll come back to their full beauty if you wear them." Roughly, Jonathan drew Prudence into his arms. "God bless you. Come home, Prue. Promise you'll come home, when you can."

"I promise."

Michael took a few steps forward to stand beside her as the coach rolled out of the inn yard. By all the saints, that was a pretty necklace. Its price would keep dozens of families in Ireland for untold years. But Michael felt no envy. Prudence was a fine girl and she deserved the pearls. For himself, he fancied a younger girl, without a jewel to her name.

Right now, there was no hope for him at all, but in time, if he could earn enough for a little piece of land, he might dare to ask. Wasn't that man Lincoln going to be President? If that could happen, so could anything!

26

Jonathan had no intention of going to New Orleans when he started his return journey. His change of plans was a spur-of-the-moment decision, but once his mind was made up, there was no deviating from it. He had been told, over six months ago, by an acquaintance who had just returned from that city, that Rebecca was there.

He had to know, to find out for himself if she were well, if she had found what she was looking for. And he had to tell her that he had let this filthy thing happen to their daughter and assure her that Naomi was going to be well cared for. Surely Rebecca would want to know that both Naomi and the child would live out their lives as free people in the North, where no one would ever know their origins.

Somewhat apprehensive, Jonathan inquired his way to the most noisome section of the city, the haunt of thieves and pimps, of low taverns and lower cribs.

He hailed a hackney, and the black coachman scowled when he heard Jonathan's destination. "You don't want to go there, not a gentleman like you! What you want is a good place, I can take you to the best."

"Do as I say."

"I charges extra to go there . . ." The driver's face showed cupidity, now. "It ain't safe, I has to be recompensed for the danger."

"I'll pay what you ask. Just get moving."

The hackman shrugged. There was no explaining the tastes of some gentlemen. As long as the fare and a handsome tip were forthcoming, how could he take it on himself to worry about the evils that might befall a well-dressed gentleman of quality in that place? You didn't argue with gentlemen, not if you knew what was good for you.

"This is it, boss. This place right here."

"Wait for me. I don't know how long I'll be."

"You'll have to pay me first."

Absentmindedly, Jonathan thrust money into the greedy hand. Encouraged by the amount, the driver decided to wait, on the chance there'd be a bigger tip, but not for too long, or somebody'd have it off him before he could get out of here, and maybe slit his throat for good measure.

The house at which Jonathan alighted was in better repair than the places around it. It had been freshly painted, and there was a gaudy sign showing a mermaid sitting on a sailor's lap, offering him a drink. The Siren's Song, the sign proclaimed.

Jonathan pushed through the swinging doors and paused. The inside was as much of a surprise as the outside. It was clean, for one thing. The sawdust on the floor of the common room was fresh, the tables wiped free of grease, and it was larger than Jonathan had expected. It was well filled with men, most of them seafarers from their appearance, and smoke hung heavy in the air, but it was reasonably quiet. The girls, too, looked unexpectedly wholesome, their gaudy clothing fresh, their faces not as dirty under the garish paint as usual for ordinary whores.

Jonathan crossed the long room to the bar, and addressed an aproned man who stood behind it, sleeves rolled up to show heavily muscled arms covered with coarse black hair. The man's face was battered, but the eyes, squinting at him through the smoke, were intelligent.

"I'm looking for Simon LaCrosse."

"You're looking at him, but what the hell for? I don't know you, and sure as hell none of your friends recommended my place to the likes of you. Unless . . . are you one of those looking for something different? If you are, you won't find it here. We got no pretty boys, or any girls that like funny business."

"I'm looking for a woman named Rebecca. I understand that she's here."

The man put his hands on his hips and showed more interest. "Are you now! She ain't for hire, Mr. Fancypants."

"I don't want to hire her, I only want to see her."

"You got a hell of a nerve! What you want to do, invite her to tea?"

"What's the trouble, Simon?"

She walked toward him from a stairway at the side of the room. He would have recognized her anywhere, despite the expensive gown she was wearing and the way her hair was piled up on top of her head in fancy coils and ringlets. And she recognized him just as quickly.

"Aren't you a little out of your natural habitat, Jon?"

The proprietor's scowl deepened. "You know this man?"

"He used to own me."

Simon LaCrosse's hand dropped to a bottle and lifted it. "Get any idea of taking her back out of your head." He turned to Rebecca. "Shall I have him taken care of, Beckie, just to make sure?"

"Calm down. He hasn't come to take me back." Rebecca nodded toward another door, and Jonathan followed her, feeling the skin on the back of his neck crawl. LaCrosse had meant it. One word from Rebecca, and Jonathan would drop from sight, and the odds were high that no one would ever find his body, at least in an identifiable state. Even the hackman would keep his mouth shut; he wouldn't dare do otherwise.

Rebecca led Jonathan to a room that was a combination office and sitting room. The furnishings were good—bright draperies covered the one window and the rug underfoot was an Oriental. Rebecca filled a glass from a cut-glass decanter and handed it to him.

"Go ahead and drink it. It isn't our bar stock, it won't poison you." She indicated a comfortable chair and waited until he had seated himself before sitting down herself in a rocking chair. A sewing case set beside the rocker with a bit of needlepoint showing under its half-raised lid.

"Now, Jon, what is it you want of me?" Sudden apprehension crossed her face, and her hands clasped more tightly in her lap. "It isn't Naomi? Has anything happened to her? You promised you'd keep her for me until I could send for her!"

"But you didn't send for her. We never heard a word from you."

"Do you think I'd bring her into a place like this? I think it's better than most. I've seen to that. But it's no place for a young girl. I bought a half-interest from Simon with the money you gave me. It wasn't enough, but I convinced him that I could double his profits by running it the way it should be run, and I've done it. What about Naomi? You haven't answered my question."

The fear on Rebecca's face stabbed him. "She's

271

alive, Rebecca. And well. But she isn't at Roselawns any more."

Rebecca got to her feet, her face paling to the color of ivory. "You promised! You swore you'd never sell her! My God, how low can a man sink, to sell his own daughter? Simon was right, I'll have him take care of you, but not until you've told me who bought her!"

"Becky, stop it! I didn't sell her! God, you know better than that! But something happened to her, something I'd cut off my right arm to have prevented. Gaylord Renault got at her, and she's pregnant. Prue's taken her back to Martin's Corners, to Miss Emily. Prue's staying there with her. They'll take care of her. They'll make a life for her, a good life, and for the child, too. If you knew Miss Emily, you'd believe that."

Rebecca sat down again and covered her face with her hands. Jonathan went to her, and put his hand on her shoulder. He could feel her trembling.

"Rebecca, I'm sorry. God knows how sorry I am! But it happened, and now we're doing the best we can. Naomi will be all right, I promise you."

"You promised me before, and see what happened!" Rebecca had regained her composure, but her face and her voice were bitter. "If only I'd been able to send for her! This place makes money, a lot of money, but half of it is Simon's, and what I wanted for Naomi was something better than a room on a back street. I wanted to make her a lady! Now it's too late, all too late."

"You can't make Naomi a lady, because she's already that. She's sweet and gentle and good, and she'll have a better chance where she is than she would have with you, in spite of everything you might have managed to give her. That's the God's truth."

He took her hand and looked into her eyes. "Rebecca, how is it with you? I've wondered, time and again, but I never knew where you were until a few months ago."

Rebecca spread her hands. "You can see how it is. I'm well established here. Simon is not my lover, if that's what you're wondering. Our relationship is strictly business; that was part of our bargain when I bought in. I run a good place here. The liquor is fit for human consumption, the food doesn't poison anyone, and my girls are clean. The sailors know they can come here and not be robbed or leave with a disease, and they're willing to pay extra. If my girls want to leave, they can; I don't let Simon stop them. Only two have wanted to leave. They're protected here, well fed, well dressed, their health cared for, and never abused. The two who left, left to get married."

She faced Jonathan defiantly. "I know you expected me to set up a dressmaking or millinery establishment, but how much money do you think I could have made at that? Enough to keep from starving, if I were lucky! Not enough for Naomi, never enough for what I wanted for her!"

"I'm not condemning you." How could he? Rebecca had done the best she could, and he believed that she ran a good place. Taking everything into consideration, Rebecca had done well for herself.

"Naomi will be all right," he said again. "You can write to her, if you want to."

"I do not want to write to her. Are you crazy? Doesn't she have enough to bear, without knowing about me? Let her think I'm dead! But if she ever needs me, and you don't let me know, don't depend on living to a ripe old age!"

She meant it. It was there in her eyes.

"I can't foresee her needing you, Becky. All her needs will be provided for. The child's, too."

"Let me know whether it's a boy or a girl. It would be nice to know if I have a grandson or a granddaughter."

"Becky!" The word was torn from Jonathan. "Are you going to go on hating me all your life?"

"I don't hate you. You're what you are, just as I was what I was. I just don't ever want to see you again. You'd better leave, Jonathan, unless you want a room and a companion for the evening."

She was bitter, and she was hard, and she was deliberately trying to hurt him. Looking at her, Jonathan realized that there was nothing he could do to help her. The feeling inside him caused a mist in front of his eyes, so that he had to grope his way from the room and through the bar and out into the open air.

The hackman had left. Cursing, Jonathan looked around for another conveyance and saw none. It was later than he had thought, it had grown dark while he had been inside. He began to walk, rapidly, mindful of the unsavory neighborhood.

Rounding a corner, he knew that someone was following him. He cursed under his breath, regretting his determination never to go armed. He'd been a fool to venture into this section of the city without his pistol. He slipped in a bit of garbage and nearly fell, and the hair on the back of his neck prickled as the footsteps behind him grew closer. Catching himself, he turned to face his would-be assailant. He wouldn't go down without a fight.

There were two of them, big and burly, stinking of sweat and rum and garlic. He didn't have a chance against both of them and he knew it, but it didn't occur to him to turn and run. He even landed the first blow, dodging in underneath the first man's knife. The regret

274

uppermost in his mind was that he should have to die in a place like this, and that Prudence and Crissy and Yolande might hear of it. Who would there be to explain to them?

The knife caught his arm as he fended it off, and he felt warm blood gush out, soaking his sleeve. With only one good arm, he knew that his strength would give out.

The others came silently, with a rush of feet. Two, three, or was it four? Cowards, Jonathan thought, kicking out at the legs of the man who was closing in again for the kill, his companion close behind him, circling around to take him from the back. How many does it take, against one man?

But it was over in a matter of seconds. Four men closed in and did their work efficiently, with a minimum of noise. They weren't out to kill, only to maim. When the two thieves were lying in the gutter, the four men looked at Jonathan without smiling.

"Start walkin', mate. We'll be behind you till you're where you can find a hack."

There was a taste of salt in Jonathan's throat. Rebecca had sent them to see that he got out of this district safely. For all her bitterness, she didn't want to see him dead.

A few blocks farther on, a hack loomed up. The four men watched while Jonathan hailed it and managed to climb in, favoring his arm. He almost forgot to take money from his pocket and toss it in their direction.

"Don't come back, mate."

Jonathan wouldn't.

On the fast packet, his arm bandaged and in a sling, Jonathan leaned against the rail, watching the water slip by. He had been so moody ever since boarding that the other passengers had left him alone, the gentlemen forbearing to try to draw him into conversation or a card game, the few ladies speculating among themselves, with languishing glances, on what great burden of sorrow the handsome planter suffered.

The group of men nearest Jonathan were gesticulating, their voices loud and excited, while a newspaper was passed from hand to hand. The talk was of the latest exploit of "that madman, John Brown." On October the sixteenth, Brown had taken a group of eighteen men and captured the arsenal at Harper's Ferry, in Virginia. From the scraps of conversation that drifted into his consciousness, Jonathan gathered that Brown had had control of the entire town but for some unknown reason he hadn't pushed his advantage. Brown had merely taken shelter in the arsenal until it was surrounded by the militia. Colonel Lee had arrived on the seventeenth, and in the ensuing battle, ten of Brown's men had been slain, including two of his own sons.

Good man, Lee, Jonathan thought absently. They don't come any better. I expect this will be the end of the road for Brown; they'll hang him for sure this time.

It was a good thing he was on his way home. If he knew his father, Jacob was probably already on his way to Virginia to witness the hanging and make sure the rope was stout enough.

Jonathan dismissed John Brown from his mind and turned again to his own thoughts. He knew he would never see Rebecca again. He wouldn't even write to thank her for what she had done, because she wouldn't want his thanks. What she wanted from him, always had wanted, was something that was not in his power to give her.

276

And there were Naomi and Prue. If Martha was looking down at him, her eyes would burn right through him. I made a mess of it, Marty, Jonathan thought. I guess there's just no hope for me.

27

Winters in Martin's Corners were long and cold, with little to occupy the time. As the cold weather progressed, Emily seemed to shrivel. Her movements grew slower, though her mind remained as alert as ever. With Prudence as well as Cleo to take the burden of housework from her frail shoulders, and Michael to take over all the outside work, Emily set herself to the task of educating the unfortunate child who had come under her charge.

Naomi was an apt pupil, eager to learn. "I never knew the world was so big and filled with so many things!" she said, her eyes wide.

"It is filled with a multitude of things, child, and there is plenty of room in it for you and your baby. You can both become anything you choose to be, as long as you prepare yourself to achieve it."

"We're black," Naomi said bluntly.

"Well, there are various laws governing such matters in different states. In Virginia, for example, a person must have as much as one-quarter Negro blood to be held legally black. North Carolina says one-sixteenth, but we are not in North Carolina. As for your child, no State in the Union could label it as black, or would even attempt such a thing."

"Mister Jacob wouldn't agree with you," Naomi argued.

"And neither would I agree with Jacob, on almost any matter you could name."

Naomi wanted to believe, but a lifetime in Georgia made her doubtful. "They never told us things like that."

"Of a certainty they did not! They also prevent any slave from learning to read, do they not, to assure that they will never learn of their own rights? Come, child, back to our lesson! We are studying Canada, where escaped slaves go. Here it is on the map."

They bent their heads over their books for another half-hour, until dusk began to gather in the room, and then Emily bade Naomi wrap up warmly and go outside for some fresh air. Naomi's face lighted up. "May I milk the cow?" she asked eagerly. "Michael isn't home from the feed store yet, and I'd like to do it."

"I declare I never saw so many people who think it a privilege to milk a cow! Certainly you may." Emily's face was soft with the love that she had come to feel for Naomi, and her resolution deepened not to let anything hurt her.

Bossy's flank was warm against Naomi's cheek, and she talked to the creature, softly, as Miss Emily had instructed her. "What will happen to me, Bossy? Is Miss Emily right? Am I really white? Silly old cow, how would you know! But Miss Emily says it's true, so it must be."

The bucket filled, Naomi left the barn, her burden heavy in her hand. She was so deep in her thoughts that she didn't notice Michael until he loomed up beside her in the dusk and took the bucket from her.

"You shouldn't be carrying anything so heavy, Miss Naomi! I'm surprised Miss Emily allowed it."

"She says it won't hurt me, for a time yet." In the crisp air, Naomi's face flushed, and she was glad that it was dark enough so that Michael wouldn't notice it. He knew that she was carrying a child. He could scarcely help but know it, not being blind. But Michael, along with everyone else in Martin's Corners, thought she was a widow, a distant cousin of the Beddoes' whom Prudence and Miss Emily had befriended in her sorrow and trouble.

"Sure and the womenfolk go right on doing heavy work, back in Ireland, but you're a lady, Miss Naomi. You aren't used to it as my sister Meg would be."

"I'm strong. I hardly have enough to do, as it is. Just sewing, and taking walks, and my lessons."

"Studying, now, that's a fine thing. I never had much opportunity, myself. But you must have had some book learning before you came here."

"Only a little." Naomi's voice was muffled.

"What was he like, your husband?" The question came without volition, and Michael was aghast at himself. But it was in his mind constantly. Had Naomi loved him? Would she ever get over the grief of losing him?

Naomi raised her face, startled, and it shone pale in the twilight. Her eyes looked enormous, and to Michael's horror, they filled with tears.

"There now, see what I've done!" He set the bucket down and groped for his handkerchief and began dabbing at Naomi's wet cheeks. "It's made you cry I have, and I'd rather have cut out my stupid tongue!" His hands on her face were tender, but Naomi shrank away.

"No. Please don't!" She turned and began to run back toward the house, but in the gathering darkness she stumbled and went to her knees.

Michael was beside her at once, helping her up.

He couldn't help himself, his arms went around her and he held her close. "Darlin' girl, are you hurt?"

"You mustn't!" Naomi struggled to free herself. "You mustn't call me that, or touch me!"

Michael's hands dropped to his sides. "I beg your pardon. I was carried away. I have no right to as much as look at you, much less dare to love you!" He'd said it, and he couldn't take it back, and now Naomi was crying harder, her shoulders shaking.

"No right! Michael, it's the other way around! I'm the one that isn't good enough for you! I never will be, I never could be!"

She was running again, but Michael caught her easily and held her, his face intense as he looked down into hers. "And what could you be meaning by that? A lady like you, gentry—"

"I'm not! I never was!" She sagged in his arms, and everything came pouring from her with an anguish that made Michael writhe. "It's all a lie, I'm not gentry. I was a slave, Michael, a slave. And I never had a husband, I was raped. . . ."

Michael released her slowly. He had to let go of her, because his hands were clenching with anger. Raped! Who could have done this to her? He'd kill him, by his own Saint Michael he'd kill him, if ever he could!

His voice was thick. "It isn't true. I'll never believe it. You, a slave? Slaves are black, Naomi! It's delirious you are, talking so crazy!"

"My mother was a slave, at Roselawns. She was almost white, but she was still a slave. And that made me a slave, too."

A terrible suspicion filled Michael's mind, and he felt the blood rush to his head, making him giddy. "It wasn't Mr. Beddoes who did it to you?"

"No, no! Mister Jon is my father!" Naomi was

weeping again, silently. She just stood there with her arms hanging limply in front of her in an attitude of despair that made Michael want to tear the world down with his bare hands and build it over again to lay at her feet, just the way she wanted it. "It was a young man from another plantation. He was drunk and he was angry with Miss Prudence and he got back at her through me. So they brought me here, to Miss Emily, but I can never marry anyone, Michael. I'm tainted with sin, and you must go away and forget me, because I can't bear it if you don't."

The roar that escaped Michael's throat made Bossy raise her head and low, and her tail switched nervously. From their stolen nests in the loft, hens that had settled for the night opened sleepy eyes and cackled.

"Go away? I'll never go away, except to take you with me! I've been loving you all this time, and thinking you wouldn't touch me with your dainty foot, I'm that far beneath you, and my heart torn out every time I looked at you. It's ignorant I am, and a clumsy fool, but I'm strong, and I'll work for you, and I'll kill the next one who tries to hurt you. An Irish name isn't much to offer you, but 'tis an honest one where I come from, with never a stain on it, and better than no name for the child. There's work to be had in Boston—I'll be going there tomorrow—but I'll come back as soon as I find a job and have a place for you."

"You're crazy! How can I marry you? How can you want to give your name to a bastard?" Naomi's voice rose and then broke with hysteria.

Michael put his hand over her mouth. "Never say it!" he commanded. "Never even think it. Just say you'll have me."

She shook her head violently, until he took his hand away. "No. I can't."

"Then it's me. You can't bear the thought of having

me for a husband." Michael looked at her, his face stricken. "And you're right, I'm thinking. You have Beddoes blood, and your family would not be happy to call an Irishman kin."

"That isn't true! We'd be proud; Mister Jon liked you, and so does Miss Prudence, and Miss Emily. And I love you, how could I help but love you? But there's no use talking about it, Michael. Let me go!"

He let her go and watched her until she entered the house through the kitchen. When he followed, she was nowhere in sight. From the iron range, Cleo looked at him with inscrutable eyes, but Prudence faced him with her face flushed with anger.

"What happened out there? Naomi ran upstairs and locked our bedroom door." Prue was out of breath, and Michael knew that she had followed her half-sister and then run down again to find out what had upset her.

Michael brushed past her without answering and entered the sitting room where Emily had risen to her feet, preparing to learn for herself what the commotion was about.

As Michael stood in front of the diminutive woman, he felt like a small boy who'd been caught stealing from the poor box.

"I've done it," he said. "I've opened my great mouth and got Naomi all upset. I'm thinking you'd better go to her and see that she comes to no harm from it."

Emily sat down again. "A few tears will not hurt her. Tell me about it, Michael."

She listened without interrupting, a great virtue in a woman and one that Michael appreciated. When Michael had finished, she nodded.

"I think you need have no fear that Naomi finds you repulsive, or objects to the fact that you are Irish.

The idea of being able to marry had simply never crossed her mind. I'll talk to her, Michael."

"Then you'd not object?" Michael's astonishment made Emily smile again.

"Certainly I would not object. What I do object to is your idea of finding work in Boston. I am well aware of the kind of work available to Irish immigrants, and you would never be happy. I understand that your dream has been to have a place, a piece of land, and I'm convinced that you could succeed at farming. Tell Prue that the three of you are to go ahead with supper. I'll be down later, after I've talked with Naomi."

Michael sat at the kitchen table, but he couldn't force himself to swallow the food in front of him. For one thing, there was Prudence, firing questions at him like one of those new guns that didn't have to be reloaded at every shot. But at least she didn't get angry, or make him feel that he'd overstepped himself. Instead, she looked thoughtful.

"If Naomi loves you, none of us would have any objections. Papa liked you, and Aunt Emily thinks the world of you, and we don't give a hang about anybody else's opinion."

"I'm a Catholic."

Prudence laughed. "We don't give a hang about that, either, if you're worried about religious prejudices. No, Mike, it all depends on Naomi." Prudence had never used his nickname before, and it made Michael feel warm inside.

Cleo was pouring Michael a second glass of milk, all he'd been able to manage, when Miss Emily and Naomi came down. Miss Emily was as calm as ever, but Naomi's breathing was rapid, and there were still marks of tears on her face.

"Naomi had some idea, probably fostered by her

284

Southern heritage, that her child could be a throw-back and turn out coal-black. She knows better now. Michael, I am not going to do your proposing for you. Take her into the sitting room, where you can have proper privacy. Cleo, that boiled cabbage and beef smells delicious." Emily sat down and helped herself liberally, but Prudence noted, even through her own excitement, that her great-aunt ate very little.

Cleo observed Prue's worried look and, later, drew her aside. "Miss Prudence, Miss Emily is sick. She's been ailing for a long time, for all she never lets on. And she drinks a lot."

"Cleo! Aunt Emily, drinking?"

"I know how much of that elderberry wine she puts away." Cleo's tone was not disapproving, just anxious. "And it's a lot. It used to be she never touched it except when we had company, but now she drinks some every day, sometimes as much as half a bottle, a little at a time."

"Has she seen Doctor Bryant about her illness?"

"Yes, she has, but she didn't tell me what he said. I think you'd better see him, Miss Prudence. I think we ought to know what we've got to face."

The next morning, Prudence put on her shawl and bonnet and walked rapidly through the cold air, her shoes crunching on a thin film of ice when she walked across puddles that had not completely thawed. Doctor Bryant was in his office, the front room of his home, and he looked at her from underneath beetling brows when she entered.

"Well, now, young lady! You look fit enough to me. Or did you just drop in to pass the time of day?"

"It's Aunt Emily. I think she's very ill, and I want to know what it is." Prudence came straight to the point.

Doctor Bryant, who had risen at her entrance, sat

down again, as though he were suddenly very tired. But he was as direct as Prudence.

"I'm breaking a professional confidence in telling you this, Prudence. I gave Miss Emily my word that I wouldn't even tell the parson. She has a cancer in her breast."

"A cancer?" Prudence groped for the chair beside her and leaned against its back for support. "But that's quite serious, isn't it?"

"She's dying."

The blunt words made Prudence feel as if somebody had taken all of her insides out.

"But you're treating her! Surely you're doing something for her?"

"There is nothing to be done. Nothing that will cure her, or even prolong her life. Cancer is a fatal disease; it always has been and it always will be. All we can do is try to ease her pain as much as we can as the disease progresses. And there will be pain, more pain than you can conceive of. That's why I'm throwing my ethics down the well and telling you this. When she gets bad, really bad, you're to come and fetch me, at any time of the day or night, do you understand?"

"That's why she drinks," Prue said, her voice catching.

"That's why. There's no harm in it, at this stage of the game. She'll be gone long before she gets like old Jeb Addison. But wine won't hold the pain back much longer, Prue. That's why you'll have to come for me. I'll have to administer more opium than is found in the usual dose of laudanum, and even that relief will be temporary."

It took two tries before Prudence could force out the words. "How long has she?"

"Young woman, I'm a doctor, a poor, mortal doctor,

not God!" The doctor's voice was harsh, and Prudence realized that the harshness stemmed from anger at his own limitations, not at her question.

He was on his feet again and now his hands clamped on her shoulders, and he shook her.

"Take that look off your face! When you go home, you're going to be smiling, do you understand me? Miss Emily has enough to bear without having to see you go around like the world has come to an end! You're going to behave in an ordinary manner, as if you know nothing at all, or you'll answer to me! Talk to her, read to her, turn a blind eye to her drinking. And see that she eats! She has to keep up her strength, although for the life of me I don't know why! Whatever damned fool doctors made up the rule that we have to prolong life as long as possible, no matter the suffering, ought to have been drowned at birth!"

I can't. The words screamed in Prudence's mind. *It's too much to ask, it's inhuman.* But she didn't say them. Her face remained calm, although the smile she forced to her lips was a trembling failure.

"That's the way. Practice smiling on your way home. You can be at least as brave as she is, girl, she's the one that's suffering!" Abruptly, he took her in his arms and kissed her cheek. "Go along now, and not a word to anyone but Cleo; she can be trusted."

Prue had no memory of walking home, although the wind had turned chill and cut through her shawl, making her draw it closer around her. Cleo met her at the front gate, a question in her eyes.

"It's cancer. She's dying." She'd said it, and saying it made it all the more' true.

Cleo's expression didn't change, but the look in her eyes was one of unbearable grief. Without answering, the older woman turned and re-entered the house.

287

Prudence sat in front of the little dresser in her room, the open jewel case and Burke's latest letter in front of her. The letter had cut Prue deeply. Burke was still in Baltimore, but he had written immediately after his last visit home. His letter had been filled with Crissy; how she had blossomed out into the most beautiful girl the county had ever seen, how many beaus camped on the doorstep at Roselawns, how jealous all the other girls were of her. There had hardly been a word of his studies, and only the last line had held anything personal. He'd asked, almost as an afterthought, when she was going to come home.

She pushed the letter aside and touched the pearls, while her lips moved in a silent prayer. "Help me, Mama. Help me."

Naomi had worn the pearls the day she and Michael were married. Prue had put them around her own neck only occasionally since her father had given them to her, to help them retain their luster. Now she clasped the necklace on, forcing her fingers to steady themselves enough to manage the intricate closure, and tucked them under her high collar. She was going to need to feel them there, in the days to come.

28

Naomi's baby was a boy, brought into the world at three-fifteen one drizzling spring morning. Emily had been prepared to deliver it, but shortly after Naomi's pains had started, she had turned to Prudence and said, very calmly, "I don't believe I'm up to it after all. You'd better send Cleo to fetch Doctor Bryant."

In the end, it was Emily who was given the opium to ease her pain, while the infant was delivered without complications and greeted the dark, rainy morning with cries of outraged protest.

"He has a temper, this one!" the doctor grunted, well pleased. "Naomi, you're a remarkable young woman. I wish all my confinement cases were as easy."

"But I cried, I cried like anything!" Naomi said, shamefaced.

"Only when you had to, and there's nothing wrong with that. You should hear some of these hefty farm women carry on!"

"Like Mehitabel Tait?" Naomi had been in Martin's Corners long enough to have heard the stories about the Taits. "But Miss Emily said she only yelled because she was sure she'd have another girl."

"And you have a fine boy, I've never seen a finer."

Naomi was lying back against a freshly cased pillow, holding her son in her arms, when Michael was finally allowed in. He took one look at the mother and child and tears filled his eyes. He went to his knees and crossed himself.

Prudence tapped him on the top of his head. "Mike! You're lucky nobody is around to see you! Crying, I vow!"

"And who has a better right? Here they are, my darling and my son. A boy it is, Cleo told me, and both of them alive and well and me thinking all this time that never could I be so lucky! Sometimes a man's faith is sorely tried, Prudence, and I need to ask pardon for doubting."

During these last months, Michael had been invaluable. Prudence felt she had to tell him the truth about her aunt, although they had kept it from Naomi. And Michael, with his Irish charm, had made a game of it, pretending that he couldn't resist picking Miss Emily up in his arms and carrying her up the stairs to bed, telling her she weighed no more than a feather. He'd regaled them with stories about Ireland, about leprechauns and Larry-go-downs, about fairy rings in the dew, that no man dared to step in on his way to fetch in the cows, and the evil fairies who snatched infants from their cradles and left changelings, strange, dark-souled children who were nothing but trouble to their families.

"Never a word of it would I believe, except that me own mither's mither told me, and would she lie? Now meself, I never saw one, but they're there, and disbelief bodes a man no good because they'll get even, Miss Emily, and there's the truth of it."

Emily had laughed, forgetting her pain for a brief while, and Naomi had listened entranced. How happy Naomi had become. And now her happiness was

290

complete. Her child was born, a strapping boy, the fuzz of hair on his head so fair as to be almost colorless, his skin, once the newborn redness had faded, as white as Prudence's own, his eyes promising to be the blue of Gaylord Renault's.

Although Prudence moved through the days with a heavy heart, she was always aware of the blessing that Emily had lived to see Arthur born and Abraham Lincoln nominated. There had been some fear of the outcome when Senator William H. Seward of New York, who contended that a war between the States was inevitable, had entered the race. Chase, Bates, and Cameron had also put in bids for the nomination, but they had not caused as much worry.

Two hundred and thirty-three votes had been needed to win, and on the third ballot Lincoln had garnered two hundred thirty-one and a half. (A half, Prudence had wondered? How could that be? But it had been in the *Clarion,* so it must be right, because Mr. Lawrence didn't make mistakes like that, especially on anything as important as the Presidential election.) At the last moment, Ohio had risen and cast four more votes for Mr. Lincoln, and the issue had been resolved.

"Mr. Lawrence says that Mr. Lincoln actually played ball, in Springfield, while he was waiting for the results!" Prudence marveled. "He must not have doubted the outcome at all."

"Mr. Lincoln is an intelligent man, and he no doubt knew that keeping occupied would be the best antidote to worry," Emily offered.

"And there won't be a war, after all." Prudence breathed a sigh of relief. "Mr. Lincoln calls for noninterference with the slave States."

"His platform also calls for a stiff tariff to protect American industry," Miss Emily reminded her. "Don't

291

count your chickens before they're hatched, Prue. We can only hope that Mr. Lincoln will be able to hold both North and South in line. I'm rather pleased with Mrs. Lincoln, myself. She hopes to save at least twelve thousand dollars a year out of Mr. Lincoln's salary of twenty thousand, and that shows that she has good common sense and a background of thrift."

Emily leaned back in her chair and closed her eyes. Rising to tiptoe from the room, Prudence planned to leave Emily to her nap so that her ravaged body would get some of the rest it sorely needed. The elections had been a godsend, keeping her great-aunt's interest at such a high pitch that it helped her to forget her pain, but it was always there, crouching like a wild beast, waiting to spring.

But Emily's voice stopped her at the kitchen doorway. "Prudence, bring Naomi and Michael to me. It's necessary that we have a family conference."

"Don't you think that you should rest a little first, Aunt Emily?"

"My dear Prudence, very soon now, I shall have an eternity to rest." Her great-aunt's eyes held Prue's steadily, without dissembling. Although it had never been mentioned between them, Emily knew that Prudence was aware of her condition. "There are things that must be settled, and I want to be sure that Naomi's future is secure before I die."

Heavy-hearted, Prudence did as she was told. Cleo went to fetch Michael from the garden, where he was using the late afternoon hours to thin and weed the vegetables, and Prudence, carrying Arthur, brought Naomi down to the sitting room.

Emily waited until they all sat down, and she motioned for Cleo to do the same. "Arthur is a month old, and a sturdy child. As the weather is mild, there is no reason to delay your departure."

292

Michael had spent the first months after their marriage searching for a suitable farm. Emily had advanced a sum of money toward its purchase, and Jonathan had sent more. Michael's protests had been quashed. "You are a strong and capable man, and you will reimburse us as your farm prospers. Prudence will be returning south in the near future, and my needs are very little. Cleo shall have this house and land after I am gone, and I have no one else to provide for. The sooner you have a farm, the sooner you will prosper and be able to provide Naomi with the security we all want for her and Arthur and the other children you will have."

Through David Lawrence, who had many acquaintances because of his antislavery articles in his newspaper, Michael had learned of a farm in Maine. He'd hired a horse and gone up to see it before the worst of the winter had set in. Prudence had objected to their moving such a distance, but Naomi had wanted to go far enough away so that no one would ever connect her son with the Beddoes family. "I don't want anyone ever to guess that he isn't Michael's own."

Now Michael smiled at Miss Emily. It would break his heart to leave her, but Naomi's happiness had to come first, and the land on the farm in Maine was so good that it made his Irish heart swell. There'd be no blight there, and he'd seen with his own eyes the potatoes that it grew. He only regretted that his own mother would never see it. Meg had written that she was dead, too weak to fight off the lung congestion that had carried her away. The money that Michael had sent, out of his wages from Mr. Hamilton, had come too late. In any case, she had refused to budge from Ireland. Her husband was buried there,

293

and all her family, and she would not leave their bones.

Right now, he could only agree with Emily. "The farm will be in fine shape, Miss Emily. The hired man stayed on, you know, and promised he'd have the crop in before ever we arrive, and he struck me as a reliable man. But you are right, I'm afraid. It's time we were leaving. My hands are itching to get into that soil."

"I have come to a decision," Emily said. Her hands grasped the arms of her rocking chair tightly, so that the veins showed through her almost transparent skin. "Cleo is to go with you." She looked at Cleo. "If she agrees, of course. Naomi will need her help, and I know from my own experience that Cleo is a tower of strength. I would never have a moment's real peace unless I knew that Cleo was there to take some of the burden from Naomi's shoulders. The life of a farm wife is not easy, as I remember from my own girlhood all too well."

Cleo started to protest, but she held the words back. Leave Miss Emily? It would be like tearing the heart out of her body. But her eyes and Emily's met, with complete understanding. In a very short time now, Emily would no longer need her, and Prudence would stay with Emily until the end.

"I'll go," Cleo said.

"Miss Emily, you can't let us take Cleo." Naomi's face had gone pale. "Why, whatever would you do without her? I can manage; I'm much stronger than I look."

"You are also very young, and there will be other babies. No, Cleo is going with you, for now at least."

Michael's face was a study in emotions. No matter what anyone said, Miss Emily was a saint. Look at all she had done for him already, taking him in, healing his hands, explaining things so that Naomi had agreed to marry him, and now to persuade Cleo to come with them as well! He was the happiest man alive. These last months had been like being in heaven, and if it was a sin to think it, then let it be, because it was true. He'd never dared to dream of such happiness as it was to have Naomi for a wife, and he loved Arthur as though the child were his own.

"Our first daughter will be named for you." It was all he could think of to say. "And the second for Prudence."

"Well, I'm glad that Crissy isn't here, because you're building quite a family for yourself, two girls on top of all those strapping sons you'll have!" Prudence had to laugh to keep from crying. It seemed that her whole life had been a series of partings from those she loved, and this one was especially bitter because she would probably never see Naomi and Michael and little Arthur, or Cleo, again. Maine was a long way from Georgia, and Burke, as a doctor, would not have time to make long journeys. Nor would Michael, as a farmer, be able to leave his land to take Naomi to visit Georgia, even if such a visit would be possible, or desirable.

"Then it is settled," Emily said. "I want you to leave the day after tomorrow. That will give you plenty of time to pack. Michael, you'd better go this evening and make sure that the two horses you bought from Sam Tait's grandson will be ready for you. And pick up the wagon the wainright sold you."

Thinking of the horses made Michael feel better. They were fine animals, big-boned and strong, and they would plow his fields for years to come.

What a letter he would write to his sister Meg! She'd think him a king, no less, with his own farm, and fine animals, and no landlord to turn him out!

He hoped there would be a Catholic church within a reasonable distance, because he felt the need to give thanks in a place of worship at least once a week for as long as he should live. The first candle he burned would be for Miss Emily, the second for Prudence, and his prayers for their welfare and souls would be never-ending.

The four travelers were ready at first light, the day they left. The weather promised to be sunny and fair, a good omen for the beginning of a journey.

Only Naomi cried, her face crumpled with grief at leaving the two women she loved. In spite of her happiness to be going with Michael to start a new life, she felt torn and tearful. Prudence held her own tears back, and Cleo sat straight and still on the wagon seat beside them, holding Arthur in her arms.

"Let me hold him just once more!" Prudence begged, and when she took the infant in her arms, it was almost her undoing.

"Hand him back, Prue. They must be on their way. Prolonged leave-takings only make it harder," Emily said, though she, too, was very still. "Cleo, thank you for all the years you gave me. And God bless you all."

Emily stood there, not moving, watching while Michael clucked up the horses and the heavy wagon rumbled out of the yard. Then she turned to Prudence.

"Come inside now. I think we will indulge in a small glass of wine, a toast to their happiness." There were deep lines of pain on her face that had nothing to do with the leave-taking, and Prudence winced, knowing what the older woman suffered.

"I'll bring it. They'll be all right, Aunt Emily."

"I know they will. I'm a little tired, Prudence. I think I'll rest a while after we've drunk our toast."

When I see Burke, Prudence thought, I'll have a

296

thing or two to say to him. Why can't doctors do something for people like Aunt Emily? I won't care how hard he works or how much he neglects me, if he can just find a way to relieve their suffering.

The hurt she had felt at Burke's numerous references to Crissy in the first letter she had received from him had long since receded. How foolish she had been to let it bother her! Crissy was beautiful, yes, but she was only a child. Burke had written her since then, still mentioning Crissy, but now Prudence could smile at his thoughtfulness in letting her know how her sister was faring.

Burke was hers, just as she was his. There was no need for words of reassurance between them; they had both known it since they'd been children. A doctor's wife with a jealous nature would have a thin time of it.

Burke was hers, but not yet. Not while Miss Emily lived. Her smile faded as she went to bring the elderberry wine, and she resolutely ignored the level of the wine in the bottle, which had been more than half-full last evening and was now less than a quarter full. She only hoped that the supply would last as long as it was needed.

29

The inn where they stopped on their third night was a poor one, for they were off the more heavily traveled roads now. The innkeeper, a wizened little man with a two-day stubble of beard, looked at Cleo sourly and then at Michael and Naomi. "Don't see many slaves up this way," he said, his disapproval evident in his voice.

"Cleo is not a slave." Michael looked the man in the eye. "She isn't even a servant. She's our friend, a member of our family."

The innkeeper thawed visibly. "Well, then, that's different. I don't hold with slavery. I'll find her a cozy place to sleep. We only have three bedrooms, and two of them are already spoken for, but I'll make her up a pallet by the fire."

"Anything will do," Cleo assured the landlord, "as long as it's clean."

The inn wasn't actually clean. The landlord was a widower, and since his wife's demise he had been slack about such matters. It wasn't a place where gentry stopped, in any case. The food was of such poor quality that Naomi could hardly eat it, but she finished her portion without complaint. Being with Michael, having a home of her own to go to, made her ashamed to complain, even in her own mind.

It seemed that Naomi had no sooner gotten to sleep on the lumpy mattress, under blankets that had not seen soap and water for too many months, than she awakened by the rapping on their bolted bedroom door. Michael was sound asleep, so she threw a shawl around her nightdress and answered it herself.

"I have to talk to your mister," the landlord said, as he brushed past her to shake Michael's shoulder.

Michael came awake with a start and flailed his arms at the man who bent over him.

"Hush! Be quiet! I don't want the whole place roused. I got to take a chance on you, seeing as your black woman ain't a slave and you called her friend. I got a man out there in my barn, escaped from the South last winter. He's been passed along from one underground station to another, but the farmer who was going to take him on has come down sick. His lad just brought me word, along with worse news. There's bounty-hunters on his trail, and like as not they'll stop off here and have a look. I got to get him out of here, right now!"

Michael was fully alert now, his eyes shining with interest. "A slave, you say? Poor devil! But it's the middle of the night, man!"

"All the better, if you'll take him. You'll get a good start and be out of danger of being overtaken. Will you do it?"

"If I were alone I wouldn't hesitate, but I have my wife and baby to think of." There was doubt in Michael's voice, and he looked at Naomi.

"Michael, of course we must take him! I can be ready in a few minutes. Go hitch up the wagon."

It took Michael but a moment to throw on his clothes, and by the time he and the landlord had the horses hitched, Cleo and Naomi joined them in the stableyard. The black man was installed under the tarpaulin in the back of the wagon, along with Cleo, who spoke to him reassuringly and learned that his name was Jube.

"Short for Jupiter, I expect, Miss Naomi," Cleo said. "Here, let me take Arthur. He'll be snug and warm under here with us and go straight off back to sleep."

"The next station's fifteen miles down this road. Olsen, the farmer's name is. You take the fork to the left, by a blasted pine tree, after fifteen miles, and then you can't miss it." The innkeeper was in a sweat to get rid of them, his fright obvious as he kept looking over his shoulder.

There was only the sound of the horses' hooves and the creaking of the wagon, and the soughing of the wind in the tree branches when a breeze sprang up. It was chilly, and Naomi pulled her shawl closer around her shoulders. The wagon jolted and bumped, for the state of the road, after the winter snows, was deplorable. Miss Emily had said that some day this country would be so populated that all the roads would be maintained in good condition, but it was hard for Naomi to envision it, and she began doing mental arithmetic as Miss Emily had taught her, to keep from worrying about the dark and the cold.

Caught up in her own thoughts, she half-dozed for an hour or two—she wasn't sure how long it had been. It was Michael who heard the hoofbeats behind them on the road, and she only stiffened to attention at his exclamation.

"It may be trouble. Honest men don't go galloping around the country in the middle of the night. Those bounty-hunters may have been closer than the landlord knew. Just hold tight, Naomi. I'll tell them that your mother's sick, and we're traveling at night to get to her as fast as we can."

The horsemen were approaching fast, and Naomi's spine chilled as she heard a shouted command for them to whoa up. They loomed out of the darkness, and Michael pulled the team to a halt.

"What's all this? We have nothing for you to steal." He made his voice sound angry.

"We're looking for an escaped slave." The men surveyed Naomi and Michael as well as they could in the darkness.

"Well, you can see for yourselves that we aren't black! Pull your horses aside and let us pass. We're in an almighty hurry, my wife's mother is dying and we're trying to get to her before she's gone."

Naomi began to cry. "Michael, are they highwaymen? Are they going to hurt us?" Even to her own ears her fright sounded convincing.

The older of the two men had the grace to look abashed. "You didn't stop at that inn back there?"

"No, we didn't. We've been traveling straight through."

"Well . . ." the man made up his mind. "Go along, then. I reckon we were steered wrong. Ten to one the bugger's still back at Jenkins's place. We'll go back and take a better look."

Michael flicked the reins as the men drew their horses aside. Naomi's breath caught, and she held it, hardly believing that the danger was past.

"We did it!" she whispered.

"You're the one who convinced them. You were fine! Being able to look pretty when you're crying is an advantage to any girl! You could have made your fortune on the stage." Michael's voice was filled with admiration.

At that precise moment, Arthur chose to wake up

and send forth a piercing, lusty wail. Behind them, they heard the slave-catchers' horses pause, and Michael cursed. They were in for it now, and he was unarmed.

"That did it! They'll be after us. Hang on, Naomi. I'm going to make a run for it. If they look under that tarpaulin, it'll be all up with that poor devil back there. I could probably handle one of them, but they'll be having guns, and there's two of them. Watch out for some place we can turn off the road. If we're lucky, we might be able to lose them."

Standing up in the seat, he laid the whip on the horses. They broke into a lumbering gallop, filled with panic at Michael's whoop. The wagon jolted and bounced from one side of the rutted road to the other, in constant danger of going off the road entirely and smashing into the trees on either side. Their progress was so noisy that Naomi couldn't hear if they were being pursued. Maybe the men hadn't heard Arthur, maybe they'd been far enough away so the sound hadn't carried to them, or they might simply have assumed that there was a baby they hadn't noticed in the wagon.

Her hopes were short-lived. The horsemen bore down on them and cut ahead of Michael's team. Shouting a wild Irish war cry that made Naomi's blood run cold, Michael laid at them with his whip, lashing furiously, defying them.

"Keep off! I'll cut you to ribbons!" Michael warned.

"Pull up or I'll shoot!" There was a pistol in the first man's hand. Cursing again, Michael tossed the reins to Naomi. "Keep going!" he shouted at her, and at the same instant, he sprang. His leap took him on top of the man with the pistol, and they both fell from the horse into a tangled heap on the ground.

Almost paralyzed with fear, Naomi struggled to

302

control the racing team. There was the sound of a gunshot behind her, and she cried out and tried to stop the horses, but the shot had further terrified them and they were out of control. Naomi's arms felt as if they were being pulled out of their sockets. "Whoa, whoa!" she cried. Michael! Had he been shot? She had to stop the team, she had to go back, and find out. Oh, Michael, Michael!

The wagon left the road, lurched, struck against the side of a tree and overturned. Naomi screamed as she was thrown from the seat. And then there was silence, except for the sound of the wagon wheels as they spun crazily in the air and the scream of a horse.

"Look! There he goes, the bastard!" A short distance back, the second horseman saw a dark figure dart away from the overturned wagon and disappear into the thick woods that lined the road. He spurred his horse after the fugitive, and in a moment he, too, was lost from sight.

Cautiously, Cleo put her head out from under the wagon. Her hand was clamped tightly over Arthur's mouth. She saw Naomi, lying like a rag doll, at the side of the road, and she crawled to her, still carrying the baby.

It took Cleo only a moment to see that Naomi was dead. In her shock, she could not even weep. Where was Michael, and what had happened to the other men? She looked at Naomi again and touched her cheek gently. Naomi's head was turned at a grotesque angle, her neck broken.

Keeping off the road, still carrying Arthur with her free hand over his mouth, Cleo back-tracked. A short walk brought her to the place where Michael had leaped from the wagon onto the shoulders of the older horseman. They were there, both of them. Both of them were dead.

Michael had been shot, but by some superhuman strength engendered by rage, his huge hands had strangled the life out of his assailant. He lay on top of the other man, his hands still clasped around the man's throat, frozen there in his death throes.

Cleo rose from her knees. She dared not even pause to say a prayer. The first horseman might come back at any moment. Murder had been done, and Cleo had no illusions that she, a witness, would be left alive. The slave-catcher would kill Arthur, too, simply because the baby would be a problem to him.

Her breath catching in her throat, Cleo took to the trees. It would be a long walk home to Martin's Corners, and she would have to walk every step of the way. She dared not take time to untangle one of the horses from the harness. The other horse was still screaming, one of its legs broken.

She would not dare to seek help from any house or settlement along the way. A black woman alone, carrying a white baby, would be suspect, and there was always the chance that the remaining slave-catcher would hear of it and claim that she was an escaped slave. Who would believe her, a black woman? She'd be charged with kidnapping, thrown into jail, and Arthur taken from her. Miss Emily and Prudence were a long way away; it would take a long time for word to reach them even if whoever caught her would agree to send a message.

Resolutely, still holding her hand over Arthur's mouth so that no whimper of his could alert the remaining slave-catcher to her presence, she began to walk.

30

Prudence was at the stove, frying the pungent codfish cakes, when Emily came downstairs. Prudence saw, with a pang, that her great-aunt's hair was poorly arranged. It hurt the elderly woman to raise her arm now, and Prudence kept her face averted so that her aunt wouldn't see that she had noticed.

"The coffee's about ready. Sit down and I'll pour you a cup."

They were at the table when the kitchen door opened and Cleo stood there, tall and gaunt, thinner even than she had been when she had left, her clothing stained and ripped in a dozen places, scratches on her face and hands. She held a bundle close to her breast, and her eyes were pools of fatigue and a grief unto death. Even before Prudence could rise to her feet, the bundle stirred, and a thin, angry wail came from the wrappings.

"No!" The word was torn from Prudence's throat, a denial of what she knew must be true, even before Cleo spoke. "Oh, God, no!"

Cleo walked to the table, and for the first time in her life, she sat down before she was asked.

"They came after us, two men on horses. Michael fought them, and the wagon tipped over. Michael was shot. Naomi was thrown from the wagon, and her neck was broken."

Her words came slowly, without expression. "They were slave-catchers, the men who did it. We'd picked up an escaped slave—an innkeeper asked us to take him on. They're dead, Naomi and Michael are dead, and so's one of the men who stopped us. The other one took off after the slave, through the woods."

Prudence had lifted Arthur from her arms and was taking him out of the shawl. The baby's angry wailing nearly drowned out Cleo's voice as she droned on, as if she couldn't stop.

"I walked. It was night and I got lost, and Arthur kept crying, once I dared take my hand from over his mouth. I kept on walking. I didn't dare stop. I was afraid the other man would come and find us. So I kept on walking, and in the morning I rested a little, and then I walked some more and I came to a farm, but I was afraid to ask for help. I hid in the bushes until I had a chance to get to a cow in the field and I milked it. I had to catch the milk in my hand and soak a piece of Arthur's petticoat in it to give him to suck, and it took a long time. But it quieted him a little, and I walked some more."

Her shoulders slumped, as if she had come to the end of her strength and couldn't go on. Emily, moving quietly, put a cup of coffee in front of her and then went to the sitting room and returned with the decanter and poured her a glass of wine.

Cleo drank, first the coffee and then the wine. "It was a long time before I dared walk on the road at all, and then I got off it whenever I saw anybody coming. But I came home as fast as I could, Miss Emily. And this morning, right after daylight, I saw a man from around here, in his wagon, and he gave me a ride. He's putting his horse up at the inn and

306

then he's coming back here to see how we are. Miss Naomi's dead, Miss Emily. I had to leave her there. I had to bring Arthur home."

Prudence sat at the kitchen table, her dark hair hanging loose, haloed in the glow of the single lamp. It was after eleven at night, and both Emily and Cleo were in bed. Upstairs, Arthur whimpered in his sleep, but there was no following roar of outrage to signal his displeasure at being wet or hungry. Prudence sighed with relief and picked up her pen again. She was writing to Burke, and the words came hard.

"I want you to tell Papa and my grandparents about Naomi. I can't bear for them to learn of it from a letter. Cleo brought Arthur home more than a week ago, and I haven't been able to bear to write about it, even to you, until now. But they must be told, and you must be the one to tell them. They'll need you, Burke. Have your mother go with you when you tell them. She'll know what to do for my grandmother.

"Aunt Emily grows frailer every day. She eats less and less, and I know that her pain is excruciating. Still she tries to move about and to be the same tower of strength for Cleo and me that she has always been. She consumes a great deal of wine, and I believe that its nourishment is all that keeps her alive."

She paused and rested her head on her hand. It was so quiet that she could hear the tick of the mantel clock in the sitting room and the last faint cracklings of the fire in the range as it went out.

"Arthur thrives. He gives every indication of being an exceptionally bright child, as well as an extremely handsome one, and he is the greatest comfort to Aunt Emily, who dotes on him although, of course, she does not spoil him as Cleo and I do.

307

"What is the latest sentiment about things political, in the South? Aunt Emily and I both read all the Boston newspapers, as well as Mr. Greeley's New York *Tribune*. The news is so disturbing that Aunt Emily is convinced that the rift between North and South can do nothing but widen.

"I send you, as always, my highest regards, and my wishes for your happiness and success. Yours of this instance, April the twelfth, eighteen hundred and sixty-one."

The next morning she burst through the front door, mindless of her muddy tracks, instead of going around to the woodshed and back kitchen.

"Aunt Emily, it's happened, the war has started!"

They spread the newspaper out on the kitchen table to read it. Prudence, still in her outdoor clothing, stood with Cleo behind Emily's chair as they pored over the headlines.

Second Edition, April 13, 1861
Half past one o'clock, P.M.

THE WAR BEGUN

Very exciting News from Charleston

Important Correspondence between General Beauregard, Major Anderson and the Northern Secretary of War

The Summons to Major Anderson to Surrender

MAJOR ANDERSON'S REFUSAL

BOMBARDMENT OF FORT SUMTER COMMENCED

Terrible fire from the Secessionists' Batteries

BRILLIANT DEFENSE OF MAJ.
ANDERSON AND HIS GALLANT
GARRISON

"It's fallen," Emily said, her voice curiously flat. "Fort Sumter has fallen." The eyes of the three women were bleak as they looked at each other, before they went on to read every word in the long account of the fort's defense and eventual surrender. "May God have mercy on them all!"

My father, my sister, Miss Yolande and Jacob, Prudence thought. Burke, Burke!

"But it will be over soon." She tried to make her voice firm. "Mr. Lincoln will send troops, and the rebellion will be put down!"

"Pray God that it is so." Emily bent her head.

She was not the only one who prayed that it would be so. The First Congregational Church, as well as the other churches in the neighborhood, was filled to capacity that Sunday morning, as people flocked to pray for an early victory and to exchange rumors and news. Reverend Smith, who was a very old man by now, preempted the pulpit from Reverend Parker and preached a long, ranting sermon, much interspersed with prayer. So excited was he that he failed to notice and reprimand Mrs. Blaisdel's headgear as he ordinarily would have done.

31

Prudence's mind and body both felt numb for the first few weeks following the outbreak of the war. Events happened with such rapidity that she could scarcely keep up with them. It seemed, in those early days, that nothing could keep the South from sweeping to an early, overwhelming victory, in spite of Mr. Lincoln's calling for seventy-five volunteers on April the fifteenth, and his blockading of Southern harbors on the nineteenth. The news of the blockade was more than offset by the Confederates' taking of the Federal Arsenal at Harpers Ferry on the nineteenth, and the U.S. Navy Yard at Norfolk, Virginia.

It was a heavy blow that Colonel Robert E. Lee had refused the field command of the Armies of the North and had hurried home to become Commander in Chief of the Confederate Forces of Virginia.

"We lost a good man there, a very able man," David Lawrence said. He had taken to dropping in nearly every evening to keep Miss Emily informed of the latest war news and to discuss its implications with her.

Prudence's nerves were stretched to the breaking point because there was no way to receive news from the South. Burke would probably not have to fight as a soldier, since both sides were desperately in need of doctors. But Jonathan and Rory, and perhaps even Jacob, would have joined up by now, riding into battle as officers. She had written to both Jonathan and Burke, the Monday after Fort Sumter, but she had no idea whether her letters had arrived at their destination, and there had been no replies. Her only comfort was that there were no reports of fighting near Roselawns. Crissy and Yolande would be all right, at least.

The days wore on, telescoping one into another, and Prudence lived in a sort of suspended animation, waiting for news, waiting for something to happen. As summer faded into fall, Emily's condition worsened, and watching her, Prudence had the dreadful conviction that her great-aunt would not live out the winter.

The nights were the worst, when Emily was asleep, drugged by elderberry wine and the laudanum that Doctor Bryant administered. Often on those interminable nights, Prudence would take out the case that contained her mother's pearls and hold them in her hands to try to draw a measure of faith and strength from them. Sometimes she would wear them to bed, just to feel them against her skin, bringing comfort.

By fall, Emily was very bad and growing worse with every day that passed. She could no longer climb up or down the stairs, but Cleo had to carry her, her weight hardly more than a small child's. Even then, no matter how gently Cleo lifted her, the old lady would cry out in pain. Still, she refused to remain upstairs in her bed. Beds, she said, were for sleeping in and for dying in, and she wasn't dead yet.

"Take the medicine Doctor Bryant left for you," Prudence begged.

"I do take it. It doesn't do much good."

"Then have some more wine."

Miss Emily would accept the wine and drink, not one glass but two or three. "I never thought to go to my grave a drunkard," she said. "It only proves how little we know."

Still she fought on, bearing her pain, speaking words of comfort to Prudence, and even rocking Arthur when she had had enough wine to ignore the pain it caused her.

"He's too heavy for you, he'll hurt you!" Prudence protested.

"All love is bound up with hurting. The hurt is well worth it."

But was it worth it? Sometimes Prudence doubted it, and her doubts were so strong that she felt sick to her soul.

A letter from Crissy, months delayed, having traveled through no one knew how many different hands, arrived on November the fifth. It was only a single sheet, folded over so the blank side served as an envelope, and it had been carried in so many different pockets that Prudence's name and address were blurred. Even the name of the sender was obliterated, where dampness had got at it and turned the ink into an illegible smear, so that it took Prudence a moment to realize that the letter was from her sister rather than from her father or her grandmother or even from Burke.

Burke! For a moment, when the letter had been placed in her hands at the post office, her heart had lurched, until her eyes made out that the handwriting of the address was not masculine, no matter how smeared. Coming from the South, there was no way the letter would have been sent through legitimate channels, and so it had had to suffer mishandling

312

and abuse until it was a wonder that it had ever arrived at all.

But it was news from home, even if it wasn't from Burke, and Prudence's hands trembled as she opened it.

"Prue, I'm married! It was all so exciting! I was in Baltimore when the war started, visiting Grandma's cousins the Vernons, and he was enlisting, of course. We didn't even have time to let Papa know, Cousin Paul arranged everything and gave me away, and it was all so romantic and patriotic, scads of people are getting married before the men have to march away to war! Oh Prue I'm so happy and I know you'll be happy for me even though we all thought for a long time that it was you he wanted but when the war came he said it had always been me. . . ."

The writing was tiny, cramped together to get all of the words in the limited space. The writing blurred in front of Prudence's eyes, the misspelled words, typical of Crissy, running together.

The letter fell from her fingers. Married! They were married! She lowered her head to the kitchen table and her shoulders shook.

All those letters from Burke, before the war had started, talking about Crissy, always about Crissy! Crissy was so grown-up, Crissy was the prettiest girl Georgia had ever seen, Crissy this and Crissy that. He must have seen a lot of her; the love affair must have progressed to the point where marriage was inevitable. The war, and Crissy's chance visit to Baltimore where Burke was still studying, had only brought it to a head. In Massachusetts, too, young people were rushing to the altar to grasp what happiness they could before the war tore them away from each other, perhaps forever.

How could she have been so blind, how could she

have been such a fool! Burke had told her, over and over, how he felt about Crissy, if only she had realized it.

Where, in all of Burke's letters, had he ever told Prudence that he loved her? He had never said it, or written it; she had taken it for granted that he felt the same way about her that she felt about him. Aunt Emily was wrong, the hurt of loving wasn't worth it, it could never be worth it, not this pain, this desolation, this stark knowledge that the world would be forever empty, for there was nothing left in it for her.

Blindly, she rose to her feet and went upstairs to her room where Arthur was napping in his cradle. He stirred as she entered, and opened his eyes, and smiled and stretched up his chubby arms for her to take him. When she failed to respond, his face puckered up and he began to cry.

Prudence lifted him then, and held him close, and wondered why her tears would not fall as his did, freely, to give vent to her grief. Cry for me, baby, she begged him silently, shed all my tears for me, because mine won't come when I need them!

"Shall I go up to her?" Cleo asked, her eyes desolate with sympathy for Prudence's suffering.

"Certainly not. We can't help her, either of us. She can only help herself." Emily rose and went out to vent her own emotions on the woodpile, ignoring the pain that tore through her shoulder and breast.

In the kitchen, Cleo snatched up the letter and threw it into the fire before she went out to take the hatchet from Emily's hand. She'd always known that Crissy was nothing but trouble.

The sound of Aunt Emily's moans tore at Prudence's nerves until they were jagged and raw, until a whisper

314

made them cringe. Worse than the moaning, the whimpers of pure anguish, and the words which sometimes poured from Emily's withered lips, draw back over her teeth in agony. She used language that Prudence had never heard or dreamed that her aunt knew.

"Stop your ears, Miss Prue," Cleo told her. "Go along now, go out to the barn. I'll sit with her."

"No. I can stand it. Let her cuss all she wants to!"

"She doesn't know she's doing it, Prudence."

Prue faced Doctor Bryant, and she screamed at him. "Do something! For the love of God, do something! It's inhuman! She's turning into an animal, my aunt is turning into an animal!"

"An animal caught in a trap," Doctor Bryant said. He looked old, incredibly old, the lines on his face etched deep with suffering. "Only, we're allowed to put animals out of their misery."

"Then do it! I swear to God, if you don't, I will!"

She didn't. She couldn't bring herself to press the pillow down over Miss Emily's face that night, although she'd entered the room determined that she would do it. Her aunt opened her eyes and looked at her.

"Damn it to hell, Prue, what are you waiting for? Do it!"

Retching, Prudence stumbled from the room. Cleo met her at the top of the stairs and put her arm around her and led her to her own room.

The doctor came later that night. He prepared a draught for Miss Emily and supported her shoulders while she drank it. "Take it all, old friend," he said.

Miss Emily took it all. There was a faint, wry smile on her face, grotesque against the dribbles that had escaped the corners of her mouth.

"Thank you, George."

315

He was still sitting beside her when Prudence crept in. "How is she? Tell me, how is she?"

"She's asleep. She won't wake up."

Prudence wept silently. He'd done it. She hadn't had the courage, but he had. Forgive me, Aunt Emily, she whispered, before she turned, blindly, to Cleo's arms for comfort.

32

The snow began to fall as Prudence paused outside the jeweler's shop in Boston. She was cold. Her loose-fitting paletot hadn't been warm enough after all—she hadn't expected snow. The big flakes were melting where they dropped, and she was beginning to get wet. Brushing the snowflakes off, she wished she had brought her umbrella, but she had left it at the Carters' house. Hester Carter, who had been Hester Lattimer, had kindly lent her her chaise and driver for this errand.

The case containing the necklace was safe in her pocket. Ladies seldom carried reticules now, as their skirts were provided with pockets for carrying small articles. She touched it to make sure that it was safe, took a deep breath, and entered the shop.

She must sell the necklace. There was no money. She had been shocked to learn how little Aunt Emily had kept to live on. The money she had loaned Michael to help buy the farm in Maine might be recovered in time, but the sellers, the two daughters of the original owners, claimed that they would have to re-sell the place before they could make any refund.

A gentleman in a morning coat approached Prudence as she hesitated just inside the doorway. "Yes, miss?" Clearly, he thought that Prudence was out of her natural orbit, with her serviceable dress and her paletot which was of good quality but hardly the latest mode, and her plain, prim bonnet framing a face that looked pale and a little frightened in spite of her enforced calm.

"I am Prudence Beddoes. Mr. Joseph Carter made an appointment for me."

Mr. Carter's name made an impression on the man. His expression was respectful as he disappeared through a door at the rear of the shop and reappeared a moment later behind a younger man.

"Miss Beddoes? I have been expecting you. If you will come into my office?"

The office was small but richly furnished, and there was a fire in a small marble fireplace. The younger man, Mr. Wentworth, was the owner of the establishment. Drawing a chair close to the blaze, he indicated that she should sit there and warm herself.

"It's turned raw, Miss Beddoes. Would you like a cup of tea?"

"Yes, thank you." His kindness, after Joseph Carter's pomposity and Hester's ill-concealed patronage toward an impecunious acquaintance, broke through Prudence's defenses, and her eyes filled with tears. She turned her head away quickly, but Mr. Wentworth noticed and he cleared his throat, distressed. While she recovered herself, he busied himself by pouring her tea from a kettle on the hearth, making a small ceremony of filling the delicate china cup.

"I know how painful this must be for you, my dear. But with so many men going off to fight, a good many ladies have been constrained to sell off pieces that they set a great store by."

How nice his voice is, Prudence thought. She blinked to clear her eyes and looked directly at him for the first time. She had no idea of the impact of that look, her face pale and forlorn, her eyes luminous with the tears that were still in them. Mr. Wentworth's heart turned over. Joseph had told him a little of her circumstances, and he felt the greatest sympathy for her.

"There's no use putting it off." Prudence's voice held a slight tremor, which she quelled, and it was firm as she went on. "Here are the pearls, Mr. Wentworth. My father told me that they are good ones."

Aaron Wentworth accepted the case, and he nodded as he lifted the necklace and examined it. "They are indeed. They are of good size and beautifully matched, although of course they should have been worn more often."

Prue smiled, a gentle smile that transformed her face. "Yes, Papa told me that, but there are few opportunities for wearing a pearl necklace in Martin's Corners. I'm afraid that Bossy wouldn't appreciate them while I'm milking her, and the bugs and the weeds in the garden would simply ignore my splendor."

Her courage impressed him. "Mr. Carter told me that you are originally from the South."

Prudence nodded, and her smile flickered again. "I was caught by the war, and now I find myself unable to get home and short of funds."

"Miss Beddoes, this necklace is worth a great deal, but it is a shame that you should have to sell it." For the past few minutes Aaron Wentworth had been thinking hard, and now he made up his mind. "There is an alternative, if you would be willing to accept employment."

"I'd be glad to accept anything, but I've never been a salesperson, and I have an infant nephew I am responsible for. You are very kind, but you couldn't

319

pay me enough for me to support my nephew in Martin's Corners and maintain myself in Boston."

"Neither of those things would be a problem. Let me explain, Miss Beddoes. My wife, Lucy, is very ill. She is also from the South, from Carolina. Since her illness, my home has become what might be called a shambles. We have servants, but Mrs. Jackson, my infant son's nurse, rules the household and leaves much to be desired. What I have in mind is for you to be a companion to my wife and take my household in hand. Would you be interested?"

Prudence's hands clasped tightly in her lap, and she drew a deep breath. "Yes, Mr. Wentworth. If I could have Arthur with me, and if Mrs. Wentworth agrees to my employment, I would be very much interested."

"Miss Beddoes?" The voice came from the wide tester bed, and straining her eyes through the dim light, Prudence made out a slight form propped up against lace-trimmed pillows. Why, Lucy Wentworth was hardly older than herself, although the hand she held out was so thin that the veins stood out, in delicate tracery, through transparent skin. Her hair was fair, and her shadowed eyes were very blue. She must have been beautiful before this illness overtook her, Prudence thought.

Now the thin face was flushed with excitement. "You're from the South! And you have a nephew the same age as my son! Please, Miss Beddoes, come and stay with us! Adam needs a playmate, someone to grow up with, and you have no idea how lonely I am! Aaron, go and bring Adam, so that Miss Beddoes can see him! Oh, Miss Beddoes sounds way too formal; I'm going to call you Prudence and you must call me Lucy!"

Prue's heart was wrung with pity. A few moments ago she had been feeling sorry for herself, despite all of Aunt Emily's teachings. But she had her health, and she knew, as certainly as if this girl's physician had told her, that Lucy Wentworth was going to die.

Aaron brought the baby, and he was so exactly Arthur's size and so like him in coloring that Prudence exclaimed with pleasure. Adam squirmed in his father's arms, wanting to be put down.

"There, didn't I tell you? Put him down, Aaron, he wants to crawl. What a mischief he is, aren't you, love?"

"Isn't the floor too dirty? This rug hasn't been taken up and beaten for a long time."

"That's what soap and water are for! Children thrive on dirt, as long as it is not carried to excess." Prudence's statement seemed to startle Lucy, so she added apologetically, "At least that's what Aunt Emily always said! A baby needs exercise to develop properly, and they can't get it if they're kept in cotton wool."

"See, Aaron? That proves it!" Lucy Wentworth's voice was triumphant. "Oh, see him go! Quick, stop him, he's going under the bed!"

It was Prudence who scooped the excited infant up into her arms and handed him to his mother. Lucy held him close, stroking his silky hair, her face a mirror of love.

"I hardly ever get to see him. Mrs. Jackson says it isn't good for him to be in my room." She sounded almost apologetic again. "We all have to mind Mrs. Jackson."

Mrs. Jackson herself entered the room at that moment. She was a formidable woman, her face long and her jaw square, and disapproval spilled from her eyes as she took Adam from his mother's arms. Adam set up a wail of protest, holding out his own arms to his mother. Why, he's afraid of the woman, Prue thought, aghast.

"There, he's been on the floor! His dress is all rumpled, and smudged with dust, to boot! Those worthless Irish girls never do half a job of cleaning. I told Mr. Wentworth when I came here that the Irish are a shiftless lot and he should get rid of every one of them! Now, you stop wriggling, young man, and behave yourself!" Her hands held Adam firmly, subduing him, and Adam cried harder, his face turned appealingly to his mother.

Prue felt fury rise inside her. Poor little Adam, with Lucy so ill, and this veritable demon ruling them all! She made up her mind. Drawing a deep breath, her eyes met Mrs. Jackson's unflinchingly, and she girded herself for battle.

"I am Miss Beddoes, and I am going to be the housekeeper here," she said. She didn't need to see Lucy's eyes widen with joy to feel elation surge up in her own breast. Prudence had found something to live for, a battle to fight, and if Miss Emily were able to look down from heaven, she would be proud of the great-niece she had taught so well.

33

Cleo would not come to Boston, no matter how Prudence urged her. Assurances that Mr. Wentworth had said she would be more than welcome made no difference. "I'd be a fish out of water. It isn't as if you'll need me. You can handle those servants without me—you were born and bred to run a large household. There's no use asking me to leave Miss Emily's house cold and empty. I'm staying here."

"Then I'll send you money out of my wages," Prudence insisted, hiding the dismay she felt, for she had counted heavily on Cleo's help in establishing her authority.

"You needn't send much. Anything left over, I'll put away," Cleo replied.

There was little to pack. Prudence hesitated over the crinolined frocks she had brought from Roselawns, and decided on taking three, no more. Mr. Wentworth had said that she would be a friend, not a servant, but she intended to earn her wages, and drifting around the house near Beacon Hill in fancy gowns was not part of her plans.

The Irish cook and the equally Irish housemaid accepted her authority just as Cleo had said they would. Before the first week was out, the rooms, which had been sadly neglected, had been swept and dusted and polished, the windows washed, the heavy draperies beaten and rehung.

Mrs. Jackson was another matter. She recognized a lady when she saw one, but Prudence's hands were rough from hard work, and the clothing she had worn the first time the nurse had seen her spoke of hard times. Mrs. Jackson decided to fight, and Prudence joined battle with sparks in her eyes.

"Mrs. Jackson, when Mrs. Wentworth wants her baby with her, she is to have him. And if she wants him to crawl about on the floor, then he shall."

"It's unsanitary! And I have two to look after now, instead of just one!"

"If the work is too much for you, I am sure that Mr. Wentworth will understand if you give notice."

Their eyes met and held, and Mrs. Jackson's were the first to waver. "I can manage, I'm sure."

"I hope so, Mrs. Jackson." Triumphant, but not showing her relief, Prudence swept both babies up in her arms and carried them to Lucy's room, where they crawled and explored to their heart's content. Lucy's thin face flushed with excitement as she watched them from her pillows.

"Look at them!" Lucy marveled. "You can hardly tell one from the other. Prue, Adam seems so happy since you and Arthur came! He used to cry all the time, but now he laughs. I bless the day that you went to Aaron's shop and he brought you here."

"I have blessings on my part, too," Prudence told her. "This position is an answer to my prayer. I was afraid I couldn't do it, but things seem to be working out, after all."

Lucy clasped her hands together, her face alight. "Oh, they are! Even Mrs. Jackson minds you!"

Every afternoon, while the children napped, Prue

read to Lucy. The sick woman was extraordinarily fond of Robinson Crusoe and only laughed when Aaron accused her of having childish tastes.

"But Aaron, on an island there would be no wars! And I would get well, because it would be warm. I hate the winters, I feel so shut in, so trapped."

"You are getting well. You look better every day." Aaron took his wife's hand and held it to his face, turning it over to kiss her palm.

But she wasn't getting better. Prudence could see her wasting away, day by day. As her pallor deepened and she lost appetite and became weaker, the physician prescribed fresh steers' blood for her to drink. So, every day, Maggie, the youngest of the Irish maids, wrapped her shawl around her shoulders and head and made the journey to the slaughterhouse to bring back a bucket of the noxious stuff, which Lucy could not swallow without gagging.

"Aaron, are we going to have a Christmas tree?"

"The biggest I can find. I'll carry it home myself, like a character in Dickens."

"You won't! I want one so big you couldn't possibly carry it!"

"Then I'll hire a man to help me. He'll take the heavy end and I'll take the light."

It broke Prudence's heart to see them. When he was with Lucy, Aaron pretended gaiety, but he no longer slept with his wife for fear of disturbing her, and Prudence often heard him pacing in his bedroom long after the rest of the household was asleep.

Lucy rested, and choked down the steers' blood, but her eyes were feverish as she counted off the days until the children's first Christmas. Aaron was unfailingly kind to the children, and Arthur had already accepted him as a father, pushing Adam out of his way as both babies tried to reach him first when he appeared in the nursery doorway. Mrs. Jackson glowered and made scathing remarks about breach of discipline.

On Christmas Eve, Aaron brought home a tree almost as large as he had claimed it would be. Aaron and Prue and the maids spent the evening decorating it, and when the last candle had been fastened in place, Aaron poured Prue a glass of sherry, and they sat together beside the dying fire in companionable silence.

"The boys are too young to appreciate all this, but Lucy will be pleased," Aaron said, running his hand through his dark hair. "Thank God she lived to see it, Prue."

Prudence rose early, because Lucy had insisted that they must be early on such a morning. Mrs. Jackson was tight-lipped with disapproval as she entered the nursery to wake the boys and dress them warmly. Maggie had been instructed to have the fireplace lighted by five o'clock, but the house would still be chilly.

A child in each arm, both of them still nodding sleepily, Prudence walked down the hallway toward the staircase. Aaron emerged from his own room, in his dressing robe and slippers, but with his trousers pulled on underneath the robe.

"Take the children on down, Prue, and make sure that Maggie has blankets warmed and ready to wrap around Lucy. Have her push the big chair close to the fire," he said. "I'll carry Lucy down as soon as I can get her robe and slippers on her. I'll depend on you to help me persuade her to go back to bed, once the first excitement is over."

Prudence arranged the blankets in the chair herself and waited. The candles on the tree had not yet been

326

lighted, but Maggie was waiting with a long splinter, ready to begin.

After ten minutes Aaron had still not appeared, so Prudence instructed Maggie to watch the children and mind that they didn't crawl too near the fire. She went upstairs and found the door to Lucy's room open. Aaron was kneeling beside the bed, his head resting close to Lucy's hand, which he held in both of his.

Prudence's breath stopped, and she thought that her heart stopped, as well. She put her hand, very gently, on Aaron's shoulder.

"Come away, Mr. Wentworth. It's cold in here. Get dressed and I'll bring you coffee and a glass of wine."

"Not yet."

"Soon then."

She started downstairs to tell Maggie that the tree was not to be lighted, that the children must be returned to the nursery. Halfway down, she changed her mind. Lucy would never have forgiven her.

"Light the candles now, Maggie," she said. "Mrs. Wentworth will not be coming down, after all, but she wants the children to see the tree and have their presents."

It wasn't a lie. It was what Lucy would have wanted.

During the first weeks after Lucy's death, Prudence could hardly bear to walk past the closed bedroom door on her way to the nursery or her own room. She caught herself, one day, going up the back stairs to avoid it and drew herself up short. What would Aunt Emily think of her? Death was part of living, something that must be faced, and to flinch from it was to deny life itself.

Lucy's room had not been opened since Prudence had helped Maggie give it a thorough cleaning after

Lucy had been carried out. Now she turned the door-knob and entered. It smelled musty, and she could hardly see through the gloom, as almost no daylight filtered in through the closed velvet draperies.

Resolutely, she crossed to the windows and drew back the draperies and opened the sashes wide to air it out. Heavy dust had already collected on the dresser top and the chest of drawers, and she went down to the kitchen for a dustcloth.

"Oh, ma'am, do you think the mister will like what you're doing?" Mrs. Murphy asked, her face red from basting a roast in the huge coal range.

"The room must not be kept closed. Think what impression it would make on the children, as they grow older. I'll explain to Mr. Wentworth."

Aaron's expression of pain made her wince when she told him, as gently as possible, that Lucy's clothes should be given to a charitable organization and her room kept open.

"I suppose you are right. Her jewelry must be locked away for Adam, of course, but do as you please with the rest." He turned his face away, and Prudence saw that he was crying.

"What is the news of the war?" she asked, in an attempt to divert his attention.

"It goes on. God, Prue, don't ask me about the war! How do you suppose I feel, spending my days in a comfortable office, my nights in a comfortable home, while other men are fighting and dying?"

"You're a father, you have responsibilities."

"Do you think that would stop me, if they would have me?" Aaron's voice was bitter. "The children would be all right, with you here to look after them. But the doctors say my heart isn't good."

He looked at her, and she saw that his face was set in lines of anguish. "I feel like a slacker! I've paid half a dozen men to fight in my place, and I felt like a murderer when I did it, even though they were eager to take the money, begged me for the opportunity."

"I didn't know, I never realized. . . ."

"Of course you didn't. Do you think it's something I like to talk about? I have no right to burden you with my troubles, Prudence. But I saw the doctor again today, and the answer was the same. Stay home, hire someone else to take your place!"

He left the room abruptly, and Prudence knew that he would go, not to his own room, but to Lucy's. He'd sit there, in the dark, for hours. She put her hands over her face and wept for him.

Hester Lattimer Carter sat in the front parlor, her back very stiff, and refused Prudence's offer of refreshment.

"This is not a social visit. I have come because it is my duty. It is well known that you were installed in this household as a result of my husband's introduction, and your continued presence here now that poor Lucy is dead reflects on my husband and myself. The situation is untenable. Worse, it is a scandal! I did not realize until Mrs. Jackson came to inform me of the facts that you were still here and, I see, show no signs of leaving."

So I have Mrs. Jackson to thank for this visit, Prue thought, but she did not answer the woman, only waited for her to continue.

"If you do not care about your own reputation, you should at least have some thought for Mr. Wentworth's good name. I can tell you, in confidence, that a good many of our friends have decided not to patronize his shop until something is done about this."

Hester stood up. "I will leave you now. I have said

what I came to say, and I trust that I will hear, very shortly, that you have made other arrangements for employment."

It took all of Prudence's will to thank Hester for her advice, but she managed it with no show of the resentment that roiled inside of her. To think that dirty-minded, scandal-mongering people should drive her away from this home where she was so much needed!

But she must go, no matter the wrench it would cause her or the grief it would cause the little boys. The thought of leaving this house, which she had come to think of as her home, made her feel hollow inside, as though her world had come to an end.

But her world had come to an end before. It had ended when her mother had died, when Burke had married Crissy, when Naomi had died, when Aunt Emily had died.

Everything seemed to be taken from her, and she wondered why the Almighty chose to make it that way, piling burden upon burden. Lucy's death had numbed her with grief, and close on that she had received a letter from Cleo, telling her that Doctor Bryant had died.

"He died of cancer. He must have known he had it, when he helped Miss Emily die. But there was no one to help him, at the end. I tried to go in and help take care of him, but his wife said she did not need me. I think that in his pain, he must have let it slip that I would bring him something from his stock of drugs, since she would not. I don't know if I could have done it. I like to think that I would have. Everyone in Martin's Corners, and for miles around, attended his funeral. His wife was very proud."

In the sitting room that evening, Prudence left her

coffee untasted and told Aaron, simply and directly, that she must leave.

"Leave? But you can't! I won't hear of it! You belong here, I couldn't go on without you!" In all the time Prudence had known him, he had never been so agitated.

"People are talking. Hester made that clear to me." Her throat hurt, but she got the words out.

"Of course. What a fool I am! I've all but ruined your good name, through my own selfish need of you. Prudence, we must be married, as soon as possible."

To Prue's incredulous disbelief, Aaron began to pace the floor. "I'm making a mess of it, I'm making it sound as if I'm concerned only for myself. I'm years older than you are. You'll want to marry a younger man, someone you will love."

"No, Aaron. There is no possibility that I will ever marry for love." Aaron deserved the truth. "I did love someone once, but he married someone else. All that is behind me now."

"In that case, is there any reason you shouldn't marry for convenience? Lucy would want us to marry, to keep the children together. She would want me to provide for you and Arthur. I'll adopt Arthur, make him legally my son, if that is what you would like."

Now Prudence's face was pale. "That would not be possible, Aaron. Arthur is my nephew, that much is the truth, but he is my half-nephew only." She would not let herself hesitate for fear of losing her courage. "His mother was my half-sister, and she was illegitimate, the daughter of my father and a slave." She kept her hands very still in her lap and met Aaron's eyes without flinching.

Aaron lifted her hands and held them. "You are a brave, wonderful girl. That is of no matter at all. Arthur is a fine boy. It does change things, though.

331

It might prove a matter of embarrassment to him, when he is older, to have the facts of his birth come out through adoption papers. But I will set up a trust fund for him, and as my wife you will be well provided for in the event of my death. The bulk of the estate would of course go to Adam, but I promise that you and Arthur will want for nothing."

"I had never thought to marry for security." A little smile twitched at the corners of Prudence's mouth. "I always believed that there were more important things."

"Prudence, if I were to die, I would not want to leave Adam in any hands but yours. We can have a marriage in name only, if that is what you prefer. We could make each other comfortable, share our interests, watch the boys grow up. I'll accede to any conditions you ask."

Now the sparkle in Prudence's eyes intensified. "Will you discharge Mrs. Jackson?"

They had been married for a month when Aaron's nightly pacing stopped, and he came to her in her room in the middle of the night.

"I need you," he said. "Don't turn me away, Prudence."

She didn't turn him away. She accepted him into her bed, into her arms, not because it was her duty, but because of her genuine fondness for him.

His passion surprised her, and since her body was young and healthy, she responded with delight. It wasn't the romantic love that she had dreamed of with Burke, but it was very satisfying, and she felt truly happy for the first time in her young life.

34

They had been in Baltimore for two weeks. At first, Aaron had objected to letting Prudence accompany him. The trip was a business one, to appraise a jewelry shop that had been forced into bankruptcy and to bid for the pieces that were offered for sale.

"It's July, Prue. It will be hot. And what of Arthur and Adam? I don't know how long we'd be gone, and you know how you hate to have them out of your sight for even a few hours."

"We'll take them with us. They're old enough to make the journey."

Aaron had been puzzled by Prudence's insistence on going with him, but in the end he had given in. His wife was young, and he had to admit that their day-to-day lives were uneventful. He had no idea, for Prudence had not told him, of the real reason she was so eager for a change of scene.

The letter had arrived a week before, headed Swanmere, Georgia, and written in Crissy's unformed scrawl.

"Of course Gay has been gone all this time, he was one of the first to enlist. And now Father John is morose all the time, and Bella does nothing but go around with a long face. I wish I could go home to Roselawns, but Grandfather has never forgiven me, or Father either, for marrying Gay. I don't even know why, unless they wanted to save him for you, and you never wanted him. I thought that it was all going to be so wonderful and romantick, and now it isn't at all. . . ."

Her hand, holding the letter, had begun to shake, and it was several seconds before Prudence could make her vision focus again.

"Of course Papa has gone to the fighting, but I hear nothing, as Grandfather will not allow Grandmother to visit me, or me to set foot at Roselawns. Oh, Prue, how I wish you were here, I am so miserable. . . ."

Blindly, Prudence had set the letter down, looking around the room without seeing anything at all. Blindly, she had picked it up again and gone upstairs to the room she shared with Aaron.

She sat at the dressing table, her fingers touching the pearl necklace as though to draw strength from it. It wasn't Burke, she thought numbly. It was Gay Crissy had married, it wasn't Burke. Her fingers curled over the necklace, holding it tight, until the pearls made deep impressions in her skin. Not Burke!

I can't bear it, she had thought. It's too much to bear, it can't be done.

But she had to bear it. She was Aaron's wife, she shared his bed, he even hoped for another child from their union, one who would belong to both of them. And Aaron loved her. Not as he had loved Lucy, but with a deep, abiding love based on respect and trust.

In the end, at her insistence, Aaron had agreed that she and the boys could make the trip to Baltimore.

Prudence was in their hotel room going through the children's clothes when Aaron returned from a session at the jeweler's shop, his face flushed with agitation.

"What is it, Aaron? What has happened?" Prue dropped the shirt she had been inspecting and reached out to him.

"There's a battle going on. At a place near Gettysburg, perhaps forty miles or so from here. Prue, I want you to take the children and go home at once."

"Without you? But why?"

"It's a very big battle, Prue. Probably the biggest since the war began, and it may very well be the decisive one. They say that General Meade has over eighty thousand men, and rumor has it that General Lee has upwards of seventy-five thousand. I've heard that the wounded are lying everywhere, that there are nowhere enough men to care for them, it's bedlam. You must take the children and return home. I am going to stay and help. I've already arranged for transportation to the scene of the action."

Prudence's face lost all its color. "Aaron, you can't! You aren't well, you know your heart isn't strong!"

"My God, Prue, don't you understand? It's my chance to help at last, to do what I can! They need me!"

"Then I shall stay here. Surely the fighting won't spread this far? There's no use arguing, I won't leave you. Go, if you feel you must, but I will be here waiting for you."

Aaron opened his mouth to protest, and then he kissed her instead, holding her close, so that she could feel him trembling. "Keep it from the children if you can. They'll be over-excited, hard to handle. I don't know when I'll be back.

Aaron was gone for more than a week, and in all that time Prudence had no word from him. Reports of the battle were alarming. The fighting had gone on for three days, and the Federal Army, Prudence heard

335

with her heart leaden, had lost over three thousand men, and the numbers of the wounded were astronomical. Over fourteen thousand, the newspapers estimated, and five thousand more taken prisoner. Prudence was almost out of her mind with worry. Where was Aaron? What had happened to him?

Where was Aaron, and where was Burke? The Confederate side had fared even worse. Had twenty-six hundred Rebel soldiers actually been slain, and was Burke one of them? Was her father? Were he and Burke and Rory among the five thousand captured or missing?

Baltimore was in a ferment. Every day wounded were brought in, until facilities for caring for them ran out. People opened their homes to them and cared for them personally in the absence of doctors and nurses. And still Aaron did not return.

When he did return late on the fifth night, his clothing was stiff with dried blood, his face and hands filthy. He was gaunt, his face hardened into sharp planes, his eyes sunken and feverish. He looked years older with his stubble of unshaven beard, and he trembled with fatigue.

"It's over, Prue. The Rebels were beaten, but at what a cost!" Aaron mumbled thickly, even as he fell across the bed. He was asleep before Prudence could lift his feet and slip a pillow under his head.

During the night his skin began to burn, and his body shook with fever. He spoke only to rave of the things he had seen, indescribable horrors.

"Arms and legs, there was no one to take them away! And blood! Oh, God, the blood, it stinks! Doctor, can't you do something for this man? Oh, God, not again, not the saw again! Make them stop screaming, I can't bear to hear the screaming!"

"Hush, Aaron, hush!" Prudence held water to his

cracked lips, but he pushed it away fretfully. She lay down beside him for the rest of the night to lend him warmth from her own body. How could he be cold, when he burned so?

"A doctor?" The hotel manager looked at her, in the first light of morning, as though she were insane. "There aren't any doctors to be had. You'll just have to do the best you can."

Of course there were no doctors. Wearily, Prudence brushed her hair away from her forehead. What medicines were to be had, she asked. Could she get some quinine?

"Ma'am, be reasonable."

"I'll pay. It doesn't matter how much."

"Money ain't worth a thing, you can't get what there isn't. I'm sorry, ma'am."

She returned to the second floor and paused to glance into the room where the boys slept. Annie O'Brian, an Irish chambermaid, was asleep on a cot, and Adam also slept, looking angelic with his face flushed and his mouth slightly parted in a smile. But Arthur wasn't there.

Prudence found him in Aaron's bed, snuggled up against his side, his chubby hand resting where it had been patting Aaron's cheek when sleep had overtaken him again.

"Arthur!" Prudence swept the child up into her arms. "This is very naughty of you! You must not come into this room again, do you understand? Papa is ill." What if it were catching, what if Arthur came down with it? In her agitation she shook the child a little and then hugged him tight. She mustn't go to pieces. Their well-being, the children's as well as Aaron's, depended entirely on her.

Aaron was desperately ill. She had to get the boys

337

away, somewhere where they would be safe from contagion. But where?"

She returned Arthur to his room and woke Annie, instructing her to wash him thoroughly and send his nightgown to the laundry. When she returned to Aaron, he was deep in delirium.

By evening his fever had worsened so drastically that every breath he took was agony. She bathed his forehead and tried again to get him to drink some water. When he refused it, she thought it was probably just as well, because everyone knew that water was deadly to a fever. Only, hadn't Aunt Emily derided that, and called the doctors nincompoops? Cool a fever, Aunt Emily had said.

Prudence went down to the lobby and asked if there were any way to procure some ice. The manager looked at her sourly.

"I'm sorry, ma'am. And I'm afraid I'm going to have to ask for your rooms. The city is desperate for rooms."

Prudence felt hysteria rise in her. "My husband cannot possibly be moved! You have no idea how ill he is!"

"Then I'll have to have the other room, at least."

"You shall not! I cannot let the children stay with their father."

"I'm sorry. One family cannot take up two rooms." The manager was harassed, but firm.

When Prudence told her, Annie's face drew up with sympathy.

"The poor little loves, sure and you're afraid, and why shouldn't you be, you poor creature? Now, me mother might take them. Our place is nothing fancy, mind. It's only a flat, on the third floor of a tenement like, but it's clean and mother loves little ones."

Prudence swallowed. Send Arthur and Adam away?

338

Place them in the care of a woman she had never seen, in a tenement? But it was better, safer, than taking them into Aaron's sickroom. She had no choice but to accept.

On the bed, Aaron's body shook so violently that the head of the bed rattled against the wall. The room stank. Aaron had had dysentery for two days. His skin was dry and withered under her touch, flaming hot. Prudence's mind was fuzzy. When she looked at her hand on his forehead, she saw two hands. Something was the matter with her eyes. Was the window open? Had the chambermaid brought clean sheets? She tried to stand up to look, but her legs wouldn't support her.

The room was dark. When had it got dark? She couldn't remember. She tried to get up, to strike a light. She was lying on the floor, the rug harsh under her cheek, and it smelled of dust.

Aaron? She struggled to her feet, her ears strained for the sound of his breathing, but she could hear nothing.

She reached for his hand. It was cold. His fever had broken. If his fever was gone, he must be better. She groped to see if he had thrown off his blankets. She was so weak because she hadn't eaten. When had she eaten last? She couldn't remember.

She had been ill. She realized that, without knowing how. The room was half-darkened, and very quiet. Only the little chambermaid, Annie O'Brian, sat beside her, her head nodding as she dozed, her mouth half open.

Aaron! Prudence reached out, but the space in the bed beside her was empty. He was up, then, and had gone out. He was well.

Annie's head jerked, and her eyes opened. "You're awake, praise the saints! And you're better, I can see that!"

"My husband, where did he go?" Prudence had to wet her lips before she could speak, and even then it was an effort.

Annie's face paled, and she crossed herself. "They took him, of course. They couldn't leave him here. Five days ago it was, they came and carried him away. And didn't I use some of the money you gave me to light a candle for his soul?"

Prudence's fingers clutched at the edge of the sheet. She lay there, refusing to accept it. She'd think about something else. She knew there was something else. Her brow furrowed in her effort to make her brain function.

The boys. Arthur, Adam. "My little boys?"

Annie was crying, her apron over her face. "It couldn't be helped, ma'am. The poor little lad, he was gone before we knew, blown out like a candle. Poor little Arthur. Me mother hasn't given over crying yet, and she on her knees at the church every day, praying for his soul, and her with the rheumatics in her joints. But the other lad is fine, ma'am."

Prudence wasn't listening any more. She had stuffed the corner of the sheet into her mouth to keep from screaming. Be quiet, be quiet, her mind insisted over and over. I don't want to hear any more!

The woman who let her into the two-room flat, stark in its poverty but respectably clean, was thin and tired and looked far older than her years. America had not been kind to its Irish immigrants.

"Sure and you're Mrs. Wentworth. You don't have to tell me, dearie, and I'm that glad that you're alive and perky! A miracle it was, brought about by the

340

saints. And here's your Adam, bless his heart, he was that sick, but he's better now. Both of you'll soon have the roses in your cheeks again."

Adam lay on a cot, his back turned toward Prudence. She felt a sob rise in her throat and fought to control it. She mustn't frighten him any more; he'd been through enough.

She had to turn sideways to work her way between the beds. There were only three, but the room was small.

"Adam?" She hoped that her voice sounded all right. "Adam, Mama's here."

He turned so that she could see his face, and she felt the room swim around her, felt herself falling, and reached out to touch the wall to give herself balance. Arthur's face, Arthur's eyes—it was Arthur, not Adam!

"There now, you just sit here, quiet like, and drink this tea. Niver a drop of whiskey is there in the house, worst luck."

Mrs. O'Brian's voice broke off as Prudence shook her head, and her face was filled with concern. The cup she proffered was cracked, but it was of fine china. Had the woman managed to bring it all this way from Ireland?

"I can manage now." Prudence stood up and found that her knees would support her.

"Your cab driver is still waiting. Here, now, my head is that empty I almost forgot! Here's the paper the doctor signed, the death certificate like. I used the last coins we had in the house to call him, you see."

Money. Mrs. O'Brian's heart was big, she'd have cared for the children without recompense, but a body had to be practical and it would be false pride not to take what was offered. Prudence fumbled in her reti-

341

cule and put a large sum of money in the work-worn hand.

In the cab, she held Arthur on her lap. He was sleepy and still weak, pale and wan from his illness, but alive.

On her lap, Arthur stirred and looked at her with confused eyes.

"Adam?" he asked.

"Hush, darling. We're going home."

The driver had overheard. "Well, so he has a tongue, and he knows his own name, he does, there's a brave lad."

"Adam?" Arthur said again.

I'm going mad, Prudence thought. I must still have fever. Still, she held Arthur more tightly, cradling him in her arms.

"We're going home, Adam," she said. "Rest now, everything will be all right."

BOOK TWO:

Prudence

Part Two

35

Standing in the middle of their Paris hotel suite, Prudence surveyed herself in the cheval glass and smoothed the gown she had been doubtful about over her hips. Her judgment had been correct. The dress was all but indecent, fitting sheath-like all the way down to the floor, with the ties under the skirt tightened to pull it back and flatten it against the front of her still youthful body.

The years had been kind to her. *I'm thirty-eight*, she thought, *a middle-aged woman*, but as she evaluated herself in the glass she could see little evidence of the passing years. Her face was more mature, but its delicate outlines were still unblurred, and her abundance of brown hair, rolled into a French twist at the back of her neck and cut into a fringe over her forehead, was still without a trace of gray.

Behind her, Adam, lounging most inelegantly on the bed, surveying her with admiration. "You'll do," he said, his eyebrows quirking. "My only worry is that people will take you for my sweetheart or my wife, and then where will I be? None of these chic little Parisian girls will give me a second look!"

"Adam, behave yourself!" Prudence reproved him.

"But it is rather nice, isn't it? Perhaps it was worth the price that salon demanded, after all."

"You'll stun Boston. Tongues won't stop wagging for months after we get back."

Adam grinned, and Prudence's heart turned over, because as used as she was to his extraordinary handsomeness, there were times when it struck her with such force that it was as if she were seeing him for the first time. His hair was still nearly as fair as it had been when he'd been a child, although it lacked that very silvery quality that Gay's had had. His eyes were of such a deep blue that in certain lights they appeared almost black, and his face was molded on strong planes, with a mouth, nearly always curved in a smile, that made young ladies languish over him.

"It seems very plain, and yet there's something about it." Prudence returned to her musing over this latest acquisition to her wardrobe.

"I should certainly hope so!" Adam rolled his eyes. "Deliver me from the gewgaws women are wearing these days! Do you remember what Marcia wore at the bon voyage party her grandmother gave for us? Frogs? Frogs all over her dress, and her earrings made in the shape of lizards, and ribbons and ruffles and doodads everyplace there was room to stick one."

"And Marcia's hat!" Prudence smiled. "Three storys and an attic, they call them, because they're so tall. I declare she was quite overshadowed by it. Hester chose them, of course. Marcia's mother doesn't dare open her mouth to defend her daughter from that woman."

The dress was perfect after all, Prudence decided, and turned to ask Adam, "What are you going to do this afternoon? Go running around the Left Bank with those disreputable friends you and Carl•picked up almost as soon as we arrived?"

346

"Certainly. I didn't come to Paris to sit about in fashion salons, or to spend hours mooning over the paintings in the Louvre. It's the sidewalk cafés for me. The real city that tourists seldom see unless they are fortunate enough to make a disreputable friend or two."

"You'll catch some filthy disease, or find yourself robbed and stabbed in a dark alley."

Adam's brows shot up. "I? Never fear! Carl and I both carry knives. Besides, I am quite proficient in the art of fisticuffs, if you'll remember."

"As if I could forget! All those months, when you took lessons from that dreadful pugilist!" Prudence made a face, remembering her fear that Adam would end up with a cauliflower ear or broken nose.

"And where are you off to, may I ask? Not more shopping, I hope. Doesn't Mrs. Richards ever tire of trying to buy out the entire stock of every dress shop in Paris?"

"No, we are not going shopping. We have a most interesting afternoon ahead of us, although of course you wouldn't think so. There is a lady in Paris who is something of an institution. She has a small and very select salon every afternoon from three until five, and an invitation to her drawing room is tantamount to being presented to royalty."

"It sounds gruesomely boring."

Prudence's eyes took on a mischievous sparkle. "Oh, but you don't understand. This is a very remarkable lady indeed. She calls herself a countess, but there are rumors that she was once a very wicked person of low origins. Still, people vie for invitations to her salon, and however Estelle managed it I'll never know, but of course her husband is acquainted with M. le Girraud, the banker, who has connections with the highest society."

"Not the Comtesse Marie de la Roche!" Adam sat

347

up and looked at Prudence with sudden respect. "Why, even Carl and I have heard of her! If she's half what they say she is, you might try to get an invitation for us, too!" Adam lay down again and put his hands behind his head.

"Go and sleep in your own room and stop rumpling my bed!" Prudence picked up her purse and brushed a kiss across Adam's cheek.

She rarely wondered any more whether she'd done the right thing when she'd substituted Arthur for Adam and taken him directly to Martin's Corners. They did not return to Boston, where the deception might have been detected, until he was old enough to attend the Boston Latin School.

Aaron wouldn't have disapproved, she was sure of that. He'd loved Arthur, he would have wanted what was best for him. All of his estate would have passed to Prue and Arthur in any case when Adam died. The opportunity to make the exchange, to rear Arthur as Adam, with no question of his legitimacy, had been irresistible, and she had never regretted having seized it. Arthur was all she had left to live for, and she hadn't been able to bear to think that some day he might be hurt by having the truth of his heritage come to light.

In the years since Aaron died and the war ended, Prudence had traveled extensively. There was more than enough money to indulge her need for change, for new experiences to crowd out memories. Aaron's estate had been far larger than she had imagined, because he had invested his money wisely and widely.

Even now, so many years later, she could not think of the period directly after the war ended without feeling pain so acute that it sickened her.

The first news of her family came well over a year after the war was over, in a letter from Crissy. Absa-

348

lom had led a slave revolt at Swanmere early in the war, and only her father-in-law standing on the gallery with a shotgun had kept him from burning the house down around their heads. As it was, he had taken all of the field hands and most of the house people away with him, and the Renaults had lived in fear and trembling that he would return and burn them out in the night.

Gay had returned home, miraculously unscathed despite having fought in countless engagements, but Swanmere was very nearly derelict. It would take years to restore it to any semblance of prosperity. Could Prudence send them some money, so that they could buy needed equipment and have a little reserve for paying field hands? Imagine having to pay them—it was a disgrace—those Yankees had ruined all their lives, and nothing would ever be the same!

Jonathan and Rory had also returned. Jonathan had been wounded twice, but his health was restored. Rory had had his right arm amputated, and he was very morose and bitter. Rory had even jilted Miss Cecelia who had waited for him all through the war. (Who was Miss Cecelia—trust Crissy not to be explicit!)

Grandfather Jacob had deteriorated in health due to the hardships he had undergone on the field, and he suffered from a cough that all of Grandmother Yolande's remedies could not alleviate. Victor Slade had returned while Grandfather and Jonathan and Rory were fighting, while Crissy had been visiting Yolande, and he'd murdered Juliette and Benjamin. He would have raped Crissy and killed her if Grandmother, who had been upstairs, hadn't come down with Grandfather's shotgun and fired both barrels right into his middle. She would never forget it, she'd be marked by the horror all the rest of her life. Prue

349

couldn't possibly know what they had suffered. . . .

And . . . here Prudence had come to the part of the letter she had been waiting for—news of Burke.

She had read it twice, three times, disbelieving, certain that she had made a mistake. Burke had married, a Miss Julia Thornton, and it was a scandal because Julia wasn't even from one of the county families. She was the daughter of a shopkeeper, and even if Coralie Amhurst pretended to be fond of the girl, everyone knew that Burke was ruined, socially.

Prudence had been making preparations to journey to Roselawns, frantic with impatience to be reunited with her family, to see Burke again. Now she unpacked. Cleo watched her suffering, her eyes dark with sympathy, but she held her peace. Once more, Prudence died a little. It was then that her restless travelings had begun, and there had been many trips since.

This visit to England and the Continent had been Adam's idea, however. He had graduated, with honors, from Harvard, and by rights he should have made the Grand Tour alone, with only a suitable older male companion, but he had derided that idea as archaic.

"I'd rather go with you. Then I can go my own way without some pedantic old scholar to lecture me on antiquities every step of the way! Ezekiel Armbruster had one all picked out for me, and he's raising Cain. He spouts 'responsibilities' at me till I could spit in his eye! He may be a capable manager for Father's affairs, but he must have come over on the Ark. So we're going together, and let's see what he has to say to that!"

"Won't you miss Marcia?"

"Marcia isn't bad, taken by herself. It's her grandmother I can't stand, and you needn't look at me like that because you can't stand Hester either, and

350

you know it! She's determined to trap me for her granddaughter, and I'm damned not ready for it, begging your pardon, if it's necessary."

"It is necessary. Adam, will you please learn to watch your language? But I know what you mean. Hester is formidable, isn't she? Very well, then, we'll go. It will please Estelle to have you for a companion for Carl."

And so they had embarked, without, as Hester had hoped, an engagement party beforehand. And Prudence had enjoyed herself more than she ever had before. Though Adam was far from being the most perfect young man in the world, he was never boring.

The Hôtel de la Roche was an imposing house, even in this city of magnificent homes. Not large as such houses went, but its lines were so graceful that it stood out among its neighbors indicating that there lived a lady of taste and charm. Estelle was volubly impressed as they were admitted to a white paneled entrance hall, decorated sparingly with small gilt chairs and one console table on which an arrangement of fresh flowers was reflected in the mirror behind it. Prudence recognized the antique porcelain bowl that held the flowers and knew it was a museum piece.

The drawing room to which the uniformed maid conducted them contained no more than half a dozen people, confirming the rumors that Madame la Comtesse's salons were very exclusive. At that, two of the men appeared to be impoverished students. Another young man was so beautiful of feature and so foppishly dressed that Prudence felt a shudder of distaste. A handsome couple, members of at least the minor nobility, were talking to an elderly man, carelessly attired in a lounge suit that was in need of sponging and pressing, with a shock of equally untidy

351

white hair, and a face so filled with benign humor that Prudence felt that he alone would be worth cultivating as an acquaintance.

Prudence looked about her, impressed by the seventeenth-century furnishings and the Aubusson carpet, and *objets d'art* so carefully selected, and so discreetly few in number, that an observer must be filled with delighted surprise when they were finally noticed.

One figure dominated the room, that of a woman sitting on a small, straight-backed chair in front of a large window so that the rose-colored draperies made a backdrop for her. The planes of her face were delicate but strongly molded; her complexion, in spite of the telltale lines, was white and firm, although she must have been at least into her late sixties. Her gown disregarded fashion; it transcended fashion, being starkly unadorned except for a magnificent emerald necklace and emerald earrings. Her hair was white and dressed in elaborate fashion, high on her head. Her hands, innocent of rings, lay on the arms of her chair, in a pose of quiet elegance.

The Countess nodded to them and spoke, her voice low and husky, musically pleasing to the ear.

"Come closer. You are the American ladies, of course? I have a particular sympathy for the United States of America. You are from Boston, I understand. I have never traveled to Boston."

"Yes, that is correct, we are from Boston, although Mrs. Wentworth was originally from the South." Estelle hesitated, not sure how to address the lady, but the Comtesse brushed her hesitation aside and directed her penetrating gaze at Prudence.

"I was born in Georgia, Madame la Comtesse, although I have not been back there since before the War between the States."

"A plantation, then?"

"That is right. I was born at Roselawns, a cotton plantation."

The Comtesse signaled to the maid, indicating two small chairs which were brought forward for her guests. The maid then offered a silver serving tray with a choice of coffee or sherry. Estelle helped herself to sherry, clearly in need of it to fortify herself to cope with the overwhelming presence in front of her. Prudence selected coffee in a cup so fragile that it was a miracle it did not shatter at a touch. The Comtesse watched her closely as she tasted it, and then she chuckled, deep in her throat, at Prudence's surprise.

"You find it to your taste?"

"Indeed, Madame, I find it the best coffee I have tasted on the Continent!"

Mischief sparkled in the Comtesse's eyes, and Prudence felt a sudden stirring of unease. There was no reason for it, but it was there, and undeniable.

"And how did you find the English coffee?" The old lady's laugh rang out as Prudence shuddered. "I pride myself on my coffee. I learned the secret many years ago, although these poor misguided friends of mine look on it with distaste and prefer Cognac, much to their shame."

"Now, now, that isn't true of us all!" the elderly gentleman protested.

The Comtesse's attention was diverted to the speaker, and without apology she began a spirited conversation with him concerning Armatine Lucile Aurore, Baroness Dudevant. Estelle looked at Prudence blankly, her face mirroring bewilderment. "George Sand," Prudence whispered, but Estelle looked as bewildered as ever.

"It was her fervent plea for socialistic revolution that most impressed me!" René, one of the young

353

students put in, on the edge of his chair in his eagerness to be included in the discourse.

His hostess transfixed him with a cold stare. "I should suggest that you become more familiar with reformation issues before you venture an opinion. Reform is all very well, but it can be carried too far." Once again her gaze flicked to Prudence. "As your country found out, to its sorrow, has it not? The freeing of the slaves was surely a great reform, but what has become of them since? To say nothing of their erstwhile masters. Reform without a background of sensible planning can end in nothing but chaos, rather than advancing the world toward perfection as idle dreamers believe." She turned to Prudence. "Mrs. Wentworth, I asked you a question."

"There was a great deal of chaos, I understand. I was not there, and so I cannot report at first hand. I know of it only through the letters I received from my father and my sister."

The elderly man chuckled. "Stand in the corner, René. It's a pity we don't have a dunce cap!"

"No, no, let him remain, but silently. How else can he learn?" The Comtesse's English was perfect, the elderly gentleman's spoken with an accent that was charming, and the young man who had been reprimanded had struggled with the unfamiliar language for the benefit of the American guests. "I must have thought he had a mind of sorts, at least, or I wouldn't have invited him, would I?"

Prudence smiled at the abashed student, and his face flushed with gratitude. Estelle still looked bewildered. She had not been able to follow the young man's conversation at all.

By the time the salon was over, Estelle had a numbed expression on her face, but Prudence was sorry to have it end. The company had been stimulating, and she wished that Adam could have been there. The Comtesse had not asked them to return, however, and so there had been no opportunity to ask if she could bring him the next time.

"Prue, whatever is the matter with you?" Estelle's plump, pretty face was annoyed. "I declare you haven't heard a word I said!"

Prue started. "I'm sorry, Estelle. I was thinking of something else." There was a frown between her well-defined eyebrows. That strange feeling had come over her again, just as they had been dismissed. Premonition? Some obscure memory that persisted in eluding her?

She shrugged and put it out of her mind. Still, it was a shame that Adam had not had the opportunity to meet the Comtesse. He would have enjoyed her most thoroughly.

36

The note arrived with her breakfast chocolate, and the chambermaid who brought it was visibly shaken. The handwriting was boldly defined on thick, crested paper. Prudence was summoned to the Hôtel de la Roche at two o'clock that afternoon. It was a royal command, with no opening left for her to decline.

"I shall expect you promptly on the hour." Prudence didn't know whether to be amused or annoyed, but at least it would spare her another afternoon of shopping with Estelle.

Prudence felt a twinge of apprehension when the maid ushered her into the drawing room, for there were no other guests present. The Comtesse rose from her chair as she entered, her hazel eyes, remarkably unfaded for a woman of her age, fixed on Prudence's face.

"Prudence." The woman had used her first name! At Prue's startled expression, she smiled.

"That is your name, is it not? Certainly you are not Christine, because you are dark, exactly like your mother, and Crissy was fair. And your name is Wentworth, not Renault."

Prudence felt chilled, although the day was warm, and her knees seemed to have turned to water. The name came to her lips as though it had been there all the time. "Rebecca!"

"Sit down." It was a command, not an invitation. "There is wine on the table beside you; you look as though you need it. Tell me, how did Naomi die? I know some of it. The men I employed to procure information for me were very able. It was not the information I had contracted for, unfortunately. I was going to send for her, so that I could at last give her all the things it was in my power to give her. A name, a life, a husband of impeccable family. Instead, I learned that she was dead and that she had left a child."

An expression of infinite pain crossed the old woman's face. "I understand that he, too, died. In Baltimore. Tell me if my information is correct, Prudence."

The wine, which was mellow, full-bodied, tasted acrid on Prudence's tongue.

Rebecca's voice was gentler, now. "It has been a shock to you. I knew that you did not recognize me. Why should you have? It's been a great many years, and you were only a young girl when I left Roselawns. But while I have changed, you have not. And our meeting was not a coincidence, Prudence. I have made it a habit to learn of any Americans who visit Paris. Unfortunately, I was ill the last time you were in this city, and on one other occasion it turned out to be a different Mrs. Wentworth.

Rebecca. Her father's mistress, the cause of her mother's leaving her father. Naomi's mother, the cause of Prudence's leaving Roselawns, leaving Burke. How had she come here, what twist of fate had made her the mistress of this house, given her the title of Comtesse?

Rebecca! Rebecca! Anger surged through Prudence.

She clenched her hands inside her fine kid gloves and ground her teeth together. Her head pounded; the pain in her temples was unendurable.

"Prudence!"

She ignored the sharp cry and turned and left the room, the house. She could not go back to the hotel. Adam might be there, and he would know at once that something was wrong. And Adam had a habit of getting to the bottom of things.

She walked, and then she sat on a bench in a park where children attended by their nursemaids played around her. Little boys rolled their hoops and sailed toy boats on the pond; little girls jumped rope or played with their dolls. Yesterday Prudence had been enthralled with French children. Today, she scarcely knew that they were there.

Rebecca! Where had she been all these years? Her disappearance from Roselawns had never been discussed. She had simply gone. Naomi had cried, and Yolande had comforted her and told her that she would soon see her again, but no mention had been made as to where she had gone.

Rebecca, here in Paris, a Comtesse! And she had tried to send for Naomi. She had, then, some love for her daughter, some sense of responsibility. Prudence sat there a long while, her blood pounding against her temples. It was growing late. The nursemaids had gathered up their charges and taken them away. Her companions would be wondering where she was. She must get back.

She and Adam attended an opera that evening, and she enjoyed it. She always enjoyed Adam's company, no matter the occasion, and in spite of Adam's pretended indifference to culture, he also had a lively interest in the arts, as well as an obvious enjoyment of Prudence's company.

After the opera, they had light refreshments at a quaint café, and Adam pretended to flirt with her, most outrageously. He was incorrigible, and there was no use trying to change him.

Later, in spite of the pleasant evening, Prudence could not fall asleep. She tossed and turned, and the very comfortable bed was intolerable to her. If only she were coming down with something, she would feel better about it, but she knew that she was not. It was her own mind that was making her ill.

Rebecca! No matter how tightly she closed her eyes, or how wide she opened them to stare at some shadowy object in her room, Rebecca's face seemed to be imprinted on the air directly in front of her.

She deserves nothing; I owe her nothing! Prudence told herself furiously. She ruined my mother's life, she ruined Papa's, and Naomi's, and mine. Yes, and Adam's life would have been ruined if I had not taken steps to prevent it. Maybe it was wrong of me, but it was something I had to do and I'll never be sorry!

Still, Rebecca's eyes seemed to look directly into her own, eyes so sad, so filled with human misery that Prudence felt like screaming at her to go away and leave her alone.

No one had ever come near to guessing the truth. No one ever would. The secret would go to Prudence's grave with her, and Adam would be safe. It wasn't her fault that Rebecca suffered, that Rebecca thought that Arthur, as well as Naomi, was dead.

I hate her, Prudence thought, pounding her pillow into still another shape and finding it as uncomfortable as before. It's ridiculous to lose sleep over her. Rebecca got what she wanted—money, position, even a title. It wasn't my fault that Naomi died before she could share it all with her. I did the best I could.

Two hours before dawn Prudence rose and dressed.

A sleepy doorman let her out of the hotel, startled and protesting volubly at a lady's going out, unattended, at such an hour. Francs changed hands and the doorman smiled and nodded with understanding. Who would have thought that such a genteel lady, and an American from that staid city of Boston, would have an assignation! But she was certainly beautiful, in her own different way. What lucky man was she meeting? the doorman wondered.

It took a long time for the maid to answer her ring, and Prudence nearly turned and left before the door was opened a tiny crack. The maid, apprehensive but valiant, demanded to know what she meant by disturbing honest people at such an hour.

"You will tell Madame la Comtesse that Mrs. Wentworth is here." There was no turning back now. If she turned back, she knew that she would never have another moment of peace. Rebecca's face, Rebecca's eyes, would haunt her forever.

Rebecca, a satin robe thrown over her shoulders, received her in her bedroom. "Prudence! What on earth brings you here at this hour? Gabrielle, bring wine. I am too old to be startled in the middle of the night, and you look about to swoon here on my bedchamber carpet."

Prudence waited only until the maid had left the room, and then she spoke directly to the point. The sooner she got it over with, the better.

"I lied to you, Rebecca. Arthur is not dead. It was Adam who died, not Arthur. The woman who was caring for them mixed up their names, and the doctor put Arthur's name on the death certificate."

For a moment she thought that her blunt statement had been too much for Rebecca, for the older woman sank back against her pillow, her face drained of color. She was chafing the old woman's hands when

Gabrielle returned with the wine. While the maid supported her mistress's shoulders, Prudence managed to coax a few drops between the white lips.

"Leave us." Rebecca recovered sufficiently to order her maid. Her eyes fixed themselves on Prudence's. "So. And he is here, in Paris?"

"You aren't to tell him!" Prudence said. "You are never to let him know the truth!"

"Of course I will never tell him. What have I to offer him that would make up to him for no longer being Adam Wentworth? Just knowing that he is alive, and happy, is enough." Rebecca's breathing was harsh, but she controlled it. "Prudence, tell me. What does he look like? I have the right to know that, as it is all I will ever have."

"He resembles his father, Gaylord Renault, somewhat. He is not quite as fair-haired, but he is very handsome. He charms everyone he meets. He is tall, and his shoulders are broad, and his eyes are dark blue. He has a fine mind. He was at the top of his graduating class at Harvard without having had to strain himself to achieve his grades. What else can I tell you?"

"It is enough." Rebecca closed her eyes. She looked very old, every year of her age, and frail and vulnerable, but her face seemed strangely at peace. "You will let me know when he marries, when he has children?"

Prudence bent her head. "I'll let you know."

"Could you send me a picture of him?"

Again Prudence nodded. "I'll see to it as soon as we return to Boston."

Adam Wentworth. Rebecca thought the name, and then whispered it, filled with satisfaction.

"I'll leave you now. You must rest. This has been a shock to you." Prudence stood up to leave.

A smile quirked at the corner of Rebecca's mouth,

and incredibly, made her look, just for a few instants, much as she had looked years before when she had been a young woman of great beauty. "I will survive it. I shall live to know that I have great-grandchildren. You will send me pictures of them, let me know their names?"

"Yes." Prudence's throat hurt with unshed tears. "I'll have Gabrielle summon my coachman."

"There is no need. I told my driver to wait."

"Goodbye, then. Thank you, Prudence." Rebecca did not cry, nor grow effusive with gratitude. And Prudence was able to leave without further talk.

The doorman let Prudence in again, a little more than an hour after she had left. She must have a stupid lover, the doorman thought, to let her go so quickly. Or perhaps they quarreled? But no, the lady looked content. In fact, she looked far happier than when she had left. They had quarreled before, then, and now they had reconciled, and all was right with the world.

The lady smiled at him, and he dared to wink. Feeling devilish, wanting to giggle, Prudence winked back. The doorman laid his fingers to his lips, indicating that he had not seen her, that she had not left the hotel that night.

So now I have a reputation as a scarlet woman, Prue thought, as she drifted off to sleep as the first light of dawn crept into her room. How Aunt Emily would laugh!

Prudence saw the carriage the next afternoon, waiting directly opposite the hotel. When she recognized the crest on the door, her heart sank. Rebecca was there, waiting! But Adam was not with Prudence, he was off on affairs of his own, getting in all the riotous pleasure he could before their sailing date, only two days away.

The carriage was there again that evening, but once again Rebecca was to be disappointed. At least she hadn't broken her word, she hadn't come into the hotel and asked for Adam or even for her, Prudence thought. She was glad that tomorrow was their last day. She would not breathe easily now until they had left Paris behind them.

But then she was ashamed of herself. Rebecca will never break her word, Prudence decided. She wants the best for Adam, just as I do. She onlys wants to see him, just a glimpse, and she had the right to that, every woman in the world had the right to see her own grandson, at least once.

The next day she informed Adam that he was taking her to lunch. "Just the two of us. A little of Estelle goes a long way, and I'll be compelled to endure her all during the crossing. Besides, I want to see all the beautiful French girls flirt with you."

"Mama, behave yourself! It's a mercy you never remarried, you'd drive a husband crazy. I know your real motive perfectly well! You want to do a little flirting of your own without Estelle to be shocked and jealous."

"You know me too well, but you are still taking me to lunch."

The carriage was there, where it had been twice before. When they had crossed the boulevard and were only a few steps from it, Prudence paused and pretended to adjust her gloves. When she looked up, her face assumed an expression of surprise.

"Why, it's Madame la Comtesse! Madame, may I present my son, Mr. Adam Wentworth?"

Rebecca extended her hand, and Adam bowed over it before he kissed it. His eyes were merry and filled with devils. "I am devastated! Here I meet the most fascinating woman in all of Paris, and it is already my last day! Mother, I shall never forgive you. But I know why you didn't cajole Madame la Comtesse into extending me an invitation to her famous salon. You were afraid that I would run away with her, now confess it!"

Rebecca tapped his hand with her folded fan. "You will do," she said. "Oh, yes, you will do very well indeed! Adam Wentworth, it has been a pleasure."

Her carriage drove on, and Adam looked at Prudence accusingly. "You know, mother, something tells me that that is a woman worth knowing. Oh, well, one can't have everything! I shall have to content myself with flirting with all those shallow little creatures we shall see while we lunch, only I'm afraid my heart won't be in it."

Laughing, they walked on together, and Adam did not notice that Prudence's laughter had a faintly bubbly sound, as though there were a lump in her throat. He still had tonight, and he intended to make it a good one. His last night in Paris, and then back to Boston to decide whether he liked Marcia well enough to ask her to marry him, in spite of her dragon of a grandmother.

BOOK THREE:

Adam

Part One

37

Adam was in Martin's Corners. He had ostensibly
come to visit Cleo and to take a short breather from
the arduous training that Ezekiel Armbruster was
inflicting on him to prepare him to take over his own
financial affairs. The real reason was that three invitations from Hester Carter in one week had been
two too many. Adam found it annoying and obvious,
the way Hester managed to send Marcia on some
trifling errand and then send Adam to find her, usually
in the garden or the conservatory or some other such
secluded place.

Adam had nothing against Marcia. She was a pretty
girl, if not actually beautiful. But he'd be hanged if
he were ready to be stampeded into marriage even
to a sweet brown-eyed girl he felt sorry for because
of her domineering grandmother.

To tell the truth, he felt at loose ends when Prudence wasn't at home. She was gone again, to England
this time. What ailed the woman that she couldn't
stay put? Didn't she know he needed her, even if he
had turned twenty-one in March of this year eighteen
eighty-two? Adam suspected, with more than a twinge
of jealousy, that Prue was much too interested in
a certain Sir Archibald Snowdon, whose estate in

Sussex was a showplace running a little to seed from lack of funds.

A widower, Archie had made it plain, last year when Adam and Prue had gone abroad together to London and Paris, that he would not be averse to taking an American wife with money behind her. Lady Prudence! Adam snorted, just thinking of it. Good Lord, what did she want with a title? Meeting that Comtesse, Maria de la Roche, must have put delusions of grandeur in her head!

Martin's Corners had grown, but not much. The *Clarion* was still there, but David Lawrence had retired the year before. David now spent a good deal of time sitting on the porch of Blaisdel's mercantile store soaking up the warmth that radiated from the wall behind him. Sometimes he played checkers with another elderly man, sometimes he just sat and passed the time of day with everyone who entered the establishment or walked along the boardwalk in front of it.

David was there when Adam alighted from the stage and stopped in at the store to buy a sack of peppermint sticks and another of horehound drops to take on to Cleo. In her old age, Cleo had developed a sweet tooth but the black woman, still erect and active, was so used to penny-pinching that she never bought candy for herself, in spite of the fact that Prudence had seen to it that she was financially secure. Adam exchanged news with David for a while before he went on to settle in at Cleo's.

Adam felt a deep sense of contentment as he sat at the scrubbed kitchen table, having waved aside Cleo's attempt to lay a cloth. Nobody made coffee the way Cleo did, and her gingerbread and apple pie were as good as his childhood memories of them. She'd fry codfish cakes in the morning, he knew, but even that would bring him pleasure.

"You know something, Cleo? Your cooking has the French cooking beat all hollow. I'd rather have your gingerbread and coffee than all the *escargots* and wine in the world!"

"Snails!" Cleo wrinkled her nose. "I'd as soon eat worms."

Adam's laughter rang out. He stuffed another bit of gingerbread into his mouth and asked, "What's new in this metropolis?"

"Old Mr. Tait, the one your grandmother knew, died last winter. Nobody knows how old he was, but it was some old. The family runs to boys now. At least he lived to see that, even though none of them is named Tait."

Adam put his hand over the top of his cup to indicate that he had had enough. "How's the fishing? Anything biting in the pond over Jones's way?"

"They're biting. You'll have to get up early, though."

"That suits me. You know what I'm going to do, Cleo? For one solid week I'm going to go fishing, and sit and chew straws on Blaisdel's porch, and play chess with Mr. Lawrence."

"He'll beat you. Only Miss Emily was ever able to beat him."

For three days, Adam did just as he'd said he would. Cleo cooked the fish he caught; he renewed his acquaintance with the Taits and Blaisdels and Hamiltons. David Lawrence trounced him soundly at chess, and he decided the taste of a blade of grass or a straw, while tilting his straight-backed chair against the wall of the mercantile porch, was better than tobacco. Boyhood revisited, he thought, with a deep and abiding satisfaction. If he had his way, he'd spend at least half of every year right here in Martin's Corners.

It was on the fourth day that the spinster Cummings, who tended the post office, called to Adam as he passed the store and told him that there was a letter for him. "It was forwarded from Boston," Miss Cummings told him, her nose quivering with curiosity that, with her New England upbringing, she dared not admit. "Somebody must have thought it was important."

Adam turned the letter over in his hands. It was not, as he had hoped, from Prudence. The postmark was Georgia, and he knew that his stepmother's family still lived there. But why would any of them write to him? In all these years, Prudence had been reticent about her family. She had never gone back to visit, and she had told him almost nothing about them.

"Dear Adam: I know I oughtn't be writing you like this, Jonathan would be angry if he knew about it. The fact is we're in a little financial trouble again. Jonathan said we weren't to ask Prue for help again, that we'll manage to get another extension on our loan, but even so it might not be enough. I wrote to Prue, but then we had a letter from her from England, so I know she didn't receive my letter.

"Father isn't getting any younger. I wish you could visit us. It seems a shame that we've never met. We'd be mighty pleased to see you. Crissy is downright put out, never having laid eyes on her own sister's stepson. It isn't like any of us can afford to travel around the way you can and, besides, Prue has never invited us to Boston. It's about time we got to know each other."

The letter was signed Rory Beddoes and dated July the seventeenth, eighteen hundred and eighty-two.

Adam studied the letter for a long time. It was odd that Prudence had never gone back to Georgia for a visit, the way she liked to gad about. From what he knew of Southerners, they were intensely loyal to family. The letter from Rory, whom he knew to be Prue's brother, aroused his curiosity.

Hang it all, they were family, even if they weren't related to him by blood. And if they were in trouble, he ought to do something about it. He didn't want to go back to Boston yet and resume his game of catch-me-if-you-can with Hester and Marcia. And it would be better all around if he found out just how much help the Beddoeses needed and took care of it in person rather than just sending them a bank draft.

Cleo looked up, surprised, when he entered the kitchen so soon after he had left.

"Cleo, I'm going to Georgia, to Roselawns. What do you think of that?"

Cleo's face changed, became withdrawn and wary. "You been invited?"

"What about all this famous Southern hospitality? Since when does kin need an invitation? Besides, I have a letter here from Rory and they're in some kind of trouble. So, I'm going. Cleo, tell me, why didn't Prudence ever go back?"

"I expect she didn't want to." Cleo's expression was still unreadable, but then she said something that astonished him.

"If you're going back, I think I'll go, too. I haven't been back there since Miss Martha brought me here to Martin's Corners."

"Well, I'll be! I never thought anyone'd be able to get you more than a mile and half from this town! But of course there's no reason you shouldn't take the trip back. You may still have friends living there, and you'll enjoy seeing Jonathan and Rory. Come along, then. I'll be more than happy to take you."

"I can pay my own way." Cleo's tone was determined, and Adam knew there would be no use arguing with her. The black woman was proud to be completely self-sufficient. "I've just taken a notion to go, that's all."

Her first glimpse of Roselawns made Cleo uneasy. If it hadn't been necessary to keep an eye on Adam and make sure that nothing went wrong, she wouldn't have come. She had never had any desire to return, even though she knew that many people had wondered, over the years, if she wasn't lonely, being the only black person in Martin's Corners.

She hadn't been lonely. She'd had Martha, and Miss Emily, and Prudence and Naomi and Adam. And after they had all left her, she had had her work. Tending to Miss Emily's place hadn't taken up all her time, and so she had helped care for sick children, she'd split wood and raked hay for men who were laid up, she'd cleaned the church and sewed with the Ladies' Christian Orphanage Association. She'd taken no pay for her work, counting it done in Miss Emily's name.

Adam had not written ahead to advise the Beddoeses of his coming. He had wanted it to be a surprise. "If they don't want to put us up, we'll stay in town, but I'm betting they'll lay out the red carpet." He hadn't added that if they didn't it would be a crushing blow to him. Prudence was wonderful, but all his life he had yearned for a real family.

He pulled the trap he had rented to a halt just where the long curving driveway turned a bend, so that the house stood directly in front of them. "I never knew it had been burned!" he exclaimed. "Did you know, Cleo?"

Cleo shook her head. The dining-room wing had been burned, the one that Yolande was so proud of, with its table that would seat twenty-four people and the sideboard covered with silver. Now the wing stood in ruins, the roof nearly gone, the broken walls looking charred and ugly in the late afternoon sunlight. It had happened during the war, Cleo supposed. Sherman must have passed this way.

Some attempt had been made to repaint the main structure of Roselawns, but the work had not been completed. The lawn was unkempt, there were weeds in Miss Yolande's rose garden, the fountain had rusted, and no water spilled from the shell that the stone nymph held shoulder-high. There was cotton growing in the fields, but it was scraggly and sparse, a poor crop. No wonder Rory had written Adam for help.

Adam spoke to Cleo again. "Are you sure this is the place?"

"I'm sure. This is Roselawns, Adam." She sat very straight beside him, inscrutable as usual. "The front door's open; you'll have to walk in and let out a yell. I'll go around to the kitchen and see who I can rouse up."

Adam followed her instructions, feeling foolish. He'd never in his life stood in an open doorway and yelled, "Is anybody home?"

"Who is it?" a voice called. And a man emerged from an open doorway halfway down the central hallway. The man stopped and looked at Adam uncertainly, and with a shock, Adam saw that his right shirtsleeve was empty. Rory, of course. This man was too young to be Prue's father, in spite of the touches of gray in his thick, dark hair.

"I'm Adam Wentworth. My stepmother is still in England, and so I decided I'd just come along. I hope I'm not intruding. You did write that you'd be glad to see me."

"Adam!" Rory's left hand thrust forward and grasped Adam's in an awkward but firm grip. His voice rose in a shout. "Pa! Come on out here, we have company! Come in and have a drink, Mr. Wentworth. Where're your bags—in the trap? I'll send somebody to fetch them." He looked beyond Adam to see Cleo returning around the outside, from the kitchen, his face filled with puzzlement that changed to disbelief.

"Cleo! It is Cleo, isn't it? Of course it is! I'm almighty glad to see you looking so well. Go around to the kitchen and stir Marta up, tell her we have company and she's to fix something fit to eat for supper or I'll skin her, you hear?"

"I've been to the kitchen. There was no one there."

"That lazy slut's sneaked off again to take a nap! It's the third cabin in the old quarters, Cleo. Tell her to stir her stumps or she'll hear from me."

Cleo nodded, but there was no servility in her manner.

"Ain't many around here that you'll remember, I'm afraid. The housegirls all left years ago, Pansy and the others you knew. Juliette was killed when that bastard Slade came back to rob us, during the war. Yolande got him, right in the gut, with both barrels of Jacob's shotgun." Rory shook his head. "She was quite a lady, my grandmother. I miss her. She just seemed to fade away after Jacob died. Marta's one of Juliette's granddaughters. Tell her to see a room's made up for Adam and to send Jasper in to fetch the luggage."

As they stood in the front hall, Adam admired the graceful staircase. Its lines were still as beautiful as they must have been when the house was built, although the treads were worn and the balustrades could have used a good dusting. He smiled, thinking that when Cleo got after this household, they wouldn't know what had hit them.

Prudence's home, he thought. She was born here;

374

her father was born here. It made him feel as if he had roots, even though they were borrowed.

Jonathan appeared then, coming down the stairs, his hand outstretched. Adam saw that his hair was completely white and that fine lines of suffering were etched on his face. "Adam Wentworth? This is a mighty fine surprise. Why didn't you let us know you were coming? But it's no matter. You're always welcome. Come into the sitting room. Rory, this calls for a drink! I hope peach brandy will do."

"What, no mint julep?" Adam's brow shot up, and he laughed.

"No ice. And no whiskey, either. Peach brandy is our local product. One thing Georgia still has plenty of is peaches. It isn't bad, Mr. Wentworth. We have survived drinking it for generations."

The sitting room was shabby, but the few good pieces of furniture that were left reflected the prosperity the plantation had once known. Adam noticed that the carpet, Aubusson if he wasn't mistaken, was frayed, and the draperies at the windows were thin and none too clean. But his hosts seemed unaware that things were not as they once had been, and their welcome filled him with exultation. He was kin!

The brandy that Rory poured from a chipped cut-glass decanter was surprisingly good, full-bodied and sweet. Adam ignored the dust that rose from a brocaded chair when he sat down to savor the brandy.

"I hope you've come to stay a while," Jonathan said. "Everyone will want to meet you. Christine, in particular. And she has children that you'll have to consider as your cousins.

Adam's happiness grew. He had a strange feeling that he had been a wanderer all his life and at last he had come home.

38

The gathering of the clan, Adam thought, and there was a tightness in his throat caused by pure sentimentality. They'd come, the Renaults, in response to Jonathan's summons. Rory had ridden over to Swanmere the morning after Adam's arrival, and by suppertime the Renaults had arrived to welcome him into the family.

Crissy was Prudence's sister, of course, but no one who didn't know of the relationship would have guessed it. Jonathan had told him that Christine took after her grandmother Nancy Curtis, who had been blue-eyed and fair. She was still fair, her complexion showing the exquisite care Southern ladies lavished on their faces, but her hair was a little faded now, for all that she was younger than Prue. She hadn't kept her figure as well, either. She was, in fact, quite matronly, although still what older men referred to as a well-set-up woman.

Crissy was dressed in her best, with an enormous bustle and lots of those doodads that Adam thought so ugly. Compared to Prudence, she looked almost dowdy. Adam felt a twinge of shame at the thought. Crissy didn't have the money to spend on clothes that Prue did, nor the opportunities to keep up with the latest trends. All the same, although he could see that Crissy had been a beauty in her time, Prue had it all over her in looks. A certain discontented sulkiness around the mouth marred Crissy's appearance, as far as Adam was concerned.

Adam liked Gaylord Renault better than Crissy. He, too, was fair, much fairer than Crissy or himself— a big man, broad of shoulder, the fairness of his hair disguising the gray. His handclasp had been as firm as Rory's and Jonathan's, his smile as broad and welcoming. Anybody would think that I was a member of the family, Adam thought, and once again he felt that wonderful sense of belonging, of having come home.

Nelson, the older Renault son, was a year or two younger than Adam, fair like his mother and father and giving promise of Gaylord's height and breadth. Jacob, the younger boy, was fifteen, going through the awkward age, but here the Beddoes side of the family came out, for he was as dark as his grandfather and Rory, with the same gray eyes.

And then there was Rosalind. Adam felt his breath catch in his throat when his eyes turned to her again, as they had turned ever since the Renaults had arrived.

It didn't matter at all that Rosalind's dress was just a trifle too small for her and had been let down, so that the marks left by the original hemline had had to be covered with braid. When she smiled, nobody on the face of the earth would notice what she was wearing, anyway. When she smiled, Adam's heart turned over and he felt that he must be dreaming.

Prue, Adam thought. She's Prue all over again, or Prue the way she had been when she was Rosalind's age. The same face, grave in repose, radiant when she smiled or was excited. The same delicate lines, the same gestures, everything about her made Adam's breath stop and then resume more rapidly than was normal. He'd found her at last, the girl who could take Prue's place in his life, the girl he'd been looking for ever since he'd noticed that no girl he met could measure up to Prue.

Don't go off the deep end, he warned himself. You hardly know her. Maybe she has a nasty disposition. Maybe her voice goes shrill when she's riled. Maybe she's stupid. She'd almost have to be stupid because the good Lord wouldn't have endowed her with everything else and then topped it off with brains—it wouldn't have been fair.

"I'm sorry. I didn't catch what you were saying."

Crissy looked at him with disfavor. She wasn't used to being ignored, especially when she was the hostess, as she was here in the absence of another mature woman of the family.

"I was asking about Prue. How often does she go abroad?"

"Every summer, ma'am. She's fond of traveling."

The discontented look around Crissy's mouth deepened. "And I suppose she has all sorts of clothes. I suppose she buys them all from Worth."

"I think so, ma'am. At least most of them. She bought a heap of them last summer when we were in Paris."

"Paris!" Rosalind's eyes were shining. "Mama, imagine, Adam has been to Paris! You'll have to tell us about it, every single thing, Cousin Adam."

"Well, there are a lot of art galleries, and parks, and of course the opera house and the Louvre. I'm afraid I didn't give them the attention I should have." Adam stopped, aware that that was a mistake. What if Rosalind asked to what he had given his attention? His haunts in Paris weren't a suitable topic for a

378

young lady, and Crissy would whisk her daughter away, out of his clutches.

Rosalind's face was rapturous. "And sidewalk cafés, and the Left Bank! That's what I want to hear about!"

"And to think that I felt sorry for Prue when she went back to Martin's Corners and got stuck there when the war broke out!" Crissy's voice was filled with envy. "I couldn't bear the place, myself. I always thought she was out of her mind to go back, until I heard that she'd married your father."

"Are you really fantastically wealthy, Adam?" Rosalind asked. "Oh, I'm sorry! I know that sounded dreadful, but nobody in the South has any money any more."

"Rosalind, behave yourself," Jonathan said, fondly but firmly. "You know better than to pry into folks' affairs."

"I know, Grandfather. But when Mama tells me how it used to be, sometimes I can't help wondering what it would be like to have enough of everything. It must be wonderful."

"It was wonderful, before those Yankees ruined our lives! Nothing will ever be the same again. You can't imagine how we suffered, Mr. Wentworth. Not only did our slaves run off, we actually didn't have enough to eat." Christine took another drumstick; even the thought of those days made her ravenous again. "And there wasn't any medicine. My grandfather died because there wasn't any quinine. And I had to nurse Grandmother through her last illness myself. I hated those Yankees like poison; it was all their fault."

"I'm sorry, ma'am."

"Christine!" Gaylord's voice was sharp. "Aren't you forgetting that our guest is a Yankee?"

"Well, that isn't the same; he was only a baby, he wasn't in the war. And he's Prue's stepson and that makes him family. Besides, why shouldn't he know how it was? Maybe he'll tell other people up North and they'll be ashamed of themselves and tell the government they have to do something about our condition now! Make those Yankees stop robbing us."

Christine drained her wineglass and set it down. It was the third time she'd emptied it since the meal started. Adam tried not to stare. She'd had a hard life, both during the war and after it, and it was none of his business how much she drank. Maybe Southern ladies drank more than Northern ones just as a matter of course.

Young Jacob, a glint of amusement in his eyes, spoke for the first time. "To hear Mama go on, you'd never guess that my other grandmother was an abolitionist, would you? She was, though. She lectured against slavery, and ended up being—" he broke off as he saw Jonathan's face. "I'm sorry, Grandfather. May I be excused?"

Jonathan's face had grown tight and strained, but at Jacob's discomfiture, it softened. "Stay where you are, Jacob. We all know that Martha lost her life in the cause of abolition." His voice was calm, but Adam noticed that his fingers were white around the stem of his glass.

"Papa, don't break that glass, we only have a few pieces left! Jonathan and Benjamin managed to bury most of the good things before the Yankees came burning and plundering, but some of it's already been broken and the silver sold off. It was a mercy that Grandmother managed to kill that awful Vic Slade. He'd have taken everything he could carry and burned the house down around us!" Crissy's eyes were wide and dark with remembering. "He bragged that he was going to rape me, to get even for being sent to prison! He killed Benjamin and Juliette—he stabbed them.

380

Grandmother made Juliette a dress to be buried in; it was velvet, one of hers that she'd been going to make over for me, and she said the service over them herself, and she made me watch and listen. Imagine, wasting a perfectly good velvet dress on a dead slave!"

"Crissy, it's over," Jonathan said. "And I suggest that we find a more pleasant topic of conversation."

"I don't care!" Christine reached for the decanter again. Some of the brandy spilled on the mended table-cloth as she poured it. She drank it quickly, her hand shaking, and then she pushed her chair from the table, and rising, hurried from the room, her shoulders shaking. There was an embarrassed silence for a moment as they listened to her footsteps stumbling up the stairs. Rosalind turned to Adam, her eyes bright with tears.

"Poor Mama, she just can't forget what she suffered in the war. Please forgive her, Cousin Adam. The rest of us don't feel that way, or at least I don't."

"Well spoken, Rosy." Jacob, who was too young for brandy, lifted his water glass in a toast to his sister. The use of the nickname drew sparks.

"Just don't call me that, you know I despise it! Mr. Wentworth will think we're all so dreadful he'll turn around and go straight home. Only, please don't, Cousin Adam, we want you to stay for weeks and weeks, don't we?" This last was directed to her father and grandfather, who both laughed indulgently and assured her that that was their uppermost wish.

"Of course he's going to stay. He didn't come all this way to make a flying visit. The whole county will want to meet him, and things like that take time. Everybody knew Prudence, and they'd take it most unkindly if they weren't presented to her stepson." Jonathan's voice held a note of finality. "Jasper, fetch that other bottle of brandy from the sideboard. We'll drink a toast to Adam's long and we hope enjoyable stay!"

And stay he did. Days passed, and Adam made no move to leave. The truth was that he had no inclination to leave. He liked Georgia, he liked the planters' way of life. He even began to think that he had been born out of his time and place, that he should have been master of just such a plantation as Roselawns or Swanmere, rather than the son of a conservative jewelry merchant who had had a knack for making money in railroads and real estate.

The loan that Jonathan needed was accomplished with a minimum of embarrassment. As far as Jonathan was concerned it might never have been asked or granted, because Adam transacted the business with Rory. But it was Rosalind who kept him there, even though his original purpose in coming had been carried out.

He joined in the plantation social life enthusiastically, meeting the families that lived in surrounding homes. Adam could not remember when he had felt so drawn to another man as he was to Burke Amhurst. As soon as their hands clasped in greeting, he felt a strong liking for the doctor. Burke was in his early forties, and he had aged well. There was not an ounce of excess bulk on his lean frame, and only a whisper of gray in his hair. A quiet man, and one who inspired confidence, was Adam's initial feeling, an evaluation he had no reason to change later.

"I knew your stepmother well," Burke told him. "That was years ago, of course. I still remember how surprised I was when I heard she'd gone back to Massachusetts. I was in medical college at the time, up in Baltimore. We wrote to each other a few times, and I expected that she'd return home to Roselawns,

382

but the war got in the way and the next I heard she was married."

There was an expression in Burke's eyes that jolted Adam. He felt a sudden, deep suspicion that Prudence's acquaintance with this man had gone far beyond casual friendship. The guarded warmth with which Burke questioned him about Prue added to his conviction. Was Burke Amhurst the reason Prue had never returned to the South?

Studying Amhurst, Adam thought that if it hadn't been for the war, Prudence might very well have returned to Roselawns and married this man instead of ending up as his stepmother. Amhurst's loss, my gain, he thought, but all the same he felt a stab of pity for them both.

His meeting with Burke didn't last long. Burke's days were full, from early morning often until late at night, for he did not cater exclusively to the so-called "better" element but was always on call to the poorer families, even to the farmers that the local people called "crackers," and to blacks who needed him.

"And they don't even pay him, except with a slab of bacon or a sack of corn, or fresh eggs or the like!" Rosalind told Adam indignantly. Adam had borrowed one of the Beddoes saddle horses to ride over to Swanmere. Chaperoned by young Jacob, Adam and Rosalind rode around the estate together.

By some miracle, Swanmere had escaped Sherman's famous march through Georgia. Although like Roselawns it was badly in need of paint and repair, the entire structure still stood. It was much larger than Roselawns, more pretentious, but with that undefinable Southern charm.

"Nelson says that Mama wept and pleaded so beautifully when the Yankees came and took all the horses that were left, and all the grain and supplies they could find, that the young Yankee lieutenant wouldn't let his men burn the house.'" There was a touch of mischief in Rosalind's eyes. "Of course, he couldn't possibly remember it, and so it's just something he picked up somewhere. But Grandmother Yolande didn't beg, and Roselawns would have burned to the ground if there hadn't been a rainstorm that put out the fire after the Yankees left."

Adam drew the subject back to Burke Amhurst. The man intrigued him, and he wanted to learn everything he could about him. They dismounted and strolled through the trees as they talked.

"Oh, everybody likes Doctor Amhurst! Aunt Prudence liked him a lot. At least, that's what Mama says. He was married once, though. His wife had consumption, poor thing. If it hadn't been for Doctor Amhurst, she wouldn't have lived even as long as she did.

"They were married during the war. She wasn't that sick back then, and she was pretty. But there were hardly any men around, and her mother nagged at her all the time. Mama says that Burke married her because he was sorry for her, just to get her away from that woman. But they were happy. She was so grateful for Burke's marrying her that she worshipped him. I don't blame her at all. When I was a little girl I used to dream of growing up and marrying him, myself."

"I wouldn't have liked that at all." Adam reached out, touched a tendril of her hair that had escaped from under her broad-brimmed hat, and wound it around his finger. The soft and silky strand felt like satin and seemed possessed of a life of its own, as vital as Rosalind herself. His breath caught with painful sharpness. Compared to Rosalind, every other girl he had ever known faded into insignificance. Try as

384

he might, he couldn't even remember exactly what Marcia looked like.

Rosalind laughed, her eyes dancing. "Why, he's old enough to be my father! But all the same, he's still terribly handsome for a man of his age, isn't he?"

"Here now, you stop that!" Adam was surprised at his jealous anger. "When a girl is with me, she isn't supposed to moon about another man."

The tendril of hair clung to his fingers, and Rosalind began to scold him. "You'll have it all in a tangle, and it'll take me an hour to brush out all the snarls! Adam, do stop . . ."

Rosalind reached up to push his hand away. But when their hands touched, he leaned down and kissed her. As his mouth covered hers, his blood leaped through his body in a headlong rush, and he seemed to hear a roaring in his ears.

Adam broke off at last, amazed at the violence of his passion. He reminded himself that Rosalind was entirely without experience, not one of those delectable young ladies he had known in the past, especially in Paris.

He was behaving like a cad, like an unprincipled animal. Another moment, and he'd have had her on the ground, tearing off her clothing. Had he gone completely out of his mind? Or did he actually want to be called out and shot? Someone had mentioned to him that Gaylord was a crack shot, that he had been a participant in more than one duel before the war and had always come out unscathed while his antagonist fell under his unerring aim.

Even though her lips had parted under his and she had pressed herself against him until he'd nearly burst with his desire, Rosalind wasn't the kind of girl you took to bed at night and forgot in the morning. She was a girl to marry.

The thought hit him like a blow to his solar plexus. And then warmth, quite unlike that which had stormed through his body a moment ago, took possession of him. Well, why not? If she'd have him, and from the way she was looking at him now, her lips still moist and parted, her cheeks flushed and her eyes like stars, she had been as shaken as he was.

Again, his native caution warned him to wait. Would Rosalind's family sit still for her to marry him and go to live in Boston, the stronghold of everything they hated? And how would his own friends in Boston accept her, a girl from the South? Hester Carter would do everything in her power to see that she was ostracized.

Of course, they wouldn't have to live in Boston. There was no law that said he had to go on living there just because he had been born there. All during his visit, the idea of staying on in Georgia had been growing in him, until he had put off even thinking of leaving, refused to think of it at all because it was so distasteful to him.

Swanmere, with both an elder and a younger son, was barred to him, but there were no boys in Jonathan's immediate household. Rory was already over forty and unlikely to marry it seemed. What feminine companionship Rory needed, he bought. As Jonathan's granddaughter and Rory's niece, what would be more natural than to bring Rosalind to Roselawns, so that their sons would inherit? Roots, continuity, the idea took hold of him and grew, bringing with it an excitement that made his face flush and his eyes take on a glow.

How he would transform the place! The dining-room wing would be rebuilt, painters and carpenters put to work throughout the house, the exterior restored to its former glory, the interior completely refurbished.

For the first time, Adam was aware of the advantages of being wealthy, of being able to spend all that was necessary to make a dream come true.

He realized that Rosalind was waving her hand in front of his face.

"Adam, come back! You've been a hundred miles away! What were you thinking of, just now?"

"Of heaven, Rosalind, of heaven!" He caught her hands and started walking her back toward the house. "We'd better go back or your father will be out looking for me with a gun. There's something I want to speak to him about, anyway."

"What is it, Adam? Can I know?" The use of his first name pleased him. No more Cousin Adam; he wasn't her cousin, and he wanted no tinge of implied relationship between them.

"Now isn't that just like a woman! As if you didn't already know. Just for that, I think I'll speak only of planting matters and compliment him on his brandy."

"I'll never forgive you!"

"Never?"

"Never!"

Laughing, their faces alight, they found their horses and remounted. From the crest of a short rise Jacob waved to them and came cantering toward them. Adam had forgotten all about the boy. How much had he seen? It was a good thing that he really wanted to marry Rosalind, because if Jacob spoke out of turn, there'd be a wedding anyway, or a shooting.

39

Prudence hoped that it would be Adam who met her in Savannah, so that she would have a chance to draw him out, privately, before she was enveloped by the family she had not seen for so many years.

When Cleo's letter had reached her at Sir Archibald's, she had booked the first available passage home. Adam, in Georgia! The tone of the black woman's letter had shown clearly that Cleo was worried. *I think you had better come,* Cleo had written. All the way across the Atlantic, during the interminable train trip and this last leg by fast packet, worry gnawed at Prue. Had her family guessed the truth, had the long years of deception come to an end, would Adam hate her for what she had done?

It was not Adam, but Rory, who came to meet her, and for a moment she did not recognize him. There were lines in his face, gray in his hair, and when she saw his empty sleeve, her breath caught. She knew that he had lost his arm in the war—Crissy had written her about it—but somehow she had never envisioned him without it.

"Glory, Prue, it's good to see you! You hardly look a day older. You didn't discover the Fountain of Youth someplace, did you? You make me feel ancient! Or are all Boston ladies forever young and beautiful? Come along, Jonathan's chomping at the bit to have you home. He wasn't feeling so pert today, or he'd have come himself."

Not only had Rory changed, but everything else, too. Prue felt a distinct shock as he handed her into the buggy, and the wiry young driver touched his head and bobbed it to her, a wide smile splitting his face. He reminded her of someone, but who? Trust Rory to bring a boy to handle her luggage, when their conveyance was an ordinary buggy!

"I'm Tod, Miss Prue. Jimmy's son. It surely is good to see you here."

"Jimmy took off as soon as that devil backwoodsman in the White House told the niggers they were free," Rory explained to her. He used his normal speaking voice, not caring whether Tod heard or not. "But Jimmy's wife refused to go with him, and she kept the boy. He said he'd come back for her, but he never did. We don't have any idea what happened to him. He went off with that fire-eating Absalom from Swanmere, so likely he got himself killed."

"I hope not." Prue frowned at him, and then sighed inwardly. Rory was thoughtless, not intentionally cruel. To Rory, black people were simply there, not persons to be considered as individuals with feelings.

"You'll find things mighty changed at Roselawns. We Southerns didn't fare as well as the North, as you'll remember." Rory spoke with a casual drawl, but Prudence sensed an underlying bitterness. "We just about get by. That Adam of yours is a godsend, and I don't mind admitting it. We didn't have enough to carry us the rest of the summer, until the crop is in. We'd have had to ask Gay to help us out, and he's almost as bad off as we are."

"How is Crissy? And her children?" Prudence asked.

389

"Crissy's as touchy as ever and just as complainin'. At least she was until Adam arrived and started waving his magic wand. The boys are fine, and Rosy's a beauty. Adam hasn't been able to take his eyes off her since he got here. It's lettin' the cat out of the bag—they want to surprise you—but it's all settled, and everybody in the family's tickled about it, even if he is a Yankee. Don't let on I told you. I'm fond of Rosy, and I don't want to steal her thunder."

It was full summer and hot, but Prue felt a chill spread through her body, and she had to exert an effort to keep her teeth from chattering. Oh, God, why had Adam taken the notion to come to Roselawns, instead of just sending a bank draft? Adam and Rosalind! Adam was Rosalind's half brother!

"Prue, are you all right? You've gone as white as a sheet! You, there, Tod, whip up that horse, Miss Prudence is sick!"

In her lap, Prudence's hands clenched until the bones ached. She was living a nightmare, and it was only beginning. She closed her eyes, but she knew that when she opened them, it would still be there. She'd spent twenty years making sure that Adam had no interest, no curiosity, about her family in the South. She'd denied herself visits to Roselawns. She'd violated every rule of hospitality by not inviting them to visit her in Boston, ignoring Crissy's broad hints when she had ached to see her. She'd sent Jonathan a small loan just before she sailed for England, more than he'd asked for, but obviously not enough. Why hadn't she remembered his pride, and sent more?

"Where is Adam? Why didn't he come to meet me?"

"He was going to, but Crissy arrived to measure all the windows for new draperies, with Rosy in tow. Crissy had him climbing up and down ladders, and then those saddle horses he bought arrived and nothing

390

would do but he and Rosy try them out. Decent horses again, Prue! You can't know what that means. There hasn't been a decent piece of horseflesh at Roselawns since before the war. He bought three strapping hunters for himself and Jonathan and me, and a mare for Rosy —it's the daintiest thing you ever saw and she was in raptures, couldn't wait to try her out. Do you do any riding, back in Boston?"

"Very little." Prudence's face was strained.

"Prue, you aren't upset about Adam and Rosy, are you? You didn't have some high-falutin' Boston girl picked out for him? I expect that's it—you've been up North so long you've turned into a penny-pinchin' Yankee! You had it fixed to marry him off to some heiress!"

"That isn't true. Please, Rory, I don't feel very well. Let's not discuss it now." ·

Rory settled back against the seat, disgruntled. Something was eating at his sister, and it wasn't all because she was tired or sick. *Northerners*! Rory thought to himself. He hadn't thought it could rub off on anybody, least of all his own kind. But then Prue had spent most of her life up there, and under the influence of Miss Emily, at that. If that was the way she felt, why the devil hadn't she just stayed away? Or had she come to break it up, if she could?

Rory's eyes narrowed. He'd be damned if she would! It wasn't just the money. They'd get along without it, they always had. But those two youngsters loved each other, and if he had anything to say about it Prue damned well wasn't going to spoil things for them!

Crissy's face was flushed, and strands of her hair had come loose from their pins, but there was a satisfied gleam in her eyes as she surveyed the living room at Roselawns. Unlike the others in her family, who had been able to ignore the shabbiness as if it didn't exist, Crissy had always been aware, with a deep and angry resentment, of what both Roselawns and Swanmere had once been and how derelict they were now.

But now all that was going to change. In a few months Roselawns, at least, would be restored to all its former glory. Rosalind would live in the manner to which she was entitled by blood and birth, and Crissy would bask in the reflected glory. Maybe some of the county people would make catty remarks about its being Yankee money, but it would be pure jealousy. Crissy felt a deep and abiding satisfaction as she pictured her daughter amid all the luxury that Adam would provide.

All these years, Crissy had hated her sister because Prudence had married money up there in Boston and lived off the fat of the land, while Crissy had had to make do with practically nothing. Oh, Prue had helped them out a few times, but not anywhere near as much as she should have. That was her father's fault, and Gay's, because they'd been too proud to ask and they got angry when she did. Finally, Rory had done the asking this last time.

Crissy brought herself up short. Be nice to her, she reminded herself. No matter how badly she's treated you, be nice to her. Remember, it's Adam's money that's going to change everything. Besides, Prue would be going back to Boston, and she wouldn't have to put up with her for very long.

She'd be as sweet as sugar, even if Prue tried to upstage her. And there was one satisfaction. She, Crissy, or rather Crissy through Rosalind, was taking Adam away from Prue, and Adam's money with him. And Prue was older than she was, and that was another satisfaction. She'd be old and dowdy like all New England women, for all her fine clothes and jewels.

Crissy had always been the pretty one, everyone had said so, and that was something that all of Prue's money couldn't buy.

She was here! Crissy made an ineffectual effort to smooth her hair and put a welcoming smile on her face as she hurried to the door. Where had Gay and Papa got to? Out in Jacob's old office, she'd be bound, and into the brandy, instead of staying in the house to be ready when Prue arrived.

But they had heard the buggy, too, and were hurrying over to help Prue down. And there, thundering down the drive like the devil was after him, was Adam on that new hunter, its nostrils flaring. Adam was laughing, his face alight with excitement as he pulled the horse up to a rearing stop and jumped down, tossing the reins to Tod.

"Cool him out, Tod, and give him a good rubdown, you hear?" After only a few weeks Adam had already picked up some of the local expressions. In his eagerness he shouldered Rory aside and lifted Prudence to the ground before Jonathan or Gay could reach her.

"Well, Mother, you didn't waste any time getting here! I don't see how my letter got to you fast enough so you could be here already! Here comes Rosalind— wait till you see her. You'll know why I fell in love with her at first sight!"

The smile froze on Crissy's face. Was that really Prudence, her prim, plain older sister? The woman in front of her looked years younger than Crissy, and she could have stepped right out of a fashion plate. And around her throat, wasn't that Mama's pearl necklace? Crissy had always resented Jonathan's giving the pearls to Prudence. If one of the girls were to have them, then she, Crissy, had had just as much right to them as Prue! It wasn't fair. Nothing had ever been fair to

393

Crissy, except that she'd got Gay, and what a commotion there had been about that!

Crissy looked at her husband, and her face relaxed a little. He was still by far the best-looking man she'd ever laid eyes on. His blond hair scarcely showed the gray, and it was as thick and softly curling as it had been when she had married him. Maybe he did drink a little too much, and maybe he'd had more than one flirtation, but he was still a husband a wife could be proud of. His temper wasn't anything to brag about, but then he rarely showed it in company. Only to her, and she'd always known how to hold her own. Prue didn't have to know about that, anyway. Crissy's smile was almost as sweet as she'd planned it to be as she kissed Prudence's cheek and said, "You remember Gay, of course?"

"And I remember Prudence! You led me a merry chase, young lady, and then you ran off and never did come back! Prue, you look wonderful. I can see why I was so taken with you when you were a girl. Living in the North certainly agrees with you. You hardly look a day older than when you left, which is more than I can say for the rest of us who stayed here."

Crissy's face flushed, and she could feel the bitter gall roiling around in her stomach. All the old jealousy that she had so carefully pushed under the surface emerged again, intensified by Gaylord's flattering banter to Prue. And the way he was looking at her, that look that tells a woman more plainly than words that she's beautiful. All her defenses were whipped away, with Prue standing there as if butter wouldn't melt in her mouth, a smile on her unlined face, radiant in spite of the fatigue of her journey.

Prue was completely unaware of the emotions that were seething in her sister. Her attention was taken

394

up with Rosalind, who had slid down from her saddle without waiting for help.

"Adam, you're a brute! Here you go on about how wonderful the South is, and you haven't a trace of Southern chivalry! Galloping off like that and leaving me behind, just when you'd let me think that I was beating you!"

Lord, how lovely she is! Prudence thought, her heart aching. Rosalind bore little resemblance to Crissy; instead, the girl looked like herself twenty years ago, only far prettier than she had been. Had she ever really been that young? It didn't seem possible.

"I'm sorry, Rosy. I just got carried away when I saw the buggy." Putting his arm around Rosalind, Adam drew her forward. Laughing, to show that she wasn't really angry, Rosalind turned to Prue, her hands outstretched.

"Aunt Prudence, I just might not marry him at all! Imagine being married to a man who prefers his stepmother to his wife! It isn't to be borne, is it?"

Her eyes were dancing, and Prue felt a chill spread through her body again. I have to hurt her, she thought. I have to hurt Adam, and Rosalind, and I'd rather die. Why did I ever allow this deception that's come home to roost! They'd hate her to the day she died and beyond. And she would hate herself, from this day forward, for having done what she thought would insure Adam's happiness and security but, instead, was going to plunge him into hell.

Cleo greeted her quietly, with deep, mute suffering in her eyes that matched Prudence's own.

Dinner, cooked by Cleo herself, was excellent, and Jonathan and Rory's appreciation of it was plainly evident.

"I never thought I'd sit down to a decent meal again," Jonathan told Prudence. "That Cleo of yours is a wonder. You know the best wedding present you could give these children of ours, Prue? Leave Cleo here to supervise the kitchen and the house!"

"Cleo is a free agent. I can't tell her what she should do." Prudence's voice was strained, and she felt as if the skin on her face was stretched as taut as a mask.

"I understand that, but maybe you could persuade her. She'd be our housekeeper, not an ordinary servant. She wouldn't have to do any of the actual work herself. I understand that she never worked for you in Boston anyway, but just stayed on in that little house in Martin's Corners."

"The house belongs to Cleo now, and if she prefers to return to it, I will not attempt to change her mind."

"La de da!" Crissy's face was flushed. She had over-indulged in the wine that had been served with every course, and now there was a dangerous glitter in her eyes as she turned them on her sister. "We might have known you'd be a turncoat, Prue! Mama and Aunt Emily ruined you, as far as the blacks are concerned. Well, let me tell you, they may be free, but to me they're still niggers and they always will be! If Cleo were my servant she'd do as I told her, or she'd be good and sorry!"

"Then it's fortunate that she isn't your servant, isn't it?" Prue kept her voice even. "Just because she is a colored person does not mean that she should have to put up with abuse."

"Colored person!" Crissy's voice rose. "Persons, she calls them, just as if they were like the rest of us. Prue, you're a caution. I just hope you'll keep such radical opinions to yourself when you meet our friends! I'd hate to have to be ashamed of my own sister!"

"I expect I'll manage to deport myself suitably," Prue said dryly.

"Mama, please don't be difficult. Don't you think you've had enough to drink?" Rosalind was close to tears. Prue cringed inwardly as she saw that her niece was a girl who would be easily hurt, dreadfully hurt, by any controversy.

Crissy turned on her daughter, her eyes flashing dangerously. "Since when has it been your place to correct your mother? You're not a married woman yet, my girl, and when you are, I should hope I brought you up to know the respect due to your elders!"

Rosalind looked down at her hands, clasped tightly in her lap, and Adam reached out to cover them with one of his own. "Come now, how did this silly argument get started, anyway? If Cleo wants to stay, it will make us all very happy, but if she doesn't, there are other capable women to be had." Always tactful, Adam had a knack of knowing the exact thing to say, and now he turned his boyishly appealing glance to Crissy. "I hope you'll train whatever woman we get, because then it will be done right and we'll have the best housekeeper in the county, outside of Swanmere itself."

Crissy subsided, almost purring. Swanmere had no housekeeper, only two shiftless girls who had to be watched every minute or they'd leave dust under the beds and the dishes half clean, but that, too, would be changed as soon as Rosalind and Adam were married. Adam would be a generous son-in-law, Crissy was sure.

The conversation turned to the repair work that was already going forward. "Crissy plans to go to New Orleans herself to choose the wallpaper and draperies and rugs," Rory told Prue. "You're leaving Monday, aren't you, Crissy? I'll bet you'll go through those fancy shops like a tornado!"

Something stirred in Prudence, a tenuous idea that had been sparked by Rory's remark. There might be a way to resolve this situation without ruining Adam's life, if she could persuade Gaylord to cooperate. The children would be hurt, but they were young, they would get over it in time. She was quiet until the meal ended, and then she excused herself and went to the kitchen to talk to Cleo.

Cleo turned from the table where she was scraping and stacking dishes. "It's a terrible thing to have happened. I sent for you as soon as I saw how things were going, but it was too late, and it wasn't my place to tell them."

"You did just right, Cleo. And I think I may have thought of something. I'm going to send Crissy out here. I'll tell her that you want to consult with her about the menus for next week, and you're to keep her here as long as you can. I must talk to Gaylord, and she must not hear what I am going to say."

"I understand. I'll keep her as long as I can. And I'll be praying, too."

For just a moment, Prudence's resolve crumbled. "Pray hard," she said, "because I'm going to need it!"

40

A single lamp stood on the marble-topped table in the small library—a room that Jacob, in his declining years, had fixed up as his own study. There he could close the door on a world that had turned upside down and retreat into the happier times of the past through the pages of books that he had never had time to read in his more vigorous days.

Gaylord's voice was choked as, reluctantly, he struggled to absorb what Prudence had just told him. "My God! Naomi's child? Adam is my son? Prudence, this is monstrous! Oh, my God, Prue, how could you have done it? It'll kill them, it'll kill Rosy and Crissy both!"

The despair in his voice set up a quivering inside of her, but Prue's voice was steady as she answered him. Her only hope was that Gay was so overwhelmed by this disaster that he would obey her instructions without question.

"Gay, you must take Rosalind with Crissy to New Orleans. Override any objections Rosalind might have. Crissy will back you up, because she'll be crazy to buy Rosalind's trousseau there with the money I will give her.

"When you are in New Orleans, tell them that Adam has something in his past that makes it impossible for the marriage to take place. You need not tell them what it is, only that you will never permit the marriage. Hint at a scandal, anything. From New Orleans you can go on to Europe, and stay there, where Adam cannot possibly find you. Gay, do you understand me? Don't allow Rosalind to write to Adam. You write to him, and tell him that Rosalind has changed her mind, that she does not want to marry him, and that nothing will make her reconsider. I'll pay all of your expenses, of course. The essential thing is that the children must be separated at once, and not allowed to see each other again. You can return here once Adam accepts Rosalind's rejection."

"It'll break Rosy's heart." Gaylord put his face in his hands, and his shoulders shook. At that moment Prudence pitied him, although it was his own actions that had made this nightmare possible. What was it the Bible said about the sins of the fathers? And the most terrible thing about it was there was no way to undo the harm.

But there was no time for self-abnegation now. The children's hearts must be broken to protect them from a greater hurt. She repeated her question. "Gay, do you understand? You know exactly what you're to do?"

"I need a drink."

"No drink. You are to stay sober. Listen to me, Gay! You are not to drink, do you understand? If you get drunk you'll let something slip." Her lips compressed into a hard line. "You may never be able to take another drink for as long as you live, unless you want to risk having Crissy and Rosalind find out the truth." This time, she felt no pity at his stricken look. He must suffer, and she must suffer, but the children must be spared the additional horror of learning the truth. "Do you think your life would be worth living, if Crissy found out? And how would you be able to look your daughter in the face again?"

"Yes, yes!" Crissy was impatient. How stupid Cleo was! But then Cleo had always been stupid. Why first her mother and then Prue had set such store by the woman was more than she could understand. Stupid and ugly, so that it was distasteful even to look at her. And now this rambling, irritating series of inconsequential questions, when much more important things were at hand, infuriated her. "We don't have to discuss it all tonight, Cleo. Besides, your mistress is here, she'll straighten it all out for you later."

She left the kitchen before Cleo could delay her any longer and walked through the covered passage between the kitchen and the main house, her thoughts racing. New Orleans! She would rather go north, of course, to buy the most essential things, but time was limited, the children were already pushing her to set the wedding date, and the sooner Rosalind was married to Adam the better. She'd spent enough years of her life in privation, and it was time they came to an end.

The dining room was empty, and only Adam and Rosalind were in the parlor, sitting together on the sofa, their hands entwined. Rosalind's face was flushed, and she was laughing as she lifted it in reply to something Adam had just said. Jonathan and Rory were nowhere to be seen, and neither were Gay and Prue.

A twinge of alarm swept over her. Gay and Prue! Where could they have got to? She didn't like the way Gay had been looking at her sister all evening, or the compliments he had lavished on her, compliments that had reflected on her, even if he hadn't meant them that way. Her voice was sharp as she asked Rosalind where the others were.

Rosalind's answer was vague, her mind still completely on Adam. "I think Grandfather and Uncle Rory went out to the office. I don't know where Daddy and Aunt Prudence are."

"Didn't they go into the study?" Adam said absently. "I thought I heard them heading that way. I'm not teasing, Rosalind, you'll be a sensation in Paris! There's a lady I want to introduce to you there, she's something right out of this world, and I'm pretty sure I can wangle us an invitation. I only met her once, but I had the impression that she liked me."

"Another woman! Adam, how could you! We aren't even married yet, and you're already thinking about picking up some old flirtation with some beautiful French creature I couldn't possibly compete with!"

Adam's eyes sparkled with mischief. "And so you couldn't, and there'd be no use trying. She's a countess, for one thing."

"Adam!"

Crissy ignored the anguished wail and, turning on her heel, hurried to the study. The door was closed, but she heard a murmur of voices from inside. It was Prue and Gay. Anger brought an ugly flush to her face and she started to fling open the door, but her hand froze on the knob as she heard Gay's words take distinctive form through the panels.

"God, Prue, I still can't take it in! Adam, Naomi's son!"

"And yours." Prue's words were clipped and cold, filled with iron. "Your son, and Rosalind's half-brother. You must take Rosalind and Crissy away without delay."

The hot anger receded, and its place was taken by an icy cold that was like dying. Gay's son, Naomi's son? But Naomi was a nigger! A nigger slave, everybody knew that, for all that she was Jonathan's natural daughter. Rebecca had been a slave, and Naomi was Rebecca's child, hers and Jonathan's. There was a roaring in Crissy's head that blotted out the hallway, that blotted out everything as it intensified.

402

Her hand moved and she threw the door inwards so hard that it crashed against the wall; her voice rose in a shrill scream that penetrated even the roaring in her head.

"What are you talking about? It isn't true; you're lying! Prue's lying, she's always hated me, she's doing this to keep Rosalind from marrying Adam! She doesn't want us to have anything—"

"Crissy, stop it!" Prue had her by the shoulders, shaking her. "Stop it this instant! How much did you hear?"

"You said Adam is Gaylord's son! You said Adam is a nigger! Gay, make her stop it, do something, don't let her do this to me . . ." Her voice rose higher and higher, echoing through the room, through the house. Prue heard running footsteps and then Adam and Rosalind appeared, white and stunned, staring at the tableau in front of them in disbelief.

"Mama, what is it? What are you saying?" Rosalind's voice was on the edge of hysteria. "Adam is Aunt Prue's stepson, everyone knows that!"

Crissy's face twisted into an ugly mask, and she looked twenty years older than she had a few minutes ago. "She says that your father is Adam's father, that Naomi was his mother. She says that Adam's your brother and he's a nigger!"

Rosalind's knees went out from under her as she started to faint. Adam caught her and eased her onto a leather-upholstered chair. He turned to Prudence, his face so changed that he looked like a stranger. His skin was stretched taut so that the bone structure showed, and his eyes burned with an intensity that frightened her.

"Prudence? Speak to me!"

They all knew, now, and it couldn't be denied, it couldn't be hidden; there was no place to run.

"Adam!" The cry was torn from Prue.

It was all the answer he needed. He turned his back on her and looked at the man in front of him. Rosalind's father, his father! "I ought to kill you," he said. That soft, charming, handsome man, his father! Rage exploded in him, and he threw himself at the older man. This man was his father—a man who had raped a slave, used her and cast her aside, and brought him into being, a bastard! Gay didn't deserve to live. He and his kind should have been wiped off the face of the earth long ago, the war had come too late . . .

"Adam, in the name of God, stop it!" In his blind rage, Adam heard Prue's voice dimly, but he took no notice as his fists pounded into Gaylord's face, over and over, punishing, crushing. He felt the skin of his knuckles break, saw spurting blood, he felt Gaylord's cheekbone crush under the impact of another blow as he knocked down and straddled the man who had sired him. He would pound him into nothing, into dust. Taken completely by surprise, Gaylord was able to offer almost no resistance to the younger man.

Hands dragged Adam to his feet, away from Gay, who was lying prone, his arms over his face, groaning in bubbling, gurgling gasps. Jonathan was bewildered. "What's going on here, what the devil are you doing? Prudence, Crissy, answer me! What's happened?" Rory, helping his father subdue Adam, had surprising strength in his one arm, but even so the two of them together could not have held him if sanity had not flowed back to replace the madness.

Crissy was gone. Prudence turned to Rosalind, who stared at her, eyes blind with horror.

"It's my fault," Prudence cried. "All of it. Rosalind, my dear, don't look like that! I'll help you, I'll try to help you both . . ."

"Yes, it's your fault!"

Crissy had returned, and she held Jacob's pistol in both hands. Shaking, she leveled it at her sister. Prudence had done this, all of it! Prudence had ruined her life! Prudence must pay! All the jealousy that had built up in her during her lifetime was compressed into one small, hard, burning ball of hatred. Prue's fault!

"Crissy, have you gone mad?" Jonathan started to rise from where he had knelt beside Gaylord, after he made sure that Adam no longer posed a threat. "Give me that gun!"

Prudence turned to face Crissy; she heard Rory shout, and then she felt a. numbing blow on her shoulder. She felt only surprise, and then the encroaching darkness and a babble of incredulous, shocked voices that receded until there was nothing at all.

"Burke." She whispered his name through lips that were so cracked and dry that she could hardly get the sound through. Her throat was dry, it burned, and her shoulder was burning, it was on fire. But Burke was there, it wasn't a dream, his face bent above hers, filled with concern.

"Be quiet, Prue. Lie still. I don't want you to move."

She was in her old bedroom at Roselawns. Sunlight came through the windows and lay in stripes on the floor and on a patch of the light coverlet that was thrown over her. She didn't mind the pain, the thirst, somehow she knew that they were unimportant. There was something else, something that she had to remember, but she didn't want to; her mind and her body recoiled from remembering.

But she remembered. She couldn't stop herself from remembering. Adam, and Rosalind. Gaylord, and Crissy.

Burke held a cup to her mouth. It tasted bitter, but it relieved the burning dryness. "Adam?" Prue pushed the cup away, and the wave of pain from moving her arm almost plunged her back into darkness.

"Don't try to talk."

"I have to know."

Burke sighed. "As far as we know, Adam is all right. He left. He was gone before I got here, and we haven't seen or heard from him since."

Prudence's forehead creased. "How long?"

"Two days. Cleo sent Tod to fetch me after Crissy shot you. Prue, you must rest. You've lost a lot of blood. Drink the rest of this and go back to sleep."

Adam, Adam! The name repeated itself, agonizingly, in her mind, but the drug that Burke had given her took effect, and she slept again.

Burke was still there, or had been away and returned, when she woke early that evening. Smile lines crinkled around his eyes when he saw her looking at him.

"You're better. The worst of it's over now, Prue. I'll go and have them send up some broth."

"Burke, I have to know."

"After you've eaten."

How could broth taste so good? She opened her mouth like a baby, and Burke fed her himself, spoonful by spoonful, until the cup was empty. "Now tell me."

"Nobody outside of the family knows. Except for Cleo and Tod, of course, and they can be trusted. I had to patch up Gay's face after I'd got that bullet out of your shoulder. He'll have a scar or two, but it won't be bad. Rosalind's all right, but I'm keeping a close eye on Crissy. I sent Cleo home with them as soon as Gaylord could travel. She's the only one who can cope with your sister at this stage of the game. We're keeping Crissy pretty heavily sedated. To tell the truth, she's locked in her room so the other servants won't hear when she raves."

Prudence swallowed, and winced. "She isn't mad?"

Burke's smile transformed his face. "As a wet hen. But if you mean insane, I don't think so. It'll take a little time for her to simmer down and realize that keeping her mouth shut about all this is to her own advantage. She wouldn't want to face charges of assault with a deadly weapon."

"Adam is gone?"

"Nobody knows. He may be in town." Burke took her hand and held it, and his touch was infinitely comforting. "Prue, Adam is a grown man. He can take care of himself. He's had a shock, but he's strong, he'll live through it."

"He hates me. He'll never forgive me."

"Never is a long time. Don't think about it now." Burke touched the tear that escaped from under her closed eyelids with a gentle finger.

"You're just the same," he said. "You haven't changed. I've wondered all these years why I loved you so much. I've told myself that I must have imagined how wonderful you were, that I was young and inexperienced, that I endowed you with all sorts of virtues that you didn't possess. I told myself that I only imagined that you'd loved me, that I was a fool to go on thinking about you."

No, Prudence thought, *no more. Not now. I can't bear it.* She wouldn't cry. It was too late for that. She was a middle-aged woman; all that old hurt was in the past.

"I did love you. I thought I'd die from loving you."

"But you married someone else."

"I thought you'd married Crissy. By the time I knew better, there was Adam who needed a home and security. I thought it wouldn't matter, since you and Crissy were married. Aaron needed me, Burke. Aaron and Adam and Aaron's baby son needed me, and I

407

thought you were lost to me, and so I married him. And later, when Aaron died, you had married, too. Were you happy, Burke?"

"Julie was a sweet and gentle girl, and I had my work."

"Aaron was a sweet and gentle man, and I had Adam." She opened her eyes and looked at him. "It's too late, Burke, Everything is gone, it was all for nothing."

"Stop that! It's never too late. Damn it, why don't you cry?"

"What would be the use? It wouldn't change anything." Her hand felt hot and limp in his, infinitely helpless. "I'm alone now, Burke. I'll always be alone. Everyone hates me, and with reason."

"You're not alone. I'm here."

"Burke, we're old. Too much has happened."

"And more is going to happen. A lot more, if you'll let it. Prue, you have to face the fact that Adam left you, that Crissy hates you, that Jonathan and Rory are shocked and resentful. But you know that you did what you thought was right at the time, and that can't be changed. It must be lived with and not allowed to ruin the rest of your life. That would be a waste, Prue, and one that I won't allow to happen if I can help it."

"How could I ever be happy again? I don't deserve to be happy."

"I never want to hear you say that again," Burke said angrily. "You can't change what's past. You can't live anyone else's life for them. But you can live your own life, and it's up to you what you make of it."

She hadn't thought that she could cry, but she did. At least it was a beginning. Feeling was living, whether she liked it or not.

BOOK THREE:

Adam

Part Two

41

Adam reined his horse to a stop in front of the biggest saloon in Albuquerque and pushed his broad-brimmed hat back on his head as he surveyed the street. His shirt was stuck to his back, and rivulets of sweat trickled from his underarms. These Southwestern towns were all alike. Hot, dusty, with a relentless sun beating down out of a molten sky on the saloons and a sheriff's office, a general store, maybe a restaurant. They had nothing to recommend them but loss of identity; they were places where a man never asked your name or your business, places where you volunteered the information or chose not to.

For two years now he had been drifting, a man with no purpose in life except forgetfulness. His quest had not been successful. Never, even for a moment, had he forgotten one jot of the bitterness that had welled up in him, when he had learned the truth of his birth, to burn like a fever that nothing could quench. Even here, in this heat and dust, with a three-day stubble of beard on his face, it was all there, right on the top of his mind, something to be relived over and over again, as he was reliving it now, as his mind went back to the past, to the day his world ended. . . .

Rory had intercepted Adam as he left the house, a carpetbag in his hand. "Where are you going? Good God, man, Prue's been shot, may be dying! Aren't you even going to wait for Burke to get here?"

"I don't give a damn whether she lives or dies!" Adam's words were cold, as cold as ice, in contrast to the fire that had consumed him. "If she lives, I never want to see her again!"

Rory's face grew a shade more pale, and he recoiled from the venom in Adam's voice. "What about Rosalind? She'll need you—"

"Need me for what?" Adam's laugh grated. "What need has she for a nigger half-brother?"

And he left, saddling his new hunter with quick, savage motions, riding away without looking back. He had to get away, fast, before the fury inside him broke loose again, before he killed someone. His hands clenched on the reins, and he had felt sweat break out all over his body as he urged the horse toward town.

God, he had loved her, that stepmother of his! Loved her, admired her, thought her a paragon among women! And all this time she'd been living a lie, forcing him to live a lie! No matter what her motive, her deception had ended in this, the shattering revelation that the girl he loved more than life itself was his half-sister!

Like Jonathan on another dark night years before, he had thundered along the road as if the devil had been on his tail, but Adam did not break his journey. He bypassed the town and went at a blind, furious gallop, heedless of anything except putting as much distance between himself and Roselawns as possible. Only his horse's faltering gait and heaving sides had finally made him slow his pace. As strong as the hunter was, he realized that it could still be ridden to death and drop under him. He stroked the horse's neck, and his hand came away covered with froth. "Easy, boy. It's all right."

The horse stood with its head down, its sides heaving. When they started on again, they went at a slow trot that still covered ground.

Adam used every ounce of his self-control not to turn the horse's head back toward Roselawns, where his enemies were still alive, still unpunished for the enormity of their sins. His hands ached with the desire to feel Gaylord Renault's throat between them, to choke the life out of him, and then to turn to Jonathan and repeat the process.

And there was Rosalind. What would she do, how would she bear this? She had no hate to keep her alive. She was soft, and sweet, and completely innocent of harm, and she was his sister. Somebody had to die for it.

But dying would be too easy. When you were dead, it was over, and no more punishment could be meted out. No, they must live, and suffer, as much as Adam could make them suffer. Prudence, too, because of all of them her betrayal of him had been the greatest, because she had been the only one who had known his true identity.

In the moonless night, Adam's thoughts had gone back, far into his childhood, seeking, probing. Arthur? He was Arthur! Scraps and wisps of memory, shrouded in mist, drove his mind into a frenzy. He'd remembered a sense of loneliness, of being abandoned. There had been someone called Arthur, someone called Adam. And then there had been only one.

And she had done it, Prudence had done it. You are Adam, she had told him over and over, until he had believed it, until he had forgotten why he had begged for a boy named Adam. "You're Adam, darling. Hush, hush, you've been sick, but it's all right now, it's over."

Over? Once again, Adam's laugh rang out into the night, making his horse shy until he brought it under control again. The hate roiled in him, until he choked with it, but underneath the hate a small particle of sanity remained.

He could have exposed Prudence. He could have subjected her to arrest, trial, conviction. But there would have been no point to it now that he, and so many others, knew the truth.

Exposing Prudence would only have added further shame and disgrace, and Rosalind, an innocent, would have suffered even more. Had it been only an hour ago that he had held her in his arms, that he had felt her warm lips parting under his, rich with promise? He groaned, and felt like retching. His Rosalind, his sweetheart, his love, his *sister*!

Dawn streaked the sky before he stopped at an inn, a shabby place, whose proprietor was amazed at being called down at such an hour to give accommodation to a gentleman of obvious means. Adam brushed aside the offer of liquid refreshment. "Tend my horse."

He slept, woke hours later, ate without knowing or caring what was set in front of him, and set out again, retracing his steps.

The hotel in town provided him a bath and a shave. A black servant sponged and pressed his clothing. Adam inquired at the desk for a reliable man with a cart or a wagon to go to Roselawns and bring the rest of his suitcases to him, and to give Rory a message that he wanted to see him.

Rory, looking drawn from fatigue and needing a shave, rode to the inn on his horse well before evening. In Adam's room, away from curious ears, Adam asked him if Prudence was going to be all right.

Rory's tone was hostile, his look, one of undisguised disgust. "Aren't you a little late wanting to know? For all you cared, she might have died while you went galloping off God knows where! Burke's tending her, and he says she's going to live. Rosalind is in a state of shock. Your rushing off like that didn't help matters any. She keeps asking for you."

Adam felt as if his guts were twisting into a hard knot, and the muscles on his jawline bunched. "Tell her I'm all right, and that I wish only the best for her. But I won't go back there, or see her again. It could serve no purpose. All it would do would be to make things harder."

"You're going home to Boston, then?"

"Only briefly. I don't know where I'll go after that, and you can tell Prudence that I don't intend to ever see her again, either."

"So you're just going to walk off and leave us holding the bag!" Rory lashed out at him. "What about all the promises of help you made? We're still kin, even if it is on the wrong side of the blanket! Gaylord counted on that loan you promised him to pay up his back taxes. He's going to be in bad trouble if he doesn't get it. He'll likely lose Swanmere, and then Rosalind will suffer as much as her father and mother!"

"They managed to get by before I came on the scene. They'll just have to go on getting by." Adam's mouth was set in a grim line. "I owe my *father* nothing, any more than he believed he owed me anything, or my mother, the innocent girl he fathered me on! Rosalind will marry, eventually. I'll leave a sum of money at the bank here. It will be enough to take care of her, but not to help Crissy or Gaylord. When and if Rosalind marries and has children, the principal will be used to set up accounts for them to assure their education." It was all he could do for her without Gaylord benefiting, and as far as Gaylord was concerned, he'd like to see him in hell!

The interview was at an end. There was nothing more to keep Adam in Georgia, and the sooner he got away, the better. He resaddled, rode to Savannah, and set out from there for Boston to wind up his affairs. Ezekiel Armbruster tried to argue with Adam, but he might have been talking to deaf ears. The Boston house was put up for sale. The sales manager of the jewelry shop was put in full charge, and Adam's lawyers and business managers were given full proxy to handle all his other affairs.

He did not see Marcia during the time he spent in Boston. Hester knew that he was back. She had left her card, but he ignored it, although he had a fleeting, sardonic moment of amusement wondering what her reaction would be if he told her that he'd be glad to marry her granddaughter, provided that she did not object to a bastard of color as a grandson-in-law. He would have enjoyed seeing the wind taken out of her sails, but there again, Marcia had done nothing to deserve being used like that. He hoped she would find and marry some young man who would be strong enough to fight her grandmother for her and who would make her happy.

He had not yet reached the point where he could hope the same for Rosalind. The thought of any other man possessing her was a torment. There had been one young man, a tall, lanky youth with soulful brown eyes, who had looked stricken when he'd learned of Rosalind's engagement. Adam thought his name was Robert Jamison. The Jamisons hadn't had two nickels to rub together, but they were quality, and Robert had been working his way through law school. Perhaps he would be the one to save Rosalind.

As for the rest of them, Adam hoped they would

416

rot in their own hell on earth, and that they would live to ripe old ages. Prudence would have nothing but her allowance from Aaron Wentworth's estate. It had been adequate, while she had lived in the Boston house, with all of her expenses paid for her, and it would keep her from starving now, but it would hardly stretch for all of them, to support them in comfort. There were some unsettled debts of Prue's, things bought on account and not yet paid for, which Adam did not pay up. Prue had, in the past, made it a habit to run over her allowance because Adam had always been there, to take care of it. She had not stinted herself, and he had urged her to use a free hand. Adam could do nothing about the allowance itself. Aaron's will had set the amount, and it would have to stand. But she would see her family suffer, and the thought gave Adam pleasure.

How would they explain it to their friends? The broken engagement, all of Crissy's bragging, Adam's sudden exit? Scandal would ride the winds, speculation would run rife, and their pride would be scalded. They would be hard put to find a suitable explanation, since Crissy had broadcast that her daughter was to marry a very wealthy man. How would their Southern pride cope with all of that? From his talks with Gaylord, Adam knew that his father was nearer to financial ruin than even Crissy had expected. There was little doubt that Swanmere would be lost and Gaylord's arrogant pride ground into the dust.

His business in the East completed, Adam had set out for the last time, on his odyssey of forgetfulness.

Now, slouched in his saddle under the relentless New Mexico sun, he realized that he was tired, hungry, and thirsty, above all thirsty. He had ridden for over twenty miles in the heat, and his body was dehydrated. Without straightening his shoulders, he turned his horse toward the livery stable, where he left it to be rubbed down and cooled out before it was watered or fed.

"See that he has oats. Not just alfalfa hay, understand?" The coin he tossed to the stable lad made the young Mexican boy's eyes pop. A silver dollar, a cartwheel, all for himself! "There'll be another to keep it company, if I see you've taken good care of him." The boy's soft brown eyes followed Adam, worshipfully, as he left the stable.

His feet had swollen inside his hand-tooled boots from the hours in the stirrups. All of his clothes were expensive, and the best quality that money could buy, but they were dirty now, sweat-stained and stiff with the salt of his perspiration. His broad hat, covered with dust, still held its shape. His hand-tooled belt, his holster and gunbelt, were heavily worked; his spurs were silver, his saddle silver-mounted. Adam had no lack of money and his recently chosen career as a gambler, perversely, had made him even wealthier. If he'd needed the money he probably would have lost more often than he won. But being possessed of a supreme indifference, he seldom lost.

There had been fights. The gun he wore was not an ornament, but a machine of the finest craftsmanship. Usually, however, no one challenged him, even if the stakes were high and the loser belligerent. There was a coldness in Adam's eyes that tended to make a man, no matter how angry, think twice about calling him out.

As he pushed through the swinging doors of the saloon, Adam saw that it was sparsely filled. It was an ornate establishment, for its kind. The bar was mahogany and had a full-length plate glass mirror behind it. A raised stage stood at the rear of the room for such entertainment as the place had to offer, but it was empty now.

Adam tipped his sweat-stained hat to the back of his head and ordered beer. The hair revealed was bleached almost white by the sun. Adam was not a heavy drinker. He had found, early in his traveling, that drinking held no forgetfulness, but only served to conjure Rosalind's image to torment him. Where was she now?

He could have found out. His resources would have made checking on the activities of the people he had left behind easy for him. But he did not want to know.

The few men in the bar looked at him speculatively, but his manner did not invite friendly advances. He finished his beer and went out again to find a hotel that looked passable.

In his room, Adam washed and shaved before he fell on the bed, closing his eyes with a grimace of distaste at the cabbage roses rioting on the wallpaper. Its garishness would have given Prue fits.

The offensive wallpaper shut out, an image of the room he had always used at Miss Emily's brought sudden, acute nostalgia—bare, austere, its dormer window open so that the curtains blew inward from the breeze. Cool air, fresh, filled with the scent of growing things, of roses, and new-mown hay, and clover, instead of dust and manure and heat.

There was a lump in his throat, hard and hurting. He wondered if Cleo had gone back there, if the kitchen smelled of baked beans and gingerbread, if Cleo still moved, erect and unhurried, through the rooms, polishing, dusting, keeping the house as a shrine to the woman who had owned it and whom Adam could not remember. Maybe Prudence had gone back there too.

Of them all, Cleo was the only one he didn't hate. He knew that none of this had been her doing. She'd be there, he told himself, in that house, and for some reason it brought him comfort. Deliberately, he turned over and slept, to clear his mind for the evening of gambling ahead of him, provided a decent game could be found.

Somewhere in his sleep, he thought that he caught the scent of new-mown hay, and he smiled. The smile transformed his face. It was young again, innocent of hurt or of hurting, filled with pleasure.

The game was unsatisfactory, but that was not unusual. Most games were unsatisfactory. His amusement came from the ill-concealed greed in the eyes of his adversaries, from their expressions of consternation when they lost more than they had bargained for. Adam had found that the much-touted poker face was largely nonexistent, except as applied to himself, and that was only because he didn't care one way or the other.

The stakes were low and the other players were a couple of cowhands in from nearby ranches, a shopkeeper, and a professional gambler whose seedy elegance disgusted Adam. Though he won pot after pot, Adam's only interest was watching the thickset rancher opposite him squirm, seeing the sweat ooze out of the pores of his hands and his forehead when he lost yet another hand. He'd taken a dislike to the rancher at first sight.

"Hey, you, bring another bottle here!" The rancher threw down his cards, his face registering disgust. Uninterested, Adam barely glanced at the girl dressed in the short, full skirt of a barroom hostess who moved to carry out the order.

Adam continued to study his hand. Two aces, two tens. It was hardly worth discarding the five and drawing another card. With his luck, he'd draw either an ace or a ten, and that would be like rubbing the other players' noses in the dirt. Except for the gambler and the rancher, he had nothing against them and the ordinary cowhands could hardly afford to lose another hand. Should he keep the five, he wondered, and give them a chance at something that would beat his two pair?

"Damn you, hurry it up! What the hell are you getting paid for?" the rancher snarled at the barmaid.

"What the hell do you think I'm getting paid for?"

Adam looked at the girl more closely. It was hard to tell what she looked like under all that paint, but the face itself was thin, finely molded, with high cheekbones and a delicate structure that even the cheap makeup couldn't entirely camouflage. The girl's body was thin, but it wasn't an angular thinness, rather one that suggested privation. Her hair was black, piled high in a pompadour, with bangs plastered to her forehead. It was hard to tell her age, but he guessed that she was no more than nineteen or twenty. Her eyes were dark, though in this light he couldn't tell if they were blue or brown. Right now, they were spitting hate.

"You're paid to work here, and it's damn well time you did something!"

"What's the matter, Otis? You still smarting because she chased you off with your drawers down, last Saturday night?" one of the young cowboys asked, his face twisting with amusement. "Bet she wouldn't of chased me off, if I'd been in your place."

The rancher's face became mottled, and a ugly look came into his eyes. "Listen, you bitch, when I say jump, you jump! No damn squaw's going to sass me!"

Adam spoke in a normal tone, but his voice was hard. "That isn't a nice way to talk to a lady."

"A lady! That breed? You're a stranger here, or you'd know better."

Adam frowned. The girl didn't look like a breed. But before he had time to ponder the point, she lifted a nearly full glass of beer from the table and threw the contents in the rancher's face.

"You vicious, mongrel bitch!" Otis sprang to his feet, his chair crashing over behind him, and raised his hand to strike the girl a blow that would have sent her spinning across the room. Nobody saw Adam move, but he was between them in an instant.

"That's enough. You need a bath, anyway. You stink," Adam told the man.

"Get out of my way!"

Adam didn't move.

Slowly, his face going through a full range of emotions, Otis turned from red to a pasty, putty-like white, and he backed off and left the saloon.

The cowhands struggled to conceal their mirth. After all, Otis was one of their own, and this cold-eyed man was a stranger. But the cowboy who had needled Otis about the girl chasing him off with his pants down felt for Adam.

"Mister, I worked for that bastard once, and they don't come any meaner. You'd better watch out, or he'll either get you in the back or bring in half a dozen of his men to help take care of you."

"I doubt it."

"What the hell's going on here?" Coming toward the table was the owner of the saloon, a tall man with a stoop and squinted eyes in an avaricious face. His hand shot out and caught the girl, and he swung her around violently. "You again! I've had just about enough out of you! What do you mean, making trouble and driving my customers off? I'm docking you for it, a week's wages!"

422

"She had cause," Adam insisted.

"Look, mister, you keep out of this! You don't know the trouble this half-breed has caused me. You got no say in it; you drifters don't bring in steady money, like Otis and my other regulars. I got a right to protect my interests!"

Adam looked at the girl. "Why don't you quit working for this bastard?"

"I can't. I owe him money."

"Fifty dollars," Adam said to the saloonkeeper, "that ought to cover any loss of Otis's patronage for one evening." The sarcasm was lost on the saloonkeeper, but not on the girl. She looked at him with loathing.

"If you think I'm going to be grateful and offer to make it up to you, you're mistaken, I'm not for sale. As far as I'm concerned, you're nothing but filth, like all the rest of them!"

"On the contrary, I bathed this evening." Adam pretended to take offense.

"He wants you to be grateful, you be grateful! I've had all I'm going to take of you! You can start being nice to my customers the way the other girls are, or you can go to jail for what you owe me!"

The girl twisted free, moving so fast that the saloonkeeper was taken off balance. Her hand darted out, and she had the empty whiskey bottle by the neck. She smashed it against the table top and faced her employer, her lips drawn back over her teeth. "Try and make me!"

Adam, too, moved swiftly, and because her attention was on her tormentor, his hand clasped over the girl's wrist and he exerted pressure until her fingers relaxed.

"I think you'd better come with me. I don't believe you can be trusted until you've calmed down."

"Get your hands off me! Damn it, I said to let me go!"

She was a wild one, all right. Adam thought for a second or two and then made his decision. He had no desire to drag her, screaming and fighting, through the streets, but neither did he have the desire to see her cut the saloonkeeper up with that jagged bottle and get herself into worse trouble than she was in already. So he slapped her a little, just hard enough to make her knees sag and take the wind out of her.

Laughter followed them as he took her arm and led her, shaking her head to clear it, from the saloon.

"Watch it, mister! She'll stick a knife in your back!"

"I'll be careful."

"Come back later and I'll lose some more to you."

"Not tonight."

The swinging doors stopped swinging, and the excitement was over. Unless, of course, the girl did just that, put a knife in the stranger's back.

42

"Hold this on your face," Adam said, handing her a cold cloth. "It'll make it feel better. Shall I send for some ice to put on the bruise?"

She stood against the wall, her eyes defiant. "Go to hell."

"It's your bruise. If you prefer it to hurt, that's up to you."

"I'm not going to."

"You're not going to what?"

"I'm not going to bed with you."

"How do you propose to prevent it? Scream for the more gallant gentlemen in town to rush to your rescue?"

She laughed, and there was a quality in her laughter that was chilling. "Gentlemen! All the gentlemen in this town are at home with their wives, who'd brain them with rolling pins if they dared lift a finger to help me. The ladies don't like me, mister. They move to the other side of the street when they see me coming and hold their skirts aside."

"Then why don't you get out, if it bothers you?"

"I told you. I owe that . . ." she used a word that Adam hadn't heard used since that summer in Paris, when he'd prowled the murkiest dives of the city with his French student friends . . . "money. He has a paper out on me, restraining me from leaving. I tried it once, and the sheriff took me off the stage."

"Then get another job."

"In this town? Mister, you're funny. The stores and restaurants won't have me. The women wouldn't have me in their houses to scrub their floors. This is the only job I can get, and I keep it or starve."

"It looks like you've starved a little anyway. What's the matter, won't the restaurants or stores sell you food, either?"

"The job doesn't pay much. I don't make tips, like the other girls, because I won't do what they do. And I get docked a lot."

"Stay put."

Adam went down to the lobby and ordered the clerk to have a meal sent up—steak, potatoes, pie, the best the town had to offer. And wine. "Not whiskey, wine. Sherry, if you can find any, or claret."

He was a little surprised to find the girl was still in his room when he returned. He'd locked the door, but there was the window. A one-story jump probably wouldn't hold her back if she'd taken a notion to go. "They'll bring up some supper in a few minutes."

"I'm still not going to."

"Where I come from, ladies wait until they're asked. It isn't considered nice not to."

Her eyes were blue, after all. He could see that now, as they widened with sudden interest.

"Where do you come from?"

"Boston."

"Boston!" Her breath caught, and she walked over and sat down on the only chair. "My father came from Boston, a long time ago."

"The saloonkeeper said you were a breed."

Her nostrils flared at the word, and for a moment

426

he thought he was going to have trouble with her again.

"My father was a Scot. Scotch and Irish. He was educated, he was a schoolteacher once, before he came west and became an Indian agent. He got kicked out for drinking. He said his family were gentlefolk, back in Scotland, and I believe it. My mother was half Apache."

She gave him an oblique look, out of the corners of her eyes, but her face remained immobile, as if his reaction to her next statement meant nothing to her one way or another. "He didn't bother to marry her. He bought her from her father for a quart of whiskey. He was good to her, when he was sober. He wasn't sober very often."

"Where are they now?" Adam's interest had been caught, in spite of himself. It had been a long time since he'd had any interest in other people's problems.

"Dead. My mother died two years ago. She caught the measles, and Indians have no immunity. It carried her off in three days; her white blood wasn't strong enough to fight it."

"And your father?"

"He brooded about her death. No one can brood like an Irishman. His last job was at the saloon. He was a good bartender, when he was sober enough. If he felt like it, he'd get the customers laughing and put them in a good mood so they'd buy a lot. But one night he got to brooding more than usual, and after he closed up he crawled under a table to finish off his bottle, and he fell asleep. He'd forgotten to blow out the lamp. All we know is the place caught fire and there was a lot of damage. He died in the fire, mostly from the smoke, according to the doctor."

"And you were held responsible for the damage?"

427

Adam's brows drew together in a frown. "That doesn't sound legal to me. Why didn't you get a lawyer?"

"I tried. I didn't have any money. It wouldn't have done any good, anyway. Feeling ran high. You see, a man was killed, helping to put out the fire. He was a teller at the bank, and he was well liked. He left a wife and three children. And after all, I'm a breed. There was a hearing, and the judge said it was all right for Slocum to make me work off the amount of the damage. If my father had lived, they'd have hanged him. I'm glad he died in the fire—at least he was spared that. He wasn't bad, when he was sober, and I learned early to keep out of his way when he was drunk."

The tray was empty. She had demolished a plate-sized steak, the potatoes, the pie, and two cups of coffee. Adam poured a glass of sherry for her and handed it to her, but she pushed it aside.

"Getting me drunk won't do any good. I still won't. It was your idea to feed me, not mine. If you're out the price of a meal, it's your bad luck. From what I saw when you were playing poker, you can afford it."

Adam studied her. "Supposing I were to tell the sheriff that I caught you in the act of rifling my pockets? What would he do, throw you in jail?"

She was on him like an animal, her lips drawn back, her face a mask of fury as she tried to stab him with the knife from the tray.

"You bastard! You low-down, conniving spawn of Satan!" She fought like a wildcat, deadly in her intent. By the time Adam had her subdued, twisting her wrist until she dropped the knife, he was out of breath and scratched and clawed in half a dozen places.

"What did you think you were going to do with that knife, blunt me to death?"

Panting, her teeth still bared, she glared at him.

Her hair had come loose in the struggle and hung thick and tangled to her waist. Adam wrapped his hand in it and dragged her to the bed.

He could feel blood dripping down his face where she had managed to cut him with the knife, as dull as it was. They'd warned him about her, and they'd been right. She was a vicious little bitch, sly, untrustworthy, biting the hand that fed her.

The thought filled him with rage. He'd had no idea of forcing her when he'd brought her to his room. He'd brought her because of the dislike he'd formed for the saloonkeeper, Slocum. He'd only been teasing her, curious to find out what she'd do. Well, now he knew.

She was up again instantly, all over him, raking him with her nails. He yelped with pain as her teeth closed on his shoulder, drawing blood. He slapped her, a great deal harder than he had in the saloon. Her head snapped back, but her lips drew over her teeth again, and she kept right on hitting out. Damned wildcat! He'd given Slocum fifty dollars, not for the pleasure of her company but to protect her. Now she could damned well give him the pleasure of her company!

All the pent-up frustration and fury of the last two years surged up in him as he subdued the girl under him by brute force. He ripped her clothes from her. Even through the red haze of his fury, he saw, without bothering to think about it, that her ribs showed, that her breasts were small but well developed and high, that her hips would have been rounded if she hadn't been so thin.

It had been a long time since he had had a woman. The kind that could be bought were like this one, cheap, tawdry, filling him with disgust even as he used them. The other kind were out of bounds for him because he would never again trust a woman who was a lady.

He took her savagely, without mercy, holding her down as he ravaged her, the blood of fury still pounding in his brain. She'd think twice before she tried to knife some other man who'd done her a good turn.

Though it was too late to stop, because by now his passion had been roused to full spate, he realized that he was hurting her a great deal more than it should have hurt her. Incredible as it seemed, the girl was a virgin. No man had ever had her before. Even as his body exploded with the force of his completion, he felt disgusted with himself for his brutality and anger.

He rolled off her, trying to think of something to say, to frame an apology. How the devil was he supposed to know that she'd never had a man before? The face inches away from his own was filled with revulsion, with pain and shame, but the eyes that stared into his own were flaming with hate. She wasn't crying, and a sudden insight convinced him that she'd rather die than cry.

He got off the bed, fighting back the nausea of self-disgust. "You can go to sleep now. I'm not going to bother you again. Damn it, don't look at me like that! Why didn't you tell me you were a virgin?"

"I didn't figure it was any of your damned business! Why would you care whether a saloon girl was a virgin or not, even if I had told you?"

"I'm going out for a while. Stay where you are. You have my word that I won't touch you again."

She pulled the sheet over her, not taking her eyes off him. They were still filled with hate.

To make sure she stayed put, he took her clothes out of the room with him and tossed them in a heap in the corner of the hall and locked the door behind him, pocketing the key. There was still the window, but he didn't think that she'd climb out of it stark naked or wrapped in a sheet.

The hotel clerk wasn't happy at being asked for hot water at that hour, but a look from Adam's steely eyes made him promise to have it sent up as soon as possible. With a renewed pang of shame, Adam realized that he didn't even know her name.

"Hot water's on the way up. You can clean up and then go," Adam told her when he returned to find her still wrapped in the blood-stained sheet. "I'm afraid your dress is torn, but I'll pay for it."

He took a hundred dollars in bills from his saddlebag. The West still preferred cartwheels, but Adam found it more convenient to carry the bulk of his cash in paper money. Crossing to the bed, he laid it beside her.

Her mouth curled. "I don't want it. Just because you forced me doesn't make me a whore."

"I didn't say you were a whore." He'd never met a woman more exasperating!

"If I took it, I'd be a whore. Get out of here and let me get dressed."

"Look, you don't have to act like this! If there's anything I can do—"

"Get out of my life. And right now, get out of this room till I can!" She had her hand on the table knife again.

Damn her. There was no need for him to feel so guilty. It had been bound to happen to her sooner or later, living as she did in this town with every hand turned against her. It wasn't his fault if she refused to accept compensation.

To rid himself of the bitter taste in his mouth, Adam went out and had a drink. When he returned, the room was empty. He threw the blood-stained sheet

431

off the bed before he undressed and got into it. He wasn't going to lose any sleep over her. From all he'd seen, she was capable of taking care of herself.

Nevertheless, it was nearly dawn before he slept.

She was in the saloon when he went back there the next evening. Otis was there as well, his beefy hand grasping her arm so hard that it would be bruised from his grasp, but she gave no indication of pain as she struggled with him.

"Look, you little breed, everybody knows that stranger had you last night! What he can have, I can have! Now quit your squirming and come along like a tame little whore!"

"You'll go with him, or you're fired," Slocum put in behind the bar. "He's right, you're a whore now, like the other girls."

"Fired or not, I'm taking her with me." Otis's face was ugly.

"Come on, Otis, leave the girl alone . . ." It was the young cowboy who had told Adam the day before about the girl chasing Otis off.

"Keep out of this." Otis yanked the girl toward the stairway at the back of the room. She kicked him, hard, and her fingernails raked his face. He struck her across the side of her head, and she would have fallen if his hand hadn't still grasped her arm.

No one had noticed Adam enter, since all eyes were focused on the scene that was being played out in front of them. Lithely and silently as a cat, Adam covered the distance between himself and the two struggling figures. In another second, Otis went spinning across the room, to drop to the floor and lie there, his eyes glazed.

"Get out of here," Adam told the girl. He tossed her his hotel room key. "Go and wait for me."

432

She went, but she didn't take the key that she had let fall to the floor.

Adam stood in front of Slocum, their eyes level.

"How much does the girl owe you?"

"Four hundred and seventy-eight dollars and seventy cents." Slocum rattled off the figure so quickly that Adam knew he had made it up.

"Write out a receipt."

"How's that again?"

"You can write, can't you? I said to write out a receipt and sign it."

"Look, you can't come in here, beating up my customers and threatening me and telling me to write out receipts—"

"I'm doing it." Adam's eyes were like ice. Slocum hesitated for a moment and then drew a torn envelope, all he had at hand, toward him.

"I'll want the money," he blustered.

"You'll get it." And he peeled off a handful of bills from the jacket he held.

Slocum's handwriting was almost illegible, but it was good enough. The two men Adam summoned, with a jerk of his head, to sign as witnesses decided to sign without protest. The young cowboy edged one of them aside, his face split in a grin. "Let me," he drawled. Adam returned his grin.

Pocketing the receipt, Adam gave one more hard look at the saloonkeeper and left.

The girl wasn't in his hotel room when he went looking for her. Damn her, why did she always have to give him trouble? He retraced his steps to the saloon and asked Slocum where she lived.

"Stood you up, did she?" There was a sneer on Slocum's face.

"I asked you a question."

Slocum decided to answer it.

433

It was only a shack, some of the boards fallen off. Inside, there were two rooms, divided by a ragged curtain. A potbellied stove, two straight-backed chairs, and a small table furnished the room that Adam entered when the girl opened the door to his knock. But Adam's eyes, accustomed to observing the smallest detail, saw that there was a bright rag rug on the floor, checked gingham curtains were at the windows, and a Mexican pottery bowl of dried flowers was on the table. Everything was meticulously clean in spite of the grinding poverty of the place.

"What do you want?"

"Nothing. I came to tell you that you don't need to work for Slocum any more. I've paid off what you owe him, and you're a free agent."

"Why?"

"If you mean why did I do it, I did it because I wanted to. I just don't happen to like Slocum."

"What do I have to do in return?"

"Damn it!" Adam exploded. "Have I asked you to do anything in return? Why can't you take what's offered without bristling like a cornered cat?"

"Because nobody ever gives anybody anything for nothing. At least in my life, they haven't."

"Well, you learn something new every day, if you don't close your mind to it. Before you go for me with a knife, I want you to listen long enough to hear that as soon as the bank opens tomorrow, I'm giving you five hundred dollars to get yourself out of this town and go somewhere where you can start over."

Her face was still hostile, filled with suspicion, and her voice echoed her feelings. "Aren't you paying a high price for one evening's entertainment?"

"I've paid higher."

"I'm a squaw. You don't have to bother to pay me

at all. Or is it conscience money? Get out, stranger. Whatever your motive is, I don't want any part of it."

"Maybe I just don't like slavery. Be at the bank to pick up the money or not, just as you like. I'm tired of playing games with you." Adam turned to leave, but he paused with his foot on the threshold. "What's your name? Nobody remembered to introduce us."

"Kate. Kate Babcock. What's yours? Not that I care, but some day I just might get curious about who it was that raped me."

"Adam. Like Adam who was kicked out of Eden. Only in my case, it was somebody else who ate the apple."

Her voice was soft, so soft that it startled him.

"You've been hurt."

"So have you, and that makes us even. Good night, Kate Babcock."

He stepped outside, leaving the sagging door open to the warm night. He started to walk away. The sooner he got out of this town, the better he'd like it. The girl was getting under his skin, and he wanted no entanglements, nothing to hold him, or hurt him, for as long as he lived.

He heard something that might have been a muffled sob, and he paused. The sound wasn't repeated, and he began to walk on. Then, cursing himself for a fool, he turned around and went back.

She was sitting in one of the straight-backed chairs, her head bent. She wasn't making a sound, but her face was soaked with tears.

"Kate?"

She looked up, her face tightening into the mask that she wore to defend herself from a hostile world.

"I'm sorry I hurt you. Take the money, and leave. I want you to have a chance."

435

She didn't answer; she just went on looking at him.

"Damn it, it won't make you a whore! Why do you have to be so stubborn?" He crossed the small space between them and pulled her up out of the chair, his hands on her shoulders, shaking her. Her hair fell loose around her shoulders. Then his arms were around her, holding her close, feeling the slightness of her body, the way it trembled.

He lifted her and carried her into the second room, brushing aside the curtain. There was a narrow bed with a sagging mattress, a small chest of drawers, and nothing else except a few clothes hanging from pegs on the wall.

"Are you going to rape me again? Wasn't once enough for you? I knew you were a bastard, like all the others—"

"Not this time," Adam said. He kissed her. She struggled, but when she tried to claw him, he caught her hands before she could leave a mark. Her hands were small and slender, beautifully shaped. He turned one of them over and kissed the palm. Then his mouth came down over hers again and he felt her deep breath shake her body, and his own caught fire as her lips opened under his.

Her body shuddered once, and then grew soft and pliable in his arms. She made a little sound in her throat, one of surrender, of wanting and longing. Adam's own breath caught as he drank in her sweetness, her warmth, all the womanly giving, the womanly loving, of her. Her hair was like a cloud on the pillow, silky and fragrant. Her eyes were tender as they looked into his.

Gently, he caressed her. He didn't want to hurt her, he wanted her to desire him as much as he desired her. He felt her body respond as hs hands played over her breasts, her waist, her hips and thighs.

436

"Adam," Kate murmured. "Oh, Adam. . . ."

She was ready for him, and he took her. Slowly at first, gently, until with one accord their tempo increased and they were climbing to the heights, still in perfect unison. Sometimes, in his dreams, Adam had imagined that it could be like this, an experience so shaking that no man who had lived through it could ever be satisfied with anything less.

The tide broke over them and washed them up and up, to leave them replete and exhausted on a high shore. Adam saw that Kate's face was wet with tears, and he kissed them away and drew her even closer into his arms. "Thank you, Kate," he murmured in a husky voice. He felt that this was the first time he had ever known complete satisfaction, and he was filled with gratitude to her.

In the other room, the oil in the lamp ran out, and the wick spluttered into darkness, and Adam still held Kate in his arms. He never wanted to let this moment end. Kate's fingers touched his cheek, his mouth, and he caught them and kissed them, one by one. He knew now that he wasn't going to leave town in the morning as he had planned. He couldn't leave her yet, he'd always feel that he had left something unfinished, that he was incomplete.

"Adam?"

"Hush," he said, before he kissed her and felt his manhood burgeon again, before her body moved to meet his as eagerly as he sought hers. This time, after the sweet tide broke over them, they slept in each other's arms.

It was daylight when Adam awoke. The tantalizing smell of coffee wafted in from the front room. Leaning on his elbow, he caught a glimpse of Kate's feet and ankles as she moved in front of the curtain that served as a door between the two rooms. He smiled, remembering the night before, as he dressed to join her.

She looked radiant in the morning light that flooded the shack, her skin scrubbed to a glow, her hair shining. She'd set the rickety table for two, and now she put slices of bacon in a frying pan where it began to sizzle and add its aroma to that of the coffee.

"I didn't expect room service."

Kate smiled at him. "It's as easy to cook for two as for one. Come and eat."

Later, as she cleared the dirty dishes from the table and washed them, he watched her. Every movement she made was graceful, sure. There was no artifice about her. She hummed as she worked, enjoying the simple tasks. Once in a while she glanced at him, her eyes reflecting a question but not demanding an answer.

"I'll go and bring my things," Adam said.

When he returned, the shack was immaculate, the floor swept, the few bits of furniture dusted, and she was sitting on the doorstep, her arms wrapped around her knees, waiting for him. When she saw him, she ran to meet him. She hadn't been sure that he would come back.

"Let's ride," Adam suggested. "I'll rent you a horse at the livery stable."

She rode as she moved, graceful and sure, a part of the horse. As nondescript a nag as it was, it responded to her every touch. She rode astride like a man, her skirts tucked under her, her long, smooth legs hugging the animal's sides. When they returned, she made a meal for them, and they made love again and slept.

"You're quite a man, Adam Wentworth," Kate told him, her head pillowed on his shoulder. "Out here, we call it *muy hombre*."

"And you're quite a woman. I won't forget you in a hurry."

438

Kate's eyes clouded and she bit into her lower lip, but she didn't protest the fact that he would soon leave her and she would never see him again. She wouldn't cry, or beg, or make a scene. She was too proud, too much of a woman, for that. Instead, she rose and pulled a battered guitar from under the bed and sat down again, cross-legged, and began to play. The tune was something Spanish that Adam didn't recognize, too expert for the cheap guitar.

"You need a new guitar," he said. "I'll get you one before I leave."

"No. My father gave this one to me, on my thirteenth birthday. He stayed sober for a whole week to make sure he'd have the money."

Adam didn't press the point. He could see that it meant a great deal to her, and he liked her the better for it. She was an unusual woman, and if he were a different sort of man, something might come of it. But he wasn't a different sort of man, and he knew he had to leave soon, because every day he stayed would make it harder.

"Come here," he begged. Kate laid the guitar aside and came into his arms, her mouth soft and warm and sweet under his. He should have left yesterday. He would leave tomorrow.

She sensed his mood, and her lovemaking had a desperate quality about it, as though she knew that this would be the last time. They didn't bother to eat that night, and it was late before they slept.

She came to the door with him in the morning, a shawl wrapped around her nakedness. "I'm going to take the money you offered," she told him. "I'll go to Tucson. I can find work there. With so much, I might be able to buy a share in a general store or a boarding house. So if you come looking for me, don't expect to find me behind a door with a red light on it."

"You're not a whore, Kate. I never thought that, and even less now. I hope you find everything you want in life."

As she watched him ride out of town, her eyes were free of tears, but her lips trembled slightly. The receipt that Slocum had signed was in her reticule, along with five hundred dollars Adam had given her, and a ticket on the next stage for Tucson.

Her body was free, she could no longer be held in bondage by Slocum. But watching Adam ride away, she knew that her heart went with him.

She ought to hate him. He had ravished her body and then ravished her heart, and now he was riding away as if it had meant nothing at all. Her eyes stung, but she refused to cry in front of the curious townspeople who had gathered to watch. Ignoring them, she straightened her shoulders and walked back to the shack that she called home. She closed the door behind her before she sank to her knees on the floor, her hands over her face, and let the floodtide of grief wash over her. She knew that she would never love another man, because having known Adam, no other man could ever measure up to him.

Carl Otis was in a rage when he learned at the saloon that Adam had left town. He'd made the long ride from his ranch with three of his men to back him up, and now his prey had escaped him.

"Mr. Wentworth ain't the only one you ain't going to be able to lay your hands on," the young cowboy who had admired Adam told him, his satisfaction barely suppressed. "Kate's leaving, too, tomorrow morning on the stage. You might as well of stayed to home, Otis."

Downing two double whiskeys in a row, Otis felt

his rage mounting. He'd been made a fool of; the whole town was laughing at him.

"Give me another," he growled. His men watched him warily, and the other men in the saloon gave him a wide berth. They knew he'd have to strike out at something, at someone, so that he could hold his head up and feel like a man again. He'd been drinking before he'd started to town, working up his rage to the point where he felt it was worth the risk to call Adam to a showdown. It had been festering in him ever since Adam had thrown the whiskey in his face and made him back down that first night. Now it had come to a head, and it had to break.

He drank the third double whiskey at a gulp and left the saloon.

Kate was folding the last article of clothing into her cheap straw valise when she heard someone enter her shack. She paused and held her breath. Her eyes, still red from her storm of grief after Adam had left town, took on a glow. He'd come back, Adam had come back! She'd go anywhere with him, be anything he wanted, just as long as she could be with him. If only he loved her a little, she'd make no demands on him. As long as he was happy, she'd be happy. Adam!

She said his name aloud, her voice lilting, filled with joy. "Adam, I'm in here!" She dropped the dress she'd been folding in a heap on top of the other clothing and began to run toward the outer room.

She'd barely reached the curtain that separated the two rooms when Otis shouldered it aside and stood staring at her, running his tongue over his lips.

The disappointment that flooded through her left her weak, and for a moment she thought she was going to be sick.

"Get out of my house!"

"Sure I will, after I've had what I came after! Maybe

you're leaving tomorrow, but tonight you're going to pay me for all the trouble you've given me!"

"Don't touch me, you pig!"

"Your hard-eyed stranger ain't here to stop me this time, so you might as well save your breath!" Otis lunged at her, and Kate backed up, her hands seeking frantically for something with which to defend herself. Then Otis was on her, his bulk pressing her back into the sharp edge of the chest of drawers. His hands were on her breasts, twisting, squeezing, and Kate screamed with pain.

Otis laughed. "Squeal, squaw," he taunted her. "You'll squeal louder than that before I'm through with you! And you won't yell rape, because who'd believe you, after you sold yourself to that stranger?"

His mouth came down on hers, loose, wet, heavy. He stuck his tongue into her mouth and she gagged. Her hands, pounding against him, her nails scratching, had no effect at all. With his mouth over hers, suffocating her, she couldn't even scream.

The glass chimney from the lamp on the chest behind her burned her hands as she grasped at it, but she scarcely felt the pain. Her one thought was to stop him, to defend herself in any way she could. She cut herself as she broke the chimney, awkwardly, on the chest, and she scarcely felt that, either. But Otis screamed, like an animal, as the jagged glass found the side of his throat.

"You bitch! You half-breed bitch!" He strangled, his eyes popping. He lurched at her, but she twisted around him, numb with horror. She was still numb as she gained the outer room and then the door and ran out into the night, with Otis stumbling after her.

He collapsed before he had gone twenty yards and sank to his knees, falling face forward on the hard sun-baked ground, his blood spreading around him.

She was standing there, looking down at him, the shard of glass still in her hand, when running footsteps approached. Several of the cowboys from the saloon came down the street.

"What the devil's going on here? Is that Otis? Damn it, Kate, you've gone and done it this time! Somebody get the sheriff, and the doc. Kate's killed Carl Otis! She'll hang, for certain."

The young cowboy knelt beside the prostrate form on the ground, his ear to Otis's chest.

"He ain't dead."

"And she'd blamed well better pray that he don't die! It'll be prison for her, in any case, even if she escapes the rope."

The crowd gathered swiftly, drawn by the shouts, to stare and add their own comments. The sheriff came, and as he led Kate toward the jail, Slocum, the saloon-keeper, slipped into Kate's shack. In the confusion, nobody noticed except Kate, and she was too numb with shock to pay it any mind.

43

They faced each other in the lobby of a San Francisco hotel, Adam and a short, pink-faced man dressed in Eastern clothes. The man's hand, as he extended it, was delicate, so that Adam had to be careful not to crush it in too strong a grip.

"Adam Wentworth? Thomas Edwards. My credentials, sir. You are, if I may say so, a hard man to catch up with."

A Pinkerton man? What the devil! As far as he knew, Adam hadn't broken any laws, or killed anyone. A sudden premonition turned his mouth dry. Someone had died. Rosalind? God, no, not Rosalind!

"Yes, indeed, a hard man to catch up with, for all you left a broad trail! It seemed that every time I entered a town, you had left a day or two before. But we're here now, so no matter. Is there some place we can talk?"

"I have a room. Will that do?"

The room was large and richly furnished and overlooked the bay. A fresh, fog-laden breeze stirred the curtains at the open windows, welcome relief from the heat of the Southwestern deserts that Adam had endured for the past several months. Adam nodded to a comfortable chair and, picking up a bottle from the mantel, raised his sun-bleached eyebrows in a question.

"Yes, I believe I will." Mr. Edwards's face registered pleasure at the quality of the bourbon. He finished it off and allowed Adam to replenish his glass, while expressing his satisfaction that this assignment was at an end.

Adam waited. He had learned patience in his two years of exile. Here in the West, time was a plentiful commodity.

"Mr. Wentworth, are you familiar with a Marie de la Roche? A countess, it says here. Madame la Comtesse de la Roche."

Adam had held his own drink untasted. Now he tossed it off and felt it burn past the constriction in his throat to his stomach. "Marie de la Roche? Why, yes, I met her once, in Paris. But only briefly."

"Just so. However, the countess seemed to have known quite a lot about you, sir, if I may be privileged to say so. She died some months ago, and she named you her sole heir. We have been tracking you ever since your own solicitors in Boston received word of her bequest. It is necessary to have your signature on certain legal papers, you understand."

"But why would she leave me her fortune?" Adam was genuinely astounded.

"I am not in possession of that information. All I require of you is that you sign these papers, apprising my superiors that I have delivered the message. It has been a pleasure, sir."

Adam signed the papers, but he scarcely noticed when Mr. Edwards departed. Marie de la Roche! It had to be a mistake. He put his glass down on a small table and stretched himself out on the bed. Why would she even have remembered him, after all this time, much less leave him her money? There was a mystery here, and one that he knew, suddenly, he needed to unravel. It was odd that of all the people he had known in his life, two that he met only briefly should have made such a deep impression on him. Marie de la Roche, and Kate Babcock, neither of whom he had ever expected to hear from again. He wanted no ties, he wanted never to care for any human being again.

Rosalind, Prudence, Jonathan, Rory, Crissy, Gaylord, Cleo—he'd belonged to them once, believed in them; now he belonged to no one, and that was the way he wanted it.

Where was Rosalind now? Had she married that calf-faced young lawyer? Was she happy? Had Prudence stayed in the South? Prudence. What did she know about Marie de la Roche?

He didn't care, after all. He would not let this legacy, however intriguing, draw him back into his old life, involve him again with those he wanted to forget.

San Francisco was suddenly intolerable to him. He rose, packed, and checked out of his hotel. The Southwestern deserts called to him—heat, dust, desolate sun-baked towns where he could lose himself.

But gambling no longer appealed to him. In New Mexico, he joined a trail herd and spent weeks in the saddle, accepting the grinding work as an antidote to his bitter thoughts. He slept, or lay awake, under the stars, every bone in his body aching. His body, already lean and hard, became like whipcord.

He left the herd at Abilene, unshaven, tanned to the color of saddle leather, still fighting his devils. He had a bath and a shave at a barbershop, changed into clean clothing, and searched for a game. He had not checked with Ezekiel Armbruster, although the puzzle of why Marie de la Roche had left him her money still chafed at him like grit under his shirt.

He was in a dangerous mood as the cards were dealt. The stakes were low at first, but even so, three of the four men he was playing with dropped out early. The fourth, a raw-boned rancher with a grim determination in his eyes, kept on. *Fool*, Adam thought. He's getting in over his head.

The game held no interest for Adam. Still he played on, for lack of anything else to do. He could have found a woman, but the thought was distasteful to him. He had nothing to offer a woman but money. Where was Kate Babcock now? Was she in Tucson, or had she gone elsewhere from there?

He cursed Kate silently. The girl meant nothing to him. It infuriated him that she came so often to his thoughts. Deliberately, he turned the memory of her off and returned his attention to the game. Kate would be all right. The money he'd given her had been more than enough to maintain her until she was able to find decent employment. If she were worth thinking about at all, she had already found another man, one who would marry her. There were still more men than women in the West; any girl who wanted to get married could find someone.

The rancher, shaken but obsessed, had signed a paper and thrown it into the pot. What the hell do I want with the man's ranch, Adam thought, but on the next turn of a card, the ranch was his.

Quietly, the rancher pushed back his chair. Quietly, he walked out of the saloon. There was the sound of a single shot, and Adam's chair crashed over as he plunged through the swinging doors.

The men stood in a circle, looking at him with hard eyes. "It's going to be hard on Mary," one of them said.

"It was a fair game. I didn't push him into putting up his place."

Their silence showed that they agreed. Still, the man was dead, and there was a widow. In his hotel room, Adam looked at himself in the mirror. The cracks in it distorted his face, made him look like a devil. His reflection sickened him, and he turned away, his stomach tightening into knots.

He went to the bank in the morning, as soon as it opened, and left the I.O.U. there, signed back to the widow. He hoped that the next man she married wouldn't be fool enough to gamble away their livelihood. Adam wondered how many other lives had been ruined by his uncanny ability to win, when winning or losing meant nothing to him?

He had made up his mind the night before that he was going back to Georgia, to find out what had happened to Prue and Rosalind. After that, he had no plans

44

Prudence picked Naomi up and put her to her breast. It never ceased to amaze her that at her age her milk was still abundant, though since Naomi had come along, Michael had had to be weaned. The babies themselves amazed her. Every morning, when she woke, she was convinced that it must all be a dream.

Michael opened his mouth and howled, and Cleo laughed.

"He has good lungs. He'll be a strong man."

Cleo picked up the thirteen-month-old infant and danced him on her knee, and he quieted, comforted by her familiar touch, the smell of soap and water, of starched clothing.

As Naomi sucked greedily, making little sounds of contentment, Prudence asked, "How was Crissy?"

"Just the same." Cleo shifted Michael to her shoulder and began to rock. "The place was like a pigpen, and she hadn't combed her hair for two days. I made her clean herself up, and I gathered up the dirty clothes for the laundress and left a good supper for Gaylord."

"I don't know why you put up with her. All you get for your trouble is abuse."

"The good Lord has put up with her all these years; I reckon I can put up with her for a few hours a week. If I didn't go, then Rosalind would have to, and that poor pregnant little thing has enough on her hands without trying to cope with her mother. She gets too upset, listening to Crissy rant and rave. We don't want anything to happen to that baby."

Naomi finished nursing and Prudence handed her to Cleo and took Michael to hold. How sturdy her son was! Cleo was right, he'd be a big man, like his grandfather and his great-grandfather before him.

A girl and a boy, and here she was a new mother when other women her age were grandmothers. It was a scandal. Tongues were wagging in the county as people still tried to digest it. Not that they weren't happy about it. It would be hard to find anyone who didn't love Burke, and seeing him happily married, with two fine children, was a satisfaction to them.

Cleo changed Naomi and put her back in her cradle. "Rory's going to talk to me about the west field. There's going to be a good crop this fall, everything considered. Mr. Amhurst took good care of his land; it isn't entirely ruined like so many places around here. The young tobacco's showing a good stand, and we should realize a profit."

Prudence smiled. It was a continual source of pleasure to her to listen to Cleo and her father-in-law, Evan Amhurst, talk crops. Evan was in town right now arranging for drying sheds to be built. They were sticking their necks out, investing so much in an untried crop, but Cleo and Evan were sure it would pay off.

Under Cleo's management, the house ran like clockwork, and between Cleo and Evan the land was being rehabilitated. The entire county was watching to see how their management would turn out. With Cleo's arrival Evan, at seventy, had taken a new lease on life, and Coralie watched the two of them with a glow in her eyes as they planned the rejuvenation of the plantation.

Prudence began to hum under her breath as she rocked the baby. Three years ago she'd have called anybody a liar who would have dared to tell her she would ever be this happy. She'd put up a fight against marrying Burke. It hadn't been fair to him; she'd thought that she was too old to make anyone a good wife.

And now, they were all under the same roof. Not only Prudence and Cleo and the children, but Jonathan and Rory as well. After a few months, Cleo had pointed out that Prudence's father and brother could live much more comfortably by moving in with them and closing up the house at Roselawns. It was more economical, for one thing, and saved Prudence the inconvenience of making innumerable trips to Roselawns to see to their well-being. Jonathan and Evan were company for each other, and either Jon or Rory rode over to Roselawns to supervise the few fields they were still able to plant.

The change in Rory had been remarkable. Prudence thought it was because he felt that he had to pull his weight as long as he accepted the Amhursts' hospitality. He was young and strong in spite of his handicap, and the added responsibility as well as the constant family companionship left him little time to lose himself in his old, bitter brooding. He was a surprisingly doting uncle to his niece and nephew, who took the place of the children he had never had.

Not that Rory didn't still have his bitter moments. Leaving Roselawns had been a shattering blow to him, and for a while Prudence had been afraid that he would go as Crissy had gone, living his life in a bottle, lashing out at fate for the blows that had crushed him, blaming Prue. But Cleo, conferring with Evan Amhurst, had seen what work was to be done, and bullied and shamed Rory into lending a hand, until he had been caught up in it and infected with enough enthusiasm to pull himself through. But those first days and weeks had been hell.

Now Prudence rocked Michael, laughing at the fatuous expression of contentment on his face. Two children, and before Christmas, Rosalind would have her child. No matter what happened, the family had a way of going on. Rosalind was going to be all right. She was fond of Robert, and he worshipped her, and she would have children to comfort her.

It was Crissy who was a constant source of worry to Prudence. Crissy, who had screamed and raved. Crissy, who had turned to the bottle and never turned away from it. Crissy, living in a small rented house in town, humiliated, hating everyone. Only her pride had kept her from telling everyone the truth. She had put it about that Rosalind had turned Adam down, and that Adam had chosen to leave without helping them in order to punish them all. What else, she demanded bitterly, whenever she could corner someone to listen, could you expect of a Yankee?

At least the children were all right. Rosalind was married, although it was doubtful if her husband would ever make a great deal of money. Nelson was in college in Baltimore, his tuition paid out of the allowance that Adam had not been able to take away from Prudence. Jacob did what he could, after school, to keep their small house livable, his patience with Crissy a marvel. Gaylord worked at the mercantile store. If it galled him to measure out lengths of calico and gallons of kerosene for people he would not ordinarily have nodded to, his native charm prevented the customers from guessing it. A natural salesman, he might

452

have earned more as a traveling man, but he could not leave Crissy.

After the debacle, after the initial period when Crissy had had to be restrained by force, by sedation, by whatever means came to hand, Crissy had never spoken to Prudence, and she would not allow Prudence in her house. The few times that Prue had tried to visit her, she had been attacked, physically, once with a paring knife so that she had come away with a deep cut on her arm. The scar still showed. And Crissy still drank, her own scars deeper, twisted and ugly on her heart.

The family was at the supper table when Cleo entered the dining room to tell them that they had a visitor. Cleo's face was calm, but Prudence noticed that her hands were clasped together as if she were concealing some inner agitation.

"It's Adam, Miss Prudence." Cleo never called her Miss Prudence unless she was upset.

"What the hell!" Rory threw down his napkin and shot out of his chair. "I'll take care of this, Prue. I'll run him off this place before he knows what hit him! Jonathan, where's my gun?"

"Rory, control yourself!" Prue, too, was on her feet, her face as flushed as Rory's. Jonathan also rose and clamped his hand on Rory's arm.

Adam was standing beside the mantel in the sitting room, an Adam so changed that she might not have recognized him unless Cleo had given his name. He was thinner, harder, his face bronzed dark by the sun. When he moved, it was with the grace of a jungle animal.

Rory, having wrenched himself free from Jonathan's restraining hand, stormed into the room. "Get the hell

453

out of here! Get moving, unless you want a bullet in your heart!"

"I wouldn't do that, Uncle. Killing a man in cold blood makes for bad dreams. I know. I killed a man. I'm not happy about it."

"Don't you call me Uncle! You bastard, after what you did!"

"You are my uncle. Whether I call you by your title or not doesn't change it. You're my uncle, Prudence is my aunt, and Jonathan is my grandfather. But I haven't come to push my claim to the relationship. I only want the answers to some questions. One has already been answered. Prudence, I'm glad that you are all right. I've wondered about you."

"Adam!" The cry was anguished. "Adam, you didn't even say goodbye! I didn't blame you for hating me, but . . ."

"Rory, get Prudence a drink." Burke's voice was strained but controlled. "Adam, you look as if you've come a long way. We've wondered about you, too. What's this about you having killed a man? If you walked away from Roselawns without killing anyone, I should think that that danger would have been over."

"I let him lose more than he could afford at cards. He lost his ranch to me, a poor place, almost ruined by drought. He shot himself. No, Uncle Rory, killing a man brings very little satisfaction. There's no way to make restitution, you see. Money won't do it, or being sorry. It's something you just have to live with."

Rory started to hand Prudence the brandy he had poured, changed his mind, and drank it himself. Adam smiled. Burke nodded to a chair, indicating that Adam should sit, and brought both Prudence and Adam brandy.

"And your other questions?"

"Only Prudence can answer them, I think. A woman

named Marie de la Roche died and left me her estate. It turned out to be a considerable fortune. I want to know why she left it to me."

Prudence took a sip of brandy. She looked at Jonathan, and then back at Adam. "She was your grandmother. Marie de la Roche was Naomi's mother."

Adam's eyes lighted up. "So that's it! That remarkable old lady! Well, I'm proud to know that she was my grandmother. A countess! That must have taken some doing. I wish I had been privileged to know her better."

"Knowing about you made her happy. As for her title, she explained that to me when we were in Paris. She had made a great deal of money in New Orleans and gone from there to England. She set up a gambling establishment in London, a very exclusive place, frequented by the wealthiest people."

A little smile hovered around Prue's mouth, echoed in her hazel eyes. "An Italian count lost a great deal of money at Rebecca's tables. Rebecca was a beautiful woman, and wealthy, which the count was not. He saw no obstacles in marrying her to cancel his debt and other debts, thinking to acquire a beautiful wife and a fortune at the same time. The wife, he acquired; the fortune, he did not. Rebecca was far too astute to let him get his hands on it. When he died, she was still a very wealthy woman, and she lost no time in liquidating the run-down de la Roche estate in Italy and setting herself up as a *grand dame* of Paris society."

Rory's face was shining with interest, but Jonathan's eyes had grown misty, and he said, "I'm glad that she saw you before she died, Adam. I know how happy it must have made her."

"Well, she was different from the rest of the family in that! Don't worry, Jonathan. I'm not about to settle here and claim my relationship with you, even though I've learned that Swanmere is up for sale and I could name my own price. It would be a strange twist of fate if I were to buy it and live here, wouldn't it?"

Rory's face grew red with rage, and Adam relented.

"You can set your mind at rest, Uncle Rory. I'm not about to buy Swanmere and take up residence there. But if you don't object to taking a favor from a nigger, I'd like to advance you and Jonathan enough money to get Roselawns back in shape. I don't want to see it go out of the family. One or the other of Prudence's children will want to live there, when they're grown."

"You can go to hell!" Rory took a step toward Adam, his expression threatening, every line of his body bristling with fury. "You put us through disgrace and embarrassment that no human beings should have to endure, and now you come back here and offer us charity! It's a wonder Rosalind didn't die of her heartbreak and shame. Do you have any idea of what she went through, you bastard? To say nothing of Prue, whose only crime was loving you a hell of a lot more than you deserved, and getting herself shot for her pains, and nearly dying!

"Did you care? No, you went belting off to God knows where—you didn't give a damn! I've changed my mind, Adam. I'm going to kill you if you aren't out of this house and off this property in five minutes!"

Prudence had risen, her hand stretched out protestingly toward her brother, but it was Jonathan who spoke. His voice was quiet, but filled with authority.

"Rory, sit down. As for me, I will be glad to accept my grandson's offer. It's more than we deserve from him, but I too would like to make sure that Roselawns will stay in the family. Given enough time, I'm sure we can make it pay again. Adam, I trust that the going rate of interest will be acceptable?"

"The interest should be put in the bank, as a fund for Michael and Naomi." No expression betrayed Adam's emotion, but Prudence knew what it cost him to keep his tone light. She knew that Adam refrained from giving them the loan without interest, or as an outright gift, to assuage Jonathan's and Rory's pride. Her fingers tightened on the stem of her glass, but she refused to weep. The time for tears was long past.

"What are you going to do now, Adam?" Prudence's throat felt tight. "Will you return to Boston and take up your life there?"

"I think not. The West has spoiled me for Boston, or even for Georgia or any other place in the South or the East. I liked what I saw of Texas. I've a mind to go back there and buy myself a cattle ranch."

Cleo, who was sitting beside Prue, had taken no part in the conversation, but had hung onto every word that had been spoken. Her life was so bound up with that of the family that her interest in what was going on was as great as theirs.

"How about coming with me, Cleo? You'd make the damnedest ramrod Texas ever saw!" Adam's eyes were laughing, but filled with his fondness for this black woman who had played such an important part in his life. It seemed that she had always been there, a tower of strength and comfort, whenever he had needed her.

"Don't think I couldn't do it." Cleo's face was covered with hundreds of tiny lines as she smiled, and there was a twinkle in her eyes. "Only, I could never leave Prudence and the children."

"Not even to go back to Martin's Corners?"

"Not even for that. But the house is still there. One of the Tait girls and her husband is looking after it for me. I'll never sell it. Maybe when the children are old enough, Prudence and I will want to take them there for the summers. Miss Emily would have liked that, to know they were there."

Rory had left the room and gone stomping upstairs, still seething, but Burke brought the conversation back to the issues at hand.

"You will stay with us while you're here, of course? You're welcome to stay for as long as you like."

Adam's face registered amusement. "I don't think I'll risk it. Rory might change his mind about shooting me. It would be an imposition of your hospitality to have to ride herd on him. But I'll be in town for as long as it takes to get everything settled. I'd like to see your children before I leave, Prudence."

"Michael and Naomi," Prue spoke their names lovingly.

"Thank you for naming your daughter Naomi."

"I loved Naomi. She was my sister. Just as I loved you, both because you are my nephew, and for yourself. When Naomi died so senselessly, I was so bitter against the world that it might have ruined my life. But Aunt Emily made me see that Naomi and Michael had several months of happiness greater than many people ever achieve in an entire lifetime. And she was happy, Adam. You have that to remember, and be thankful for. She had found her place in life, and her dying advanced the cause of abolition one step farther because the people around Martin's Corners were outraged by it and not only took up a collection to hunt the murderer down, but supported the underground railroad even more strenuously than they had before. My mother and your mother both died for the cause."

Their eyes met, and a burden seemed to fall from Adam's heart. The bitterness was gone. He was glad that Prudence was happy. He was glad that he could help to restore Roselawns and make sure it stayed in the family.

But there was no place for him here. Even if they were ready to accept him, and Adam thought that with the exception of Rory they were, his presence would be a constant embarrassment to them because of Rosalind. He didn't want to cause her any more pain, or even a twinge of regret. She, too, had made a new life for herself.

There were too many bitter memories; the past was still too much with them to make remaining feasible. No, he would return to the West and build his own life.

45

Adam stayed in town for three weeks. The transfer of ample funds for repairs and improvements at Rose-lawns was arranged. Adam walked the overgrown fields with his grandfather, their easy companionship pleasing them both. Adam was moved, more than he would have thought possible, to realize that Jonathan was proud of him. Bastard or not, slave blood or not, he was Jonathan's grandson. He found himself telling Jonathan everything he knew about Rebecca, and he was surprised at the pride in his own voice when he described her.

"She was a remarkable woman, Jonathan." He did not call Jonathan Grandfather; the word would have seemed unnatural to both of them. "I wish I could have known her better. The relationship would have meant a lot to both of us."

But he no longer blamed Prue for the deprivation. She had done what she thought was best for him, and Rebecca had agreed with her. At least Rebecca had known that he was alive. She had seen him. He had that to comfort him.

"Prudence told me that Rebecca wrote to her before she died and told her to make up any story that seemed plausible for her leaving me her money. Any story would do so long as I didn't learn the truth."

"Won't you be lonesome, Adam?" Jonathan asked with real concern. "It doesn't seem right that you should live in what amounts to exile, because of other people's mistakes."

"Texas is a big place. I'll make friends. And I'll be busy. I'm looking forward to the challenge. Maybe you'll come and visit me when I have my place going. It's an experience worth having, just to see the West, the vastness of it. There's room for everybody out there."

Jonathan's face lighted up. "I think I'll do just that, as soon as Roselawns is back on its feet."

They looked at each other, and Adam felt the burden of his aloneness lighten. Jonathan loved him and accepted him. And Prue had gone on loving him even after he had run off without waiting to see what would become of her.

Prudence and Burke gave a family dinner for him the night before he left. Neither Crissy nor Gaylord was there, and Rosalind too was absent, although she had been invited. But Rosalind had sent a note in her own hand explaining that her acceptance would upset her mother, and she was sure that he'd understand why she couldn't come. She added that she wished him nothing but happiness. Rosalind, too, had come to terms with life and harbored no bitterness.

Adam had seen her once, briefly, and her resemblance to Prue was even more marked now. He thought he knew, now, why he had fallen so desperately in love with her. He had been more than half in love with Prue all the time he was growing up. He was sure that he would hate the man Rosalind had married. He felt, instead, only gratitude that she had married someone who so obviously worshipped her. Rosalind could

461

scarcely fail to return that love, and soon she would have her child to bring her happiness to completion.

Prudence looked radiant that night as she presided at the dinner table. Coralie had insisted that she sit at the head of the table for this one night in spite of convention. This was her night, and Adam's, who sat beside her. She wore Martha's pearls, and they glowed in the candlelight.

And, to Adam's intense pleasure, young Jacob joined them. He explained that Nelson was still at school in Baltimore. The initial liking that Adam had felt for the younger boy increased. Jacob was taller now and broader, and it was easy for the others to see that he was going to be the image of old Jacob when he was fully grown. It gave Adam a glow of great satisfaction that Jacob cared nothing for the old family scandal and quarrels and had wanted to see him again.

Jacob leaned forward, his eyes alight with excitement.

"Adam, when you get your spread going, may I come out to Texas and help you work it? I'd go with you right now if you'd have me, but Mother and Father say I have to finish school. Mother's against my going, of course, but Father says I can go after I've finished school, if you'll have me."

It took Adam a moment to digest that. He knew that he could never be a friend to Gaylord Renault, but he realized now that his father was a product of the time, of a society that had lived by its own rules. If Gaylord could be big enough not to stand in Jacob's way, in spite of all the bitterness between them, it proved that he had breeding as well as the arrogance that had been the seed of all their enmity.

Jacob was still talking. "Nel wants to stay here, in Georgia. He wants to be a planter. But not me. I want to get out there where there's room to breathe.

462

I'm willing to work as a common hand until I learn to pull my weight. I won't expect concessions just because you're my brother."

Adam's heart constricted. Jacob's brother. He had said it naturally, with no traces of self-consciousness.

"I don't see why not. The West is the place for a young man like you. I don't have any doubt that you'll pull your weight, and I'll be glad to have you."

"A cattle empire!" Jacob almost breathed the words. "That's the place for me!" As their eyes met, Adam felt this young brother of his was a boy to be proud of. They'd work well together. The old Jacob had been an empire builder, and this young one would follow in his footsteps, maybe go him one better.

Yes, he'd have Jacob with him in Texas, and when the time came for Nelson to buy a piece of property, he'd see about helping him. It was no fault of the boys that there must always be an unbridgeable gap between him and their common father. He had brothers, a sister, a family. It was a good feeling.

Jacob held out his hand and Adam took it. Their clasp was firm. If there were tears in Prudence's eyes, the candlelight masked them. Jonathan stood up and raised his glass.

"To the new generation," he said. "And remember, I want you to get that place of yours as fast as you can, Adam. I'm almost as eager as Jacob to get a look at it, even if I come back and remain a staid Southern planter the rest of my life while you youngsters take your turn at pushing forward the frontiers of this land of ours."

Adam set off on the first stage of his return journey westward with more peace in his heart than he would have thought possible. Although he had to leave them behind, he had the satisfaction of knowing that he had a family, and knowing that his brother, young Jacob, would join him in Texas.

Still, there was a sense of something lacking, and it ate at him as he covered the miles. Prue had her family, Rosalind had hers. He had no doubt that Jacob would marry and do his part in populating the West. A wife and children, a close-knit family unit—without them a man was nothing, no matter what else he achieved. He could leave his holdings to Jacob's children, but as he intended to make Jacob a full partner in his enterprise, it would be an empty gesture.

What he needed, what he must have, was a family of his own. He wouldn't find another Prue, or a Rosalind, and he wouldn't want to. That part of his life was behind him. What he needed was a tougher woman, one who would match his own strength for the task ahead.

One face kept intruding its image into his thoughts, a face that he hadn't been able to forget no matter what distance he'd put between himself and its owner. A squaw, a breed, as wild as her half-Apache mother, as sweet as honey in the comb. He remembered her defiance, the pride that could not be conquered, the love that she'd offered freely once she had stopped distrusting him. She was beautiful, and she was strong enough, she had what he wanted and needed. Kate Babcock!

Where was she now? For all he knew, she might already be married. There was only one way to know for sure, and that was to find her. Whether she would accept him, even though he'd walked out of her life once, remained to be seen. Remembering that last night with her, when their passion had soared to incredible heights, made him curse himself for a fool. Why hadn't he realized then that he couldn't do without her? Why had he ridden away without looking back? If she hated him, he wouldn't blame her. He'd used her, taken the warmth and passion she had to offer, and cast her aside.

Amusement replaced the grimness in Adam's eyes, as he imagined how Kate would probably meet him with a dagger in her hand, when and if he located her. It would be up to him to persuade her not to use it.

When he had ridden out of Albuquerque, Kate had been holding a ticket for Tucson, and so Adam changed course and went there.

Nobody in Tucson had seen or heard of Kate Babcock. But Adam continued his search until he was convinced that she had never come to Tucson at all, or even passed through it.

Albuquerque, then, to pick up her trail where he had left her. Damn the girl! She'd told him she was going to Tucson, and he had believed her. All this backtracking was losing him time.

The saloon, the obvious place to start his search in Albuquerque, was just as he remembered it. Slocum himself was behind the bar, placidly polishing a glass when Adam entered. Slocum recognized Adam immediately and moved toward him.

"I don't want you in my place, mister. There's other saloons in town."

"I'm not here as a patron. I'm looking for Kate Babcock."

"You're looking in the wrong place. You can see for yourself, she ain't here. She ain't been here for over a year."

Slocum knew something, Adam was convinced of it. He leaned across the bar and took a handful of shirtfront in his hand.

"Where is she?"

Slocum's face turned a sickly putty color. "Get your hands off me, or I'll send for the sheriff! Kate's none

465

of my affair. You can't come in here and manhandle me for no reason, we got laws!"

One of the three other men in the bar started to edge toward the door to get the sheriff, but a look from Adam stopped him. Still Slocum glared at him defiantly.

"*Señor.*"

The word was spoken with a soft Mexican accent, and Adam felt a tug at his shirtsleeve. He looked down and saw the lad from the livery stable, his eyes wide and brown.

"*Señor*, she's in jail."

With his free hand, Adam reached in his pocket for a silver cartwheel and handed it to the boy. The white teeth flashed in the brown face.

"*Gracias, amigo.* But I would have told you anyway, 'cause I don't like Mr. Slocum much. I like you, though. What are you going to do to Mr. Slocum?"

Adam answered the boy's question by pulling the saloonkeeper across the bar and throwing him against the far wall. Adam stood over Slocum, who lay sprawled on the floor, his nose gushing blood. "What did she do?"

"She cut up Carl Otis. He almost died. If he had, she'd have been hung and it wouldn't have done you any good to come looking for her."

"When did it happen?" Instead of letting Slocum get up, Adam put one booted foot on his chest and applied a little weight. The three patrons of the saloon watched with lively interest, still making no move to fetch the sheriff. The Mexican boy's grin spread from ear to ear, and he'd completely forgotten that the owner of the livery stable had sent him to fetch a bucket of beer.

"Right after you left. That's all I know, mister. You want to know more, you'll have to ask her," Slocum answered.

466

"I'll do that. And I'll expect you to be here, in case I have to come back."

Fifteen minutes later Adam stood looking at the girl behind the bars in the jail. She was thinner, her face planed down to sharp lines. Her eyes looked black in this light, but they were still spitting fire.

"I had one hell of a time finding you. What happened?"

"Didn't they tell you?" Her bitter voice asked no sympathy, expected none.

"I want you to tell me. I think it'd be closer to the truth."

"You bought me a ticket on the stage, and gave me money, and rode out of town. I went to my place and started packing. Carl Otis came. He was drunk, and mean, and he attacked me. I fought him off and slashed his throat with a broken lamp chimney. It was all I could lay my hands on."

"Why didn't you hire a lawyer? I left you enough so you could have hired one."

"Slocum stole the money. It had to be Slocum; he was the only one that went in my place after I stabbed Otis. When the sheriff went to find the money for me, it wasn't there. The receipt for what I owed Slocum was gone, too. The sheriff is honest, so it had to be Slocum."

Kate crossed her arms over her breast and looked at Adam. "They gave me two years. It's a small price to pay for sticking that pig. I wish I could have castrated him instead. As for Slocum, he'd better watch all the dark corners once I get out. I have a score to settle with him."

"You'll play hell."

"Won't I just! I don't give a damn if I have to spend the rest of my life in prison, if I can just get at that bastard first. He has the gall to think that I'll

467

go back to him when I get out of here, to pay off that debt! He says I have to, and that I have to entertain his customers, too. I'll kill him first."

Adam looked at her and cursed the bars between them. It was too soon, at any rate. He had business to attend to before he could shake some sense into this girl who could actually laugh when she was in jail.

"Stay put."

"I'm not going anywhere, Adam. My talents don't include walking through iron bars."

In the sheriff's office, Adam faced the lantern-jawed man, who met his glance squarely.

"What kind of a trial was it? Was it fair?"

"As fair as it could be, considering the girl had no witnesses. Her reputation wasn't the best—she was known as a firebrand. And Otis got a couple of his men to swear that she'd invited them to her shack on more than one occasion, for money. There wasn't any way she could disprove it, and they were under oath. No, the trial wasn't fair, Mr. Wentworth. How could it be? I'm only the sheriff, I don't pass judgment. As things stood, she'd have drawn a lot longer sentence if I hadn't had a word in private with a couple of the jurors. Some of them were good men. They couldn't disregard the evidence, but they recommended leniency.

"I convinced them that Otis had used unnecessary brutality on the girl. I didn't want her sent to the women's prison; it's a hellhole from what I've heard. The jury gave her just enough time to serve so she could serve it here in jail where she wouldn't be worked half to death and starved."

"You did a lot, considering the way things stood. This trial is going to be reopened, Mr. Benson, with the best lawyer money can buy. And I want the names of the men Otis had perjure themselves for him."

468

The sheriff gave him the names, and the two men shook hands.

"I'm glad you came back," Sheriff Benson said. "I've sort of taken a liking to the girl. You needn't spread that around; it might get back to my wife. But Kate has a lot of spirit, and I didn't want to see her broken."

"You can do me another favor. If you hear a ruckus at Slocum's place, don't be in too much of a hurry to investigate."

"Matter of fact, I'm pretty busy right now. I have a pile of paperwork to do, and it takes all my concentration." He rolled a cigarette and looked around for a light. "I hope I won't have to throw any stranger in jail for disturbing the peace; it would be disruptive to my work."

Adam entered the saloon quietly. Just as quietly, he spoke to Slocum. "You're selling out. Name your price."

Slocum bristled and his face turned a mottled red. "Like hell I am! This here place is a moneymaker. It ain't for sale at any price."

"Have it your way, then." Once again Adam grasped the man's shirtfront and pulled him across the bar. He held him with his feet dangling six inches off the floor. With his free hand, Adam slapped Slocum's face, first on one side and then on the other. Slocum's head jerked violently. One of the customers edged forward, but Adam's voice stopped him in his tracks.

"I wouldn't if I were you, mister."

"Get the sheriff! Somebody get the sheriff!" Slocum screamed. Adam slapped him again, and this time the man spat out a tooth.

"The sheriff's busy. How much for your saloon?"

"Go to hell."

Adam threw him back across the bar. He landed

469

against the row of bottles and they crashed into the mirror and onto the floor, shards flying wildly.

"Name a price."

Getting to his hands and knees, Slocum wiped blood from his face. A man who had started to come into the saloon when the altercation began, and backed off, returned, panting.

"The sheriff's office is empty, there ain't even a deputy around! I didn't see hide nor hair of any of them! What the hell's going on here, anyway?"

Adam smiled. "Slocum and I are coming to an agreement on the price he wants for this saloon."

Slocum saw death in that smile. "Five thousand dollars."

"I'll give you one. Write out a receipt."

"You can't do this! I'll have you behind bars!"

"That's your privilege. I'll soon be out again. I'm not a helpless girl, without resources. And I won't be leaving town when I get out."

"Four thousand." There was desperation in Slocum's voice.

"Five hundred. You've already stolen a thousand from the girl. Start writing, or I'll go down to a hundred."

"You're all witnesses! You'll all testify against this man!" Slocum's face paled under the blood smeared on it, as he saw every man in the place head for the door. There wouldn't be any witnesses. They too had seen Adam's smile.

With his hand shaking, so that his writing was scarcely legible, Slocum wrote out a receipt. Adam pocketed it. "If you will step down the street with me to the bank, I will pay you the rest and have the bank witness the receipt. And I would not advise you to make any complaint about me, either at the bank or elsewhere. As I told you, I am not without resources."

470

Slocum did not need to look at Adam's face again to decide to take his advice. Nor did he protest when Adam informed the banker that Slocum was leaving town, the reason for the hurried sale. The banker, who had done business with Adam the last time he was in Albuquerque, asked no questions. He was fully aware of Adam's fortune and being a man who dealt in money, gave Adam his full respect.

"I meant what I said about you leaving town. If Kate ever has to see your ugly face again, I'll have you bound over for trial for robbing her. Your generous terms in selling your saloon take care of any money you owe her, with a little interest. I believe she'll be satisfied. If she isn't, I'll come looking for you."

Slocum believed him. He decided that he would go as far as the thousand dollars, and his savings, would take him. He wondered what it was like in Australia. Whatever it was like, it would have one advantage—Adam Wentworth would not be there.

It was evening by the time Adam arrived at Carl Otis's ranch. The place seemed prosperous, the house unpretentious but large enough to accommodate a family in comfort. The outbuildings and bunkhouse stood at some distance from the house, close by the corral.

Adam tied his horse to a cottonwood tree a good distance from the house and the bunkhouse. Moving as purposefully and as quietly as a panther, he located the tack room and carried two saddles and bridles to the corral. Still silently, his murmuring voice soothing the horses within the enclosure, he cut two of them out and bridled them. Leading them outside, he saddled them and tied them beside his own mount.

Pausing for a moment, he listened outside the bunkhouse door before he opened it. Then he stepped just

471

inside the doorway, his left hand holding two lassos, his right hand poised over the gun that was slung low on his hip.

A dozen men were in the bunkhouse, some of them playing cards with a dog-eared deck, greasy from years of use. One man was reading a months-old periodical, a hand-rolled cigarette dangling from his lower lip. Another man, obviously suffering from toothache, lay on one of the bunks with his jaw painfully swollen.

"Johnston, Lester?" Adam asked, his voice clipped and cold.

The man with the swollen jaw sat up, and the card-players stopped their bidding to stare at him. "I'm Lester. You got business with me?"

"I want Johnston, too."

A lanky, middle-aged man laid down his cards and stood up. "I don't recollect seeing you before. What's your business with us?"

"You gave false testimony at Kate Babcock's trial. You are going to retract that testimony."

"What the hell does that mean?" Johnston's eyes narrowed suspiciously, hostility tensing his muscles.

"It means that you are going to admit, under oath, that you lied."

Johnston stared at him, his face incredulous. "The hell you say! You got another think coming, mister. Now get the hell out of here!"

From the corner of his eye, Adam saw the fat man who had been thumbing through the periodical start edging toward a peg on the wall where a gun hung in a holster. Adam's hand moved faster than light.

"Hold it right there." His Colt .45 covered the room and everybody in it. "Lester, get off that bunk and get over here. That's far enough. You too, Johnston."

"Now you see here, you can't come in here and take these men away at gunpoint! Who the hell do

472

you think you are, anyway? There's laws in this country!"

Adam's voice was as pleasant as if he were asking the time of day, when he said, "You feeling inclined to enforce them?"

The fat man started to back off, but Adam jerked his head and tossed the ropes at his feet. "Cut these into lengths, and tie up your friends, all of 'em. Hands behind their backs, and run the ropes from their ankles to their wrists. You've hog-tied enough steers to know how to do it."

"Mister, you're plumb crazy!" The fat man was sweating profusely, and his eyes rolled nervously.

"Then you'd better hurry, hadn't you, before I go all the way over the edge and this gun goes off!" His eyes bored into one of the card-players who had opened his mouth to shout. "Don't do it," Adam advised. The man's mouth clamped shut.

The fat man worked quickly, his hands shaking. This was the first time he'd ever seen Adam, but he'd heard about him from the men who had been in Slocum's saloon the night he'd made Otis back down. And now that he'd seen him, he concluded that Adam might just be able to best Otis. He didn't owe Otis his life for his monthly wages, and this cold-eyed stranger looked as if he'd as lief shoot a man as look at him.

There was swearing and protests as he went about his work, efficient in spite of his shakiness. One bearded cowbow raged, "Otis'll have your hide for this! He ain't a healthy man to cross! If you got any brains you'll let Lester and Johnston go, and make tracks!" as he was trussed up by the fat man.

"Gag him," Adam ordered. "Use his bandana. Gag the others, too." A slight movement of his gun made the man hurry with his task. When it was done, Adam forced Johnston to tie and gag the fat man in turn, and then he herded his two prisoners outside and kicked the door shut after them. Otis would find the others in the morning, when they didn't appear for breakfast or the day's work. By then it wouldn't matter.

It took less than an hour for Adam, with Sheriff Benson's cooperation, to break the two men down, in spite of their fear of Otis. At the moment, it was Adam who was threatening them, and it was plain that he was much more to be feared.

"Do you have any idea of how long a sentence you'll have to serve for perjury? Don't make the mistake of thinking that I can't procure a lawyer who will see that you draw the maximum penalty. Whatever Otis paid you to lie for him isn't worth it. You aren't dealing with an amateur; I'll make it my business to see that you pay the full penalty."

Adam's voice was deadly, and Benson nodded agreement to everything he said, assuring them that it was true.

"But luck is with you," Adam continued. "I happen to be in a hurry and I'm willing to sacrifice the pleasure of seeing you put where you belong in return for your testimony against Otis. You can take your choice. Otis is going to prison in any case, because the lawyer I'll procure to reopen Kate's case will know just how to extract the truth from him, truth that will implicate you. It's up to you whether you go to prison with him, or are free to pull up stakes and get yourself other jobs with a more honest man."

A statement was drawn up, and two reputable towns-men were brought in to witness the signatures. Once that was done, Benson sent a deputy to arrest Otis and bring him in. Red-faced, bursting with fury and swearing vengeance on the two men he called liars and traitors, Otis was held until Adam and the sheriff contacted Judge Carlisle and arranged for the trial to be reopened.

The courtroom was packed to capacity as Adam's lawyer made mincemeat of Otis's representative's efforts to exonerate him. Kate was quiet and attentive, her hands folded in her lap, her back proud and straight. When she was called to testify, her voice was clear and firm. She didn't flinch when Otis's lawyer sought to discredit her by questioning her relationship with Adam.

"It wasn't for money. I loved him. He was the first, and he'll be the last. Yes, he gave me money, but it was so I could go to Tucson and find an honest job. Men don't give that much money to a girl for a night or two of love. It was for friendship. I was never a whore, and I never will be."

As Kate faced the jury and the spectators, her pride unassailable, Adam knew he hadn't been mistaken in her. It was no wonder he'd never been able to put her out of his mind all those months before he'd had sense enough to come after her. Her courage would match his own, no matter what the future held for them.

At the end of less than two hours Kate walked out of the courtroom a free woman, while the judge ordered Otis held over for his own trial.

Adam was shaking hands with Benson and Dan Matthews, the lawyer he'd hired for Kate, when Kate slipped out of the courtroom. The men spent another half-hour discussing Otis's coming trial and arranging for sworn, witnessed statements so that it wouldn't be necessary for Kate or Adam to be present. Adam didn't want Kate to have to go through another public exhibition. She'd already been put through more than any woman should be. Besides he was getting impatient to be on his way to Texas to start building the ranch he was determined to turn into a cattle empire.

He found Kate in her shack. She was just strapping her straw valise closed when he entered.

"There's no need to close it up so soon. It's too late to get started tonight, so we'll be spending the night here. It's more private than the hotel," Adam told her, grinning.

There was no answering smile on Kate's face.

"No, Adam. I'm not going to take up where we left off. You said you'd put the thousand dollars you got from selling Slocum's saloon in the bank in my name, and it'll get me a long way from this town."

Catching her arm, Adam controlled his urge to shake her. "Have you gone crazy? Do you think I went to all this trouble just to let you walk out of my life again?"

Kate faced him, her expression resolute. "As I recall it, you were the one who walked out, over a year ago. It's no good, Adam. I'm not going to go through that again. Thank you for getting me out of jail—I'll always appreciate it—but we aren't going to take up where we left off. I couldn't stand it, and you have no right to ask me to. I don't think I'll ever be able to forget you, but I'm going to give it a darned good try!"

"Kate, you are the most exasperating woman I ever knew! What makes you think I'm going to walk out on you again? We're going to be married."

Kate winced, but she answered him levelly. "Before you rode out of Albuquerque that time, I'd have married you at the drop of a hat. I'd have followed you anywhere, lived any way you wanted to live. I'd have worked for you, gone cold and hungry without complaining. But things are different now. I didn't know then that you were a rich man, that you could have your pick of any girl in the world. You can't marry an ex-saloon girl, an ex-prisoner! And I won't

476

be your squaw. You deserve a lot better than me, and I deserve a lot better than that, and there isn't anything else to talk about. So just let go of my arm."

"The hell I'll let go of your arm! Do you think I give a damn that you had to work in Slocum's saloon, that you did time in jail for protecting yourself? As for your being my squaw, I never heard such a pack of nonsense!"

"I'm a quarter Indian, Adam. My mother was a half-breed, and you don't realize what that means out here. I'd never be accepted."

"And my grandmother was an octoroon, but if you think I'm ashamed of it, you're as insane as you just accused me of being! I'm proud of her—she was a very great lady. Some day, when we have time, I'll tell you all about her. We'll make one hell of a combination, won't we?"

"You're still rich; we come from different worlds. Adam, don't do this to me! It isn't fair!"

"I love you, and it is fair. I don't intend to lose you. You can talk yourself hoarse and voiceless, and it won't mean a thing. On second thought, you're wasting a hell of a lot of time talking! Words don't solve anything, but this does!"

He had her in his arms, holding her so hard against his body that she couldn't breathe. His mouth came down over hers. She struggled, she kicked out at him, but he went right on kissing her until her knees sagged and she went limp in his arms. Under his mouth, hers became warm and soft and parted, and elation flooded through him. She loved him! And he loved her. She hadn't been out of his mind since the day he'd left her, she'd haunted him even though he'd tried to deny it, distrustful of all women, distrustful of love. God, what a fool he'd been, to waste so much time!

"Adam, you're being unfair. . . ." Kate accused him

when he finally took his mouth from hers. She was shaking and he was shaken.

"We're going to be married, here in Albuquerque. Unless you'd rather travel from here to Texas without being married," Adam insisted. "One way or another, you're coming with me. Kate, I have plans, and I need you to help carry them out. We're going to have a ranch, the darnedest cattle ranch you ever dreamed of! We're going to build an empire, and we're going to do it together!"

"In Texas?" Kate's eyes widened. "Adam, you're insane! People in Texas are even more prejudiced than they are here! They'd never accept me . . ."

"They aren't going to be given a choice!" Adam told her. "We're going to build that empire, and we're going to have sons to help us rule it, and if anybody takes exception to it, we'll run them clear out of Texas."

Kate fought for control, her hands on his chest now, trying to hold him off.

"And I suppose you'll dress me in silk and satins," she laughed.

"You can have all the silks and satins you want, but whatever the gown, you'll wear these with it," Adam told her.

He released her to take a slim velvet case from his pocket. He put it into her hands.

"Open it."

Her fingers trembled as she lifted the hinged lid, and she gasped. There, on their blue velvet bed, was a string of pearls, each one perfect. She gasped as she touched them. She'd never seen anything so beautiful in her life.

"They're a little dull now, but they'll come to life when you wear them. Pearls have to have contact with warm, human flesh to achieve their full beauty. I bought them when I decided to marry you. Another very great lady, Prudence, has a string just like them. I'll tell you about her someday, too, so you'll understand the tradition that goes with pearls in our family. Our family, Kate, yours and mine! My grandfather bought the original string for his wife Martha, when she presented him with their first child."

Adam took the pearls from their case and clasped them around her neck. Kate's eyes were filled with tears.

"You aren't giving me much choice," she accused him, wiping the tears away with the palm of her hand.

"I'm not giving you any choice. You're my woman, and you might as well understand it."

"If you think I'm going to be a meek and respectful wife and let you walk all over me, you have another think coming!" Kate flashed back at him. Her head was swimming; things were going too fast. "No man's my master, Adam Wentworth, not even you!"

"God forbid! I wouldn't want you if you were meek and submissive! Where we're going, what we're going to do, calls for strength, and you have it, and I wouldn't have it any other way. Damn it, Kate, stop talking!"

His mouth came down over hers again, and he lifted her in his arms and carried her to the bed. Her arms entwined around his neck as he went on kissing her; then she released him and they began to undress. Her body pulsed and flamed, aching for him. She was his woman, and he was her man, and she'd ride beside him and help him build that empire he talked about.

Wearing only the pearls, she opened her arms and her body to receive him, to give, to take, to love, to die a little only to be reborn. The shack, all of their surroundings, faded away and there was nothing but their two bodies, entwined as one, their pledge of eternal love and loyalty to each other, their promise to the future.